Workhouse Angel

ALSO BY HOLLY GREEN:

Workhouse Orphans

HOLLY GREEN

Workhouse Angel

EBURY
PRESS

1 3 5 7 9 10 8 6 4 2

Ebury Press, an imprint of Ebury Publishing
20 Vauxhall Bridge Road,
London SW1V 2SA

Ebury Press is part of the Penguin Random House group of companies
whose addresses can be found at global.penguinrandomhouse.com

First published in the UK in 2017 by Ebury Press

www.penguin.co.uk

A CIP catalogue record for this book is available from the British Library

ISBN 9781785035685

Typeset in India by Integra Software Services Pvt. Ltd, Pondicherry

Printed and bound in Great Britain by Clays Ltd, St Ives PLC

Penguin Random House is committed to a sustainable future for our
business, our readers and our planet. This book is made from
Forest Stewardship Council® certified paper.

Prologue

Mist lies thick over the Mersey and, beyond the crowded buildings, the first faint lightening of the sky shows the dawn to be near. It is very cold. The streets are empty, save for one heavily cloaked figure, who walks with an uneven stride to the doors of the great building that squats menacingly at the top of Brownlow Hill. He carries in his arms a shawl-wrapped bundle, holding it close to his chest within the folds of his cloak. The doors of the workhouse are closed and no light burns in the window of the porter's lodge. The man hesitates, looking down at the burden he carries and then back over his shoulder towards the river. From out of the mist a ship's whistle sounds a warning.

'It will be light soon. Then someone is bound to open the gates. You won't be left alone long.'

His voice is choked with tears. He stoops and lays the bundle tenderly on the flagstones in front of the gate.

'I'm sorry! I'm sorry! I don't know what else to do. I have to go. You will be cared for – and I shall come back to find you when I can.'

He kisses the small face, looks up for a moment at the grim outline of the building, then turns and hobbles away as fast as he can towards the river.

It is cold and she is hungry. She begins to cry. For a long time nobody comes. She wants her mother, wants to be picked up and held and comforted. She cries louder. There is movement and light falls on her; then unfamiliar hands pick her up. She is carried, passed into other hands; strange faces peer down at her.

'Left outside like a parcel. Might have been there all night for all I know! Who could do such a thing?'

'Plenty have done worse. Let's have a look at her.'

She is unwrapped by brisk, ungentle hands.

'Well, it's a girl. Pretty little thing. How old would you say?'

'Not a newborn, that's for sure. A year, maybe a bit more.'

'Anything left with her, to show who left her here? No note or anything?'

'Nothing at all, except this rag doll.'

Raggy! She reaches out, feeing for the familiar shape. It is not there. She begins to cry again.

'Oh, shut your noise! I can't be doing with it.' The voice, like the hands, is harsh.

'Here, give her this. Maybe that will quiet her.'

The rag doll is thrust into her grasp. She holds it tight. It smells of home, and Mother.

Time passes. She is dumped in a chair and a spoon is pushed into her mouth. The food tastes strange and she spits it out. The spoon is pushed in again, more forcefully. She screams in anger and distress.

'Do without then, see if I care!'

She continues to scream. She is picked up and shaken roughly. Then, suddenly, other arms go round her, holding her gently, rocking her and a soft voice begins to sing:

'Lavender's blue, dilly dilly, lavender's green.
When I am king, dilly dilly, you shall be queen ...'

She goes quiet. The arms that hold her are thin, the shoulder against which she lays her head is bony; not like her mother's, but she feels safe here. She looks up into a narrow, pale face and a lock of hair falls across her cheek. Her mother's hair was golden. This is more like the colour of polished wood. Voices go on over her head.

'I shall call her Angel. Don't you think she looks like a little angel?'

That is not her name. Her name is Amy. She tries to tell them, but it comes out as 'May-me'.

'She's trying to say my name! It's May. Say May.'

'May-me! May-me!'

'There's a clever girl!'

Days pass. Sometimes the girl called May is there, some-times she is not. She is always gentle. She helps her to eat, changes her, plays with her. But when she is not there the woman with the hard hands takes over. She does not like that. She screams in protest. The nights are worst. Alone in the dark, listening to the cries of other children nearby, she clutches her rag doll and cannot help crying; and then she is picked up and shaken and dumped down again.

One night is different. May takes her with her, up some stairs, into a room where other faces peer down at her. There is a lot of chatter. 'What have you got there, May? Who is she? Do they know in the nursery you've got her?

Why have you brought her up here?' Then she is laid in a bed and May lies beside her and cuddles her close. She shuts her eyes and sleeps.

She wakes to shouts of alarm and a strange, frightening smell. Someone shouts 'Fire!' She is grabbed out of the bed and thrust into unfamiliar arms. There is noise and confusion. She cries for May, but May does not come. Then she is back in the nursery.

More days pass, but still May does not come. One day, a new face peers down at her. This one is framed in dark hair. The eyes are bright, but not gentle like May's.

'This one! I want this one.'

'Are you sure, ma'am? She's over a year old. I thought you were looking for a baby.'

'I don't care about her age. Just look at that golden hair and those blue eyes. She will be a beauty when she grows up. What is her name?'

'Angela, ma'am. She was baptised Angela.'

'Angela? That's rather a common name. Perhaps Angelina would be more suitable. Yes, Angelina will do very well. I'll take her.'

One

'I won't! I won't! Take it away. I don't like it. I hate you!' The pretty face was scarlet with fury, the golden curls dishevelled and matted from the struggle.

'Angelina, please!' The governess's voice was harsh with desperation. 'Just try it. You've had nothing to eat all day, and your mama has ordered that you are to be given nothing until you drink your medicine. It's for your own good. The doctor says it will strengthen you, so that you do not have so many stomach upsets. Now, be a good girl. Drink it up.'

'But I don't like it. It makes me feel sick.'

'That's nonsense. It isn't nasty. I'll try a sip to show you. There! See? It's quite nice really.'

'You drink it then. If I drink it, I shall be sick.'

'That will not help, will it? You are the one who needs it. Now, come along. You are not a baby any more. You are eight years old, old enough to understand reason. Stop being so disobedient. Drink!'

She grasped the squirming child by the back of the neck and held the cup to her lips. For a moment they remained obstinately shut. Then they opened and the draught was swallowed.

'There you are! You see … oh, you little beast!' Angelina had twisted her head and vomited over the governess's skirt. 'You little horror! You did that deliberately.'

'I told you what would happen! I said if you made me drink it I should be sick.'

'What is going on here? What is all this noise about?'

Marguerite McBride stood in the doorway. The governess scrambled to her feet, trying to wipe the vomit off her skirt with a pocket handkerchief. 'I'm sorry, ma'am, if we disturbed you. I was just trying to persuade Angelina to drink the medicine the doctor prescribed.'

'And she is still refusing?'

'She swallowed it and then brought it all up again, all over me.'

'Angelina, come here!' The child moved unwillingly towards her mother. 'I have had enough of this. You are a naughty, disobedient little girl and disobedience has to be punished. Kneel down at the end of your bed.'

'No, Mama! Please! I couldn't help being sick.'

'Do as you are told at once! Or it will be the worse for you. Miss Garvey, the rod, if you please.'

'Ma'am, are you sure? Is this really necessary?'

'Have you never heard the maxim, "spare the rod and spoil the child"? Give it to me.'

The governess handed her a thin cane. She pointed to the bed, and Angelina, after a last mute gaze of appeal, went and knelt at the foot. Her mother stooped and lifted her skirts, then raised her arm and administered four stinging blows with the cane. Angelina endured them in silence.

'Get up.' She got to her feet. 'Now go to your room and stay there. Your supper will be brought to you on a tray, together with a fresh dose of the medicine. I shall come too. If you take the medicine and keep it down you may eat your supper. Otherwise it will be removed and you will continue to go hungry. Go!'

Alone in her room Angelina buried her face in the pillow. She did not weep. Crying did not help. It did not explain what was happening to her. Once, it seemed a long time ago, her mother had treated her differently. She had spent hours combing her hair and dressing her in pretty clothes. She had taken her with her to visit friends and they had all said what a lovely child she was and had asked her to sing for them. She thought her mother had loved her then. She never cuddled and kissed her, as she had seen other mothers do with their children, but she had been kind.

Then something had changed; something had happened, which she could never quite remember. They had been in a shop, and there had been a young woman who called her 'Angel' and her mother had been angry and sent her to wait outside. Since then, life had been different. Miss Garvey had arrived and all Angelina's time had been spent in the schoolroom. There were no more visits and no more pretty dresses, and if she did not do exactly as she was told she was punished.

Sometimes, just before she fell asleep or as she was waking up, images came into her head. She could not tell if they were dreams or memories. The face of the young woman who had called her Angel came back to her, though when she was fully awake she could not recall it. With it came a sensation of comfort, of being held and cared for;

and sometimes, from even longer ago, came the flickering image of another face and long, golden hair, which fell around her and shut off the outside world.

Angelina got off the bed, wincing at the pain in her bruised and swollen buttocks, and went to a cupboard. It was full of toys – soft woolly lambs and puppies, beautiful dolls with porcelain faces and rich clothes – but she ignored them all. At the bottom of the cupboard was a box filled with a jumble of old toys and torn doll's dresses. She rummaged through it until, hidden at the bottom, she found what she was looking for – a rag doll, grubby and stained. She took it back to her bed and lay down, holding it against her cheek. It had a faint smell, which she could not name but which brought closer than ever that memory of being held in loving arms. Softly, she began to sing:

'Lavender's blue, dilly dilly, lavender's green.
When I am king, dilly dilly, you shall be queen.'

Downstairs in the drawing room, Miss Garvey was facing her employer.

'You are telling me that you wish to give notice?'

'Yes, ma'am. I'm sorry if it is not convenient, but I cannot remain here under the circumstances.'

'What circumstances?'

'I cannot stand by and watch a child being mistreated.'

'Mistreated! How dare you? Are you accusing me of mistreating Angelina?'

'I feel that you are altogether too harsh on her. She is only eight years old.'

'Old enough to know the difference between right and wrong, to understand the necessity for obedience.'

'There are better ways of inculcating that virtue.'

'So now you set yourself up as better able to judge how my daughter should be brought up, do you? Well, the sooner you leave this house the better.'

'On that point I agree with you. But I am prepared to work out my notice.'

'You will not! You will pack your bags and be gone by tomorrow morning. And you need not expect a reference from me!'

When her supper was brought to her room, Angelina still refused to drink the medicine. She went to bed hungry. Next morning the maid brought up a tray on which there was a boiled egg, some delicate slices of bread and butter, a dish of honey and a glass of milk. Marguerite arrived at the same time, with the medicine in a cup.

'Well? Are you hungry enough to see sense? Drink this and you can eat.'

Angelina looked from the cup to the tray. Her stomach rumbled. She reached for the cup. The smell of the contents turned her stomach but she took a sip, and then another. Somehow she managed to keep it down. Her mother smiled triumphantly.

'So, I hope you have learned your lesson. We will have no more scenes like the one we had yesterday.'

'No, Mama.'

'Very good. Eat your breakfast. I want to see you in the schoolroom in half an hour. Miss Garvey has decided that she cannot endure your bad behaviour any longer and has given in her notice. For the time being I shall teach you myself.'

As soon as the door closed behind her, Angelina pulled the chamber pot out from under the bed and vomited up the medicine. Then she set to on the boiled egg.

A week passed, during which Marguerite took charge of Angelina's lessons in a haphazard fashion. She soon tired of the atmosphere of the schoolroom and left her to read and copy out passages from improving books or memorise verses from the Bible. Then, one afternoon, Angelina was summoned to the drawing room. A small woman in a grey dress was with her mother.

'This is my daughter, Angelina. Angelina, this is your new governess, Miss Drake.'

Angelina curtsied, as she had been taught. 'How do you do, ma'am?'

Miss Drake looked her over critically. 'So this is the young lady who is to learn proper respect for authority?'

'Yes,' Marguerite said, with a regretful sigh, 'I fear her last governess was far too lax. She needs a firm hand.'

'Have no worries about that,' Miss Drake said. 'I have handled some rebellious spirits in my time. The young are like horses. They have to be broken in.'

'I am sure we shall see eye to eye in that respect,' Marguerite replied. 'But I make one proviso. If there is to be any corporal punishment, you will refer it to me. I do not regard it as fitting that an employee should chastise the child of her employer.'

Miss Drake looked at Angelina with narrowed eyes. 'Have no fear, ma'am. I do not think we shall need to resort to anything so crude as beating.'

Marguerite rang for the parlourmaid and instructed her to take Miss Drake upstairs and show her where she would sleep. 'You can wait in the schoolroom, Angelina, until Miss Drake is ready to begin your lessons.'

It was some time before Miss Drake appeared and Angelina fidgeted restlessly, first sitting, then wandering round the room. She had a fluttering sensation in her stomach as she wondered what she could expect from this new governess. The expression on her face when she said 'I do not think we shall need to resort to anything as crude as beating' had frightened her.

Eventually the door opened and the small woman came in.

'What are you doing over there? Sit down at once!'

Angelina scurried to her place at the table and sat.

'I expected to find you usefully employed, not wandering like an imbecile. Have you no sewing to do, no books to read?'

Angelina shook her head dumbly.

'Speak up when you are spoken to!'

'I … I'm sorry, ma'am. I didn't know what you would like me to start on.'

'You should not need to wait for me to tell you what to do. You should always have work in hand. Well, I shall make sure that in future you will not have time to sit around in idleness. Now, let us see how far your education has progressed. What is seven times eight?'

Taken by surprise, Angelina struggled to respond. She had been made to recite her tables over and over but she still needed to repeat them to her herself before arriving at the correct answer.

'Come along, come along!' Miss Drake took up a ruler and rapped it on the table, making Angelina jump.

'Please, fifty-six,' she gasped.

'At last! I was beginning to think I was dealing with a half-wit. Nine times four!'

The questions kept coming; tables, mental arithmetic, then, 'What is the capital of Poland?'

'Please, ma'am, I don't know.'

'You don't know? How long was your previous governess with you?'

'Please, two years, I think …'

'Two years? You seem to have learnt very little in that time.' The governess delved in a bag she had brought in with her and took out a book. 'Read the first paragraph of this.'

It was a book she had never seen before and some of the words were unfamiliar. It took her some time to struggle through the paragraph.

Miss Drake sighed deeply. 'I see we have a long way to go – but I am not deterred. We shall make up for lost time.' She looked at Angelina. 'Sit up, girl! Have you never been taught not to slump?' She moved round behind the chair and took hold of Angelina's shoulders, pulling them back painfully. 'There! That is correct posture, and correct posture is essential in a young lady. That is another thing which has obviously been sadly neglected.' She set a pen and inkstand in front of Angelina and turned a page on the book. 'Copy that, in your best handwriting.'

Angelina began to write, but Miss Drake kept a grip on her shoulders, forcing her to sit bolt upright. The unnatural position made it difficult to control the pen and inevitably she made a blot. Miss Drake reached down and grabbed her hand. 'That was careless! You will learn to be more careful, or this is what happens.' She took hold of Angelina's little finger and bent it back so that she yelped with pain. 'Now, begin again, and take more care this time.'

Angelina burst into tears and her tears created fresh blots. Miss Drake whisked away the paper and set a clean sheet in front of her. 'Begin again. There will be no tea until you have achieved a clean copy.'

It took four attempts, and, by the time she had finished and was allowed to have the milk and biscuits that had been brought up for her, Angelina's hands were shaking.

It was customary after tea for her to be taken down to the drawing room to spend half an hour with her mother and her father, when he returned from his business. She did not know what that 'business' was, except that it had something to do with tea. She was never sure what to expect at this time. Her mother had never played with her or made a fuss of her and lately she had become even more distant, but sometimes her father would sweep her up into his arms, if he was in a good mood, and tickle her or rub her face with his moustache to make her squirm and giggle. Occasionally he even allowed her to sit on his lap. He was the only person who showed her any affection and she tried hard to please him, but there were days when he came home grim-faced and irritable and she had learned then to do nothing to attract his attention.

On this particular evening he seemed pleased to see her and picked her up in his arms.

'Well, well,' he said. 'So how are you getting on with your new governess?'

Angelina drooped her head. 'I don't like her. She's not kind.'

'Not kind, eh?' He looked over her head at his wife.

'Take no notice,' she replied. 'Angelina has been spoiled. Miss Garvey was much too lax with her. Now she is being made to buckle down and she doesn't like it.'

'Is that it?' He set Angelina down. 'Well, hard work never hurt anyone. You'll get used to it. You'll never grow up to be a credit to us if you don't do as you are told.'

Next day, Miss Drake set out the routine that Angelina was to follow from then on. The first hour of the morning would be devoted to arithmetic and practising her handwriting; the next hour would be divided between the study of history and geography, and the last would be devoted to 'deportment', a mysterious subject on which Miss Drake placed a great deal of emphasis. After luncheon Angelina would sew, while Miss Drake took her afternoon rest. Then, weather permitting, they would go for a walk, returning in time for tea. Angelina hoped that the walk might take them into Princes Park. She had happy memories of being taken there by her nursemaid, before the advent of Miss Garvey. Something had happened there, something she could not quite remember, but the park had suddenly been placed out of bounds and her walks had been confined to the local streets.

Overnight, Angelina had made a resolution. She would try to do as Miss Drake asked. After all, she did want to be a credit to her parents. Perhaps, if she worked really hard, her mother would love her again.

She tried hard to keep to it, but there was little encouragement. The governess barked mental arithmetic questions at her and rapped the table angrily if she was slow to answer. She was given long lists to learn by heart; the kings and queens of England; the capital cities of all the countries in Europe; verses from the Bible. She could remember them perfectly when she was alone, but under the basilisk stare of Miss Drake they vanished from her mind like a flock of birds scared by a cat. The constant refrain of 'sit up, don't slouch' only served to make things worse. Very often Miss Drake came to stand behind her, pulling her shoulders back, making it harder than ever to concentrate. The lessons in deportment were even worse. She was made to walk around the room with a book balanced on her head while Miss Drake snapped instructions. 'Chin up! Shoulders back! Pull your stomach in!' If the book slipped she had to stand on a stool facing the corner of the room until her legs ached and she began to feel dizzy. Then, one morning, the governess came into the room carrying a leather strap.

'You have got to get out of this bad habit of slouching. You do not seem to be able to correct it yourself so we shall have to resort to other methods. Stand up. Put your arms behind your back.'

Trembling, Angelina obeyed. The governess seized hold of her upper arms and pulled them back until her elbows were almost touching. Then she passed the strap around them and fastened it tightly. Angelina cried out in pain and struggled to free herself, but her efforts only made it worse.

'Be still!' Miss Drake ordered. 'If you learn to sit correctly it will not hurt. Now, sit down and we will begin our lessons.'

'I can't!' Angelina protested. 'I can't breathe properly. It hurts!'

'This position expands the chest. Of course you can breathe. Sit down and stop making a fuss.'

'Please,' Angelina begged, 'when can I have it off?'

'When we stop for luncheon. Then, if I judge you have worked to my satisfaction, you may have it off for the afternoon. But if you start to slump again, it will go back on.'

Angelina endured the torment for four days, but when Miss Drake advanced on her with the strap on the fifth morning she pushed her away so violently that she staggered back and almost fell. In the moment it took for her to recover, Angelina ran out of the room and down the stairs. Her mother was in the hall, talking to another lady, and Angelina threw herself at her feet, clutching her skirts and sobbing.

'Please, Mama, don't let Miss Drake put the strap on my arms! Please! It hurts so much.'

Her mother looked over her head at the governess, who had followed her down the stairs.

'What is all this?'

'It is merely a form of restraint recommended for correcting bad habits of posture. Angelina has been allowed to slouch, so she finds it uncomfortable, but it will have its effect eventually.'

'Show me.'

'No! No, please! Don't let her do it!' Angelina wept, but she was pulled to her feet, her arms were twisted behind her and the strap was fastened.

'You see?' Miss Drake said, turning her to face her mother. 'You see how much her posture is improved? You know how important it is for a young lady to carry herself correctly.'

'Yes, indeed,' Marguerite responded. 'Stop making a fuss, Angelina. It is for your own good.'

As a punishment for this act of rebellion, she was forced to wear the strap for the rest of the day, with the threat that if there was any repeat she would be made to sleep in it at night as well.

From that day on, Angelina's only thought was of how to get rid of this tyrant who had been given charge over her.

Her only respite was the hour after luncheon when Miss Drake took her afternoon nap and she was supposed to get on with some sewing. Miss Drake's bedroom opened directly off the schoolroom, as did Angelina's, and she always left the door ajar, so that she would hear if Angelina 'got up to any mischief'. But Angelina soon realised that very quickly after retiring her governess began to snore softly. Before that happened, she always heard the clink of a glass and the sound of liquid being poured, and later, when Miss Drake bent over her to fasten her coat for their walk, she smelt an odour which was somehow familiar, although she could not at first think why. One evening her father came home looking weary, and, instead of going straight into the drawing room, he went to the dining room. When he came out she smelt the same odour that she had noticed on Miss Drake's breath. After that Angelina made a habit of waiting to greet him in the hall when he arrived home, with a curtsy and a demure 'Good evening, Papa.' That seemed to please him. One day, when he came in looking tired, she followed

him into the dining room and saw him go to the sideboard, on which stood two cut-glass decanters contained
in a curious cage-like construction, which made it impossible to remove them. She watched as her father delved
into a waistcoat pocket and produced a tiny key. This he
inserted into a lock; there was a click, a bar swung back
and he picked up one of the decanters and poured a measure of the liquid it contained into a glass.

'Please, Papa,' she ventured, 'what is that you are drinking?'

'This?' He took a mouthful and swallowed and smacked
his lips. 'This is a very special medicine for grown-up gentlemen, to help them to relax after a hard day.'

'A sort of tonic, like that medicine I had to drink?'

'Perhaps, a bit like that.'

'And what is that thing called?' She pointed to the cage.

'That is a tantalus. Do you know why?'

'No.'

'There is a very old story about a man called Tantalus
who displeased the gods, so they condemned him to a terrible fate. He had to stand up to his neck in water, but if he
tried to drink, the water flowed away from him. Over his
head was a branch loaded with fruit, but if he tried to pick
any of it the wind blew it out of reach. That is where we
get our word "tantalize" from. It means that you can see
something you want but you can never quite get hold of it.'

'Oh, I see.' She thought about it. 'Why did you say
"gods". There is only one God, isn't there?'

'We know that now, but in the old days people believed
there were many. They were heathens, who had not been
taught the truth.'

'So what happened to Tantalus was like being sent to hell.'

'Yes, I suppose that is one way of putting it.'

Angelina considered, frowning. There was still something she did not understand. 'But why do you keep your special medicine locked up? You are not like Tantalus, because you have the key so you can have it whenever you like.'

'So I can. The point is other people can't, unless I let them.'

'Other people? Do you mean Mama?'

'No, no. Your mama would never touch this. But sometimes servants might take a fancy to try it.'

'But Jane and Betty are girls. You said it was only for grown-up gentlemen.'

'Precisely. That is why they must not be tempted to try it.'

'What would happen if they did?'

'It would be a matter for instant dismissal. Now, come along. Let's join your mama. She will wonder why I am such a long time in here.'

When they entered the drawing room, Marguerite looked up crossly from her sewing. 'There you are at last. How many have you had?'

'Oh, come on, Maggie,' he said, with an edge of annoyance, 'a man's entitled to a drink after a long day.'

'Don't call me Maggie!'

Her father's voice took on a satirical note. 'Oh, pardon me, your highness! For a moment I thought I was addressing the simple Irish girl I wed ten years back. I forgot she'd metamorphosed into a great lady.'

Angelina listened to this exchange with only half her mind. She was working something out. Miss Drake drank the same kind of medicine every afternoon, even though it was only supposed to be for gentlemen. She was tempted to tell her father that, but some instinct made her keep it to herself for the time being.

In bed that night she turned the information over and over in her mind and by morning she had a plan.

The following evening she waited until her father had had his usual drink and was settled in his armchair. She climbed onto his lap and begged, 'Tickle me, Papa.'

'Really, Angelina!' her mother exclaimed. 'Don't bother your father when he's tired after a long day.'

'Oh, I don't mind,' he said with a laugh. 'It's all a bit of fun, isn't it, kitten?'

'You spoil her. No good will come of it, mark my words.'

He took no notice and began to tickle Angelina's ribs. His fingers were too strong to tickle her properly, but she pretended to giggle and wriggle with pleasure and in the process managed to slip her fingers into the pocket of his waistcoat. The key was there. Carefully she extracted it and slipped it into the pocket of her pinafore.

Next morning she endured the pain of having her arms strapped behind her without complaint. When luncheon was over she waited on tenterhooks for Miss Drake to take her usual drink and fall asleep. As soon as she could hear from her gentle snores that the governess was unconscious she crept into her bedroom.

Her heart was thumping so hard that she felt the noise of it must wake her, but she did not stir.

A little flask was on the floor beside her. With a hand that shook, Angelina picked it up and tiptoed out of the room. She undid the stopper and sniffed. If it was not exactly the same as the stuff her father drank, it was very similar.

She crept to the door of the schoolroom, opened it and listened. The house was silent. She knew that at this time of day her mother would be visiting friends, and the servants would be eating their midday meal in the kitchen.

On silent feet she padded down the stairs. The hall was deserted. Carefully, she opened the door of the dining room and looked in. It, too, was empty. She had to pull a chair up to the sideboard to reach. Then she took the tiny key from her pocket and inserted it in the lock, as she had seen her father do, and pushed aside the bar that lay across the top of the decanters. She took up the one her father had used. It was much heavier than she had expected and it nearly slipped through her fingers. She steadied herself and took the small flask from her other pocket and carefully poured the liquid from the decanter into it. It soon filled up, and when she looked at the decanter the level did not seem to have gone down perceptibly. That would not do! She looked round the room. A large evergreen plant stood on the windowsill. She climbed down off the chair, cradling the decanter, and poured a good measure of its contents into the pot. That was better. Her father was bound to notice the difference now.

She climbed back onto the chair and replaced the decanter and locked the arm in position. Then for the first time it occurred to her to wonder what to do with the key. The chances of getting it back into her father's pocket without him noticing were small. In the end, she dropped the key onto the floor in front of the sideboard. Then she replaced the chair, slipped out of the room and ran soft-footed back up the stairs. As she entered the schoolroom her heart was thudding so hard that it made her feel dizzy. If Miss Drake had wakened and found her gone she dreaded to think what her punishment might be; but the room was empty and the governess's breathing was as regular as when she'd left. Holding her breath, she crept back into the room and replaced the flask where she had found it.

When Miss Drake came into the schoolroom, Angelina was stitching industriously at her sampler.

It was time for their walk. It was almost winter, and a cold wind was blowing up from the Mersey, but Miss Drake was not deterred. She marched Angelina briskly along the road and into Princes Park. Angelina had been pleased the first time she had taken her there. She remembered sunny afternoons playing with other children, while their nursemaids sat and gossiped. This was very different. In an unvarying routine, they circumnavigated the lake while Miss Drake drilled into her into the names of the various trees and shrubs they passed, her remarks interspersed with regular commands to stand up straight, pull her shoulders back and walk 'like a lady'. If they encountered any other children with their nurses or governesses, polite greetings were exchanged, but then Angelina was hurried on without any chance to talk. Normally, she would have tried to prolong the walk, anything to be away from the schoolroom, but today she was eager to get home, afraid that they might not be there when her father returned.

She need not have worried. There was time to change her dress and have her face washed and her hair brushed, so that she was 'presentable'.

In the drawing room her mother was sewing, as usual, and Angelina sat rigidly upright, answering her random questions about what she had learned that day, being careful not to fidget because that might result in being sent back upstairs. Her father was later than usual, but at last she heard his key in the lock and ran into the hall to greet him.

Jane, the parlourmaid, was there, taking his hat and coat, and before Angelina could speak she said, 'Beg pardon, sir, but I found this on the floor of the dining room when I went to set the table for dinner.'

Angelina's heart jumped in her chest as she saw the maid was holding out the key to the tantalus.

'Good gracious!' her father exclaimed, his hand going to his waistcoat pocket. 'I must have dropped it last night. How careless of me. Thank you, Jane.'

The maid bobbed a curtsy and retired, carrying his hat and coat. Angelina curtsied in her turn. 'Good evening, Papa.'

He patted her on the head. 'Good evening, kitten.' He yawned and turned towards the door to the drawing room. This was not part of the plan.

Angelina said, 'You look tired, Papa. Why don't you have a glass of your special medicine?'

He smiled at her. 'Do you know, I think that is just what I need.'

He went into the dining room and Angelina waited, scarcely daring to breathe. A moment later he came out with a face like thunder and bawled, 'Jane! Here, at once!'

His wife came out of the sitting room. 'Connor! Whatever is wrong? Why are you shouting?'

'Someone has been at my whisky.'

'Nonsense. How could they have been? You keep it locked.'

'But yesterday I must have dropped the key and now the decanter is half empty. Jane!'

The parlourmaid reappeared at the run. 'Sir?'

'When did you find this key?'

'Just now, sir, when I set the table, like I told you.'

'Did you notice that the decanter of whisky was half empty?'

'No, sir. I didn't look.'

'Have you taken some?'

'Me, sir? No, sir!'

'Come here.'

She went closer and he took hold of her arm and bent his head close to hers.

'Hmm. No smell of it on your breath. Where's Betty?'

'She's in bed, sir, with an attack of the croup. She's not moved all day. I've been doing her work for her.'

'Fetch cook.'

'Oh, really, Connor,' his wife exclaimed. 'Do you want us to lose our cook? If you accuse her she will give notice, I guarantee it. I'm sure she would never dream of taking your whisky.'

'Then who has? It didn't just vanish into thin air.'

'You probably drank it yourself and you've forgotten.'

'Do you think I'm so far gone? If I'd drunk that much I'd have been incapable of standing on my own two feet.'

Angelina decided that the moment had come for which she had been waiting.

'Papa, if you need some more medicine, I think Miss Drake has some. She keeps it in a little bottle in her room.'

Her father went up the stairs two at a time and Angelina hurried after him, ignoring her mother's instruction to stay where she was. Miss Drake was sitting at the table in the schoolroom, about to start her dinner. She jumped to her feet as her employer entered.

'Mr McBride! What can I do for you?' Then seeing Angelina behind him, said, 'What has the child been saying? If she has been complaining ...'

'This has nothing to do with Angelina. I am told you have a flask of some alcoholic beverage in your room.'

Miss Drake's eyes went from him to Angelina and then to the door of her room. 'A little tonic wine, that is all, to fortify me against the rigours of my profession.'

'Bring it to me, if you please.'

For a moment Angelina thought she was going to refuse, then she turned away and went into her room. She returned carrying the flask and looking alarmed.

'This ... this is not as it was when last I ... someone has tampered with it.'

Mr McBride held out his hand. 'Give it to me.'

She handed him the flask and he removed the stopper and sniffed. 'Tonic wine, you say?'

'Yes, that is all.'

McBride lifted the flask to his lips and took a draft. 'You are a liar. This is fine Scotch whisky, which was taken from my decanter sometime today.'

'No! How can it be? I have not touched your decanter. Do you not keep it locked away?'

'I do, but last night I must have dropped the key and you must have found it. How much of this stuff do you drink?'

'Very little. Only when I feel the need.'

'She has some every afternoon, after luncheon,' Angelina said. 'Then she goes to sleep.'

Miss Drake turned on her. 'Why you … You are responsible for this, you little …'

Mrs McBride had made her way upstairs by this time. She pushed past her husband. 'How dare you accuse my daughter? You have wormed your way into this household under false pretences. You are a liar and a thief. You will leave this house first thing tomorrow morning.' She looked round at her daughter. 'Angelina, you had better sleep in my room tonight, away from the influence of this … this woman.'

Angelina curtsied submissively. 'Very well, Mama.'

Two

James Breckenridge stood on the quayside and strained his eyes to follow the progress of the SS *Royal Standard* as she stood out into the Mersey, and turned her bows towards the open sea. She was not as beautiful as the sailing clippers that thronged the harbour, with her tall funnels belching smoke instead of the graceful spread of white sails, but that was not important. What mattered to her passengers was that they would have a speedier and safer journey to Australia. What mattered to James was that she was carrying away, faster than any other ship, the person who, he had realised too late, meant more to him than anyone else in the world. To add to his distress, he had just made a promise he knew he could not keep.

He turned away with a sigh and began to plod heavily towards the solicitor's office where he was an articled clerk. As he walked he castigated himself for a being fool and a snob. What did it matter that May had been brought up in the workhouse? It was true that she had only told him that a few days earlier, when he had asked her to marry him. Until then he had believed that she came from a respectable family, which had fallen on hard times so that, on the death of her mother, she had been forced to take a position as a milliner's apprentice. Like a fool, he had tried to persuade her to stick to that story after they were married; but she had, quite rightly he saw now, refused to live a lie.

He took out of his pocket the letter he had received that morning. It had arrived just in time for him to rush to the dockside to see the ship sail, but not soon enough to persuade May to disembark. Could the extraordinary story she had told there be true? According to the letter, the father she had always assumed to have drowned at sea had in fact been transported to Australia for some trivial offence, had served his sentence and had then turned prospector and struck gold. Her brother, Gus, was already in Melbourne and the two had met by pure chance. Now, her father had sent money to pay her passage out to join them. It all seemed to be too much of a coincidence. Was it possible that May had made up the story, to give her a reason for leaving him? He would never have thought her capable of such a deception. On the other hand, she had maintained a false story about her upbringing for years, until she had confessed the truth a few days earlier. But, he reminded himself, he had seen her on the deck reserved for First Class passengers as the ship left. There was no way she could have afforded that if her father had not sent money for the ticket. So perhaps it was true.

He thought about the girl he had known for two years and fallen in love with. Circumstances had forced her to hide the shame of her childhood in the workhouse, but in everything else he knew her to be honest and without guile, in total contrast to the artificiality of so many of the young women of his own class. It was that openness which had first drawn him to her. She was brave and self-reliant and he appreciated that more than ever, now that he knew what her life had been like until they met. Educated just sufficiently in the workhouse to fit her for a life in service, she had been subjected to the deprivations of a job as a maid-of-all-work, at the beck and call of a cruel housekeeper. She had been lifted out of that servitude by her talent as an artist and designer, and had made use of every opportunity of improving herself until, finally, her true nature was revealed as an intelligent, lively, affectionate person, open to every new experience that was offered to her. It was that very openness which had drawn him to her. He knew his life had been easy in comparison. The son of a sea captain, who had, it was true, gone down with his ship when James was fifteen; but who had left him and his mother comfortably off and enabled him to receive a good education and then to acquire a position that would, once he had passed his final examinations, open up a respectable career as a solicitor.

That brought him to the nub of the matter. A solicitor was expected to have an equally respectable wife, from a respectable family: a wife who would be acceptable to the sort of society in which he moved. A girl brought up in the workhouse, however charming, would not meet with approval. That she had once worked as a milliner's apprentice was bad enough, without that additional shame. His mother knew that, which was why she had made her disapproval of their relationship clear. May knew it too, and that was why she had fled to Australia.

There was something that stabbed at his conscience beneath all this, and he forced himself to face it. He had made a promise which he knew he could not keep. Standing on the dockside, shouting across the widening expanse of water, he had begged May to come back. It was impossible, of course. She had shouted back, 'If you love me, get the next boat!', and he had responded, 'I will! I will!'

From James Breckenridge to May Lavender

Liverpool
October 27th 1867

My dearest May,

I hardly know how to begin this letter. This morning, as your ship was drawing away from the quay, you shouted to me that if I loved you I should get the next boat, and I, desperate at the thought of losing you, promised that I would. The receipt of this letter will be sufficient evidence that I have not kept my promise, since it will be carried on the ship I should have taken. If this comes as a blow to you, I can only offer my deepest and most heartfelt apologies; but I believe you will have realised by now that it was a promise I could not keep. We both know that my mother has only months, possibly weeks, to live. How could I leave her to suffer alone? I must stay at her side until the end, whenever that may come.

There is another consideration: my solicitor's articles. I am bound to Mr Weaver until the end of next year. He might, possibly, let me go before that time, but then I should have wasted four years' hard work. If I stay here until I have passed my final examination I shall be a qualified solicitor and able to set up in business anywhere. I am sure there must be openings for me in Melbourne, or wherever in Australia you have decided to settle. That way I shall be in a position to support a wife and family and offer them a respectable place in society. I know that now your father is, by all accounts, a wealthy man, you may feel that this is an irrelevant consideration; but to me it is not. If I were to come and ask for your hand in marriage as a penniless man with no qualifications, I might well be regarded as a 'gold digger', and with some justification. It is vital for me to be able to stand on my own feet, and not to depend on the support of my father-in-law, however freely offered. I am sure that, knowing me as you do, you will understand that.

Dearest May, a year is a long time and I cannot ask you to promise to wait for me. I am sure there are a great many young men who will be eager to court you, who may have talents and attributes that I lack. If you should fall in love with such a one, then it would be unfair and cruel of me to put you in a position of having to choose between breaking a promise to me and following your heart. I can only hope that the memory of the time we have spent together is as dear and as potent for you as it is for me, and that you will still be free when I arrive. I <u>shall come,</u> that I swear. Nothing will keep me here once my obligations have been discharged.

My darling, I think of you every day and dream of you every night. I shall miss our expeditions together and our long talks. I shall miss the way you look at me, with those beautiful eyes, and the touch of your hand in mine. The months ahead seem very lonely and dull. I wish letters did not take so long to travel across the oceans. I long to hear from you that you have arrived safely and found everything to your satisfaction. Write as soon as you can.

Remember me to your brother. I hope he is well and prospering.

With all my love,
James

Three

My dear James,

This is the second letter I have written to you within the space of twenty-four hours. In the first I told you that I could see no future for us as a married couple and begged you to forget me. I had every intention of doing the same and making a new beginning in Australia. But then I saw you on the dockside, swearing your love to me and offering to marry me without any conditions, and I felt as if my heart was being torn out of my body. I was almost tempted to throw myself overboard in the hope that I might somehow get back to the shore and feel your arms around me again.

I have had time to think more sensibly now. What I said in my first letter is right. Marriage between us could never have worked in England. For you to wed an orphan girl, brought up in the workhouse, would have caused a scandal and broken your poor mother's heart. You would have found yourself banned from polite society and your only clients would have been criminals and down-and-outs.

And the alternative would have been worse. If we had tried to hide my background and persist with the fiction that I am the daughter of a sea captain with a respectable family, we should have been afraid all the time that someone would recognise me and give the game away. And I should always have had that sneaking fear that you might end up regretting having married me. But Gus writes that in Australia no one cares about who your parents were or where you were brought up. Perhaps there, we could marry without fear of scandal.

As the ship drew away I shouted to you that if you loved me you should get the next boat, and I heard you say 'I will.' I know that that is not possible and I should never have asked it. You could never leave your mother, in her poor state of health. She needs you beside her for as long as she lives.

Quite apart from that, you have to finish your solicitor's qualification. You cannot throw away all the work you have already done. You must stay in England until that is complete. I pray that you have realised this as well and have not been impetuous enough to take the ship before you receive this letter.

That means it will be more than a year before you can even think of joining me and in that time many things may change. It is very likely that you will meet another young lady who would make you a far more suitable bride. I know your mother has already introduced you to several in the hope that you might fall in love with one. It would certainly set her mind at rest. I know she has never regarded me as a suitable prospect. If that should happen, you must not feel bound by that promise you shouted across the water in a moment of great emotion. You might well feel you would prefer to marry this other girl and settle in England, where you are almost guaranteed a successful career and a recognised position in society, rather than embarking on an unknown future in a strange land.

But if, in the end, you still feel about me as you did this morning, I shall be waiting for you. I know that I shall never love anyone else as I love you. I shall keep the memory of the times we have spent together close to my heart and dream that one day I shall feel your arms around me again.

Take care of yourself, dear James, and write to me as soon as you can. I know the letter cannot reach me until another ship arrives in Melbourne, so it will be nearly Christmas before I receive it. I shall post this letter at our first port of call, which I believe will be Cape Town, so you will not have to wait quite so long.

I shall go to bed now, and dream that you are kissing me. I long for the day when that dream may become reality.

With all my love,
May

Four

On the evening of Miss Drake's departure, Connor McBride and his wife sat facing each other in his smoking room.

'So, what do we do now?' he asked.

'Look for another governess, I suppose, though where we shall find anyone suitable at this short notice heaven only knows.'

'I am wondering if a governess is the answer. The two we have had so far do not seem to have made much progress.'

'Because she is a wilful, disobedient child. She has to be taught discipline.'

'Perhaps we are going the wrong way about it. She is kept so much in seclusion. I do not see how she is ever going to learn how to conduct herself in society if she never sees anyone except a crabbed old governess and the servants.'

'So what do you suggest?'

'Perhaps we should send her to school.'

'And remove her entirely from my supervision, to mix with lord knows who? It's too much of a risk.'

'Then perhaps there is a halfway house. She needs to learn some of the accomplishments of a young lady.

We could employ tutors to teach her music, drawing, that sort of thing. And then she might be able to meet people … carefully selected people. What do you think? We cannot keep her shut up in this house for ever.' Mrs McBride chewed her bottom lip in indecision. 'Come,' her husband went on, 'she's a pretty little thing and she can be charming when she puts her mind to it. She may yet be a credit to us.'

'Well, perhaps it might be possible now. Now that that chit of a girl is no longer around to spread her gossip.'

'To whom do you refer?'

'That little milliner's apprentice, the workhouse girl. May something or other. The one who remembered … who thought she remembered Angelina.'

'What has happened to her?'

'Gone off to Australia, by all accounts. She'll fit in well there, among the felons and barbarians.'

'How do you know all this?'

'I happened to meet Laura Pearson the other day and remark upon her new bonnet. She tells me there is a new milliner at Freeman's now. The old woman has retired and the girl has left.'

'Are they the only ones who … who guessed?'

'So far as I know. I made it pretty clear at the time that if the story spread I should know who to blame.'

'Well, then. Shall we try my idea?'

Angelina's first emotion as the door closed behind Miss Drake was one of triumph. She was the victor and her foe had been removed from the field. This was rapidly replaced by apprehension. She had succeeded in getting rid of one tyrant, but who might follow? She woke up the next morning with a sense of dread.

It seemed at first that there was to be a return to the short interregnum which had occurred between Miss Garvey leaving and the arrival of Miss Drake: Jane brought up her breakfast, she was left to dress herself and then her mother appeared with a large, leather-bound book. She dumped it on the schoolroom table.

'This is called the Encyclopaedia Britannica and it has all the facts in it that anyone could ever want to know. You can learn a great deal from a book like this.' She opened it more or less at random. 'Egypt. That should be quite educational. Copy that out in your best handwriting. I will be back soon to see how much you have done, so don't sit there wasting your time.'

She left and Angelina took up her pen and began reluctantly to write. Some of what she read was quite interesting, but there was a good deal she did not understand. An hour passed. Her hand ached and her shoulders were stiff. She longed to get up from the table and look out of the window, but she was afraid that her mother might return at any moment and she knew that if she was not working she would be punished. Her mother came back at last and cast a cursory glance over the pages she had written.

'You have made three blots. Not good enough. You will have to do better than that. Now, do you have a sampler to stitch?'

'Yes, Mama.'

'You had better get on with that until luncheon. But make sure you wash your hands first. You don't want ink all over it.'

Angelina did as she was bidden. Stitching the sampler was even more boring than copying, and she wished there was someone she could talk to. She almost began to regret the departure of Miss Drake, but the memory of the pain of having her arms bound behind her back soon dispelled that thought.

She had just finished her luncheon, brought up to her on a tray and eaten in solitary silence, when her mother reappeared, bringing with her a young woman with fair hair and a soft, delicate face.

'Angelina, this is Miss Elizabeth Findlay. Her father is one of your papa's employees and she has agreed to come and take care of you until other arrangements can be made. She will help you with your reading, spelling, sewing and so forth. I trust you will behave yourself, but I have made it clear to Miss Findlay that if she has any complaints she can refer them to me and I will deal with them. Don't stand there gaping! You know how to greet a stranger.'

Angelina curtsied hurriedly. 'How do you do, ma'am?'

'Oh, please!' The young woman's face had flushed. 'You don't need to curtsy to me, or call me ma'am. My family always call me Lizzie. I think you can call me that, too.'

'Huh.' Mrs McBride's brief exclamation made it clear what she thought of that, but she said only, 'Well, I'll leave you to it. I have other matters to attend to.'

When the door had closed behind her, Lizzie turned to Angelina with a smile. 'Your mama tells me you usually go for a walk in the afternoons. It's cold today but the sun is shining. Shall we go?'

For a moment Angelina was unsure how to react. All her life she had been told what to do next. She had never been offered any choice in the matter. Briefly, she wondered what would happen if she said 'no', but the habit of acquiescence was hard to break.

'Yes, if you please.'

Lizzie helped her on with her bonnet and cape and wrapped a scarf round her neck. 'We don't want you to get cold, do we?'

This solicitude was new, too. Miss Drake had advocated a brisk, invigorating walk as the best way to keep warm and had no patience with complaints.

Once outside she was offered another choice. 'Where would you like to go?'

'To the park, if you please.'

'Good. I like the park, too. Off we go then.'

Once among the bare trees and the drooping evergreens, Angelina began to wish she had opted to stay indoors. It was November and the cold nipped at her toes and the tip of her nose.

'Are you interested in Nature Study?' Lizzie asked.

'I don't know what that means.'

'Learning about plants and flowers and insects and that sort of thing.'

'Miss Drake made me learn the names of all the trees.'

'Well, that's a start, I suppose. But there's more to it than knowing names of things. It's about keeping your eyes open and noticing things. Look over there, under that tree, for example. Do you see those fungi with red tops and white spots?'

'They're toadstools, not … not what you called them. Miss Drake said never to touch them.'

'Well, she was right. They are poisonous. But aren't they pretty? I used to like to think that they were umbrellas for the fairies to shelter under when it rained.'

'I don't believe in fairies. That's just superstition.'

'I don't believe in them, either, but I still enjoy fairy stories.'

'What do you mean?'

'You must have read fairy stories – or had them read to you, surely?'

'No.'

'Oh, you poor little thing! I'll bring you a book from home with wonderful stories in it. I live quite close. I can pop back easily.'

'I'm not a poor little thing!'

'No, of course you're not. I just mean it's a shame you have never heard a fairy story.' She shivered. 'It's really cold, isn't it? I tell you what. Let's run to warm ourselves up. I'll race you to the end of this path. Come on!'

She set off, running swiftly, her skirt gathered up above her ankles. Angelina followed, but she had never been allowed to run. Her legs did not seem to know what to do and she was soon out of breath. Lizzie reached the end of the path and turned, her face glowing.

'Come on! Lazy bones! You can do better than that.'

Angelina stopped running and stood still. Lizzie came back to her.

'What's wrong? Is there something the matter with you?'

'No. I don't like running. It's not ladylike. My mama wouldn't like me to do it.'

'Wouldn't she? Oh dear. I didn't know that. Perhaps we shouldn't tell her?'

Angelina saw a trace of alarm on Lizzie's face. She was afraid of what Mama might say. She stored the knowledge away for future use.

'I'd like to go home now.'

Later that afternoon, when she went down to the drawing room, her mother asked if she had been for her regular outing.

'Yes, we went to the park. Lizzie ran away and I couldn't catch up with her.'

'Ran away?'

'She said it was a race. She picked up her skirt and showed her ankles.'

Her mother tutted and murmured, 'I suppose it's to be expected when you employ that class of girl. But we shall have to make do with her for the time being. At such short notice it's impossible to find a suitable governess. But I have made other arrangements. I have decided it is time for you to concentrate on the sort of accomplishments that are expected of a young lady of quality.

'I spoke this morning to Mrs Pearson. Mr Pearson sits on several of the same committees as your papa. She has two daughters, Mary and Louisa, about your age, and she employs a Mr Latimer to teach them drawing and painting. She is happy for you to join them every Tuesday morning. On Friday afternoons they go to dancing classes with a Mrs Fairchild and I have enrolled you as well. On Wednesday mornings I have engaged a Mademoiselle Duchovny to give you lessons in French conversation.

'Finally, I have arranged for a Madame Corelli to give all three of you music lessons. The Pearson girls will come here for that on Thursday afternoons and I have ordered a piano for that purpose.' She fixed a stern gaze on Angelina. 'You will understand that this represents a considerable financial outlay. I shall expect you to make good use of the lessons and do me credit in front of the Pearson girls. I am told that the elder girl, Mary, is already highly accomplished in all disciplines.'

'I'll do my best, Mama,' Angelina said. The words were spoken automatically as she strove to comprehend what this new turn of events would mean. Painting and music and dancing sounded much more interesting than Miss Drake's regime of mental arithmetic and learning by heart, but she was not sure if she would like being compared with two girls she had never met. It was easy to guess from her mother's last words that she was going to be expected to do as well, if not better, than them.

Returning to the schoolroom, she found Lizzie clasping a large book. She held it out so that Angelina could read the title. '*Wonderful Stories for Children* by Hans Christian Anderson, translated from the Danish by Mary Howitt.'

'I slipped home while you were with your mama, as I promised. I'll read you one of the stories at bedtime. Should you like that?'

Angelina frowned. She had not forgotten being called a 'poor little thing'.

'I'm not sure I shall like that. I think they are stories for little children. I'm growing up. I'm going to learn to dance and sing and paint.'

'Well, I still enjoy them. And I'm pretty well grown up. Why don't we try them anyway.'

'If you wish.' Angelina turned away, determined to conceal her curiosity, but when she was ready for bed, and Lizzie sat down by her side and opened the book, she did not object. Lizzie chose the story of the Ugly Duckling and within minutes Angelina was engrossed.

She woke next morning to a confusion of emotions. She had to acknowledge to herself that she liked Lizzie. The walk and the bedtime story had given her more pleasure than she wanted to admit. But at the same time there was resentment at being called a poor little thing and a lazy bones. She did not like being either pitied or criticised – and there was her mother's remark about employing someone 'of that class'. That meant that Lizzie was a servant, and servants had to know their place. It came into her head that she had to show Lizzie who was the mistress and who the servant.

So when Lizzie came to help her dress, she rejected the frock laid out for her. 'I don't want to wear that. I want the pink silk with the lace.'

'Oh no, I don't think that would be suitable. That's a party dress, much too fine for every day.'

'I don't care. That's the one I'm wearing today.'

'Now, Angelina, don't be difficult. You know that dress is only for special occasions. Come along now, let me help you.'

'No! I won't get dressed at all if I can't wear that one.'

'That would be very silly. This dress is pretty. Put it on, there's a good girl.'

'No!' Angelina snatched the dress out of her hands so violently that a seam tore. 'There, look what you made me do! It will have to be mended now and Mama will be cross. I shall tell her it was your fault.'

Lizzie looked at her for a moment, then she sighed and turned away. 'Very well. But if the dress gets spoiled, your mama will be angry.'

Victory having been achieved, Angelina set about consolidating her position. She fidgeted and complained while Lizzie brushed her hair, insisted on having it done in plaits and then said they weren't done properly and wanted them taken out again. At breakfast, she refused to eat her boiled egg on the grounds that it was too hard and made Lizzie go down to the kitchen for a fresh one.

By the time they sat down at the schoolroom table for lessons, she had worked herself into a thoroughly bad temper and Lizzie was no longer smiling.

At that moment Mrs McBride came into the room.

Lizzie stood up and curtsied.

'Good morning, ma'am.'

Mrs McBride acknowledged the greeting with a nod. 'Well, Angelina? Have you quite forgotten your manners?'

Angelina rose reluctantly and curtsied. 'Good morning, Mama.'

'Good heavens, child! Why ever are you wearing that dress? Really, Lizzie, I am amazed that you have no more sense than to dress her in something so unsuitable!'

Lizzie looked uncomfortable. 'Angelina insisted, ma'am.'

'Insisted! A child does not insist, she obeys! You must exercise more authority or I fear we shall have to part with you. Put her into something more suitable at once.'

She swept out and Lizzie turned to Angelina. 'Do you want me to be sent away?'

Angelina bit her lips and shook her head.

'Then we had better get you properly dressed.'

When the frock had been exchanged for another one and they returned to the schoolroom, Lizzie laid a small book on the table.

'I thought we would read from this book and afterwards you can copy some of it to practise your handwriting.' She passed it to Angelina. 'Read me the first few pages.'

The book was called *An Infant's Progress, or from the Valley of Destruction to Everlasting Glory* by Mrs Sherwood. Angelina began to read. The main characters were children called Humble Mind and his sisters Playful and Peace, and there was a being called Sin who was 'as ill-favoured and ill-conditioned an urchin as one could see', who whispered in their ears tempting them to do all sorts of wicked things. The message that to achieve everlasting glory it was necessary to be humble and obedient was clear enough but it left Angelina puzzled.

'What is everlasting glory?' she asked.

'I suppose it means going to heaven.'

'And what happens to people who are not humble and obedient?'

'Well, if they go on all their lives doing bad things, the Bible tells us they go to hell. But the point of this story is that it is never too late to mend your ways and learn to be good. But you know this, don't you? You say your prayers every night. You ask God not to lead us into temptation but to deliver us from evil.'

'Oh yes …' Angelina had been taught her prayers by rote by her nurse as soon as she was able to repeat the words, but she had never thought about the meaning. 'So it doesn't matter if someone is naughty, as long as they make up their mind to be good in the end?'

'We are taught that God is merciful and he doesn't punish those who are truly repentant.'

'Are we?'

'Haven't you learned that at Sunday School?'

'What is Sunday School?'

'Don't you go to church?'

'No. Miss Drake used to go, I think – and Jane and Betty.'

'What about your mama and papa?'

'Oh, no.' In Angelina's mind church-going was for servants and suchlike people, not for ladies and gentlemen.

'That's strange.' Lizzie looked as if she found it hard to believe.

Angelina pushed the book away. 'I don't want to read any more. I want to do something else.'

'As you please. I think we should practise our spelling next.'

'I hate spelling!'

'When you are grown up and have to write letters, people will laugh at you if you cannot spell correctly.'

Angelina struggled for a moment with warring impulses, then she shrugged and muttered, 'Oh, very well. If I must.'

It rained all afternoon so there was no question of a walk. Lizzie hunted in the cupboard where Angelina's toys were kept and found a game of snakes and ladders.

'Shall we play this?'

'I don't know how.'

Lizzie gave her a look that she was coming to recognise, but all she said was, 'It's easy. I'll teach you.'

In bed that night Angelina pondered their conversation about temptation and redemption. Miss Garvey had been apt to tell her that Jesus would not be pleased with her if she did not do as she was told, and she had been made to learn the Commandments and the Beatitudes by heart, but there had never been any discussion of religious matters. She vaguely recalled the governess saying that, as her mama and papa were Catholics, she had better not put her own ideas into Angelina's head, but she had not understood what that meant. She decided on the strength of what Lizzie had told her that it would be best not to be naughty, but comforted herself with the thought that, if she could not manage it, she could always say sorry later.

Next day being Tuesday, Lizzie walked with her the short distance to the Pearsons' house. The parlourmaid had been told to expect them and led them upstairs to the schoolroom, where the two Pearson girls were waiting for them. The elder of the two stepped forward with the air of a seasoned hostess.

'Good morning. I'm Mary Pearson and this is my sister, Louisa. Say "how do you do", Lulu.'

The younger girl gave a giggle and put her finger in her mouth, so that the greeting came out as a mumble.

'This is Angelina,' Lizzie said. 'I'm sure you are all going to be great friends. I'll leave you now, Angelina. I'll be back to collect you at midday.'

It was on the tip of Angelina's tongue to ask her to stay, but she was determined not to appear a baby in comparison to the self-assured Mary. She put on the tone of voice she had heard her mother use when dismissing servants.

'Thank you, Lizzie. I shall not need you until then.'

Lizzie gave her an odd look but said only, 'Enjoy your lesson,' and departed.

'I'm nearly eleven years old,' Mary said. 'How old are you?'

'Eight.'

'Oh, you're only a bit older than Louisa, then. She's still a baby.'

'I'm not!' said the indignant Louisa.

'I am not a baby,' Angelina said firmly.

'Have you had drawing lessons before?'

'No.'

'Shall I show you some of my paintings?' Mary led her over to one side of the room where a number of watercolours of flowers and fruit were pinned along the dado rail. 'These are all mine. Mr Latimer likes them very much. He says I am extremely talented.' She waved a hand at the opposite side of the room, where a series of slightly distorted images of dogs and kittens were displayed. 'Those are Louisa's,' she said dismissively. 'They are not very good.'

Angelina looked at the flower paintings. They were very large and painted in brighter colours than any she had ever seen growing.

'Mr Latimer will be here soon,' Mary said. 'He's nice but he gets a bit impatient at times. Don't worry. I won't let him be cross with you. He never tells me off.'

Angelina looked at her. She was tall for her age and rather thin, with bony shoulders and a nose that was slightly too large. Her hair was brown and dressed into elaborate ringlets and her eyes were brown as well and rather small. Angelina wondered what made her so sure of herself. Mary might be older, but Angelina knew she was prettier.

There were footsteps outside the door and a middle-aged gentleman with untidy greying hair hurried in.

'Apologies, my dear young ladies! I was delayed at my last lesson.' He looked around. 'Now, you must be Miss McBride. I was told to expect an extra pupil. How do you do?'

'How do you do, sir,' Angelina responded, with a small curtsy.

'Now,' Mr Latimer was already unpacking items from a large leather bag, 'let us not waste any more time. Sit down, if you please. Miss Pearson, I know this is your usual place, next to me, but for today I think it will be better if our new student sits here. Bring that blue jug over here, if you please.' Mary turned aside with a haughty shrug, clearly displeased at being displaced, and Mr Latimer fetched the jug himself. 'Come, Miss Louisa, leave the kitten alone and come up to the table, please.'

For the first time Angelina noticed that the younger sister had picked up a black kitten from a basket and was cuddling it. She felt a stab of envy. She had never been allowed a pet, on the grounds that animals were unhygienic and caused a distraction.

Sheets of paper and pencils and paints had been laid out in readiness and the teacher was busy arranging a branch of holly and some trails of ivy in the blue jug.

'Now, we are going to draw what is called a still life, a picture of an assemblage of objects such as this. Let me see what you make of it.'

Mary set to work immediately, her expression suggesting that something so simple was almost beneath her. The image of the vase and its contents grew rapidly under her pencil. Angelina tried to emulate her, but somehow the two sides of the jug never seemed to be symmetrical and the holly branch, to be in scale, would have had to extend beyond the margins of the paper. It took Mr Latimer some time to cajole Louisa into putting down the kitten and taking up her pencil and then she demanded his full attention to every line. Mary leaned across the table to look at Angelina's efforts and gave a high-pitched squeal of laughter.

'Oh dear! Mr Latimer, do look at Angelina's drawing! It's all lopsided.'

The teacher came over and gave Angelina a new sheet of paper and showed her how to correct the proportions of her drawing, but it was too late. She had decided that she hated the whole business and had no wish to try any further. By the time Lizzie came to collect her she was in a sulk, and had to be prompted with difficulty to thank him and say a polite goodbye to her two young hosts.

'I'm not going back there again!' she declared as they walked home.

'Whatever makes you say that?'

'That Mary Pearson is hateful! She thinks she is brilliant and Mr Latimer just agrees with her. And Louisa is a spoilt baby. And they have a kitten! Why cannot I have a kitten?'

'Well, who knows,' Lizzie said gently. 'If you please your mama and do your lessons well, she might let you have a kitten as a reward. But if you refuse to go back, I think that is very unlikely.'

'But I can't draw!' Angelina burst out, on the verge of tears.

'You have only just started to learn. It will come, if you persist. And I'm sure Mary and Louisa are quite nice really. You just need to get to know them.'

Next morning, Mademoiselle Duchovny arrived to give Angelina her first French lesson. She was a small, grey woman: grey hair, grey dress, with a permanent expression of weary resignation. Angelina, still disgruntled from her experience of the day before, was not in a compliant mood.

'*Bonjour, ma petite*,' Mademoiselle began. 'Now, you must say "*bonjour*, Madame".'

'Why?'

'Because that is the French for "good day, madam".'

'Why can't I say it in English?'

'Because a French lady would not understand you.'

'You understand me.'

'That is because I have lived a long time in England. But if you went to France you would not be understood.'

'But I'm not going to France.'

'Nevertheless, it is regarded as an essential accomplishment for a well-educated young lady to be able to converse in French. Now, repeat after me: *Bonjour*.'

'Boojoo.'

'No, try again. Listen carefully: *Bonjour.*'

'Bong joo. It sounds silly. I don't want to say it.'

At the end of the hour Angelina had reluctantly managed to get her tongue round half a dozen words and Mademoiselle Duchovny's expression was wearier than ever.

'French is stupid,' Angelina declared when Lizzie came in with her luncheon. 'People just ought to learn English.'

Lizzie shook her head and sighed but said nothing.

As they reached the front door, ready to go out for their usual walk, they found their way blocked by three men who were struggling to fit a large, unwieldy object through the doorway.

'What is it?' Angelina asked.

'I think it must be the piano your mother ordered so you can learn to play. You are a very fortunate girl, you know. Such things cost a great deal of money.'

Angelina tossed her head. 'Oh, that's all right. Papa has plenty of money.' Then she caught the look on Lizzie's face and thought that perhaps she should not have spoken so dismissively.

The men eventually succeeded in getting the piano through the door and carried it into the drawing room, and Lizzie and Angelina set out for their walk. The weather was milder and there were more people about and before long Angelina's attention was attracted by excited shouts. A short distance ahead a group of children were darting among the bushes around a small clearing. She saw three or four girls about her own age and a small boy. Nearby, two young women in nursemaid's uniforms sat on a bench chatting. One of the girls took up a position in the centre of the clearing with her hands over her eyes and began to count aloud.

'What are they doing?' she asked.

'Playing hide and seek by the look of it. Would you like to join in?'

'I'm not sure. I don't know them.'

'I expect that can be arranged. Come along.' Lizzie took her hand and led her over to the bench.

'Good afternoon. My name is Elizabeth Findlay and this is Miss Angelina McBride. I was wondering, could she join in the game with the other children?'

One of the nursemaids got up with a smile. 'Of course she can. Grace! Come here a minute.'

The children had scattered among the bushes but now they were reappearing, one by one, as they were found. The tallest girl responded to the summons and came to join them.

'Grace, this is Angelina. She would like to play with you. You wouldn't mind if she joined in, would you?'

'Of course not.' Grace held out her hand to Angelina. 'Come on.'

Angelina allowed herself to be led into the clearing where the others were assembled.

'Whose turn is it to be "on"?' someone asked.

'Georgie,' came the reply.

'No,' Grace said. 'He's too young. It will take him ages to find us and we'll be frozen before he does. Prue, you do it.'

'Oh, very well.' The girl thus addressed took up a position in the centre and began to count. The others scattered again, leaving Angelina gazing about her doubtfully.

'Come on!' Grace called. 'You have to hide.'

She followed the others into the bushes and saw them secreting themselves under overhanging branches or behind tree trunks. It took her a while to find a place that was not already occupied but she finally settled on a spot in the middle of dense group of rhododendrons. She crouched down and suddenly the strangest feeling came over her. She had been here before! This had happened before, a long time ago. She could not remember the occasion, or who else might have been involved; but the sensation was deeply unsettling. Without waiting to be found she broke cover and ran back to Lizzie, who was chatting to the nursemaids.

'I don't want to play this game! Let's go on with our walk.'

Lizzie looked at her with a frown. 'What a strange little creature you are, to be sure. Come along, then.' She turned to the other young women with a shrug. 'Sorry about that. She's not used to having anyone to play with.'

When they got home, an unexpected sound arrested them as they crossed the hall. A single, clear note, repeated two or three times on a slightly varying pitch; then a ripple of other notes and the single note repeated again.

'What is it?' Angelina asked.

'I think the piano is being tuned. Shall we look in and see?'

In the drawing room stood a gleaming piece of furniture with an open lid propped up by a stay and a keyboard of black and white notes. A small man was stooping over it, pressing the keys and peering into the interior. Angelina tiptoed over to him.

'What are you doing?'

He looked round with a start. 'I'm tuning it, miss. After it's been moved around the notes are sure to have gone out of pitch.'

'What does that mean?'

For the next twenty minutes or so Angelina listened, fascinated, as he showed her how the notes were sounded by a small, felt-covered hammer striking a string and how that string could be tightened or relaxed to alter the pitch.

'Now,' he said at length, 'here's a test for you. Listen to this.' He produced a tuning fork and tapped it on the side of the piano, producing a ringing note. 'Now, can you tell me if this note I'm going to play is the same, or is it a bit higher or lower?'

He struck a note. Angelina listened hard. 'It's a tiny bit higher.'

'Well done, you've a good ear. It's what we call a bit sharp, so I need to ease the string a tiny bit. Now, is that better?'

'Yes. It's right now.'

'Good!'

The door opened and Mrs McBride swept in. 'Angelina! What are you doing in here? Lizzie, she should be in the schoolroom, not bothering this man and stopping him getting on with his work.'

The piano tuner straightened up. 'She's not bothering me, ma'am. It's good to see someone taking an interest. You've done well, if you'll forgive me saying so, to get this little lady a piano. She has a good ear. She will make an excellent musician, given time.'

'Oh, well, I'm glad to hear it.' Mrs McBride was mollified. 'But you must run along now, Angelina. You will be able to play the piano tomorrow when you have your lesson.'

'Did you like that?' Lizzie asked, as they made their way up the stairs.

'Yes, I did.'

'So, are you looking forward to your lesson?'

'Yes, except those horrible Pearson girls are coming too. I don't want them to play my piano.'

'You mustn't be selfish. After all, they let you share their art lesson.'

'That's not the same. It's only paper and pencils.'

'Well, remember you are extremely lucky to have such a fine instrument. The Pearsons may not have a piano at all. I expect you will be allowed to practise on it every day.'

'Shall I? And they won't be able to, if they haven't got a piano, will they?'

'I imagine not.'

'That's all right, then,' Angelina said with satisfaction.

Mary and Louisa Pearson arrived promptly the following afternoon. Angelina greeted them graciously.

'And this is my new piano. My papa has bought it specially for me. I talked to the man who came to tune it yesterday. He says I have a very good ear. Have you got a piano at home, Mary?'

'No, but I expect we will have soon.'

Mrs McBride ushered in a plump lady in a purple dress and a turban, decked out with a plethora of ribbons and scarves and feathers.

'Girls, this is Madame Corelli, who is going to teach you music. I'm sure you will all give her your full attention.' This last with a meaningful glare at Angelina.

'I am sure we shall have a delightful afternoon,' Madame Corelli responded. She moved to the piano. 'But what a splendid instrument. You are indeed fortunate.'

She sat down on the piano stool and ran her much beringed fingers over the keys, producing a succession of chords that made Angelina clap her hands in delight. Mrs McBride, finding herself no longer attended to, took herself off.

'So – ' Madame turned towards the three girls '– who do we have here?'

'I'm Mary.' The oldest girl was quick to seize the initiative. 'And this is my sister Louisa.'

'So you must be Angelina, the fortunate owner of this lovely instrument,' Madame said, turning to her with a smile.

'Yes, I am,' she responded smugly.

'Well, let us see what sort of voices you have. Listen.' She sang an ascending scale. 'Doh re mi fa so la tee doh. Mary, you first.'

Mary took a deep breath and sang the first four notes, then had to be prompted.

'Well tried. You have a strong voice but you were slightly flat. Now, Angelina, you try.'

She repeated the scale and Angelina sang it back to her. Madame Corelli clapped her hands. 'But such a lovely little voice! As true as a bird. You will do very well.'

Angelina looked at Mary and Mary glared back.

Louisa, persuaded with difficulty to take her finger out of her mouth, sang in a breathy whisper.

'Courage, my child!' Madame encouraged her. 'No one is going to bite you. Now let us see how you all get on with the piano.'

She showed them how to play a simple scale. Mary went first again.

'No, no! There is no need to thump the keys so hard. You are not kneading bread!'

'I've never had to knead bread.'

'Try to remember the piano is not your enemy, to be beaten into submission. Now, Angelina.'

Angelina laid her fingers on the keys. For the first time in her life her whole attention was engaged and as the first note sounded she felt a shiver of pleasure.

'Bravo! You have the right touch. Try it again, a little faster.'

By the end of the lesson Angelina could play the whole C major scale with both hands. Mary tried to emulate her, but she tried to play too fast and constantly hit wrong notes. Her temper grew progressively worse as the hour passed. Louisa was permitted to stick to the simple five-finger exercise and paid little attention to what the other two girls were doing. Finally, Madame Corelli taught them a simple little tune and left them with instructions to practise every day. 'Mary can't practise,' Angelina said. 'She hasn't got a piano.'

'Perhaps she could come here,' Madame suggested, to Angelina's dismay.

'I shall not need to,' Mary said grandly. 'My papa will get me a piano of my own.'

Angelina went to bed humming the tune and insisted next morning on going down to the drawing room to practise before she started her lessons with Lizzie, much to the annoyance of Jane the parlourmaid, who was waiting to clean the room.

Five

Friday was the day of Angelina's first dancing lesson. She had viewed the prospect with some trepidation, but after her triumph of the previous day she felt ready to attempt anything that involved music. Her confidence was reinforced when her mother came up to her room and ordered Lizzie to dress her in the pink satin she had been forced to take off a few days earlier.

She then took the care of Angelina's hair into her own hands – an attention unknown in recent years – and dressed it in a mass of ringlets. Even more surprisingly, she came with them to the dancing class.

Mrs Fairchild had turned a large room at the top of her house into a dance studio, clearing it of everything except a piano and a row of chairs along both sides. Those on one side were occupied by half-a-dozen fond mamas. Eight girls, including the Pearsons, and six boys sat along the opposite side, the girls giggling together and admiring each other's dresses, the boys fidgeting awkwardly in their best suits.

Mrs Fairchild clapped her hands. 'Now, children, let us begin. Since we do not have even numbers, one of you girls will have to take the gentleman's part. Mary, you are the tallest. You had better be a man for now. So, gentlemen, take your partners for the *schottische*.'

The boys came forward and it was clear that most of them had regular partners who were waiting for them. They made awkward bows and offered their arms. Only Angelina and Louisa were left for Mary and the one remaining boy to choose between. Angelina saw Mary look from her to her sister and shrug disdainfully. She cringed as Mary came towards her, but before she reached her the boy stepped forward.

'May I have the honour?' The expression of fury on Mary's face was enough to convince Angelina that this was a triumph. Blushing deeply, she made a curtsy and took his arm.

They took their places on the floor and Angelina whispered, 'I don't know how to do this.'

He smiled at her. 'Don't worry. Mrs F. always goes over the movements before we begin.'

It was true, and Angelina picked up the simple steps very quickly. When the teacher seated herself at the piano and they went through the dance to the music, she felt her pulse quicken with pleasure. When it was over, her partner, who told her his name was John, led her back to her chair and thanked her with another bow.

'Now, gentlemen,' Mrs Fairchild said, 'choose a new partner for the *polonaise*.'

Angelina looked around, afraid that she might find herself having to dance with Mary, but another boy came forward and led her onto the floor. As they passed the assembled matriarchs, she heard one whisper to her mother, 'Such a pretty child! Why haven't we seen her before?'

After the *polonaise,* Mrs Fairchild instructed one of the other girls to take Mary's place as a gentleman, and when she announced the next dance, Angelina saw Mary cast a coquettish look towards John. He ignored it and asked Angelina to dance instead.

The next dances were a little more complicated and Angelina made some mistakes. As they passed Mary and her new partner, she heard her say condescendingly, 'Oh, she is doing quite well, poor thing, considering the fact that her mama has never let her out of the house before.' In the next interval she drew two other girls into a corner and they giggled together and cast glances across the room in Angelina's direction. Angelina could not imagine what they were laughing at, but she felt her face burning with embarrassment.

At the end of the class her mother called her over and introduced her to two other ladies.

'I can't believe you have never had a lesson before,' one said. 'You look so much at ease on the dance floor.'

'Such a pretty girl,' the other said. 'She won't want for beaux when she's a little older.'

Her mother smiled and stroked her cheek. Angelina went home well satisfied.

Two weeks followed without any major disruption. Angelina's efforts at drawing evoked mocking comments from Mary, until Mr Latimer told her that such remarks were unbecoming from one as talented as she was to someone less able. Mary relapsed into smug silence and Angelina seethed inwardly, but the peace was maintained. The French lessons continued to be a trial for both teacher and pupil, but almost in spite of herself Angelina learned a few phrases.

It was the music and the dancing that compensated for frustrations elsewhere. On her next visit Madame Corelli gave her and Mary a song to learn. It was called 'The Last Rose of Summer'. On the following Thursday she told Mary that singing loudly did not make up for singing flat; but she clapped her hands at Angelina's rendering, which she called true and delicate. When Mrs McBride came into the room at the end of the lesson, she said, 'Your daughter has a delightful voice. It is a talent that should be encouraged.'

Next morning, Mrs McBride's dressmaker appeared in the schoolroom to measure Angelina for a new frock and two days later she delivered a gorgeous creation in pale-blue taffeta which, everyone agreed, suited her even better than the pink satin. On her mother's next 'at home' afternoon, when she was entertaining several ladies of her acquaintance, Lizzie was given instructions, instead of the usual walk, to dress Angelina in the blue taffeta and send her down to the drawing room. Her appearance was greeted with exclamations of delight.

'Oh, how pretty she is!'

'Marguerite, she's a beauty. Where have you been hiding her?'

Her mother lifted an eyebrow. 'I felt it would be a mistake to introduce her to society before she was ready. Now, Angelina, I want you to sing for the ladies. Sing the song Madame Corelli taught you last week.'

Angelina's knees were shaking but she took a breath and began to sing, and once the first note was out the sound of her own voice gave her confidence and she sang with real pleasure. The ladies applauded and insisted on an encore. When it was finished her mother did something unprecedented. She called Angelina to her and kissed her on the forehead. After that, she was rewarded with one of the delicious cream cakes, which were set out on the tea table, and sent back to the schoolroom.

The dancing classes helped to reinforce this newfound confidence. John always claimed her for the first and the last dance and got angry when another boy tried to take his place. She had noticed that the other girls vied for his attention, and she felt flattered. He was the oldest amongst them and, she decided, the best looking. When she wore the blue taffeta, he said, 'I like your new dress. You look pretty.'

At their next music lesson, Mary declared triumphantly, 'My papa is going to buy me a piano, *and* I am going to have a puppy dog for Christmas.'

All Angelina's pleas fell on deaf ears. A dog would make a mess, require feeding and walking, and generally be a nuisance. Exactly how it happened that on the following Tuesday a jar of water was upset all over Mary's almost finished painting was never satisfactorily established.

Next morning, Angelina refused point blank to speak a single word of French and insisted on playing with her dolls while Mademoiselle Duchovny tried vainly to engage her interest. At length, the teacher heard her murmur to her doll, 'We don't want to say silly French words, do we? Only stupid, ugly people talk like that.' Mademoiselle left the room in great indignation and complained to Mrs McBride, who came up in a fury. She was no longer the indulgent mama who had kissed and praised her in front of her friends; this was the mama who had beaten her and committed her to the keeping of Miss Drake.

'How dare you behave like this? I had begun to think that you had learned the proper conduct of a girl in your position.' At moments like this her Irish accent, normally overlain by a carefully cultivated gentility, became dominant. 'Now I see that it was all a pretence. You had better mend your ways, or I shall give you reason to regret it. You are not too old to have your backside tanned!'

Angelina, shaken, bowed her head and begged her mother's pardon.

One Saturday afternoon, on her usual walk with Lizzie, they passed the small lake in the middle of the park. Three boys were sailing model yachts on it and Angelina recognised John.

'Let's go and watch what they are doing,' she suggested.

'If you like,' Lizzie replied, 'but don't go too near the edge. The ground is muddy and you might slip.'

The boys took no notice of their approach, their attention focussed on the progress of one of the boats. That was not part of Angelina's plan. She moved closer and said boldly, 'Good afternoon, John.'

He glanced round, annoyed, and blushed. 'Oh, it's you.' The tone was brusque. The other two boys, who did not attend the dancing classes, nudged each other and sniggered. 'Come along, Angelina,' Lizzie said. 'It's too cold to stand around.'

'But I don't want …' she began.

Lizzie took her hand firmly. 'I said come along. We are going to finish our walk.'

Angelina hung back, but something in Lizzie's expression told her that she was not going to win this particular argument. She twisted her head as they began to move away and called, 'Goodbye, John. See you at dancing class.'

He did not respond, and the next Friday he allowed another boy to claim her for the first dance.

Next morning it was clear that Lizzie had developed a bad cold, and on Sunday, when Jane brought up the breakfast tray, she announced, 'You'll have to dress yourself this morning, Miss Angelina. Miss Findlay is not at all well and she is staying in bed.'

Lizzie left instructions for her to continue reading a story from 'The Children's Friend', a periodical full of improving tales about children who withstood pain and sickness with fortitude through their faith in Jesus, but Angelina ignored them and spent the morning playing with her dolls. She found the shabby rag doll and tried to dress her in a frock from one of the much more expensive dolls she possessed, but the limp limbs would not go into the narrow sleeves and she gave up. Instead she wrapped her in a shawl and cradled her, singing softly, 'Lavender's blue, dilly, dilly.'

At lunchtime, Jane said, 'Your mama says I've to take you for your walk, so you'd better get yourself ready.'

Her tone was grudging and Angelina understood why. Normally Jane had Sunday afternoons off.

She smiled sweetly.

'Very good, Jane. I'll be ready.'

As soon as she had eaten, Angelina went to her room and put on the blue taffeta dress. When the maid came up to fetch her, she exclaimed, 'Now, Miss Angelina, surely that's not the right sort of dress to be wearing for a walk.'

'Isn't it?' she responded innocently. 'It is Sunday, so I thought I should put on my best clothes.'

'I'm sure it's not what Miss Findlay would have put you into,' Jane said doubtfully.

'Well, it's too late to start all over again now,' Angelina said. 'Let's go, shall we?'

Once in the park she headed for the clearing where she had seen the other children playing. They were not there, but she did not let that deter her.

'Let's play a game, Jane. It's boring just walking.'

'What sort of game?'

'Let's play hide and seek. You be "on" first. You have to close your eyes and count to a hundred and then come and find me, and after that I count and you hide. Now, close your eyes! And start counting.'

She darted away before the parlourmaid could argue and, looking back after a few paces, she saw that she was doing as she had been told. Angelina dodged through the bushes until she was sure she was out of sight in case Jane decided to peep, then she picked up her skirts and ran towards the lake. As she had hoped, John and the other two boys were there again with their model yachts. She arrived, panting, at their side.

'I want to play. Can I sail one of your boats?'

The three looked at her in consternation. 'You don't know how,' John said.

'You can show me.'

'Girls can't do this sort of thing,' one of the others said.

'Why not?'

'Because you'd be frightened of getting your feet wet or spoiling your clothes.'

'No I wouldn't!' She pushed back her cape so that John could get the full benefit of the blue taffeta. 'If this gets spoiled my mama will get me a new dress.'

John looked at her and then glanced round at the other two. 'All right, prove it. See that yacht just out there? That one's mine. It's got stuck on something. You have to take a stick and give it a shove. Go on!'

She looked from him to the boat. It looked a long way out. 'I can't reach it there.'

'I told you, you have to use a stick. Here, take this one.'

He held out a slender branch. She took hold of it, feeling it damp and slick through her glove.

'Go on,' he prompted.

Gingerly, she approached the edge of the pond. As Lizzie had warned, the ground was slippery with mud. She reached out with the branch, but she was a good foot short of the yacht. She stepped a little closer, feeling the damp oozing up around her boots. She still could not reach. Behind her she could hear the boys sniggering. She made a last, despairing lunge, her feet slipped, and a second later she was on her knees with water up to her waist.

John was at her side quickly, offering his hand. 'I warned you. Girls can't play games like this.' But his expression showed that he was alarmed at the consequences of his teasing. He pulled her up and helped back onto the bank, where she stood dripping and shivering and choking back tears of humiliation.

'Miss Angelina! There you are. Whatever have you been doing?' Jane arrived out of breath and furious. 'I knew you were up to something, so I came looking. A gentleman walking his dog told me he'd seen you heading this way. Otherwise I might have been looking for you all day. Now look at you! Look at your nice dress. Your mama is going to have something to say when we get back! Come along now. We'd better get you home before you catch your death. And you – ' she turned her attention to John '– you should know better!'

She grabbed Angelina by the hand and dragged her unceremoniously back along the path. By the time they reached home, Angelina was sobbing. Jane marched her through the front door and ordered, 'Stand there till I fetch your mama. I can't take you into the drawing room in this state.'

In a very short space of time Mrs McBride came out of the drawing room and gave a cry of horror at Angelina's appearance.

'I found her by the lake, ma'am,' Jane said. 'She was playing with some boys, trying to get one of their boats ashore and she'd fallen in. It's a marvel she hasn't drowned herself.'

'Playing with boys? And in that dress? Why is she wearing that dress?'

'She put it on herself, ma'am. I didn't like to insist she took it off.'

'Insist? You foolish girl. You were in charge. If you had any doubts you should have consulted me. Angelina, go to your room. Take off that dress, which you have now ruined, and wait for me. You can expect to be severely punished.'

*

In her bedroom, Angelina shivered with cold and apprehension. Her worst fears were realised when her mother came in carrying the cane.

'Over the back of that chair!'

Her shift was pulled up, her bare buttocks exposed, and she was subjected to the most severe beating she had ever experienced. She pressed her face into the cushions and stifled her cries. When it was over she was sent to bed, where she stayed without any supper.

Later, Lizzie came into her room, her voice thick with catarrh.

'Oh, Angelina! What on earth possessed you? You must have known how angry your mama would be.'

'I wanted to play,' she mumbled.

'You could have played with those girls a few weeks back, but you chose not to. I think you just wanted John to take notice of you. Good girls don't go chasing after boys. Don't you know that? And it doesn't do any good, anyway. Men don't like women who run after them.'

'I don't care! I hate him anyway.'

'You shouldn't say things like that, but listen to me. If you want to go on with your music lessons and your dancing lessons, you are going to have to show your mama that you are really sorry for behaving so badly and you will never do such a naughty thing again. Do you think you can do that?'

'Don't know.'

'Well, I think you had better make up your mind to try your hardest otherwise – ' Lizzie broke off and when she spoke again there were tears in her voice '– otherwise I do not know what is going to happen to you.'

Over a long night, while pain prevented her from sleeping except in snatches, Angelina resolved to make a fresh effort to propitiate her mother. When she came into the schoolroom next morning, she knelt down and murmured, 'Please, Mama, I am very sorry for what I did yesterday, and I promise that I will be a good girl from now on. Will you forgive me?'

Mrs McBride looked down at her sternly. 'That will depend on your conduct. You will apply yourself to your drawing and your French lessons as well as to your music, and if I feel that you are sufficiently reformed, you may go on with the dancing lessons. If I have any further reason to complain of you, the results will be extremely serious. Do you understand me?'

'Yes, Mama.'

'Very well. You may get up and get on with your lessons.'

For a week, Angelina was a model pupil, even disregarding Mary's spiteful jibes about her drawing and making a genuine effort to speak French. On Thursday, Madame Corelli began to teach them how to read music and lavished praise and encouragement on her. As a result, she was permitted to return to her dancing class.

At the end of the class, Mrs Fairchild made an announcement.

'As next week will be the last lesson before Christmas, we are going to have a proper ball. It will be held in the evening and I am inviting all the parents to join in and perhaps bring older brothers or sisters along. It will be a special occasion and I am sure you will all show yourselves at your best.'

Angelina looked forward to the ball with mixed feelings. John had studiously ignored her during the last class, and she felt that she would not be able to bear it if he continued to do so. On the other hand, she knew that she was now one of the best dancers and also one of the prettiest and she looked forward to showing herself off. She hoped she might be given a new dress for the event, but the blue taffeta had been cleaned and repaired and her mother declared it 'perfectly serviceable', so she had to make the best of it.

When the night came, Lizzie was left to dress her and do her hair without her mother's attentions, but when she went downstairs to join her parents, her father exclaimed, 'Well, who is this delightful young lady? Surely, we have a princess amongst us.'

'Don't be foolish,' her mother said with some asperity. 'This little madam has a good enough opinion of herself. The last thing she needs is that kind of flattery.'

Nevertheless, Angelina hugged the words to her as the hansom cab took them to the Fairchilds' house.

The big room was crowded with people. John was there with his parents, and she tried to catch his eye, without success. She would have gone over to speak to him, but her mother insisted on her staying by her side.

Instead of playing the piano herself, as she usually did, Mrs Fairchild had employed a trio of piano, violin and cello, who were playing softly as the guests arrived, and Angelina thrilled at the sound.

When the first dance was announced, she waited tensely for John to approach her, but he chose one of the other girls instead. Mortified, she accepted the invitation of another of her usual partners. The dance was the *polonaise*, one that she knew showed her off to best advantage, and as she danced she forgot John and began to enjoy herself. She was used to hearing flattering comments from the watching ladies, but this time she caught one that disturbed her slightly.

'Such a pretty little thing! But don't you wonder how it is that her parents, who are both dark, managed to produce such a golden-haired child?'

As the evening progressed some of the adults joined in the dancing and the floor became crowded. Angelina did not want for eager partners, but in spite of all her efforts to attract his attention, John continued to ignore her. Mary was there, in a new dress, wearing a beautiful aquamarine pendant on a gold chain. Angelina saw her showing it off to her little coterie of friends. Then, just before the supper dance was announced, Mary somehow persuaded her mother to introduce her to John's parents, so that he had no option but to offer her his arm for the dance and then take her into supper, which had been laid out in another room on the floor below. Seething with resentment, Angelina scarcely spoke to her own escort and all through the meal she watched her rival chatting animatedly and saw John respond. Then she heard a burst of laughter and saw that they were both looking in her direction. It was easy to guess that John had told her the story of Angelina's mishap. Mary beckoned to two of her friends, and they whispered together and began to giggle and point towards her, and from their gestures Angelina knew that they were laughing at the fact that she was wearing a dress which had been damaged and refurbished. It was insupportable. Ignoring her partner, and her mother's warning looks, she marched across the floor to confront them.

'What are you laughing at?'

'What, us? Laughing?' Mary pretended to be unable to stifle her giggles.

'Yes, you are!' Angelina persisted. She turned on John. 'What have you been telling them?'

'Me?' He looked embarrassed.

'Yes, you. It was all your fault. You made me go in the water after your beastly boat.'

'No, I didn't. You wanted to play boy's games. I warned you.'

'Boy's games?' Mary gave a screech of laughter that drew eyes in her direction. 'Oh, Angelina, how unladylike!'

'You're unladylike, not me!' Angelina said fiercely. 'A lady doesn't go and steal someone else's partner.'

'Steal him? I didn't steal him. He doesn't want to dance with you. Can't you see that? He thinks you're a stupid, vain little baby.'

'I'm not! I'm not! How dare you speak like that to me?'

'Why shouldn't I? You're not even your mother and father's real child. My mother told me. You're just a foundling.'

The last word ended in a scream as Angelina launched herself bodily at her enemy, sobbing, 'It's not true! It's not true!'

They went down in a struggling heap on the floor, clawing at each other's clothes and hair. The gold chain round Mary's neck snapped and the pendant rolled away and she ran her nails down Angelina's cheek. Then she gave a howl. 'She bit me! She bit me!'

Hands pulled them apart. Mary was sobbing and holding her hand to her cheek. 'She bit me!' she repeated. Her mother pulled her hand away and sure enough there was a clear imprint of teeth on the flushed flesh.

'You little monster!' she exclaimed. Then, turning to Mrs McBride who had arrived breathlessly from the other end of the room, she said, 'You should not allow this child to come into genteel society. She is like a wild thing.'

Mrs McBride took Angelina by the shoulders and shook her hard. 'You have shamed yourself and shamed me. This is the last time you will be allowed out to mix with civilized people. Come along.'

Angelina felt herself half lifted, half dragged out of the room and down the stairs. Behind her, she heard her father expostulating, 'Marguerite, for pity's sake, pull yourself together. You are making a show of us.'

'I? *I* am making a show? It is this little monster who has made a show of all of us. Get us a cab, quickly. I am ashamed to let people see us.'

A cab drew up at that moment and Angelina was bundled into it. As they moved off, she managed to recover her voice.

'It's not fair, Mama! It was Mary's fault. She said … she said something horrible. She said you and Papa were not my real parents.'

Her mother gripped her by the shoulder again and glared into her face. 'She said what?'

'She said you aren't really my mother. She said I was a foundling.'

Marguerite McBride sat back in her seat and looked at her husband. 'What did I tell you? I knew we were making a terrible mistake when we took her.'

'If I recall, my dear,' her husband replied, 'you were the one who was set on the idea. I tried to point out the pit-falls but you would have none of it. Bad blood will out. However, we are where we are and there is no going back. We have to consider now what to do for the best.'

'Since you are so far-sighted,' Marguerite said caustically, 'you had better take charge. I've done my best with her. I've no wish to trouble myself further.'

Angelina shrank into her corner, looking uncomprehendingly from one to the other. The cab arrived at the house and she was unceremoniously hauled out. She expected another beating, but instead Lizzie was called down and instructed to take her to her room and shut her in, and not to let her out on any pretext until given express orders.

Up in her room, Lizzie looked at her, wide-eyed with alarm. 'Whatever happened? What have you done?'

Angelina burst into tears, shaking her head wildly from side to side. 'It's not fair! Not fair!' was all she could say.

Lizzie calmed her sufficiently to get her undressed and into bed, where she lay exhausted, her face swollen from crying. Lizzie stroked the hair back from her eyes and murmured, 'Try to get some sleep.'

She was about to leave but Angelina caught hold of her hand. 'Lizzie, what's a foundling?'

'A foundling? It's a baby who has been left somewhere, on a doorstep or in a church, for someone to find.'

'Left? Who by?'

'Its mother, usually. Some poor woman who cannot look after it, so she leaves it in the hope that someone else will take care of it. Why are you asking about this now?'

Angelina shook her head and said nothing and after a moment Lizzie said, 'Say your payers and go to sleep now. Goodnight.'

She went away, taking the candle with her. Alone in the darkness Angelina tried to make sense of what had been said that night. 'Bad blood will out'. Did she have bad blood? Was that why she was always in trouble? Her mother had called her a little monster. Was she not a human child at all, but some kind of changeling, the offspring of some ill-intentioned demon? If so, how could she ever be good? She had bad blood, and nothing she could ever do, however hard she tried, would be right.

On that thought she finally fell asleep.

Six

Freshfields
Rutherglen
Victoria
Australia
December 28th 1867

Dear James,

I cannot tell you how much joy the receipt of your letter gave me, when it was redirected here from Croft's Hotel. It came as the most delightful of my Christmas presents. Of course, my joy would have been even greater if the ship that brought it had brought you instead, but I always knew that was not possible, so I was not disappointed. But I cannot help worrying about the length of time that letters take from the day they are written until they reach here. It is a relief to know you were well when you wrote the letter, but there is no way of knowing what may have happened between then and now. I can only pray, as I do every night, that God has kept you safe.

I know you will be eager to learn about my journey and what I found on my arrival, so let me begin. I have mixed memories of the voyage out here. The first-class ticket my father had paid for introduced me to a luxury I had never experienced, as you will understand; but there were times when I felt I should have been more comfortable in steerage. My fellow passengers were all ladies and gentlemen of means, accustomed to the kind of food and service provided in first class; but as you know, I am more used to serving than being served, and there were many times when I had to restrain myself from jumping up to clear away the dishes at the end of a meal. At least, having watched how Mr and Mrs Freeman behaved while I worked for them, I knew which knives and forks to use! Most of the others treated me with courtesy and made some enquiries about my home and my reason for travelling to Australia, but these were questions I found it hard to answer, and after a while they seemed to feel it would be more tactful to leave me to myself. I was tempted, once or twice, to tell them that they were dining with an orphan girl brought up in the workhouse, who was once a maid of all work, just to see what their reaction would be; but I thought better of it.

One thought that disturbed me all through the voyage was the fact that I had taken ship so precipitately that I had had no means of letting Gus and my father know I was coming. No other ship is faster than the Royal Standard, *so any letter I might have written could not arrive before me. Accordingly, there was no one to meet me when the ship docked in Melbourne. I remembered that Gus had been working at Croft's Hotel when he met our father, so I took a cab straight there. I was received with great kindness by Mr and Mrs Croft, who told me that Gus had left with Father immediately after posting the letter asking me to join them.*

That was over four months ago. However, by the miracle of this modern invention, the telegraph, they were able to send word of my arrival and within a day I had a reply. I was to reserve a place aboard one of Cobb's coaches, which would take me 'up country' to Rutherglen, and Gus would be there to meet me.

You will not be surprised to learn that I found the prospect rather daunting. To sit on a ship, even when it is tossed by contrary winds, as ours frequently was, does provide some sense of security, especially when you are surrounded by every luxury. Travelling alone in an unknown country seemed much more frightening. But I need not have worried. Mrs Croft took me to the inn from which the coaches depart and introduced me to three other ladies who were bound on the same journey. They were the kindest people you can imagine and I felt much more at ease with them than with my former travelling companions. The coach was much larger than I had expected, and was drawn by a team of four magnificent horses, who took us at a gallop along the dusty roads. It had a separate compartment for ladies and as we went we exchanged confidences about our lives hitherto and our reasons for being in Australia. Gus is right about one thing. Here no one cares about where or how you were brought up or what work you have done. They take you as you are, for better or worse.

I will not say it was a comfortable journey. The roads are rough and full of potholes and, even though the coach has some arrangement of straps that evens out the worst of the jolts, it is still very tiring. Every few miles we stopped to change the horses and were able to get out for a few minutes to stretch our legs and take a drink, and in this way we covered a long distance remarkably quickly; but even so the journey took two days. We stopped overnight at an inn in a small town whose name I do not recall. What I do remember is that one of the ladies called me over to look at something in one of the trees that shaded the building. There I saw a grey, furry creature, sitting in a fork of the branches and apparently asleep, quite undisturbed by our presence. They call them koala bears and they live on the leaves of the eucalyptus trees that grow in abundance here and, I am told, spend most of their lives asleep, only waking at night to eat when the weather is cooler.

Which reminds me – how strange it is to celebrate Christmas, while it is hotter here than on any day in mid-summer at home! The heat is rather trying, I have to admit; but at least the sunshine makes everything so much brighter than the grey skies we are used to.

On the second day I was most thankful when the coach galloped into the little town of Rutherglen, and there, waiting to meet me, were Gus and a man I knew must be the father I could hardly remember.

We were a little strange with each other at first, but he took both my hands in his and looked into my face and exclaimed, 'By God, you remind me of your mother!' Then he kissed me on both cheeks and suddenly I remembered the big, jolly man who used to come home from the sea and swing me up into his arms, and I knew I had found him again. I must admit we both shed some tears, and he said more than once how sorry he was that he had not returned to England to take care of us when he had served his sentence. I suppose if he had done, he would have taken me out of the workhouse and saved me from the hard times I spent in service; but when I think about it, it would have meant my life taking a completely different direction and I should probably never have met you – so I cannot have any regrets about the way things turned out. I said something like that to him and he agreed that if he had returned to England he would never have struck gold and would not have been able to provide the sort of life he can now offer us.

Which brings me to the point you have probably been waiting for: the description of the place I must now learn to think of as home.

First of all, did you read the address at the top of this letter? The house my father has built is called Freshfields! Do you remember the day you took me there on the train from Liverpool and we saw the red squirrels? Of course you do. It seems that Papa – how strange it feels to write that – took Mama there when they were first married and it was one of the happiest days of their lives, so he named the house in remembrance of that. Is that not a wonderful coincidence? It is a beautiful house, built like a ship of overlapping boards and painted white, with a large porch at the front and a veranda at the back, which runs the full length of the house and makes a beautifully cool place to sit in the evenings. It stands on a slight rise with gardens sloping down to a lake they call Moodemere, and all around the land is planted with vines, now heavy with grapes. In a month or two it will be time to harvest them and Gus says we expect a good crop. (Gus has taken to this new life with enthusiasm. He spends a good deal of his time with Pedro, father's Spanish manager, talking about growing grapes and the techniques of wine making. It is good to see him so eager and involved.) Pedro's wife, Maria, acts as housekeeper.

She pretends to defer to me, as 'lady of the house', but in truth she is so efficient that I would not dream of interfering. But at least here I do not feel awkward about clearing the table or helping to wash up and we get on very well.

The countryside all around is very beautiful. I imagined Australia as an arid, desert sort of country, but here we are in a green landscape of gentle rolling hills, rising to distant misty mountains. I am told that this area reminded the first settlers of parts of southern England, which is why many of the small towns have English names like Chiltern and Beechworth, alongside others with strange aboriginal names like Wodonga and Wangaratta. Of course, I have never seen the south of England so I cannot tell if the comparison is justified, but I cannot imagine it could be lovelier than this.

As well as vineyards, there are farms with cattle and hens and horses. Do you remember how amazed I was the first time I saw a cow? But that is nothing to compare with the animals I have seen here. On the first evening a troop of kangaroos came bounding down to drink at the lake. They bounce along on their hind legs, which they use like springs, and they can cover an enormous distance with one leap. There are little creatures called possums that live in the trees and remind me a bit of squirrels, though they are not so pretty. But it is the birds that I love best to watch. I have never imagined that birds could be so vividly coloured. There are red and blue rosellas, and rainbow lorikeets that live up to their name in shades of green and red and orange, and white cockatoos with yellow crests. Of course, there are less attractive things too. I have been warned to watch where I walk because of snakes, and not to put my hand into hidden corners for fear of poisonous spiders, but so far I have seen neither.

Rutherglen itself is, or was, a gold rush town, and it is easy to see that many of the houses were thrown up in haste and not intended to be permanent, but it is becoming more settled now and the centre has some solid buildings with some attempt to make them attractive – though after the glories of St George's Hall they appear very humble. That is the one thing I miss – not being able to wander into some of our great buildings and gaze at the wonderful artwork that went into them. Well, no – it's not the one thing I miss; but if you were here it would be the only thing.

It has taken me all afternoon to write this and my hand is aching. I think I have told you enough to give you some idea of life here, and to convince you that I am well and happy. I pray that the same is true for you. I long to hear from you. God speed the ship that brings your next letter!

Your ever loving,
May

Seven

Angelina spent Christmas and the succeeding days confined to her room, with only Lizzie for company. There were no presents, and no Christmas dinner – no goose, no pudding, no sweetmeats. Instead she received beef broth and bread and rice pudding, which she detested.

At first she cared little for this deprivation. She existed in a state of suppressed terror, expecting at any moment to be subjected to some violent punishment; but days passed and no one came near her except for Lizzie and she began to think that this confinement was itself her punishment. That being so, her attention focussed on how long it might last. No longer paralysed with fear, she veered between tearful pleas to be allowed out, to go for a walk or to play the piano; or sulky silence, refusing all Lizzie's attempts to interest or amuse her, sitting cuddling her rag doll and rocking to and fro. Lizzie herself, subjected to the same confinement except for a brief hour every afternoon, became increasingly short tempered and uneasy about what the future might hold for both of them.

At the beginning of January, Connor McBride received a letter. He opened it at the breakfast table and gave grunt of satisfaction.

'I have solved our problem.'

His wife looked up from her bacon and eggs. 'Solved it? How?'

'Angelina will go away to school. She will go to the convent of the Faithful Companions of Jesus in Limerick. I have written to the Reverend Mother and this is her reply, agreeing to take her as soon as she can be got there.'

'You are sending her to Ireland? To the nuns?'

'Yes.'

'Have you forgotten what they did to me? Forgotten why we fled Ireland in the first place?'

'Do you not think that a dose of that kind of discipline is what she needs? Besides, desperate situations require desperate measures.'

'And this is the man who swore when he left Ireland that he would never set foot in a church again.'

'With good reason. I have no intention of doing so now, but this is the solution to our problem. Angelina will be out of the way of all gossip, unable to make a show of us any longer. She will be looked after and educated. The school is run by nuns from France. She will learn to speak French like a native, but, more importantly, they set great store by proper deportment and behaviour. She will have to learn obedience and self-control, both qualities that she signally lacks at the moment.'

'And how long do you intend her to stay there?'

'Until her education is finished. I have explained that it will not be possible for her to return home during the vacations. By that time, either she will have acquired suitable habits and accomplishments to make her acceptable in polite society or, and this is an outcome devoutly to be wished, she may have been so influenced by the nuns that she will wish to take the veil.'

'You are saying that she will be out of our lives for good – or at least until she is grown up.'

'Is that not the best outcome?'

Marguerite McBride lowered her eyes to her plate and said nothing for a moment. Then she sighed. 'I had such hopes of her to begin with. She seemed just like her name, a little angel. But then that girl recognised her and I realised we could never be at ease, that at any moment the secret of her origin might come out. Just lately I had begun to think that my fears were unfounded but her behaviour … You were right. It was a terrible mistake. We know nothing of her parentage and, as you say, bad blood will out. It is better that she should be somewhere where she can do no more damage. And, who knows, it may be the best thing for her, too. When will she go?'

'Tomorrow. I will take her. I am going now to buy tickets for the ferry.'

Angelina's head drooped. She longed to sleep, but every time she dropped off the jolting of the gig on the rough road woke her up. Confused thoughts floated in and out of her mind. She still did not really understand what was happening to her. Just the day before Lizzie had come into the room and told her that she had to pack her things for a journey. 'You are going away to school. It will be fun for you. You will have lots of friends to play with.' She had tried to make it sound as though she was pleased for her, but Angelina had heard the anxiety behind the cheerful words. All her questions – 'Where am I going? When will

I be coming back?' – were answered with a brusque, 'I know no more than I have told you. You must ask your papa.' But Papa had not come to the schoolroom to answer. And when she tried to insert her beloved rag doll into the suitcase, she was told, 'You won't need that. You're a big girl now.'

Lizzie had woken her early next morning and, almost before she had time to take in what was happening, she was wrapped in her warmest coat and taken down to the hall, where her father was waiting for her. With the briefest of farewells to Lizzie, she found herself in a hansom cab, heading at a smart trot for the docks. Her mother had not come to see her off.

When she saw that they were going on a ship, she held back. 'Where are we going, Papa?'

'We are going to Ireland.'

'Where you and Mama came from.'

'Yes, that's right.'

'Are we going to stay with someone from your family?'

'No. You are going to school.'

'But where will I live?'

'In the school. It is called a boarding school. Other girls will live there too.'

The ferry crossing had been miserable. The weather was bad and the boat plunged and yawed until she was so sick that she thought she was dying. On dry land at last, they went to an inn where she was unable to eat the supper she was offered and had to sleep in a crib beside her father's bed. He slept quietly, but the consciousness of his presence was disturbing and she lay awake most of the night. This was not the Papa who used to let her sit on his lap and tickle her. This man was silent and forbidding. He had hardly spoken to her on the journey.

Next day they boarded a train. Angelina had never seen a train before and the locomotive, with its smoke and sparks and noise, terrified her. They chugged across countryside shrouded in rain. Finally, they reached a town, which her father told her was called Limerick, but even then the journey was not over. Her father hired a gig to take them to a place called 'The Laurels'.

It was dark when they reached their destination and Angelina had a confused impression of a large building standing at the end of a long drive. She was so exhausted by the time the gig drew up in front of a pillared portico that she had to be lifted down and her legs almost refused to support her. A woman in a long black dress and a white head-covering that completely hid her hair led them into a large hallway and then to a smaller room where a good fire burned. Here another lady similarly attired stepped forward to greet them.

'I am Mother Mary Benedicta. Welcome.'

'Thank you, Reverend Mother. It's good of you to receive my daughter so promptly.' Angelina detected an unusual stiffness and formality in her father's tone.

The lady turned to her. 'So you are Angelina.'

Angelina managed to collect her wits enough to curtsy. 'Yes, ma'am.'

'You need not call me ma'am. You should address me as Mother.'

Angelina's confusion deepened. This woman was not her mother, so why should she call her that? And her father had used the same form of address, but this lady was surely too young to be his mother.

The nun looked over her head at her father and then back at her. 'Your father writes that you are known to bite people.'

'Not people!' Tears rose to her eyes at the injustice of the accusation. 'I only did it once, when a girl said something horrid.'

'So there's no danger of you biting me?' There was a smile in her voice, if not on her lips.

'Of course not.'

The nun touched her cheek with warm fingers. 'You poor child, you're perished with cold. Let's have this bonnet and coat off, and you can warm yourself by the fire.' She deftly undid the ribbons that held Angelina's bonnet and helped her out of her coat. 'Now, sit yourself down by the fire while I speak to your father.' She pulled a low stool closer to the hearth and Angelina sank onto it and held her hands to the flames.

'Will you stay for the night, Mr McBride? There is a room for you in the guest house if you would like it.'

'Thank you, no, Mother. The gig is waiting to take me back to Limerick.'

'Can I at least offer you some refreshment?'

'No, thank you again. As I said, the gig is waiting.'

'Then it is time for you to say goodbye to your father, Angelina.'

Angelina scrambled to her feet with a sudden sensation that her life was about to be ripped apart. 'When will you come to fetch me back, Papa?'

A strange contortion passed across her father's face and vanished. 'That has not been decided yet.'

She went towards him. She felt herself trembling, and not only from the cold. 'How long do I have to stay here?'

91

'Until your education is complete.'

'When will that be?'

'That remains to be seen. Apply yourself and do everything the sisters ask of you. I shall want to hear good reports of you.

'I will! I will be good, I promise. Please fetch me home soon!'

Mother Mary Benedicta stepped forward and put her hand on Angelina's shoulder. 'Don't distress yourself, child. You will be well looked after. Our girls are happy here, and you will be too. Now, I think you must be tired and perhaps hungry?' She raised her voice. 'Sister Berthe.' The nun who had admitted them to the house must have been waiting outside the door, since she came in at once. 'Take Angelina to the refectory and see that she is given some warm bread and milk. Then you can see her to bed.' She returned her attention to Mr McBride. 'We have given her a bed in the infirmary for tonight, rather than putting her through the ordeal of meeting strangers in the dormitory.'

'Very thoughtful, I'm sure,' he replied, as if his thoughts were already elsewhere.

Sister Berthe held out her hand to Angelina. 'Come with me, little one.'

Angelina took the outstretched hand and followed her out of the room. At the door she looked back, but her father was already putting on his coat and collecting his hat.

The bread and milk soothed her churning stomach, and, as soon as she had eaten it, Sister Berthe led her along a long passage to a room with four small beds in it. All were empty, but her suitcase was waiting for her beside one of them. Sister Berthe helped her to undress and waited while she used the chamber pot, then when she was in bed she pulled the covers up to her chin and stroked her hair gently.

'*Bonne nuit, ma petite.*'

The words triggered a memory in Angelina's befuddled brain and she mumbled, '*Merci, Madame.*'

She was asleep before the nun had tiptoed out of the room.

Angelina was woken by the sound of a bell ringing insistently somewhere. For a moment or two she continued to drowse. The bed was warm and comfortable and she felt safe. 'Lizzie?' she mumbled. Then memory came back. She opened her eyes and looked around a strange room. It was still dark outside, but lamplight coming under the door showed her the three empty beds and bare white walls. She wondered if she should get up and get herself dressed and what she should put on. The lamplight came closer and Sister Berthe came in.

'*Bonjour, mon enfant.* Come now. It's time to get up. I have brought you your school clothes.'

Very soon Angelina found herself clothed in a dress of black cashmere with long black stockings and a blue pinafore. After a quick scrub to her face and hands in cold water, her hair was brushed back, parted in the centre and secured in a tight plait.

'There!' Sister Berthe surveyed her handiwork. 'The dress is not a bad fit and there is room for you to grow. Now, follow me and I will show you where we have breakfast.'

She led her down a wide staircase and into a big room with long tables around three sides. On the fourth side there was a platform, with another table. Girls of varying ages were sitting on benches along the tables and Angelina saw that the smallest ones were ranged along the table to her right and they got taller as they progressed round the room until the table on the dais was occupied by big girls who looked to her eyes like grown-ups. A nun sat at the head and foot of each table and at the centre of the one on the dais there was an empty chair. Everyone sat in silence. 'Ah, our new arrival,' a voice called. 'Come here, child.'

A tall nun with a pale face and a stern expression stood near the platform. Berthe gave Angelina a gentle shove and she went forward, painfully aware of the concentrated gaze of fifty or sixty pairs of eyes. The nun put a hand on her shoulder and turned her to face the rest of the room.

'Girls, this is Angelina McBride. She is new here and no doubt finds it all very strange, as some of you will well remember from your first day. I know that you will all make her feel at home and help her to settle in. Now, Angelina, you will be in second preparatory class, who are all sitting over there. Rosa O'Malley, I want you to look after her and make sure that she knows the rules and where she should be at any time.'

A dark-haired girl with cheeks that suited her name got up and came over. 'Come along, Angelina. You can sit here, next to me.'

Angelina took her place and looked along the row of girls. It puzzled her that no one was talking. Then a small bell sounded and everyone stood up.

Mother Mary Benedicta came in from a door beside the dais and took the vacant place at the top table. She made a gesture with one hand, moving it from her brow to her chest and then from left to right and pronounced words in French that Angelina did not understand, and all the girls made the same gesture and pronounced a response that was equally unintelligible. Then they sat down and conversation broke out all round the room, creating a din that was almost as unnerving as the silence.

'Angelina, this is Anna and this is Wilhelmina,' Rosa was saying. 'They're my friends. When did you arrive?'

'Last night.'

'Where are you from?' Anna leaned across to ask.

'Liverpool.'

'Liverpool? All the way from England. Why have you come here?'

'I don't know.' Angelina felt the too-ready tears swelling in her throat.

'I expect she's come because her mother and father know this is a really good school,' Rosa said helpfully. 'Isn't that it, Angelina?'

'I suppose so,' Angelina mumbled. She thought she understood why she was here. It was because she bit someone and her parents were ashamed of her, but these girls must never know that.

Food was being set on the table. There were baskets of freshly baked bread and funny shaped rolls in a crescent shape and dishes of butter. In each girl's place there was a large cup and monitors were passing along the rows, filling them with a dark, fragrant liquid. Jugs of milk were passed along and added to it.

'Is that tea?' Angelina asked timidly.

'No, coffee. Don't you have coffee at home?'

'I think my mama and papa have it. I've always had milk.'

Anna leaned over again. 'You'll get used to it. Because a lot of the nuns are French we get French food. It takes a bit of getting used to but it's not bad, most of the time.'

The coffee certainly took a good deal of getting used to, but the fresh bread and the rolls, which the girl called crois-sants, were really good. Angelina could have eaten more than her ration.

All too soon the little bell sounded again and all the girls stood up and crossed themselves. Angelina stood too and some more strange French phrases were repeated, and then Mother Mary Benedicta left the room.

The girls were filing out and she walked with Rosa along a path lined with pillars opening onto a courtyard and then into another building.

The first thing that struck her was the smell: a pungent, aromatic scent that tickled her nose. They were in a vaulted room, with long benches on either side, which had rails in front of them and little cushions hanging on hooks. At the far end was a table covered in an embroidered cloth. On it was a gold crucifix and two tall candles and there was a large vase of flowers on either side. Angelina deduced that they must be in a church.

She followed Rosa to a bench near the front and saw that she made a curtsy to the table, which seemed odd as there was no one there. However, it seemed wise to copy. Rosa also made the same gesture she had made in the refectory, moving the fingers of the right hand to her brow, then her chest, then to her left shoulder and finally to her right. Then she unhooked the little cushion and knelt down on it. This at least was familiar. She had been taught to kneel by her bed every night and say the Lord's Prayer. She knelt and murmured the words to herself.

From then on all sense of familiarity vanished. The nuns came in in procession and words were said in a language that was neither French nor English. They stood and sat and knelt and Angelina copied Rosa and wondered if she understood what was going on. She seemed to know what to do, at any rate.

Then the singing started and Angelina was transported. The nuns and some of the older girls were sitting in seats at right angles to where she was and nearer to the table with the cross on it, and they were the ones who sang. The tune was not familiar and she still could not understand the words, but as the voices rose to the vaulted roof she thought she had never heard anything so beautiful.

When it was over and they were filing out, she whispered to Rosa, 'Why do you do that with your hand?'

'Ssh! We'll lose marks for silence.'

Once they were outside, Rosa looked at her. 'What do you mean, do that with my hand? Do what?'

Angelina imitated the gesture.

'I'm crossing myself. Surely you've been taught to do that.'

Angelina shook her head and Rosa looked shocked.

They followed the others up a very grand staircase to a huge room with desks arranged down both sides and a table in the middle of one side. Above it, in a niche, stood a plaster bust of a nun.

'This is the *salle d'études*,' Rosa said. 'This is where we do private study and where we meet every Sunday evening for Marks.'

Angelina wanted to ask what sort of marks she meant, but at that moment her name was called. The tall nun who had directed her to her place in the dining hall was standing by the table. Angelina went over to her.

'I am Mother Mary Andrew. I am Mother Scholastic, which means I am in charge of the educational aspects of the convent. We need to talk so that I can find out what standard you have reached. Sit here, by my table.'

Angelina sat. The other girls were opening desks and taking out books and pens and paper before heading off down the grand staircase again.

'Now,' Mother Mary Andrew said. 'I assume you can read?'

'Yes, ma'am – I mean yes, Mother. Please, can I ask something?'

'What is it?'

'Why do I call you "Mother"? You are not my mother, nor is the other lady who sat on the platform at breakfast.'

Mother Mary Andrew frowned. 'Have you never been in a convent before? All our choir nuns are called "Mother". Only the lay members are called "Sister".'

'Oh.' It struck her as a strange convention but it was obviously something she had to accept. 'And why are you all called Mary something?'

'That is in honour of Our Lady.'

'Which lady?' She looked up at the bust above her. 'Is that her?'

Mother Mary Andrew cast her eyes heavenward. 'Heaven protect us! Have you been taught nothing of Christian doctrine?'

'I know the Commandments, and the Beatitudes.'

'Well, that is something, I suppose. Do you know your catechism?'

'My what?'

Mother Mary Andrew looked at her for a long moment in silence. 'Have you ever been to church?'

'Not till this morning.'

'And your mother and father, do they go to church?'

'No. My governesses both did – and Lizzie who looked after me after Miss Drake left. But they said as my mother and father were Catholics they had better not put their ideas into my head.'

The nun shook her head in despair. 'No more understanding than if she'd been brought up among godless heathens,' she muttered. She got up. 'This must be brought to the Reverend Mother's attention. Come.'

She marched through the passageways of the great house with Angelina in her wake until they came to a door, on which she knocked. A voice from within bade them enter. Mother Mary Benedicta was sitting behind a desk spread with papers and looked up in surprised inquiry.

'Forgive me for interrupting you, Reverend Mother,' Mary Andrew began. 'But I have just been talking to this child and I have made a horrifying discovery.'

'Horrifying?' Mother Mary Benedicta's eyebrows shot up. 'Surely that is rather strong language about one so young?'

'Old enough to have some understanding of Christian doctrine. This one has never even heard of the catechism, does not know who Our Lady is … has never set foot in a church.'

Mother Mary Benedicta looked at Angelina. 'Come over here. Now, is this true?'

Angelina wriggled her shoulders uncomfortably. She was aware that she had admitted to some terrible failing but she did not understand why it caused such consternation. 'Yes, Mother. I suppose it is.'

'You have never been taught your catechism?'

'No.'

'Never been to church?'

'No.'

'The child is a little heathen,' Mother Mary Andrew said. 'She has no business in a school like this.'

'Come now, that is a little extreme. She has been baptised. Her father sent me a copy of the certificate.'

'That's as maybe, but since then she has been in the grip of heretics and apostates. Who knows what sinful ideas she may spread if she is allowed to stay here.'

It flitted through Angelina's mind that the nun's speech had become like her mother's when she was angry. She recognised it now as an Irish accent. Mother Mary Benedicta's accent was different, more like some of the ladies who came to call on her mother.

'You are suggesting we should send her home?'

'I am saying she should never have been allowed to come here in the first place.'

Mother Mary Benedicta stood up. 'I think you are forgetting yourself, Mother Mary Andrew. The decision to admit her was mine.'

Mary Andrew bowed her head. 'Forgive me, Reverend Mother. But I believe you have been misled. This child is not suitable to mix with the girls we have here. They have been committed to our care to be given a good, Christian upbringing, not to mix with the likes of this.'

While Angelina listened to this exchange, contrary emotions chased each other through her mind. She wanted to be away from this strange place where everything was so incomprehensible. But if she was sent home, her mother and father would be angry. They would say it was her fault. And what might happen to her next?

Mother Mary Benedicta came round her desk and put her hand on Angelina's shoulder. 'Mother Mary Andrew, have you forgotten the parable of the lost sheep? "There is more joy in heaven for one sinner that repents than over ninety and nine just persons". This is a little lamb who has strayed from the true path and it is our duty, and our joy, to return her to Christ's flock. And to that end, I know that you will exert every effort. I am sure I can rely on you for this.'

There was a momentary silence, in which Angelina heard Mother Mary Andrew draw a long breath. Then she said, 'Of course, Reverend Mother.'

Mother Mary Benedicta patted Angelina's shoulder lightly. 'Go along now. Mother Scholastic will assign you to your class. But sometime soon I shall send for you and we will have a long talk. Thank you, Mother Mary Andrew.'

Back in the *salle d'études*, Angelina was given a time-table of lessons. She would learn English, geography, history, French, needlework and music. She greeted this last with delight.

'Will I be able to go on with my piano lessons?'

'You have learnt the piano before you came here?'

'Yes. Well, I had only just started, but I want to go on.'

'Well, we shall see. Mother Marie Thérèse is in charge of music and we have a teacher who comes in twice a week to give piano lessons. If you are deemed worthy of such tuition it may be possible. But now, pay close attention to me. Each girl is awarded marks for various aspects of her behaviour. There are a possible twenty marks for conduct; twenty for silence; twenty for politeness; ten for exactitude; ten for order and ten for application. Marks can be lost for any failure to abide by the rules. Each Sunday evening these marks are read out for each pupil and for those whose marks reach seventy-five there are rewards. I should warn you that any loss of marks for conduct would result almost inevitably in your expulsion from the school. Do you understand?'

'Not really. What does marks for silence mean? Do we have to be silent all the time?'

'No. It means that at certain times of day, or night, you are required to maintain silence. If you break it, you will lose marks. Likewise if you are rude to anyone, you will lose marks. The other marks refer to the quality of your work and the tidiness of your person and your belongings. Now, come with me and I will introduce you to your class teacher.'

For Angelina, her first weeks at the Convent of the Faithful Companions of Jesus was the beginning of a way of life that seemed at first unbelievably complex, but which resolved itself as the days passed into an orderly routine.

She found she was behind most of her classmates in many subjects, with the exception of arithmetic and spelling, where Miss Drake's drilling bore fruit; but the experience of being properly taught, by women who knew their subjects, instead of being made to learn by rote, was invigorating, and, for the first time in her life, she took pleasure in learning.

The constant company of other girls was a challenge at first. Her only interaction with her peers had been the fraught contact with the Pearson sisters and brief meetings with other girls and boys at dancing class. The complex maze of different relationships was difficult to negotiate. There were intense friendships and bitter, though covert, enmities. Some of the older girls were looked up to, almost idolised. Others were dismissed as 'common'. She was unsure where she fitted in this hierarchy and was aware that she was viewed in some quarters with a degree of suspicion, largely because of her English accent.

There was little chance to escape these pressures by seeking solitude. Instead of a room of her own, she had to sleep in a dormitory with a dozen other girls. She had a curtained cubicle, which provided some privacy, but there were puzzling rules surrounding that, too. It was forbidden for any girl to go into another's cubicle. Likewise, as she began to make friends, she was told that it was against the rules for two girls to be alone together at recreation times. This prohibition did not worry her too much. She got on well with Rosa and Anna and Wilhelmina and usually spent her time with them, but she did not have a special friend.

She found it hard to accept that some girls were better at certain things than she was, or seemed to get more of the teacher's attention than she did, and there were occasional flair-ups that resulted in a severe reduction in her marks for politeness; and she frequently lost marks for breaking silence. But slowly she came to terms with her new situation and learned to comply with its demands. After a few weeks her marks improved. Her biggest complaint was that at dinner they were all required to speak French. Her few phrases meant that she had to spend a good deal of the meal in silence, but slowly, by a process of something like osmosis, she began to understand and then to make stumbling efforts to join in. It helped that the French teacher was an amiable elderly nun who never scolded her.

Most of the girls came from families who lived in the surrounding area and on Sunday afternoons, provided their marks were good enough, they were allowed to meet their parents in a room designated as the parlour. It was expected on those occasions that the parents would bring sweets and cakes and afterwards these could be shared with friends. Angelina had no visitors and she was acutely aware that if she was offered such treats there was no way she could repay them. Her friends were generous and never left her out, but it was a source of embarrassment, and a keen reminder of her estrangement from her family.

Religion remained her chief stumbling block. Mother Mary Benedicta sent for her, as promised, and questioned her gently about what she knew and believed about Christianity. Finally she said, 'You are old enough to be confirmed, but first there is much for you to learn. Mother Mary Andrew will teach you your catechism and when she feels you thoroughly understand it we will ask Father O'Reilly to prepare you for your first confession. But that will not be for a while yet.'

The sessions with Mother Mary Andrew were the least enjoyable part of her week. She had never been required to deal with symbols or abstractions and her only acquaintance with the supernatural came from the fairy stories

Lizzie had read to her. It was clear from the beginning that the Mother Scholastic disapproved of her and was only teaching her under sufferance, and that made Angelina more inclined to question what she was told.

'In the Commandments it says we should only have one God. The trinity sounds like three gods.'

'How could Mary have a baby when she didn't have a husband?'

'How can bread turn into someone's body, or wine into blood?'

Mother Mary Andrew gritted her teeth. 'It is a matter of faith. You are not here to question the word of scripture.'

Once a week, Father O'Reilly, who was the parish curate, came to lecture them on Christian doctrine and they all had to assemble in the *salle d'études*, wearing their Sunday dresses and white gloves. He was a young man, and quite good looking, which was the cause of much whispering and giggling among the older girls. He was clearly aware of it and often blushed scarlet. Angelina felt sorry for him. As to the substance of his lectures, most of it went over her head. She stopped listening and spent her time looking around her and observing the reactions of her fellow pupils.

As at home in Liverpool, the highlight of her week was the music lesson. Mother Thérèse taught them to sing the psalms and responses used in the chapel, and, soon after Angelina joined the class, she stopped them in the middle of a psalm.

'There is a new voice here, one I have not heard before. Where is the new girl?'

'Here, Mother.'

'Angelina, come forward. Now sing that phrase again, solo.'

Angelina sang.

'Truly the voice of an angel. You are well named, child. We must cultivate this gift.'

From that day on she was often asked to sing a few bars alone and was soon recruited into the choir. There she found she had a rival. Eloise McLaren also had a good voice and hitherto had been Mother Thérèse's pet, but Angelina's clarity of tone and innate musicality put her in the shade. She clearly resented her demotion and it was only the tight discipline of the convent that prevented an unseemly row.

Eight

Freshfields
Rutherglen,
Victoria,
Australia
March 30th 1868

Dear James,

*Your letter arrived this morning and as always gave me
great joy. I am so glad to know that you are well – or
at least were so when you wrote. Oh, how long the time
seems between writing and receiving! I was glad, too,
to learn that your mother's condition seems a little better. It is so difficult for both of us, knowing that you cannot come to join me while she still needs your care, but
please believe me when I say that. She was kind to me
when I worked at Freeman's, especially when I had that
trouble with Mrs Connor McBride, and it was largely due
to her that I did not lose my job. And it was through her
help then that I met you, so I cannot wish her anything
but well. I know she does not approve of our engagement
and would much rather see you married to a young lady*

of a suitable background and education to be the wife of a rising solicitor; but she only wants the best for you and I cannot blame her for that. I would say give her my best wishes, but I think you may not have told her that we are writing to each other. Do not, on any account, say anything to her that might disturb her.

So, what news can I give you of our life here? The grape harvest is in and Pedro says we have a bumper crop. The grapes have been pressed and now the complicated business of fermenting the juice and making wine is in process. I don't understand much of what is going on but Gus is becoming very knowledgeable. For a boy whose only interest was in seafaring he is turning into a remarkably dedicated vintner! He, Father and Pedro spend their days poring over the vats, and seem to be very happy in each other's company, which pleases me greatly.

The more I come to know my father, the more I love him. Whatever faults or foolish mistakes he may have committed in the past, he is a good man, kind and generous and full of humour. We have had many long talks and he has told me about the smuggling for which he was convicted to be transported. He knows it was a very wrong, and very foolish thing to do, but I think he was led into it by others who took advantage of his good nature. He only wanted to have a little extra money, to make life easier for us, and for our mother. He talks a lot about her and I'm sure he loved her very much and was terribly hurt when he had no letters from her while he was serving his sentence; but he understands now how the shame of his conviction affected her and why she chose to tell us he had been 'lost at sea'.

He convinced himself that she must have married again, which is why he chose not to return when his sentence was up.

On a slightly lighter note, he is full of anecdotes about his fellow prisoners and some of the more amusing or uplifting events that occurred, both while he was a prisoner and afterwards when he was working as a prospector. I am sure he has not told me the bad things that happened, but when he is not talking I see a shadow come into his face and I know that he is a man who has suffered a great deal. He worries that we blame him for not coming back to save us from the hardships we suffered in the workhouse and afterwards, but I tell him that we do not and never have. There is nothing that I regret about the past, and Gus feels the same.

I saw my first snake the other day! I was walking with Gus on the far side of the lake and it came straight across our path. It gave me quite a shock, I can tell you. Father says they are more afraid of us than we are of them and will always get out of our way if they hear us coming, or feel the vibration from our footfalls. But I still find it hard to accept that whenever I go out I need to keep a wary eye open, just in case. I also saw my first echidna in the woods. They are like great big hedgehogs and burrow around in the undergrowth. The animal life here never ceases to amaze me.

We are beginning to get to know our neighbours. There are several other vineyards in the area, most of them owned by settlers from Britain. They come from all sorts of backgrounds but they all have one thing in common, they came here for a new life and they want to make a success of it.

I thought there was no snobbery here, but I have discovered there is one element that disturbs me a little. There is a division between those who came here voluntarily and those who were sent here, as my father was. Those who came of their own free will tend to look down on the ex-convicts, though Gus says that is much more marked in Melbourne than it is out here. Fortunately, our neighbours do not seem inclined to make a distinction and we have been invited to dine with several of them. That, of course, means that we have to entertain in our turn. Imagine me, as hostess at a dinner party! For once, I am grateful for what I learned in service. At least I know how to set a table, and which cutlery to put out. Not that that matters much out here. Most people seem to have a pretty happy-go-lucky attitude to things like that.

If I have one complaint, it is the lack of occupation. I am not used to idleness and I feel guilty if I am not busy with something. Maria cares for the house and she is a far better cook than I am, so I would not presume to interfere in that department. I do do the household accounts, for which I am grateful to Miss Bale who drilled me in arithmetic back in the workhouse, but that does not take up much of my time. There is one good thing. I have gone back to drawing and painting. I'm so glad you encouraged me in that direction. There is certainly no shortage of fascinating subjects to paint here. By the time you get here I should have quite a gallery to exhibit to you!

Please take care of yourself, my dearest. I hope your studies are going well. You have to pass those examinations to become a fully-fledged solicitor. I am looking forward to being a lawyer's wife.

Write soon.

All my love,
May

Nine

As winter gave way to spring, the girls at the convent were allowed to take their recreation periods outside and Angelina discovered that the house stood in extensive grounds, which fell away to the shores of a large lake. There were lawns and flower beds, shrubberies and a rose garden, and a kitchen garden and a yard where chickens were kept. Ancient trees spread their branches protectively over the whole. In the open, grassy area designated as a playground for the girls of Preparatory Two, Angelina learned to play rounders and discovered she could run much faster than she thought.

Lent brought certain puzzling restrictions: no sweets, and a more limited diet than the French lay sister in charge of the kitchen was normally proud to provide.

Angelina struggled with the story of the Crucifixion and Resurrection. Mother Mary Andrew told her repeatedly that it was a matter of faith and hinted at dire consequences for those who refused to believe, but she found it hard to accept.

As Easter approached, however, religious faith was not the consideration uppermost in her mind. The other girls were talking about going home for the holidays. Those whose parents lived too far away to visit on Sunday afternoons wrote home regularly and received letters in return. No one wrote to Angelina. Even her birthday passed unremarked. Now she watched with mixed feelings for a letter telling her that her father was coming to take her home. When he left her at the convent she had longed for the day when he would return to fetch her, but now she was not at all sure that she wanted to go home. Rules here were strict, but not difficult to understand, and no one was ever beaten. There were nights when she dreamed that she was back home again and her mother was flourishing the cane and threatening to punish her, and she woke shaking. But on the other hand, she had a vague feeling that to be left behind when the other girls went would be somehow shameful. She would be the odd-one-out: an object of pity or worse.

On the last day of term all the other girls were packing their trunks. Angelina had not seen her case since the day she arrived, so she asked Sister Berthe where to find it.

'What do you want that for?' the lay sister asked. 'You're not going anywhere.'

'Am I not going home for the holidays?' Angelina asked tremulously.

Berthe stopped what she was doing and looked shocked. 'God help us! Has nobody explained to you? Your father thinks the journey is too long for you to be going backwards and forwards. You are to spend the holidays here.'

That night Angelina fell asleep with a sense of relief. When the other girls expressed surprise, she pretended that she had always understood the arrangement.

Later that day, Mother Mary Benedicta sent for her.

'I know you must be feeling a little disappointed about not going home, Angelina. But you are not the only one. Juanita is staying. It's too far for her to go home to Mexico. And little Margaret has no home to go to. So you will not be alone. We will find things for you to do; enjoyable things, I hope.'

Juanita was fifteen and clearly not interested in the company of a nine-year-old and Margaret was a strange child who seemed to live in a world of her own, obsessively arranging and rearranging her collection of seashells. So Angelina was lonely, in spite of Reverend Mother's reassurances. She found, in practice, she did not mind. Some activities were organised for all three girls, but their level of maturity was so disparate that they tended to be undertaken separately.

Angelina had long conversations with Mother Mary Madeleine, the elderly nun who taught French, and became quite fluent. Sister Catherine, one of the younger lay sisters, played ball games with her and taught her the rudiments of tennis. But for a large part of the time she was left to herself. She was free to wander wherever she liked in the grounds, and this in itself was more freedom than she had ever known. There was an extensive library in the *salle d'études* and, though she was only allowed access to the section that the nuns regarded as suitable for her age group, she discovered for the first time the joy of reading. She read *The Water Babies* by Charles Kingsley, and *Alice in Wonderland*, and *At the Back of the North Wind*. Best of all was the fact that Mother Marie Thérèse allowed her to play the piano whenever she liked and sometimes gave her some extra lessons. One way or another, the two weeks of the holiday passed pleasantly enough.

Over the Easter weekend itself she was expected to attend some, though not all, of the services in the chapel. She saw that the nuns were genuinely moved by the story of the Crucifixion and equally rejoiced in the celebration of the Resurrection. The crucifix, with the body of Christ hanging on it, and the agony it represented, terrified her and she wondered how the nuns who knelt before it could bear to think about it; but there was no escaping the proof of their dedication. She had come to like many of them, even to love a few, and she tried hard to enter into their devotion but she still could not bring herself to believe.

She saw the other girls arriving for the new term with mixed feelings. It was good to have company again, but it meant the end of her freedom and a return to a regular timetable of lessons. Once they had all settled into the usual routine, however, she decided that on balance she preferred this.

In mid-May a frisson of excitement ran through the school. Three senior girls had decided they had a vocation and wished to become nuns. There would be a special service and the bishop would come to receive them as postulants. After that, there would be a special sung Mass. Mother Thérèse was in a flurry, chivvying the choir to greater and greater efforts. At the third rehearsal she said, 'I have decided that the "Agnus Dei" will be sung by a solo voice. It will be either you, Eloise, or you, Angelina. Come to my room at private study time and I will teach it to you both.'

From that moment, Angelina's whole desire was focussed on one thing. She must be the one to sing the solo! She rehearsed with Eloise and then alone and two days before the service they were both summoned to the music room.

'I want each of you to sing for me once more, and then I will make my decision.'

Eloise sang first and, listening, Angelina knew that she could do better. Eloise was good, but she had to strain for the high notes. When her turn came she reached them effortlessly.

When she had finished Mother Therèse said gently, 'You have both done very well but on this occasion I am going to ask Angelina to take the solo. Your turn will come, Eloise, at another time but for now I want you to hold yourself in readiness in case Angelina should, heaven forfend, catch a chill before Sunday and be unable to perform. Now, I do not want you to talk about this to the other girls. Let it be a surprise on Sunday.'

As they left Eloise hissed, 'It should have been me! I've been here for two years and you're just a jumped-up little show off of a new girl.'

'I'm sorry you're upset,' Angelina said, and meant it. 'But I'm sure you will get a chance next time.'

All night she hugged the thought of the service to herself. She did not want to tell the others. It was too precious to be shared as common gossip.

On the Saturday there was a final rehearsal with the full choir and, to preserve the secret, Mother Therèse asked them both to sing the 'Agnus Dei' as a duet; but as they left the chapel Angelina heard someone whisper, 'It should be Angelina. She's much better.'

That evening she was surprised to be summoned to Mother Mary Andrew's office. The nun's expression was grim.

'I have just learned that Mother Marie Thérèse is considering allowing you to sing the solo in tomorrow's Mass. I have explained to her that this is quite unacceptable. You are not in a fit state of grace to take such a prominent role. Eloise, who has made her first confession and been confirmed, will sing it.'

Angelina stared at her in numb disbelief. 'But I'm better than she is.'

'Your voice may be better, possibly. But that is not the only consideration.'

'Please, Mother Mary Andrew –' tears surged up in her throat '– please let me! I want it so much.'

'What you want is of no importance. You have yet to learn self-denial and obedience. This will be a salutary lesson.'

'But …'

'That is enough! You have already said enough to lose you five marks for politeness. Go before I have to deduct any more.'

Angelina ran through the building until she reached the music room. She burst in without knocking, already in tears.

'Mother Marie Thérèse, Mother Mary Andrew says I am not to sing the solo tomorrow.'

Marie Thérèse took hold of her hand. 'I know. Mother Mary Andrew has already been to see me. It is unkind, but there is nothing to be done. Next year, I promise, you will be the one to sing.'

'I don't care about next year!' Angelina declared passionately. 'I'm better than Eloise. It ought to be me. Don't you want the singing to be the best it can be?'

Mother Thérèse stepped back with a sigh. 'Of course I do.'

'I'm going to ask Mother Mary Benedicta,' Angelina said with sudden resolution. 'She will understand how important it is.'

'No, Angelina! Stop. Wait!'

She had already left the room. The nun hurried after her but did not try to stop her. Angelina knocked and was through the door of the Reverend Mother's office before she had been given permission to enter.

'Reverend Mother!' Angelina sank to her knees in front of the astonished nun. 'I'm supposed to sing the solo in the Mass tomorrow. Mother Marie Thérèse has chosen me because I'm the best. And now Mother Mary Andrew says I am not allowed to do it. Please say I can!'

Mother Mary Benedicta looked over her head at Marie Thérèse. 'Is this so?'

'Yes, Reverend Mother. Angelina's voice is definitely best suited to the piece in question.'

'And on what ground has Mother Mary Andrew countermanded this arrangement?'

'I believe she feels Angelina's spiritual condition is not … does not merit such prominence.'

'I see.' Mother Mary Benedicta considered for a moment. 'Mother Marie Thérèse, would you be so good as to ask Mother Mary Andrew to join us?'

'Of course, Mother.'

Left alone, Reverend Mother raised Angelina to her feet. 'Now, child, stop crying. It is not fitting to shed such bitter tears merely because your personal ambition has been thwarted. We all have to meet setbacks and disappointments and the correct path is to offer your sorrow up to God and pray that you may be strengthened by it. Do you understand?'

Angelina shook her head miserably.

'Do you know why Mother Mary Andrew has forbidden you to sing?'

'She says I'm not in a sufficient state of grace.'

'Do you know why she says that?'

Angelina hesitated. 'I think ... I think it's because I don't always understand what she says when she is teaching me the catechism.'

Brisk footfalls heralded the arrival of the Mother Scholastic. Her face was white and rigid with fury.

'Do I understand aright that this child has taken it upon herself to question my decision? And that you, Mother Marie Therèse, have abetted her in this act of disobedience?'

'Angelina has much the better voice.' Marie Therèse's own voice shook. 'I thought that we should offer up the very best we have on such an important occasion.'

'The child is a heathen!' Mother Mary Andrew overrode any opportunity for comment. 'She questions every tenet in the catechism. She is vain and self-willed. We would sin by encouraging such traits.'

Mother Mary Benedicta looked from her to Marie Therèse and then at Angelina, who experienced a flare of hope at the hint of indecision. At length she said, 'Angelina, go back to the *salle d'études* and get on with your work.

I need to talk to the two Mothers privately. I will send for you when I have made my decision.'

With dragging steps, Angelina obeyed, but it was impossible to concentrate on her work. She sat watching the door, waiting for the summons, aware that her tear-stained face had already aroused whispered comment among the other girls. After a long time Sister Berthe came in and murmured, 'Reverend Mother will see you now.'

Mother Mary Benedicta was sitting behind her desk, her face grave but composed. 'Come here, Angelina. I have talked to Mother Scholastic and to Mother Marie Thérèse and I have decided that I must uphold the authority of Mother Mary Andrew. She is, after all, in charge of everything connected with the school, and she also has the best understanding of where you are on your spiritual journey.' She raised a hand to silence the plea that burst from Angelina's lips. 'I know this is a great disappointment and that to you it seems unjust. You must try to look upon it as an opportunity to learn, and to vanquish those impulses of vanity and self-importance that Mother Mary Andrew has detected in you. Perhaps you may also wish to consider that, although it is good to question what we are told in general terms, there are certain facts that have to be accepted as a matter of faith. You are very young, and you must acquire the humility to accept that older and wiser heads have knowledge and understanding that you lack as yet.' Her face softened. 'Your time will come. I promise you that. Meanwhile, you must try not to annoy Mother Mary Andrew. Now, go to bed and when you say your prayers ask God to give you a humble and contrite heart. Will you do that?'

'Yes, Reverend Mother.' The words sounded meek, but in her heart Angelina felt anything but contrite. She had been dealt an injustice and this was something she could not accept. She prayed before she got into bed, but not for humility. Instead she asked God to bring down vengeance on Mother Mary Andrew and to make sure that Eloise had a terrible cold by the next morning.

As the choir took their places for the service Angelina made sure that her bearing was unimpeachable. Overnight she had formulated a plan and nothing must get in the way of its execution. The school assembled and the parents of the three postulants took their places in the front pews. There was an atmosphere of subdued but febrile excitement, which rose to a climax when the three girls made their entrance. Dressed like brides, in white satin and lace veils, they seemed to float down the aisle to take their places before the altar, and they knelt in turn before the bishop.

'My child, what do you demand?'

'The holy habit of religion, my lord ...'

Angelina frowned in puzzlement. Why would these girls wish to go straight from their schooldays into the seclusion of the convent? She could understand, just, the attraction of remaining in this place of quiet security; but she had heard from the other side of the lake, which was open to the public, the shouts of children at play and the laughter of young people out to enjoy themselves. There was another life out there. Not one that she had ever experienced, but the mere fact that she knew it existed meant that she could never be content to shut herself away without at least the opportunity to taste it.

The service proceeded. Each of the three girls received the folded habit, the coif and veil she would wear as a nun, and then they made their way back up the aisle and disappeared.

'What happens now?' Angelina whispered to her neighbour.

'They have all their hair cut off and then they get dressed in their new habits.'

Angelina shivered.

A hymn was sung and after another long wait the three postulants reappeared, almost unrecognisable with their hair hidden and their faces framed in the white coif. They knelt again at the *prie-dieu* they had occupied earlier and the Mass began.

The choir excelled itself, voices blending in praise and supplication. The moment arrived for the 'Agnus Dei' and not one but two girls stood up, and two voices were raised. One began confidently, then wavered for a moment, then strained for volume to drown out the other and finally cracked and faded into silence, while the other flowed on, pure and effortless, rising to the vaults of the roof and on to the heaven beyond.

Ten

One spring morning a fair-bearded man with a slight limp entered the offices of Weaver and Woolley, Solicitors, in Liverpool. The solicitor's clerk rose from behind his desk to greet him.

'Good morning. I'm James Breckenridge, at your service. How can I help you?'

'My name is Richard Kean,' was the response, 'but to be entirely honest with you, I'm not sure how you can help, or even if you can. Is it possible to speak to Mr Weaver, or Mr Woolley?'

'Mr Woolley is unavailable at the moment, but Mr Weaver is in his office. He usually only sees people by appointment but he might be able to give you a few minutes. Shall I ask?'

'Please do.'

James went into the inner office and returned a few moments later. 'Mr Weaver will see you. Please come this way.'

Josiah Weaver was a small man with pince-nez and a sharp nose that twitched when he was interested in something. He rose and shook hands with the visitor and offered him a chair.

'James, I think it might be helpful if you stayed, in case I need you to take notes. You don't mind, do you, Mr Kean?'

'No, no. Of course not.'

James took a seat at a little distance and got out a notepad and pencil from his jacket pocket.

'Now, what can we do for you, Mr Kean?' Weaver asked.

'It is a long story and one that does not reflect well on me as a person, I fear,' Kean began, 'but I will tell you the whole of it and then you can tell me whether you can see any way forward.' He shifted in his chair and settled himself. 'I am by profession an engineer specialising in mining. Until ten years ago I was mine manager at a colliery in Neston on the Wirral peninsula. One terrible day there was an explosion below ground. I went down to investigate and to help in the rescue of survivors. In the course of that operation, a slab of rock fell on my leg and fractured it. It took a long time to heal, and during that time I was, of course, unable to work. I was married, with a baby daughter, and times were very hard for us, as you may imagine. I had some savings, but we soon got through them. When my leg was sufficiently healed I started to look for a new job.

'Unfortunately, the mine at Neston never recovered from the explosion and had been closed down, so there was nothing there for me. We moved to Liverpool, hoping I might find work of some other nature, but I had no success, and to add to our difficulties my wife was now pregnant with our second child. I was at my wits end. Then one day I met a man in an inn near the docks, where I had gone in a moment of despair to, as the saying goes, drown my sorrows.

'We got talking and it transpired that he had just got off a boat from South Africa. He owned some land on which a recent survey had discovered a deposit of coal. He knew nothing of mining and had come to England expressly to recruit someone with expertise in that area.' Kean had been looking down at his hands. Now he paused and raised his eyes. 'You can imagine that it seemed a most providential meeting. I invited him to my home, we talked, and in matter of hours he had offered me a five-year contract. There was only one difficulty. He wanted me to leave for Africa at once, but my wife was in poor health. I am afraid the privations she had suffered while I was unemployed had weakened her and the pregnancy had been difficult.' He paused again and drew a deep breath.

'Now I come to the most difficult part of my story. It was agreed that I should take ship at once for Cape Town and she would remain in Liverpool with our little daughter until the new baby was of an age to be able to withstand the journey. My prospective employer advanced me some money to cover her expenses in the interim. It was far from ideal but I dared not let the chance of a good job slip away from me, so I booked my passage.' Kean's voice had become more and more strained as he spoke and now it cracked and he had to pause.

'Some water for Mr Kean,' Weaver ordered.

James fetched a glass and Kean took a sip and cleared his throat. 'On the day before I was due to sail my wife unexpectedly went into labour. There were ... there were complications. To tell it briefly, she died and the child with her.' Weaver made a noise indicating sympathy and when Kean looked up there were tears in his eyes. 'I was left with my other daughter, who was only just over one year old. What was I to do? I had no close family to turn to, no neighbours who might be in a position to take on a child, and I had to get on that ship. God forgive me, I took her to the workhouse. It was long after midnight. The gates were shut. I wrapped her in a shawl and laid her outside the gate, where she must be seen as soon as they were opened. And then I ran to the docks and just caught my ship before she sailed.'

James leant forward sharply. 'How long ago was this?'

'Almost eight years. I served out my contract and was offered an extension. I was doing well and making money, so I agreed. I tried to forget the child I had left behind me. I told myself she would be looked after, that to reappear in her life would be a disruption, but I knew I was only trying to silence my own conscience. As time passed and I thought of Amy growing up without me it became harder and harder to bear. Then my employer decided that we needed better machinery and he suggested I should come back to England, to study the latest developments and find out where the best examples were to be found. We came to an agreement. I had six months of my extended contract to run. I would come back here and spend that time locating and purchasing what we needed. After that, I would be free to stay or return, as I chose.' He heaved a deep sigh. 'So here I am, gentlemen, and my one desire is to find my daughter.'

'I take it,' Weaver said, 'that you have applied to the workhouse.'

'Of course. It was my first action on leaving the ship. They told me that she had almost certainly been adopted soon after I left her, but when I asked by whom I was told that such matters were confidential and they could not reveal the identities of adopting couples. That is why I have come to you. Do I have any redress in law?'

Weaver pursed his lips. 'Adoption has no legal standing, of course. It is an informal relationship between the consenting parties, in this case the governor of the workhouse and the adopting couple. Theoretically, if you can prove paternity, there is nothing to stop you claiming the child. But does it not occur to you, Mr Kean, that your daughter may now be enjoying a very happy life with a loving couple whom she believes to be her parents? For you to burst onto the scene now could only cause her distress.'

Kean hung his head. 'I was afraid you would say that. And of course you are right. But if I could only be sure that she is in good hands ...' His voice tailed off.

'Excuse me, sir,' James said. 'Do you mind if I ask Mr Kean a couple of questions?'

'As you wish,' Weaver said.

'Do you remember what your daughter looked like, Mr Kean?'

'I not only remember, I have a likeness of her. My wife, God rest her soul, was an amateur artist and before she died she drew Amy.' He reached into an inner pocket and took out a wallet. From this he extracted a slip of paper and handed it to James. The paper was yellowing and the lines of the picture were faded, but the likeness was still vivid.

'Was her hair golden? I see you are fair.'

'Yes, she had my colouring. Why do you ask?'

James looked across at his principal. 'Sir, I believe I may have seen this child.'

'Seen her? Where?' Kean demanded.

Weaver inclined his head. 'Go on.'

'It was a couple of years ago. The story is a bit convo-luted, so bear with me. My mother buys ... used to buy ... her hats from Freeman's Department Store. One day I found myself at liberty rather earlier than usual – if I remember rightly, sir, we had been in court and the case had ended sooner than we expected – and I recalled that my mother had an appointment to try on a new hat, so I decided to call in and escort her home.

'When I arrived, I found a small girl sitting outside the milliner's room, apparently in some distress. She was a pretty little thing, with golden hair and blue eyes. When I asked what the matter was she said her mama had sent her out of the room and she didn't know why. I went in and found my mother and another lady, who was clearly in a very bad temper, plus of course the milliner and ... and her apprentice, a young woman called May Lavender. The other lady collected her hat and left, taking the little girl with her. What had happened, I was told, was that, when she arrived, May, Miss Lavender, claimed to recognise the child. I didn't understand the circumstances at the time but now I think I can fill in the missing pieces of the jigsaw.

'She – Miss Lavender – was sure that the child was one she had looked after as a baby. She became very attached to her, but then one day the child disappeared and she was told she had been adopted. She was convinced that this lit-tle girl was the child she had named Angel because of her looks, and who was now called Angelina. The lady who claimed to be her mother, however, was extremely angry and subsequently did her best to get May dismissed from her post. I know now that May was brought up in the work-house, so that must be where she encountered the child – and it explains, I imagine, why the adoptive mother was so disturbed when she recognised her.'

'Lavender?' Mr Weaver mused. 'The name rings a bell.'

'You subsequently agreed to speak on behalf of her brother, who had been arrested for being drunk and disor-derly. We managed to persuade the magistrate that justice would be better served by a fine rather than imprisonment, so that he could take up a position he had been offered with one of the shipping companies.'

'Ah yes, I recall the incident. Your involvement with the family seems to have been quite long established.'

'I helped to arrange a petition asking Mr Freeman not to dismiss May.'

'This young woman,' Kean broke in, 'is it possible to speak to her?'

'I fear not. She emigrated to Australia about six months ago.'

Kean shook his head in disappointment.

'Do you recall the name of the lady who claimed to be the child's mother?' Weaver asked.

'I don't, I'm afraid. But I am almost sure that my mother would.'

'Could we speak to her?' Kean asked.

'She is in very poor health, I'm afraid. But I'm sure she would be happy to help if she can. I could ask her.'

'Would you? Please? I shall be grateful for any clue.'

'One moment.' Weaver raised a warning hand. 'Before we proceed any further, I think we should be clear what you are intending to do with any information you may glean, Mr Kean. If this is not the child you are seeking you might cause a great deal of trouble for yourself and for her.'

'I understand that,' Kean said, 'but if I could just see her, I'm sure I should know her.'

Weaver lifted his shoulders. 'I cannot prevent you from making any enquiries you wish to make. But as a lawyer I should warn you of the possible consequences.'

Kean looked from him to James and rose heavily to his feet. 'I understand. I'm sorry to have wasted your time.'

James rose also and cast a look of appeal at Weaver. 'Sir ... ?'

'However,' Weaver conceded, 'as I said, there is nothing to stop you making enquiries. Now, if you will forgive me, I have work that I need to get on with.' He rose and held out his hand. 'I'll wish you good day.'

'Good day, and thank you for your time,' Kean responded.

'I'll see you out.' James conducted him to the outer office and detained him with a hand on his sleeve. 'If you could come back here at half past five, when we close, I could take you to meet my mother.'

'Are you sure? I thought you said she was in poor health.'

'She is, but because of that she is unable to go out very much. She lacks diversion. I think she would enjoy a visit from someone new.'

'And you think it would not tire her too much? It seems an imposition to ask her to recall what must have been a trivial incident.'

'On the contrary.' James paused, then went on with a wry grin, 'The fact is, the thing she misses most is gossip. A chance to relive the incident will appeal to her.'

Kean's rather gloomy expression was replaced by a sudden warm smile. 'In that case, I shall be delighted to entertain her. Five-thirty, you said? I'll see you then.'

James watched him walk away, his uneven steps bearing witness to that old injury. He returned to his desk with frisson of excitement. If this was, indeed, Angel's real father, how delighted May would be to learn of it when he next wrote.

Kean was at the door when James locked up for the night. As they walked towards his house, he asked, 'This young lady, did you say her name was May?'

'May Lavender, yes.'

'Would I be right in guessing that she is more than just a casual acquaintance?'

James glanced sideways at him. This was a little too personal for his liking. 'We are … friends.'

'I'm sorry. I shouldn't pry. I was wondering what made her decide to emigrate.'

'Her father, whom she believed to be dead, wrote out of the blue. He had struck gold and was now a rich man. He asked her to go out to join him.'

Kean gave a low whistle. 'What an amazing story! From the workhouse to riches!'

'Yes, it is, isn't it?'

'It could be the same for Amy – Angel as you call her – if we can find her. I am also now pretty well off.'

'I believe the people who adopted her are quite comfortably off, too,' James said. 'That is, if Angelina is really your Amy.'

'Of course.' He sighed. 'I had this dream of coming home and taking her out of the gloom of the workhouse to a life of sunshine and flowers. I suppose I shall have to forget that now.'

They reached the modest but well-proportioned house where James had grown up and were met in the hall by the parlourmaid.

'Flossie, this is Mr Kean. He wants to meet Mama. Is she well enough for a visitor?'

'The mistress is dressed and resting in the drawing room, sir. Shall I ask?'

'Yes, please do.'

The maid returned quickly. 'Missis says will you please walk in, sir.'

Mrs Brackenridge was reclining on a chaise longue and James was glad to see that her colour, sometimes hectically feverish, was normal. He went to her and kissed her cheek.

'Mama, this is Mr Kean. He has just returned from several years in South Africa and he has something very particular he wants to ask you about.'

She stretched out a hand and Kean took it with a small bow. 'I'm very grateful to you for sparing the time to see me, ma'am.'

'Oh, as to that, time is something I have plenty of these days. Please take a seat. James, ask Flossie to bring tea.' The two men seated themselves and she went on, 'Now, what was it you wanted to ask?'

Kean looked at James for guidance and he said, 'Mother, do you remember, about two years ago, there was that unpleasant business when May Lavender thought she recognised a little girl and the girl's mother tried to get her sacked?'

'I certainly do!' Mrs Brackenridge replied. 'The woman made a ridiculous fuss and the poor little girl was most upset.'

'Why was the mother so annoyed, do you think?'

'I never understood that. Everyone knows the child is adopted.'

James and Richard Kean exchanged glances. 'You're quite sure about that?' James asked.

'My dear boy, I may be a semi-invalid but I'm not in my dotage. Of course I'm sure.'

'Mother, we think that Mr Kean here may be the child's true father. He was forced to abandon her when his wife died just as he was about to take ship for South Africa. Now he has returned and he has asked me, well asked Mr Weaver, to help him find her.'

Mrs Brackenridge turned her gaze on Kean. 'Are you an Irishman, sir?'

'Irish? No. Why do you ask?'

'From what I remember, the story was that the child was the daughter of an Irish relation whose wife had died and left him to care for her alone.'

Kean looked crestfallen. 'Then perhaps I am looking in the wrong place. I have never set foot in Ireland.'

'Do you remember the woman's name? The adoptive mother?' James asked.

'Marguerite Connor McBride. He's something in the tea trade, but there is supposed to be an estate in Ireland somewhere. The McBrides have always given themselves airs. I believe it was his brother who was the child's father.'

Kean reached for his wallet. 'Mrs Brackenridge, do you recall what the little girl looked like?'

'Pretty little thing with golden curls.'

'Does this look anything like her?'

He handed the worn paper with the sketch to the old lady, who scrutinised it through her pince-nez. 'Yes, it could be her. Of course, it was some time ago and the child was a good deal older than she is here, but yes, it could be her.'

'If I could just see her,' Kean said. 'I'm sure I should know her.'

'Do you know where the McBrides live?' James asked.

His mother shook her head. 'Not precisely. We were never on visiting terms. I believe it was out Toxteth way somewhere. Let me think. Devonshire Road, I believe.'

'How did you say Miss Lavender knew the child?' Kean asked, looking at James.

James rose hurriedly. 'We mustn't tire my mother any more. I'll see you out.'

In the hall he said in a low voice, 'I should prefer it if you didn't mention the workhouse to my mother. May tried to keep her background a secret, once she had obtained her place as a milliner's apprentice.'

Kean looked at him sharply and then nodded. 'Understood. Your mother wouldn't approve of your … friendship … if she knew.'

'Quite,' James said briefly. 'What will you do now?'

Kean sighed. 'I don't know. I may be on a wild goose chase. But I think I'll find Devonshire Road and just hang around a bit. Even if I knew the precise address I could hardly ring the doorbell and ask to see little Miss McBride.'

But there's a chance I might see her out for a walk, or going to school or something.'

'Well, I wish you luck,' James said. 'Look, can we keep in touch? I may not be able to help in a professional capacity but I'd like to know how you get on. Can we meet for a drink sometime?'

'I'm staying at the Adelphi,' Kean said. 'Why don't you drop in after work tomorrow and I'll tell you if I've discovered anything?'

Next evening, when they were both settled in the hotel bar with a glass of beer, James said, 'Well? Any luck?'

'None at all, I'm afraid,' Kean replied. 'I found the address easily enough, by asking a delivery boy who was passing. I hung around for a while, till I realised I must look rather suspicious. Then I had an idea. I saw a woman go out and get into a cab, obviously the lady of the house, so I waited until she was well out if the way, then I went and knocked on the door and asked if Mrs McBride was at home. Of course, she wasn't, so I said, bold as brass, perhaps I could speak to Miss McBride. The maid gave me a bit of an odd look and said Miss Angelina was not there either. That struck me as a bit odd. I'd been there since early morning and I'd seen a man I assume was Mr McBride leave and then his wife, but I swear no one else went either in or out.'

'Perhaps the maid thought it was best to say she was out,' James said. 'She must have wondered what you could possibly want with a girl of, what eight, nine?'

'I suppose you're right,' Kean agreed reluctantly. 'I seem to have hit a dead end. I've got to get on with the job I came to do. I can't stand around in Devonshire Road all day hoping for a glimpse of her.'

'You'd probably get yourself arrested anyway,' James said. 'I'm sorry, but I can't see any way forward at the moment.'

Later, over dinner, his mother said, 'Has your friend got any further with his enquiries?'

'I'm afraid not. He found the address in Devonshire Road but there was no sign of the little girl.'

'What will he do now?'

'I think he may give up. It's a shame, because I really think Angelina may be his child.'

'Hmm. A pity. Poor man.' Mrs Brackenridge thought for a moment. 'I tell you who might know more about her than I do. Laura Pearson. Her husband sits on the same committees and goes to the same club as Connor McBride and I fancy she knows the family quite well.'

'Could I speak to her?'

'She might find it odd if you approached her directly. But I've known her for years. Why don't I invite her to tea and see what I can find out?'

'Are you quite sure you're up to it? I don't want you to tire yourself.'

His mother gave him a slightly mischievous smile. 'It's something to take my mind off my aches and pains. You don't know how tedious it is to be an invalid. This will make me feel I'm not quite useless.'

'You're not useless, mother. You never have been. But if you can help Richard Kean to find his daughter it will be an act of kindness.'

'I'll send Laura an invitation tomorrow. Perhaps you could get away from work early and just happen to come home in time to meet her?'

'Let me know which day, and I'll do my best.'

Three days later James put his head into Mr Weaver's office.

'I wonder if I could leave half an hour early, sir. I've dealt with all the outstanding items and my mother has invited someone to tea whom she wants me to meet.'

'Indeed.' Weaver gave him a knowing look. 'And on this occasion you are happy to make the acquaintance?'

James smiled a little sheepishly. He knew what was in Weaver's mind. His mother had been trying to introduce him to suitable young ladies for a year or more and normally he did his best to avoid them. 'Oh well, I don't like to disappoint her,' he said.

'Off you go, then.' Weaver smiled. He had developed a soft spot for James. He had been with him for several years and he was a good pupil.

James found his mother presiding over the tea table with a lady who struck him as being rather over-dressed for the occasion.

'Oh, James!' his mother exclaimed. 'You're home early. How nice. This is Mrs Pearson. Laura, this is my son James. He is studying to be a solicitor.'

James took the offered hand and bent his head over it. 'Delighted to make your acquaintance, ma'am.'

'James, do you remember that time you came to collect me from Freeman's and Mrs Connor McBride was there with her little girl?'

137

James feigned an effort of memory. 'Yes, I think so. Pretty little thing with golden hair.'

'That's right. I was just asking Mrs Pearson if she knew what had become of her. I've never seen her since that day. Has something happened to the poor child?'

'Poor child indeed!' Laura Pearson gave a grimace. 'Don't be fooled by that angelic face. She's turned into a little monster.'

'Surely not!'

'Oh yes. I made the mistake of inviting her to join my girls in some of their lessons and she was nothing but trouble. She bit my Mary.'

'Bit her?'

'Yes. She went to the same dancing class and at Christmas time there was a kind of ball. You know the sort of thing. All the parents were invited and the children were all dressed up in their best clothes to show off what they had learned. In the middle of supper she suddenly attacked Mary like a little fury and bit her on the cheek.'

'Do you know why?'

'Well –' Mrs Pearson gave a small shrug '– I suppose I have to accept some blame. Mary must have heard me telling someone that Angelina was not the McBrides' natural child. They got into an argument, you know how children squabble, and I think Mary said something to that effect. But that is no excuse for attacking her like a wild animal. No wonder they sent her away.'

'Sent her away?' James leaned forward in his chair. 'Do you know where?'

'To school somewhere. I've no idea where. I've had very little to do with the family since the incident. Why do you ask?'

'Oh, just idle curiosity. The parents must be distraught.'

'Well, my husband and I always said they were taking a risk, bringing someone else's child into their home.' Mrs Pearson was obviously enjoying the opportunity for a good gossip.

'But wasn't the child related to them in some way?' Mrs Brackenridge prompted.

'Connor McBride's brother's daughter, so they said.'

'Do you doubt it?'

'I always wondered how such a dark-haired family produced a child like that. Of course, I suppose the mother may have been fair.'

'The brother lived in Ireland, didn't he?'

'On the family estate. I presume he was the elder brother and inherited the land.'

'Do you think it's possible that Angelina was sent back to live with him?' James asked.

'Sent away to school, was what I was told.'

'Where was the family estate?' Mrs Brackenridge asked.

'Oh, Marguerite did tell me once. Some unpronounceable Irish name. Let me think. Bally something. George always laughed and said it sounded like a euphemism for a swear word. Ballymagorry, that was it!'

After a few more exchanges, James excused himself on the grounds that he had arranged to meet a friend.

At the Adelphi he enquired for Richard Kean and in a few minutes they were settled again in the bar.

'My mother has undertaken some detective work on your behalf,' James began. He gave Kean the gist of what he had learned and the other man shook his head sadly.

'I hate to think of my little girl behaving like that. What must they have done to her to turn into such a little termagant?'

'It does make you wonder,' James agreed. 'But if she's at a good school now, perhaps the harm can be undone.'

'Maybe. Is there any way of discovering the name of the school?'

'Mrs Pearson didn't know it. But listen –' James put down his glass and leaned forward '– I think there is one line of enquiry we could pursue. The family is supposed to have land in Ireland, in a place called Ballymagorry. If you could go there, you might be able to find out if there ever was an elder brother whose wife died and left him with a daughter. If the story is true, then Angelina is not your child. If it's not ...'

'Then she still might be.' Kean's face brightened, then fell. 'But I can't go off to Ireland. I've got meetings set up over here, arrangements to view new machinery in all sorts of places. Could you go?'

'I've got my job to do, too. But look, it shouldn't take long to check. If I take the night boat on Friday I could be back in time for work on Monday morning.'

'I don't like to ask you to give up your weekend.'

James felt his pulse quicken at the idea of getting out of the office and setting off on such a quest. 'I don't mind. I'd enjoy the change. I've never been to Ireland.'

'Well, if you're sure ... I would meet all your expenses, of course.'

As it happened, the following day was a Friday. James needed to leave the office early so he thought it best to keep his employer up to date with the progress of his enquiries.

Weaver's nose was twitching. 'McBride, you say? I've heard the name before. He has a business importing tea, I think. I can't remember the exact context but it was in connection with some kind of shady dealing. It wouldn't surprise me to learn that the whole story was a fiction. Are you happy to go and make these enquiries, James?'

'Yes, sir. I'd be glad to help in any way I can.'

'You'd better get on your way, then. But have a care. I fancy McBride is a bad man to cross.'

They shook hands and James promised to report back as soon as he had any information. His first action was to go to the library and look up Ballymagorry in an atlas. It took him a while to find it but eventually he located it a few miles south of Londonderry, in the far north of the island. His next stop was the ferry port, where he booked a ticket on the overnight boat to Belfast. That left him just time to go home, pack a case, explain what was happening to his mother and leave instructions with Flossie and Mrs Brown, the cook, to take care of her in his absence. As evening fell, he set off for the port with a sense of excitement he rarely experienced in his well-regulated life.

Ballymagorry, when he eventually reached it after enduring a rough crossing, changing trains and then hiring a gig, was not what he expected. It was a tiny hamlet of no more than a dozen houses, poor stone-built cottages with peat roofs and small gardens. He got out of the gig and tied the pony to a convenient post and strolled down the single street. Two woman in dark clothes with shawls over their heads cast suspicious glances at him and scuttled away down a side alley. Another one, singing while she hung washing on a line, stopped abruptly and carried her washing basket into the cottage. Three small children sitting on a doorstep stared in silence as he passed. There was a poor-looking shop halfway down the street. An elderly woman with straggling grey hair looked up in alarm as he entered.

'Excuse me. I'm looking for a Mr McBride. Can you tell me where I might find him?'

The woman stared at him for a moment in silence, then said something in a language he did not understand.

'I'm sorry. I didn't understand what you said. Do you speak English?'

The woman turned her head aside and spat onto the sawdust that covered the floor. Then she fixed James with a basilisk stare and said nothing. After a brief hesitation, he turned and left the shop. This mission was clearly going to be more difficult than he had imagined.

At the far end of the street was the only building that rose above the general impression of abject poverty, the church. It occurred to James that the tombstones in the churchyard might provide some information. He let himself in through the lychgate and looked around. It was obvious that many of the tombstones were very old and he thought that the information he was seeking would most likely be found in some of the more recent ones. He worked his way round to the back of the church, where the stones seemed to be newer, and began to study each one in turn. Not one of them carried the name McBride.

'Is it something particular you are looking for?'

The question brought him round sharply and he found himself facing a priest, his black soutane covered against the perpetual drizzle by a waterproof cape. James moved forward and held out his hand.

'Good day, Father. I'm sorry. I didn't realise there was anyone here.'

'I only just arrived.' The priest indicated a pony and trap waiting by the gate. 'I look after two parishes and my home is in the other one. Can I help you?'

James reached into his pocket for his card case. 'My name is James Breckenridge. I'm clerk to a firm of solicitors in Liverpool. I'm trying to trace any member of the McBride family.'

'McBride?' The priest frowned. 'To my knowledge there is no one of that name in this parish.'

'No one? But I understood the family owned a substantial estate here.'

'An estate? No. All this land belongs to the Earl of Antrim. I am afraid you have been misinformed.'

'So it seems,' James said. 'I am here on behalf of a Mr Connor McBride. It's a question of an inheritance.' (The white lie was justified under the circumstances, he decided.)

'Connor McBride, you say? There was a family named O'Connor in the village a while back. Old man Patrick O'Connor kept the village store. But he died several years ago.'

'Did he have children?'

'Oh yes. There were three girls, all married and gone from here long ago, and a son, Finn. A wild boy, I'm afraid. Did you say the people you are acting for are in Liverpool?'

'Yes.'

The priest lifted his eyes to the clouds. 'Why are we standing here in the rain? Shall we go into the church?

At least it's dry in there, though it won't be soon unless I can get the roof fixed.'

Inside, the priest genuflected to the altar and then turned to James. 'Now, where were we?'

'You were asking if the people I am enquiring for are in Liverpool.'

'Ah yes. The reason I ask is that Finn O'Connor was sent to Liverpool to get him out of the way.'

'Was he in trouble?'

'Not so much him as the young girl he was going out with, if you take my meaning.'

'He had got her pregnant.'

'Not to mince words, yes.'

'How long ago was this?'

'Let me see. It must be ten, eleven years ago. Is that significant?'

'I thought it might be, but no, it's too long ago. There is a child involved in the matter, but she is only eight or nine, at the most. Do you know what happened to the young woman?'

'She was sent to the Convent of the Sisters of Mercy. They took it as their mission to give shelter to girls like that until they gave birth.'

'And then? What happened to the children?'

'Given up for adoption usually. But if I remember rightly that would not apply to the girl we are speaking of. I heard that she lost the child.'

'Would she have stayed in the convent?'

'No. She came home and the family moved away to hide their shame. I don't know where they went.'

'Do you remember her name?'

'It was Margaret, I think. Yes, Maggie. Maggie O'Dowd.'

'And Finn, what became of him?'

'Well, he never showed his face round here again. But I did hear he was in India.'

'India?'

'The cousin he was sent to live with was something in the tea trade, I believe.'

'Was he! The Connor McBride I am asking about is in the tea trade.'

'Perhaps he's your man, then.'

James nodded, thinking hard. 'It sounds like it, but it still doesn't solve my problem. The child who is the subject of my enquiry was supposedly born here, the daughter of Connor McBride's brother. The child's mother died and she was then adopted by Connor and his wife.'

'Well, if she was born in the parish she will have been baptised here. We could look in the register of baptisms if you like.'

'Oh, yes. That sounds like a good idea. Can we do that?'

The priest led him into the vestry and took a large, leather bound volume from a cupboard.

'When did you say the girl was born?'

'It must have been 1859, I think.'

The priest turned the pages. 'There are not many names to look through. The population of this village was never large, but is has shrunk over the last twenty years. The famine, you know. Ah, here we are. There were only five children christened in fifty-nine. Three were boys, one was a wee girl who only survived a couple of weeks, as I recall, and the fifth was Katie Donovan, who still lives here in the village.

'Well, that seems conclusive,' James said, feeling a tremor of triumph. 'Angelina was not born in Ballymagorry.'

'Could you be wrong about the year?'

'I suppose it could be eighteen sixty.'

But a brief glance at the record for that year showed no entry that could possibly refer to Angelina. James straightened up and held out his hand to the priest.

'I'm most grateful for your help, father. Thank you.'

'Will you come back home with me for a little refreshment?' the priest offered.

'Thank you, but no. I've got a long journey to get back to Liverpool and I think it will be best if I start straight away.'

'Well, I've parishioners to see in the village. Do you have transport?'

'I left a gig at the far end of the street – if it's still there.'

'Oh, it will be.'

The two men walked up the road together until the priest stopped. 'This is where I leave you.'

They shook hands again and James went on to where the pony was grazing contentedly at the side of the road. He untied it, climbed into the gig and flicked his whip over the pony's back. He was eager to get back to Liverpool and convey his news to Richard Kean.

Eleven

My dearest May,

A remarkable thing happened here the other day, something that will particularly interest you. A man walked into the office and told us that he was looking for his daughter, whom he had abandoned as a baby outside the gates of the workhouse. Now I have your interest! Not, I hasten to say, that I was in any doubt about that before. Your first reaction, I'm sure, will be to censure him for such an unfeeling act, and it was my first instinct, too. But when he related the circumstances I could only sympathise. I will not go into all the details. Suffice it to say that he had fallen on hard times but was given the chance of a new job in South Africa, and on the very day before he was due to leave his wife died giving birth to their second child, which also died, and leaving him with a baby daughter. He had no time to make any other arrangements before his ship sailed, so he left her outside the workhouse.

*His name is Richard Kean. He has done well in Africa
and has now returned a wealthy man to find his daughter.
However, when he applied to the workhouse they told him
she had been adopted, but refused to say by whom. I immediately thought of your encounter with the child you called
Angel and suggested we might make enquiries in that
direction. My mother recalled the name of the woman who
said Angel was her daughter – Marguerite McBride. I'm
sure you remember it only too well. I expect you know, too,
that Angel was supposed to be the child of Mr McBride's
brother, born in Ireland.*

*Well, I have turned detective! I have been to Ireland, to
the village the McBrides were supposed to come from, and
there is no sign whatever of anyone of that name, and no
record of the baptism of a child who might be Angel. In
short, I believe that you were right all along. She is the baby
you cared for in the workhouse, but the McBrides want to
hide that fact and have made up this story. (Incidentally,
I don't think their name is really McBride. I seems likely
that he is one Finn O'Connor, sent from the village in disgrace for getting a local girl into trouble. That child, however, did not survive.)*

*The thing now is to prove that Angel, or Angelina as she
is now known, is Richard Kean's missing daughter. He has
a little sketch done by his wife and the resemblance to the
child I remember seeing is strong. Do you, by any chance,
have a drawing of Angel? Or can you suggest any other
details that might confirm her identity?*

*We have one major difficulty in progressing further.
Richard feels sure that if he could only see Angelina he
would know if she is his child – incidentally, he calls her*

Amy. But it seems the McBrides have sent her away to school and no one knows where. However, I presume she will come home for the holidays, so we may have to wait until then before we can proceed.

Now to matters closer to home. My mother weakens a little every day, but her mind is active and the drugs the doctors prescribe seem to keep the pain at bay. It is hard, watching her decline, but the enquiry into Angelina's identity seems to have caught her fancy and given her something to think about other than her own condition, so it has a double benefit.

I am well and studying hard for my exams – though I have to admit this business has come as a welcome distraction. But I must knuckle down again now.

Write as soon as you can, and give me any useful information you may have. I know you will rejoice if we can reunite Angel/Angelina/Amy with her real father. He is a nice chap and desperate to make good the wrong he did her.

I pray that you are still in good health and have not had any further encounters with snakes! Take care of yourself, my darling girl.

> *Your ever loving,*
> *James*

Twelve

'Your conduct has been completely unacceptable. There is no place for you here. I shall write to your father and ask him to come and fetch you.' Mother Mary Benedicta's face was stern and pale.

'But I only sang!' Angelina stared up at her in bewilderment. 'And I sang well, didn't I? Didn't I?'

'You committed an act of flagrant disobedience.' Mother Mary Andrew, by contrast, was flushed with an emotion that looked very much like triumph. 'You have never been interested in anything but your own self-aggrandisement. You are a spoilt, wilful child. The school will be better off without you.'

Angelina looked up at her through her tears. 'But I thought God wanted the best. I did it for Him.'

'What God requires, of all of us,' Reverend Mother said quietly, 'is that we have humble and contrite hearts. You have no right to say that you are the best. That is for others to decide. Your part is to obey those set in authority over you, whatever you may think of their decisions. You have given an example of the very opposite of the virtues we are trying to inculcate into our girls and I cannot allow that to pass without severe sanctions.'

'Then take away a conduct mark, give me a punishment, only please, please don't send me home!'

'I'm sorry, the matter is decided. You will be kept in solitary confinement in the sanatorium until your father arrives. Now, go with Mother Mary Andrew.' She raised a hand to forestall further protest. 'That is enough. Go!'

Alone in the sanatorium, Angelina dried her tears and tried to think. God, she decided, if He existed, was very unjust. She had tried, really tried, to be good and she had wanted to do something wonderful for Him; and this was the result. All her life she had been told she must be 'obedient' but what good had obedience done her? From now on, she would not allow other people to dictate what she should do and how she should behave.

This was an easy resolution to make, but very hard to implement. Her father was coming to take her home, but home to what? To further punishment, for certain. She remembered the last beating her mother had given her, and both body and spirit cried out against the prospect of a repetition. Even if she escaped that, the only prospect she could envisage was a life of confinement under a regime similar to that imposed by Miss Drake. There would be no more music lessons, no more dancing, that much was certain. So what was the alternative?

There was only one answer. She had to escape somehow. She must run away and find some way of making a life for herself. She had heard that poor children were often set to work in various ways, so there must be some form of employment that she could take up. Her own position had been held up to her as enviable, by contrast, but she could not conceive that any kind of work could be worse than what she might have to endure once she was back at home. In the meantime, it was summer. There must be things growing that she could eat, and it would not be too uncomfortable to sleep outside. Maybe some kind person would feel sorry for her and take her in, as a servant perhaps.

She turned thoughts like these over and over in her mind until evening came. From time to time she heard voices outside and the sound of carriage wheels on the drive. The visitors who had attended the ceremony in the chapel and the celebrations that followed were leaving. She wondered what they had thought of her singing. Had the bishop been told that it was not supposed to be her? Would he have been as angry as Mother Mary Andrew?

Sister Berthe came in with a tray. 'Bread and water for you. Reverend Mother's orders.'

She dumped the tray and went out. Angelina listened to her retreating footsteps, then she went to the door and tried it. It was not locked. Obviously it had not occurred to anyone that she might try to leave. She ate some of the bread, then wrapped the remainder in the napkin that covered the tray and pushed into her pocket. She heard the chapel bell ring and the distant sound of singing. The convent was going about its normal routine. It was almost mid-summer and darkness fell slowly. The clock in the *salle d'études* struck ten and she knew that everyone would have retired to bed, but still she waited. Normally she would have been sleepy by now, but she was too keyed up for the implementation of her plan to feel tired.

At last it was fully dark, or as dark as it would ever get. Angelina knew that her cloak would be hanging in the cloakroom by the side door that led out to the garden. She opened the door of the sanatorium cautiously and peered out. The corridor was silent, lit only by moonlight coming in through uncurtained windows. Soft-footed, she padded along to the staircase that led down to the main hall. Here, too, all was quiet. She found her way to the cloakroom, which was in darkness. There was no window here to help but she knew that her peg was the fourth along on the right-hand side. She felt from one to the next, found what she was sure must be her cloak and put it round her. Then she went to the side door. It was locked.

She should have expected that, but for some reason it had not occurred to her. She stood still, thinking. The big front doors would inevitably be locked as well. There was the kitchen. There was a door from there, which Sister Martha used when she went to feed the hens or pick vegetables. Perhaps that might be open. She crept down the back stairs and into the large kitchen. The big range had been banked down for the night, but it gave off just enough light to make out the long table down the centre of the room, the sinks along one wall, the hams and bunches of herbs hanging from the ceiling.

Angelina felt her way along the table until her head struck something and set off a loud clanging. She had knocked into a pan hanging from a beam and it in turn had struck others which rang like gongs in the silence. She froze, her heart pounding. Surely that noise must wake someone. But she heard no sound of movement, no voices called out, and at length she crept forward, keeping low to avoid any other obstacles. She reached the door and tried it. It, too, was locked.

Angelina stood biting her lips in frustration. There had to be a way out somewhere! Then a breath of air wafted over her face, bringing with it the scent of the chicken coop. There must be a window open somewhere. She felt her way along the wall and into a scullery. The smell was stronger here. She reached up and found the open window. It was above her head, impossible to climb up to; but having found it she was not going to give up. Under the kitchen table there were stools where the kitchen staff sat to eat meals. She groped her way back, found one and carried it into the scullery. Standing on it, she could put her head and shoulders through the window. She heaved herself up until she was lying across the sill, but her skirt and petticoat caught on the latch and made her too bulky to fit through. She slid back and pulled her petticoat from under the skirt, wrapped it in her cloak, then climbed up and dropped the bundle out of the window. Then she leaned out again and wriggled forward. Without the bulky petticoat her dress was slimmer and this time she made better progress, but the drop from the window to the ground below looked frightening and she could see no way out except to let herself fall head first. She twisted her body so she could reach up and managed to grip the window frame above her. Holding tightly to this she pulled the rest of her body out. Once her full weight was only held by her fingertips she lost her grip, but she landed on the bundle of her cloak, which broke her fall. It took her a few seconds to get her breath back, but she scrambled to her feet with a sense of triumph. Her fingernails were broken and her fingertips were sore; her skirt had a ragged tear down one side; but otherwise she was unhurt. She pulled on her petticoat, wrapped her cloak around her and began to make her way cautiously along the side of the building.

A sudden cackle brought her up short, shaking. Her movement had disturbed the hens in their coop; but once again there was no sign of movement inside the building. She moved on, round to the front, where the drive led to the main gates. The drive was gravelled, so she kept to the grass alongside where her footsteps made no sound. There were no lights on in the gatekeeper's cottage by the main entrance. The big gates were shut, and Angelina guessed it would be impossible to open them without waking someone, but there was a postern gate to one side. She tried it and found to her relief that it opened. In a moment she was outside and walking away down the road that led to the town.

At first her mood was excited, even triumphant. She had done it! She was free, and they would not catch her and punish her any more. She thought of her father arriving to fetch her and being told that she had disappeared. She imagined him returning to Liverpool and passing on the news to her mother. What would they feel? They would be angry, yes, but worried too. Would they realise that it was their harshness that had driven her to do what she was doing? Would they blame themselves? She hoped they would.

As she walked on, the excitement evaporated. She had never been out at night in the countryside and there were scufflings in the hedgerows that were not due to the wind. Stories she had read flickered through her imagination. Did they have wolves in Ireland, or bears? She had a sudden impulse to turn and run back the way she had come. Only the thought of what might be done to her if she went back kept her walking onwards.

The summer night was short and very soon she was aware that she could see further ahead than she could before.

A bird began to sing, and then others joined in. The light grew and the horizon ahead of her flushed pink and then was shot with gold. As she came to the top of a rise she saw the first houses of the town a few hundred yards distant. She was tired and beginning to be hungry and her first thought was that there might be someone there who would give her something to eat; but that was followed by the realisation that the local people would immediately recognise her by her dress as coming from the convent. They would ask questions and try to detain her and very soon the nuns would be up and her disappearance would be discovered. The first place they would look would be Limerick. She must avoid it at all costs.

A stile led over the fence at one side of the road. Angelina sat down on it and took out of her pocket the bread she had saved. She ate some of it and felt a little stronger, but she was getting sleepy. She needed to find somewhere to hide during the daylight hours, somewhere safe to sleep. A path led from the stile across a field; in a hollow on the far side, she could just make out a roof. It was probably a farm, she thought. She had never seen a farm but she had read about them. There ought to be a barn where hay and straw were kept. If she could slip into one before people were up and about, she might be able to hide. She climbed over the stile and set off along the path.

The house, when she came to it, proved to be not a farm but a substantial residence, with a pillared portico at the front. Behind it there were outbuildings, which seemed to offer the best chance of shelter.

A gate led from the path into a courtyard. Angelina slipped through it and stopped to listen. The sun was not yet quite up. It was very early and no one was stirring in the house, as far as she could tell. A wide, open doorway led into one of the outbuildings. She crossed the yard and went cautiously inside. The interior was in deep shadow and at first it was difficult to make out what was kept there, but as her eyes grew accustomed to the change in the light she saw in front of her a four-wheeled carriage. She climbed onto the step and looked inside. There was a padded seat, which would make a perfect bed. She opened the door, climbed in, wrapped herself in her cloak and lay down. Within minutes she was asleep.

She woke with a start at the sound of men's voices close by. She huddled down on the floor of the carriage and held her breath. Then there was a sudden jolt and she felt the carriage roll forward. The light changed as it was pushed out into the yard. She contemplated jumping out and running, but there were still men moving around, horse hooves and a jingle of harness. 'Whoa, easy there, my beauty,' a voice said. 'Stand still, damn you!' Then she heard the owner of the voice climb up onto the box and click his tongue and the carriage moved forward. Before Angelina could make any decision about her next action, they were heading out at a smart trot.

She lay still, listening to the rumble of the wheels and ringing of the horses' hooves on the hard ground, and wondered where they were going. She felt a moment of panic when the idea came to her that they might be heading for the convent, but she could see no reason why an equipage like this should go there, and as the minutes passed she reckoned that if that were their destination they would have reached it long ago. So they were going somewhere else, and much faster than she could have gone on her own two feet. It would make the inevitable search for her more difficult. That was good, but another danger presented itself. This carriage was not being driven for pleasure. It had a purpose. It was not the sort of vehicle used for deliveries, or to collect goods of some kind. This was a carriage for people, so why was it empty? Sooner or later, someone was going to get in, and then she would be discovered.

At length the carriage swung to one side, the sound of the wheels changed and the pace slowed until it drew to a standstill. A woman's voice said, 'You're prompt, Michael. The ladies have not finished breakfast yet. It'll be half an hour at least before they're ready for you to take them home. You'd best take the carriage round to the back. The horses can get a drink and I daresay Mrs Riley will find you a bite to eat while you wait.'

'Right you are, missus,' the man responded, and the carriage moved on again at a walking pace.

When it stopped again, a new voice spoke. 'Ay, take them to the trough. They'll be fine there.'

The carriage jerked forward and stopped, the driver jumped down and she heard the two men walking away. She stayed still for a few minutes, then carefully raised her head and peered out of the window. They were in another courtyard, much like the one they had started from. She shrank back as two girls carrying pails crossed it, laughing together, and disappeared into a barn. Angelina twisted round and looked out of the other window. There was no sign of anyone else. Very carefully, she opened the door and slid to the ground. She could hear buckets clanking and the sound of sweeping, and someone whistling from somewhere, and the voices of the two girls, muted now inside the barn, but the yard itself was empty. She hesitated in the shelter of the carriage. What should she do now? Her stomach rumbled and she realised she was ravenous. She remembered the woman's words: 'I daresay Mrs Riley will find you a bite to eat.' She must be the cook and if there was food to spare for the coachman, there might be some for her, too. Angelina knew she had to find something to eat soon, and this seemed as good a chance as any.

Peering round the coach, she saw an open door at the back of the house. Perhaps that led to the kitchen. She looked around once more to check that no one was watching and ran across. Inside, a big woman with brawny arms was kneading dough on a table and a man, the coachman presumably, was sitting on the far side slurping something out of a bowl. The cook looked up in surprise as Angelina tapped timidly on the door frame.

'Who are you? What do you want?'

'Please, ma'am –' Angelina's voice shook '– do you have a little food to spare?'

'Food, is it? What do you think this is, a charity kitchen?'

'No, ma'am. I could work for it, if you have any jobs you need doing.'

'Jobs, is it, now? Get away with you. I've met your likes before. Let you into the house and I'll be looking for the silver spoons in half an hour. There's no place for you here.'

'Then, please, can you let me have something to eat?'

'You get back to your own folks, ask them to feed you.'

'I haven't got any folks.' Tears rose in her throat at the words. 'I'm all on my own.'

A maid came into the kitchen and dumped a tray on the table. 'The ladies have finished with this.'

'Finished?' The cook inspected the tray. 'They've not eaten half of it.'

'Not surprised, after the amount of wine that got drunk at the ball last night,' the maid said.

'It's a waste, so it is,' the cook muttered. She looked round at Angelina. 'Here.' She grabbed a boiled egg out of its cup and a slice of buttered bread and thrust them into her hands. 'Now get along before the master sets the dogs on you. He doesn't hold with giving food to beggars.'

Angelina grabbed the food and turned to run, then turned back. 'Thank you! Thank you!'

A narrow passageway led from the courtyard out to the open country. She took it and found herself on a cart track. One way led out to open fields, the other towards the front of the house and the road along which the carriage must have travelled. Angelina took that direction at a run, casting glances behind her to make sure that no dogs were on her trail. Where the track met the road a rough plank had been laid across two tree stumps to form a seat. There was no sign of any pursuit so she sank down on it to eat. As she peeled the shell off the egg she remembered how often she had made Lizzie take one back to the kitchen because it was not cooked to her liking. This one was hard-boiled but, wrapped in the slice of bread, it was the best she had ever tasted. For the first time she experienced a sense of guilt at her own behaviour. Remembering Lizzie brought a sharp pang, not exactly of homesickness, but of longing for her care and cheerful companionship.

As she ate, she heard the sound of carriage wheels on the gravel of the drive. The gates were a short way off to her left and she saw the carriage come through them and turn in her direction. In a moment of panic she looked around for somewhere to hide, but it was too late. The carriage reached her and swept on past. Neither the coachman or the occupants had taken any notice of her. It made her think about the cook's words. The master 'doesn't hold with beggars'. That was how she was seen. She looked down at her clothes. Her skirt was ripped where she had caught it climbing out of the window. There was mud on it from somewhere, and dust from crouching on the floor of the carriage. For the first time she realised that she had left her cloak behind. Well, there was no help for that now. She put her hands up to her hair. Her braids had come undone and it was hanging in a tangle round her face. No wonder she looked more like a street urchin than a respectable convent schoolgirl. So much the better. A little stream ran under the road close to where she was sitting. She scrambled down to it and rinsed her hands in the clear water, then scooped some up to drink. After that, she rubbed her fingers in the mud at the edge and wiped them across her face. For good measure, she rubbed some dirt into her hair as well. There was no way she could see her herself, but she felt sure that her disguise must now be complete.

Climbing back to the road, she looked about her. The coach had headed past her, presumably going back the way it had come, so she turned in the opposite direction. She had been shown a map of Ireland in her geography lessons and she knew that Limerick was in the west and Dublin was on the east coast. If she could find her way there, there might be a better chance of finding work of some kind. It was still early, and the road was heading towards the newly risen sun. That, then, was her way, though she had only a vaguest idea of how far it might be.

All morning she walked. The road ran between fields but all she could see growing were weeds and there was no one about. From time to time, she passed a derelict cottage, tiles missing from the roof, a door hanging open, no sign of occupation. She had heard the other girls talk of the terrible famine that had struck the country a few years earlier, but had not paid much attention. It had something to do with potatoes, but it puzzled her why the failure of that crop should have had such a devastating effect. Potatoes were all very well as an accompaniment to a meal, but she could do without them if need be. There were plenty of other things to eat, surely. She had put that point to the other girls, but they were the daughters of well-to-do professional men or big landowners. The famine had not affected them and they had little more understanding of it than she did. Now she was seeing its effects all round her.

Towards midday she came to place where the road bridged another stream. She was thirsty and her feet were aching, so she climbed down and scooped up water to drink. Then she leaned her back against the side of the bridge and closed her eyes. The day was warm and very soon she was asleep.

The clip-clop of hooves and the rumble of wheels woke her with a start, and she shrank back under the shelter of the bridge, but the vehicle, whatever it was, passed on without stopping. She got to her feet and shook grass seeds from her clothes. The sun was beginning to dip towards the horizon and she realised she had slept for several hours. If she was going to find anywhere to shelter for the night she must hurry on.

She was stiff from sleeping in an awkward position and her stomach felt hollow. Her courage was at a low ebb and she was beginning to wish that she had stayed in the convent until her father came to collect her and endured whatever punishment he chose to mete out; but it was too late to go back now. She took another drink from the stream, climbed back up to the road and plodded on. As the light faded and the blisters on her feet grew worse, she started to whimper aloud. She was hungry and frightened and there seemed no prospect of finding shelter. She thought of the nuns and wondered if they were looking for her, and of her own bedroom back in Liverpool, with Lizzie bringing her bread and milk for supper. Why was she here, on her own like this? she asked herself. What had she done that was so terrible? 'I did try to be good,' she sobbed. 'I did really!'

Sometime later her attention was caught by a glimmer of light. Up ahead, a fire was burning. At last it seemed she was nearing some form of human habitation. She limped forward, expecting to come to a house of some sort. Instead, she saw a caravan and a rough shelter formed of twisted branches with a canvas roof thrown over them. In front a campfire burned brightly and a group of people were sitting round it. She drew closer, hesitantly. There were six adults and three children. A woman of middle age or older was bending over the fire, stirring something in a blackened pot. Another, younger, had a baby at her breast. There were four men, one older and three younger. They were all sitting at their ease in the warmth of the fire, while the children chased each other round the wheels of the caravan. None of them had noticed Angelina on the road beyond the circle of firelight. There was something on a spit over the fire and the smell that rose from it brought the saliva into her mouth. She approached timidly, and at once a large dog rushed out from under the caravan, barking furiously. Angelina turned to run.

'Hey, hold on there! He won't harm you. Come back.'

It was the oldest man who had called her. She stopped and looked round. The dog was chained to the wheel of the caravan and at a command from the man it slunk back to its former position.

'Don't worry. There's nothing to be afraid of,' the man said. 'Come to the fire.'

Angelina went cautiously forwards. The older of the two women looked up.

'It's late for a young maid like you to be out alone. Where are your folks?'

'I haven't got any.'

'Come now, that can't be so. You haven't sprung out of the ground like a weed. Would you be fancying a bowl of soup, lassie?'

'Yes, please.' As she spoke weariness swept over her like a wave and her legs seemed to give way under her.

'Whoa now!' The man caught her as she stumbled. 'Sit you down. Dervla, give her some soup. The child's famished.'

There was a heap of blankets near the fire, and he guided Angelina to it and lowered her gently down. A bowl of broth and a spoon were placed in her hands. It was a moment before the mists cleared from her brain sufficiently for her to raise the spoon to her mouth, but then she did not stop until the bowl was empty.

When she finally looked up, she found she was being studied by six pairs of eyes, but, although there was curiosity in them, there was no hostility.

'Now then,' the older man said, 'tell us what you are running away from.'

The kindness in his voice and her own exhaustion swept away her defences. 'I was at the school, in the convent, but they were angry with me. They sent for my father to fetch me home, but I can't go home. I can't!'

'In the convent, you say,' the woman said. 'Did the nuns beat you?'

'No, but my mother will, if I go back.'

'Your mother beats you?'

'Yes. They sent me away because they were angry with me, but if I have to go back I don't know what they will do to me.'

The woman said something to the man in a language Angelina could not understand. He replied, and the woman said, in English, 'You can stay here with us for tonight. Don't be afraid. We'll not give you to the authorities. We've no love for the polis. You can rest easy and in the morning we'll talk more. Now, try a bit of this.'

One of the younger men had taken whatever it was that was roasting off the spit and was carving it up. Angelina was given some on a plate, with a piece of flat bread. The children were called to the fire and they all settled down to eat, talking amongst themselves in their own language. By the time she had finished eating, Angelina's head was nodding, and the woman touched her arm.

'Come. I'll show you where you can sleep.'

She took her into the caravan and sat her on a bunk set into the side. 'Let's have those boots off.'

She pulled off her boots and clucked in disapproval. 'You're not used to walking, that's easy to see. Your poor feet are in a terrible state. Never mind, we'll deal with them in the morning. Lie yourself down now.'

Angelina lay down and the woman put a blanket over her. For a while she lay awake, listening to the soft voices outside. Her stomach was full; she was in a warm, safe place. Her instinct told her that these people meant her no harm.

Very soon she slept.

Thirteen

'We can be pretty sure about one thing. Angelina is not the daughter of Connor McBride's deceased sister-in-law, as he makes out.'

James was sitting with Richard Kean and Mr Weaver in the solicitor's office.

'Just a moment,' Weaver said. 'All we really know is that Connor McBride is not the owner of a large estate in Ballymagorry. It is possible that he is the same person as Finn O'Connor, who was sent to England in disgrace, but we cannot be sure of that. If he is not, then it is still possible that he has, or had, a brother somewhere in Ireland whose wife gave birth to Angelina.'

'But why would he tell everyone that he had land in Ballymagorry? Why that tiny, out-of-the-way village rather than anywhere else?' James was annoyed that his conclusions were being questioned.

'Perhaps because it is tiny and out of the way. He thought no one would ever go there to discover his deception.'

'It seems to me,' Richard put in, 'that the whole matter rests on the question of whether Connor McBride and Finn

O'Connor are one and the same person. If they are, then his whole tale is a pack of lies.'

'True.' Weaver's nose was twitching violently. 'James, did your informant say he was sent to a cousin who was connected to the tea trade?'

'Yes, he did.'

'You remember I said the name rang a bell?

'Yes?'

'While you were away I had a drink with my old friend Inspector Vane. I asked him if the name McBride meant anything to him. It did. About nine or ten years ago he received a complaint from a Mr Michael O'Connor, a tea importer. His warehouse had burnt down, and he accused Connor McBride of being behind it. There was never enough proof to take the matter further so the case was dropped; but I think we may have found the cousin.'

'If so, why would McBride burn down his cousin's warehouse?' Richard wondered.

'Why did he change his name from O'Connor to McBride?' James said. 'Presumably he had a reason to conceal his identity. Perhaps O'Connor threatened to reveal it.'

'Is this O'Connor still in business?' Richard asked. 'Can we speak to him?'

'It seems he went bankrupt soon after the fire,' Weaver said. 'But Vane did have an address for him. Whether he is still there, who knows, but we could find out.'

The address given by Inspector Vine was in Pownall Street, not far from the docks. As soon as James could get away from the office, he and Richard made their way there. They found a solidly built, respectable house, which nonetheless bore signs of neglect in the cracked paint of the front door and the grimy windows. Their knock was answered by a thin-faced young girl in a dirty apron.

'Good afternoon,' James began. 'We are looking for Mr O'Connor. Does he still live here?'

The girl wiped the back of her hand across her nose. 'Who wants him?'

James produced his card. 'You might tell him that we are enquiring about the fire that burnt down his warehouse.'

The girl took the card and disappeared down a dingy hallway. A few minutes later she reappeared and invited them to walk in. A white-haired old man rose from a chair by the hearth, in which a small fire smouldered, although the atmosphere in the room was close and stuffy.

'I'm Michael O'Connor. What do you want?'

Richard took the lead. 'We need your help, sir. It is a matter of considerable importance to me. I wish to establish the true identity of the man who calls himself Connor McBride.'

'What's this got to do with the fire that ruined my business? I thought you said you had come about that.'

'I understand,' James said, 'you told the police that you thought McBride was behind the fire.'

'So? There was never any proof. I know who was responsible, but what good does that do me? I've no wish to meddle with that man. I've suffered enough already. So unless you have come to offer me some form of compensation I'll bid you good day.'

'Do you have children?' Richard began urgently, 'because if ...'

James cut across his appeal. 'We cannot offer compensation in monetary terms, sir. But would it be some comfort to you to see McBride unmasked?'

'Unmasked, you say? How?'

'As an imposter, for one thing. We believe that his real name is Finn O'Connor and he was sent here from Ireland to work for you, to get him out of the way because he had caused trouble there.'

'How do you know this?'

'I have been to Ballymagorry and spoken to the local priest. I believe O'Connor, or McBride if you prefer, had some reason to wish to conceal his identity and you threatened to expose him and that is why your warehouse was burnt down.

The old man sank back into his chair. 'Sit down, both of you and I'll tell you what I know. Short of murder, there's nothing more he can do to hurt me now, and I should be glad to see him held up before the world for what he is.'

Richard caught James's eye and nodded appreciation. They drew two chairs closer and the old man looked from one to the other before fastening his gaze on James. 'You say he was sent here because he was causing trouble? What sort of trouble?'

'I understand he got a local girl pregnant.'

O'Connor gave a derisive snort. 'Oh aye, very likely. But that wasn't the real reason. He'd got himself involved with the Fenians.'

'Fenians?' Richard said, puzzled.

'You've been out of the country, so you won't have heard about them,' James said. 'It's a group of men who want Ireland to be an independent country. There was some sort of rising last year, but it went off at half cock and all the leaders were arrested. But there's been trouble over here, too. They attacked Chester castle, and planted a bomb in Clerkenwell.' He returned his attention to O'Connor. 'McBride was involved with them, you say? So what happened when he was sent here to work for you?'

'Finn O'Connor was his name then, as you've rightly guessed. I could see he was going to cause more trouble here if he got the chance, so I sent him off to India. I had an interest in a tea plantation out there, so I sent him out as an under-manager, to learn the trade from the bottom up. I hoped that would knock the Fenian nonsense out of him.'

'Do you think it did?'

'I have no idea. He'd not been there more than a year when he disappeared.'

'Disappeared? How?'

'Just walked off the plantation and was never seen again, until he turned up here with a pocket full of cash and a new name.'

'Have you any idea what he had been doing?'

'None at all. Those were troubled times in India. The East India Company was still angry about losing its monopoly of the tea trade, still throwing its weight about. It was about the time of the Indian Mutiny that Finn went missing. I assumed he'd been caught up in it and killed.'

'So what happened when he came back here?'

'He set himself up in the tea trade and made a bid to drive any competition out of the market. He was undercutting prices and intimidating workers. He'd changed his appearance, but I recognised him. I went to see him and told him that if he went on as he was doing I'd report him to the authorities and tell them about his history with the Fenians. The next night, my warehouse was set on fire. I wasn't insured and it bankrupted me. So now you know the story. What's your interest?'

Richard leaned forward in his chair. 'Did you ever come across his adopted daughter?'

'I heard tell of her. Never saw her.'

'His story was that she was the child of a deceased brother.'

'Finn O'Connor never had a brother.'

'That's what we discovered in Ballymagorry,' James said.

'The point is,' Richard went on, 'I believe she is my daughter, who I was forced to abandon in the workhouse. I was down and out at the time, but now I'm in funds again and I want her back. We just want to prove that the child he adopted came from the workhouse, not from someone in his family.'

'I can't help you there,' the old man said.

'You have helped,' Richard told him. 'We know now that McBride is really Finn O'Connor and that Angelina cannot have come to him in the way he says. And perhaps you have given us a lever to use to persuade him to give her up.'

'If you take my advice, you won't mess with that man. He's dangerous and he never forgives anyone who crosses him.'

Richard got up. 'That just makes me all the more deter- mined to get my daughter out of his clutches.' He held out his hand. 'I'm very grateful to you for talking to us, sir.'

'Talk is cheap, as they say. But heed my warning. He did for me and he'll do for you, if you're not careful.'

Walking back towards the river, Richard's step was light. 'That proves it. Angelina is my daughter. Now all we have to do is find her.'

'Not so fast,' James said cautiously. 'We can prove that McBride's story about her origin is false, but that does not necessarily mean that the child he adopted is your daughter. We don't even know that he found her in the workhouse.'

'There must be some way we can establish that,' Richard said. 'I've a good mind to go there and shake the information out of that sanctimonious bastard of a governor.'

'And get yourself arrested?'

'What then? We seem to be going round in circles. Someone, somewhere, must know the truth. What about your … what about May? She was sure she recognised her, you told me. Is there no chance she could produce some conclusive evidence?'

'I have written to her, asking exactly that, though it's hard to know what that evidence might be. I've asked her to draw a sketch of Angelina as she remembers her. She's a talented artist but we're asking her to go back years, so it may not help. Either way, my letter will not have reached her yet and we cannot expect a reply for several months.'

'So why don't we go and confront McBride, and demand that he tells us the truth. We have a lever we can use, as you said.'

'You heard O'Connor. He's a dangerous man. I don't want my house burnt down, and I don't want to see you fished out of the Mersey with a gash in your skull. And we have to consider Angelina herself. He has already sent her away somewhere. We need to know where.'

'I see your point,' Richard conceded. He sighed and kicked a pebble in a gesture of frustration. 'So how do we do that?'

'I don't know, at the moment ... short of contacting every girls' boarding school in the country and asking if she has been enrolled there – and I doubt if they would tell us without some strong legal proof that we had a right to know.' He touched his companion's arm sympathetically. '*Nil desperandum*, old chap. We'll find a way. Something will come up.'

Arriving home, Richard found his mother in bed, her face pale and drawn. He gave her a draft of the laudanum, which the doctor had prescribed, and she rallied a little.

'I had a caller today with some news that will interest you.'

'A caller, Mama? Who?'

'Laura Pearson. She really seems to have taken a dislike to the whole McBride family, particularly the daughter, and she can't resist a chance to gossip about them. And she did have some quite surprising news.'

Mrs Brackenridge closed her eyes for a moment and shifted uncomfortably. James leaned over and shook up her pillows and settled her more comfortably. 'Don't tire yourself, Mama.'

'No, I must tell you before it slips my mind. You knew the child had been sent away to school ...'

'Yes, but we don't know where.'

'Somewhere in Ireland, it seems. But this is the point. Of course, it's all at third hand, like most gossip. Laura's cook was told by the McBride's cook that the house has been in an uproar because Mr McBride was summoned to Ireland to fetch the girl back. Apparently she had committed some misdemeanour serious enough for the school to expel her.' A faint smile crossed the old lady's lips. 'Laura is convinced she must have bitten someone, but that's by the by. The real surprise is this. When McBride arrived at the school he was told that the girl had run away in the middle of the night and disappeared.'

'Disappeared!' James sat back in shock. 'When did this happen?'

'I'm not sure. Some days ago, at least.'

'And she has not been found?'

'Not as far as Laura's cook knew.'

'Is it possible she may have got hold of the wrong end of the stick somehow? It is only servants' gossip, as you said.'

'Laura thinks not. Nosy character that she is, she went to call on the McBrides on some pretext, but the parlourmaid told her that Mrs McBride was not receiving. When Laura asked why the girl said her mistress had had some very upsetting news.'

'I suppose the police have been informed. There must be a search going on.'

'I suppose so, but that's all I know for now. I suspect if there are any developments Laura will be round here again to pass on the news.'

'As long as she isn't upsetting you. I don't want you to over strain yourself.'

His mother reached out and pressed his hand. 'I appreciate your concern, my dear, but as I said the other day, I am really glad to have something to think about other than my own aches and pains.'

'Well, as long as you are sure. I value any information you can get for me. Poor Richard is at his wits' end and this news is going to upset him further. I am afraid he may go and do something desperate.'

'Poor man,' his mother murmured. 'I wish we could help more. I was wondering, do you happen to have an address for … for May Lavender? I know you were … close. She may have some information that could be useful.'

James looked down at the wasted face. It was his mother's disapproval that had prevented him from marrying May and he had not told her that they were still in touch. He decided that it was time to be honest.

'I have already written to her. We exchange letters regularly, as far as the great distance and the speed of a ship allows. I don't know if she will be able to help, but I know she will do all she can.'

His mother looked at him for a moment, seeming to search for some deeper meaning to his words, then she sighed and closed her eyes. James sat beside her for a while until she drifted into sleep, then he rose and stretched and wished, as he did every evening, that May was out there somewhere in the city, waiting for him.

Richard's reaction when he heard the news was predictable. 'We must go and look for her! I don't trust the police to search properly. Dear God! Anything could have happened to her.'

'It's all very well to say that,' James responded, 'but I cannot go racing off to Ireland. I have a job here, and so do you. Besides, where would we start? We don't even know where she was at school.'

'I've been cudgelling my brains to think of a way to find out,' Richard said. 'Is it any good asking this Mrs Pearson, do you think?'

'She said she didn't know, but it sounds as if her cook has a good source of information. She might be able to find out.'

'Can we ask?'

James pursed his lips dubiously. 'She is bound to wonder what our interest is. Gossiping with my mother is one thing, but responding to a direct enquiry might seem a step too far. On the other hand, she clearly likes nosing out secrets. I'm wondering how we could approach her without giving away your position. I think we can guarantee that if we told her you think you are Angelina's father the news would be all over Liverpool within a couple of days and that would put McBride on his guard.' They were sitting as usual in the bar of the Adelphi Hotel. He got up and loosened his shoulders. 'I should go home now. My mother is not at all well today, but if she seems stronger in the morning I'll ask if she can think of any pretext for our enquiry.' He laid a hand on Richard's shoulder. 'You won't do anything foolish, will you? We need to keep our own counsel until we are on firmer ground.'

Richard sighed deeply. 'Very well. You need not fear for me. We'll meet again tomorrow?'

'Yes, of course. I'll see you here, about the same time.'

Next evening when they met he was able to present a more optimistic face.

'My mother, it turns out, would make an excellent spy. She's not well enough to go calling herself so she sent me to Mrs Pearson as her emissary, to deliver a pot of her home-made raspberry preserve. I went during the lunch hour, expressed my thanks for the fact that she has taken the trouble to visit my mother, and remarked casually that I was intrigued to hear about Angelina's disappearance. She was very willing to chat, but still had no idea where the school was, except that it must be in Ireland. However, she volunteered the information that the one person who might know is a young woman called Elizabeth Findlay, who was employed by the McBrides as something between a nursemaid and a governess to Angelina.'

'Where can we find her?' Richard asked eagerly.

'That's not quite straightforward. She was dismissed by the McBrides as soon as Angelina was sent away. But her father is one of McBride's employees. If we can track him down he might let us talk to Elizabeth.'

'Where is McBride's place of business?'

'He has a warehouse down by the docks and an office above it. I suppose if we hung around outside when men are going home at the end of the day we might get someone to point Findlay out to us. It's a bit of a long shot but it's the best I can think of.'

The plan was agreed and the next evening James and Richard made their way down to the docks and located the McBride warehouse without difficulty. They had timed their arrival well and within a few minutes the gates opened and men and women came out, calling goodbyes as they split up into twos and threes to head for home. One of the first to appear was a boy of around twelve or thirteen. Richard attracted his attention with a whistle and began tossing a shilling coin up in the air and catching it. The boy approached doubtfully.

'It's all right,' Richard said. 'You're not going to get into any trouble. Do you happen to know a Mr Findlay who works here?'

'Yeah, I know 'im,' the boy replied. 'What about it?'

'Can you point him out to me? I need to talk to him.'

The boy looked around at the crowd issuing from the warehouse. 'Don't see 'im at the moment. But that's 'is daughter, Lizzie, over there.'

'Where? Which one?'

'Her over there, with the green bonnet, talking to the tall woman in brown.'

The coin left Richard's hand and found its way into the boy's. 'Well done, lad. Thank you.'

'What do you want with her?' the boy asked, but Richard, with James at his heels, was already threading his way through the crowd.

'Let me, Richard,' James said as they approached the two women. 'Miss Findlay?'

The girl turned with a start. 'Yes? What do you want?'

James held out his card, knowing that to most law abiding people the sight of the name of a well-respected firm of solicitors was reassuring. 'My name is James Breckenridge. I'm making some enquiries about Miss Angelina McBride.'

'Angelina?' The girl caught her breath. 'Have you found her?'

'So you knew she was missing?' James said.

'Yes, I heard. Are you working for Mr McBride?'

Instinct told James that to agree to this would not be helpful. 'No, I am enquiring on behalf of a third party, someone who wishes Angelina nothing but well.' He glanced at the other woman, who was watching him suspiciously. 'I wonder, could we talk somewhere privately for a few minutes?'

'Don't trust him, Lizzie,' her companion advised. 'You don't know anything about him.'

'I work for a very respectable firm of solicitors,' James said. 'I can assure you that you will be quite safe.'

Elizabeth looked from him to her friend for a moment in indecision. She glanced over her shoulder at the warehouse and seemed to make up her mind. 'Very well, but only a few minutes. There's a pub just down there, the Baltic Fleet. It's a decent place. We could go there.'

'I'm coming too,' the other woman said and in response to James's frown she added, 'all right; I'll wait outside. But I'm not leaving her alone with strangers.'

'You're absolutely right,' Richard said soothingly. 'Come along if you like. It's quite right your friend should have a chaperone.'

In the pleasantly furnished saloon of the Baltic Fleet, James led Elizabeth to a seat and Richard installed her friend at another table, out of earshot but where she could watch them. He came back from the bar with two glasses of port and lemon and two tankards of beer and seated himself beside James.

'Now then,' Elizabeth said, 'what's it all about?'

'Am I right in thinking that you worked for the McBrides for a short time?' James asked.

'I did.'

'As a governess to their daughter Angelina?'

'Not a governess exactly. I looked after her, poor mite, until her father decided to send her away. Then I was out on my ear with no character and no option but working in the packing shed.'

'I get the impression that you do not much care for the McBrides.'

'Too right I don't. The way they treated that poor child was evil, if you ask me. No wonder she kicked over the traces.'

Richard leaned forward. 'What do you mean, the way they treated her?'

'It was her mother mostly. One minute she was dressing her up, showing her off like some prize pet, getting her to sing for her guests, next minute she was treating her like dirt. I'll never forget the way she beat her for damaging her best dress.'

'She beat her?'

'Caned her on her bare behind. I saw the marks. I don't wonder she's run off.'

James saw that Richard was working himself up into a fury and put in quietly, 'Miss Findlay ... may I call you Elizabeth?'

'Lizzie. I'm always called Lizzie.'

'Well, Lizzie, we know that Mr McBride sent her away to school ...'

'Yes. I thought it would be better for her in the long run, get her out of Mrs McBride's clutches, but the nuns must have been cruel to her. Otherwise she wouldn't have run away.'

'How did you know she had run away?'

'I heard it from Jane, the parlourmaid. We got quite friendly while I was there and we've kept in touch.'

'Miss Findlay ... Lizzie,' Richard said urgently, 'I think you really cared for Angelina. I believe I can trust you with a secret. Did you know that Angelina is not the McBrides' real daughter?'

'Everyone knew that, except Angelina herself. It was when another girl told her she went for her and started a fight. Why do you ask?'

'I am Angelina's true father. That is why I am so anxious to find her.'

'Her father? I thought he was Mr McBride's brother.'

'No,' James put in, 'that was not true. It was a story they made up. We think they took Angelina from the workhouse, but they did not want anyone to know that.'

'Why was she in the workhouse?'

Richard hung his head. 'I left her there because I was desperate. My wife had died and I had no money. I could not look after her. It shames me to admit it, but I thought it was best at the time.'

Lizzie looked at him for a moment. Then she said gently, 'People fall on hard times. It's often not their fault. You did what you thought was best for her. But now you want her back?'

'And I can promise you she will never suffer at my hands in the way you have described.'

'Well, she'd have to be better off than what she was, but she's missing. Well, of course, you know that.'

'That is why we need your help to find her,' James said.

'I don't see how I can help.'

'Do you, by any chance, know the name of the school she was sent to?'

'Ah, now you're asking.' Lizzie frowned. 'I saw a letter once, left on the hall table to be taken to the post. That would be just after the Christmas ball, where Angelina disgraced herself. I reckon that could have been to ask the nuns to take her.'

'You think it was a convent, then?'

'Oh yes. I overheard him say to Mrs McBride that the nuns would teach her discipline.'

Richard shivered. 'God help us!'

'Can you remember the address? James asked.

'I'm trying. Oh, I know. It was somewhere in Limerick. Is there a place called Limerick? I thought it was just a funny sort of poem.'

'No, there is such a place,' James assured her. 'Do you remember anything else?'

'It was a real mouthful. Something about Jesus, Faithful Friends of Jesus, something like that.'

James sat back. 'Thank you, Lizzie. I'm sure we can locate the place from what you've told us.'

'But will that mean you can find her?'

'It gives us a place to start. But isn't Mr McBride looking for her?'

'He's back in his office. I asked Jane if she knew what was going on. She says he's set the police on it, but he doesn't trust them so he's called on some of his contacts over there to help.'

'Some of his contacts,' Richard echoed. 'Well, we can guess who that might be.'

James got to his feet. 'Lizzie, you've been a great help. We're very grateful.'

'Will you let me know if you find her? I'm that worried about her I can't sleep at night. She could be a right little madam at times, but I got really fond of her. I'd like to see her happily settled with someone who'd take proper care of her.'

'Where can I contact you? Will you give me your address?'

'Do you have a bit of paper. I'll write it for you.'

James produced his notebook and Lizzie scribbled an address in it.

'I must go now,' she said. 'Or my dad will be looking for me.'

As they shook hands on the pavement, James said, 'It would be best if you didn't tell anyone why we are looking for Angelina. Can I rely on your discretion?'

'I won't tell a soul,' Lizzie promised.

As they parted from the two young women, Richard's expression was grim. 'God help me, I'll never forgive myself for leaving her in the hands of those monsters!'

'It's hard to believe anyone can treat a child so harshly,' James agreed. 'I've heard the adage "spare the rod and spoil the child", and I guess you and I have had a taste of the rod in our time at school, but to beat a small child like that … Do you think Lizzie might have been exaggerating?'

'It didn't look like that to me.' Richard squared his shoulders. 'But at least we know now where to start searching. It can't be difficult to locate that convent.'

'I assume the police search must have started there,' James said. 'I'm not sure I can see why anyone else should find clues that they have missed.'

'Are you suggesting we should sit back and do nothing? That's not an option as far as I am concerned.'

'That's all very well, but neither of us is free to go chasing off to Ireland on a search that might last weeks.'

Richard glanced at him with an expression of contrition. 'Of course. I'm sorry. You have obligations here, which you cannot abandon. But that doesn't mean I cannot go.'

'What about the work you are doing here?'

'To hell with that. What is new machinery for a mine thousands of miles away, compared to the life of my daughter? I'll make up the time after I've found her.'

James was silent for a moment. It was hard to voice the thoughts that were uppermost in his mind. 'Richard, I think we have to accept that you might never find her. She's what, nine years old, and she has been missing now for days. Unless she has been taken in by somebody, it's unlikely she can have survived.'

'But that's just it! Don't you see?' The anguish in Richard's voice was hard to bear. 'There's a chance – a good chance – that someone has taken her in, but for what purpose? Anyone with good intentions would surely have reported finding her to the authorities. That's the thought that has been tormenting me since we heard the news. I know you can't get away, James, and I have no right to ask you to anyway. You've already done more than your professional capacity requires. But I'm going to Ireland on the next boat. I shan't rest till I know ... till I find her and bring her home.'

'Believe me,' James said, 'if I was at liberty I would come with you. I know we only met a few days ago, but I feel we have become friends. It isn't anything to do with what you call "my professional capacity".'

'No, I'm sorry. I didn't mean it like that. Of course we are friends, and I value that greatly. Without your help and companionship these last few days would have been dreary indeed. But I have to go. You do see that, don't you?'

'I do,' James said, 'but it worries me. If McBride has applied to his Fenian friends for help, you don't know what you might be getting into.'

'I'll take that chance,' Richard said. 'I cannot do otherwise.'

Fourteen

'So, my little colleen, you were at school with the nuns. Where was that, then?'

Angelina was sitting on the steps of the caravan and the man who seemed to be the head of the family was seated opposite her on a battered chair. She had woken to find sunlight streaming through the window and the caravan rocking gently as people moved about. She knew at once where she was, and memories of the previous day came flooding back. Her first emotion had been one of relief. She had found safe shelter, and she pushed the thought of what might happen next to the back of her mind. She was about to climb out of bed when the woman who had taken off her shoes the night before came in and told her to bide where she was for the moment. She spread some sort of salve on Angelina's blistered feet and bandaged them, and gave her some shoes that were too large but accommodated the bandages. She hobbled awkwardly down the steps and was given a bowl of porridge sweetened with a little honey. The man waited for her to finish eating before beginning his inquisition.

'It was near Limerick,' she said. 'It was called the convent of the Faithful Companions of Jesus.'

'I know the place. And the nuns decided to send you home. Why was that?'

'They said I was disobedient.'

'Disobedient? What rules did you break?'

'I didn't ... not exactly. I just wanted to sing.'

'To sing? Was that so wrong? Is singing a sin, then?'

'No. But I was told not to. It was in a special service and I was supposed to sing the "Agnus Dei" all by myself. Mother Marie Thérèse wanted me to do it, because I had the best voice, but Mother Mary Andrew said I shouldn't because I wasn't ... wasn't in a state of grace. She told another girl to sing instead.'

'But you did it anyway?' She could see the beginnings of a grin underneath the man's beard.

'Yes. When the time came I just stood up and sang along with the other girl. Her voice isn't as good as mine, and she just stopped, so I went on singing by myself.'

He leaned back in his chair and looked at her. 'Well, you're a character, and no mistake. So, the nuns sent for your da to fetch you home.' Angelina nodded, feeling a lump in her throat. 'And that frightened you so much that you decided to make a run for it. Is it so bad at home that you'd rather be out here, alone, with no money and no friends?'

She nodded again. 'Yes.'

'Is it true that your ma beats you?'

'Yes.' She paused. Thoughts she had been repressing were resurfacing in her mind. 'The thing is ... I'm not sure she is my real mother.'

'Why do you say that?'

'Another girl, before I was sent away, she said my mama and papa weren't really mine. She said I was … a foundling. I don't know what that is.'

The woman, who Angelina thought was the man's wife, had come to sit nearby and she saw the two of them exchange glances.

'We've many tales here in Ireland,' the man said, 'of bairns left by the fairy folk to be exchanged for human children. Are you a fairy child, do you suppose?'

She looked at him in consternation until the twinkle in his eyes told her she was being teased.

'I think I'd like to be,' she said. 'Then I wouldn't have to go home, ever.'

'So what would you do?'

'I suppose I'd have to look for my fairy mother and father. Or perhaps they might be looking for me.'

'So they might, indeed.' He gave a laugh. 'But until then, would you like us to be your family?'

Angelina looked around her. The three young men had disappeared somewhere, but the younger woman was rocking her baby nearby and the children were playing. There was a feeling of contentment and ease. 'I think I should, very much,' she responded.

'It's not an easy life, I should warn you,' the man said. 'It's fine on a morning like this, when the sun shines and we've a little money in our pockets for food. There are rabbits to be snared for meat and milk from our old nanny goat, and we can find eggs and soon there will be wild berries in the hedges. It's not so good in the winter, when the rain gets into the bothy there and the van is cold and damp, but we get by. Don't we, Dervla?'

'Aye, we do,' the woman replied.

Angelina gazed around at the small encampment. 'Do you always live like this, then?'

'It's the only way we know to live,' he replied. 'We're travelling folk, and so were our fathers and their fathers before them.'

'So how do you earn your living?'

He smiled. 'Come, I'll show you.'

He rose and Angelina got to her feet also, but she stumbled over the outsize shoes and nearly fell.

'Lord ha' mercy on us,' he exclaimed, 'you'll go nowhere in those boots. Come here, I'll carry you.'

He picked her up in strong arms and she put one of hers around his neck. His beard tickled her cheek and he smelt of sweat and the earth, but she did not mind. He carried her round the caravan and over to a stone wall at the edge of a field.

'There. See?'

In the field there were around a dozen horses. Most were grazing quietly but on the far side three were being ridden by the young men she had seen the night before. They were riding round in circles and their mounts were snorting and sometimes bucking.

'We're horse dealers,' the man said. 'Those three are being broken in. They are Irish cobs, fine horses for all sorts of uses. When they are ready we shall take them and a few others to the Cahirmee horse fair and sell them and, God willing, the profit we make will keep us in sugar and flour and salt for the winter months.'

He lifted Angelina up and sat her on a flat stone on the top of the wall. 'They haven't got any saddles. Won't they fall off?'

'Not them! Our boys don't need saddles. They've been sitting on horses since before they could walk and they're as much at home there as you are in an armchair by the fire. Like that, you can feel the horse and the horse can feel you. You know if he's nervous or out of sorts and he can tell if you're in a bad mood. It's like you and the horse are one creature.' He smiled at her. 'Would you fancy a ride?'

'No!' she said in alarm. 'I'd be frightened.'

'Oh, I don't mean on one of those wild young things. There are horses and mares here would look after you like you was one of their own. Irish cobs are the sweetest natured breed in the world. One day I'll put you up on one and you'll see.'

'Oh!' she exclaimed, pointing, 'there's a baby horse.'

He laughed. 'That's what we call a foal.'

'His legs are all thin and wobbly.'

'That's 'cos he's only a month old.'

'Is that his mama?'

'His dam. Yes. Queenie's one of my best brood mares. She gives me a fine colt or filly every year.'

'She's pretty. I like the way they all have lovely long manes and furry legs.'

'We call that feathers, not fur. To be a real, true-bred Irish cob a horse must have long hair like that all down its legs to the hoof. Would you like to pat her?'

Angelina furrowed her brow dubiously. 'I don't know.'

'There's no need to be afraid. I'll bring her over to you.'

He swung himself over the wall and walked towards the mare, whistling softly. She lifted her head from grazing and greeted him with a whicker. He took something from his pocket and gave it to her, talking to her in a low voice, then took hold of her forelock and led her across to where Angelina was sitting.

'Here we are. Just lean over and pat her neck. No sudden movements, and no squealing, right?'

Angelina stretched out her arm and laid her hand on the soft, warm coat. The mare nudged her leg gently with her nose.

'She's asking for a titbit. Give her this.' He produced a piece of carrot from his pocket. 'Hold your hand out flat, like so. Now just offer it to her. Don't be afraid. She won't bite you.'

He guided her hand towards the horse's muzzle and she felt velvet lips lift the carrot from her palm. 'Oh! She's so gentle.'

'What did I tell you?'

'Oh look, the baby's come with her.'

'Yes, he'll never be far away from his dam until he gets a lot older.' He held out his hand to the foal, who nuzzled it hopefully and allowed him to stroke his neck. 'We bring them up to be used to people. That way, when they're ready to be ridden it's not hard to break them in.' He patted the mare on the rump. 'Off you go now, my lovely.'

The mare moved away and the foal followed, giving a small, experimental buck. The man watched them for a moment, then turned and lifted Angelina off the wall.

'Come along. I've work to do. I'll take you back to Dervla. I've no doubt she'll find some occupation for you.'

The two women had been joined by the eldest of the three children, a girl a year or two older than Angelina. The baby was lying on a rug at their feet and all three were busy weaving baskets from thin strips of some kind of wood. The man set Angelina down in a chair.

'There. She's been introduced to the horses. Now it's over to you.' He straightened up and then something seemed to occur to him. 'I'm Leary, by the way. Leary Donovan. This here is my wife Dervla, as you know. That –' he indicated the second woman '– is our eldest son's wife. Her name is Moira. And this scamp is our youngest, Sorcha. So now you've met most of the family, I'll leave you to it.'

'Can you weave a basket?' Dervla asked.

'I don't know. I've never tried.'

'Sorcha, you can show her. Let her start with the reeds, it's easier on the fingers than willow.'

The girl delved into a large sack and produced a circular wooden base with spokes sticking up all round it and a bundle of reeds. 'You wind them in and out, like so. It's easy.'

It looked easy, but Angelina found that her fingers were much less deft than Sorcha's and she struggled to produce work as neat.

'Can you sew?' Dervla asked, after watching her for a while.

'Oh yes. I learned to sew in the convent, and I can embroider. I had to embroider samplers when I lived –' she was going to say 'at home' but the words seemed wrong '– before I was sent away.'

'I'll find you something to stitch another day,' Dervla promised.

The baby had been sleeping peacefully but now he woke and began to grizzle. Moira put down her work to pick him up.

'You'll be all day with that basket,' she commented. 'Better you hold Sean for me and let me get on with mine.'

She moved to where Angelina was sitting and held the baby out to her.

'I don't …' she began. 'I've never held one before.'

'There's nothing to it. Just make sure you support his head. Hold out your arms. That's right, like so. There, you see?' She settled the baby in Angelina's arms and he immediately stopped crying. The feel of a warm, living creature in her embrace gave her a strange feeling, as if something inside her was swelling up. She felt suddenly grown up and responsible. When Sean began to grizzle again Moira showed her how to hold him up against her shoulder and pat his back until he belched.

'There you are, you see? You're a proper little mother,' Dervla said.

'You never held a baby before?' Sorcha looked at her in amazement.

'No.'

'You got no brothers and sisters, then?'

'No.'

'Why not?'

'I don't know. I suppose Mama and Papa did not want any other children.'

The two younger children, both boys, had disappeared, but as midday approached they came running into the little circle by the caravan.

'Look!' the elder of the two cried, holding out his cap in both hands. Moira peered into it.

'Eggs! Where from?'

'Laird's farmyard, over yonder,' the boy said, jerking his chin over his shoulder.

'You want to have a care!' Moira said. 'Farmer catch you, you'll know all about it.'

'He's gone to market,' the younger boy said. 'We watched him go. Can we eat the eggs for dinner?'

'How many you got?' Dervla asked.

'Dozen.'

'Right. Go fetch me a pan of water and put it on to boil.'

'Boys, say hello to Angelina,' Moira said. 'These are my two, Angelina. This one is Quinn and this is Danny.'

The two looked at her shyly and mumbled a greeting. Then Quinn, the elder of the two, said, 'Can we call you Angel? I can't get my tongue round the other bit.'

Something stirred in Angelina's memory, a half-heard voice, elusive as a dream. 'Yes, if you like.'

Shortly Leary and the three young men came back from the field for their midday meal. Leary was carrying a brace of rabbits, which he tossed to his wife.

'We'll eat well tonight.'

By the end of the meal Angelina had discovered that the young men were called Fergal, Killian and Brendan. They were all Leary and Dervla's sons. Fergal, the eldest, was Moira's husband, then came Brendan and Killian, who was only a couple of years older than Sorcha. As they sat around eating the eggs Quinn had stolen, she was aware that they were looking at her, and once Fergal said something in their own language to Leary, who replied in a tone that conveyed reassurance but also authority. Fergal looked at her again and shrugged, but then his wife said something and he seemed to relax. It made her uneasy. She had the feeling that he was questioning her right to their hospitality.

The afternoon was spent in the same way as the morning, and Angelina was increasingly frustrated by the difficulty of moving around in her out-size shoes. Dervla counselled patience and told her that by next morning she would probably be able to put her own boots on again. As the sun sank towards the horizon, preparations began for the evening meal and she watched with a mixture of fascination and disgust as Dervla skinned and gutted the two rabbits and put them on a spit over the fire. The atmosphere as they sat round the campfire to eat was more relaxed than at midday and afterwards Leary produced a fiddle and began to play. He began with a lively jig and Sorcha and Killian jumped up to dance; then Moira and Fergal joined in and Quinn and Danny imitated them, while the others clapped to the rhythm. Angelina clapped, too, and wished she could join in the dancing.

After a while, the mood of the pieces became more reflective and Moira sang a poignant lament. Leary lowered his fiddle and looked across at Angelina.

'Do you know any of these songs?'

She shook her head. 'No, I'm afraid I only know what we sang in chapel.' Then, remembering, 'Oh, there is one English song I know. It's called "The Last Rose of Summer".'

Leary laughed. 'Sure, that's no more English than I am. It was written by an Irish poet.' He raised his fiddle and played a few bars. 'Come on, then. You told me you can sing. Let's hear you.'

Angelina began hesitantly, but the sound of her own voice reassured her. She sat up straighter and gave herself up to the music. Even as she sang she was aware of a change in the atmosphere around her. Now she was the focus of all attention. When the song was over there was a brief silence. Then Leary said, 'And sing you can, like a thrush on a cherry tree. What else do you know?'

'Only the "Agnus Dei", like I told you.'

'Can you sing that without accompaniment?'

'Yes.' She cleared her throat, took a breath and sang.

As she fell silent there was a murmur of approval. Dervla said, 'That's a rare gift you have, child. It's a long time since I heard anything so beautiful. Thank you.'

The thanks were echoed by others and Leary said, 'Would you like to learn some other songs – songs our people sing?'

'Yes, I should, very much.'

'Then I'll teach you, but not tonight. You've done enough for one night.' He took up the fiddle and began to play again and the others began to talk amongst themselves, as if resuming conversations that had been suspended while she sang.

At bedtime she occupied the same bunk as before, but this time she was aware that Sorcha had the one opposite, and Quinn and Danny slept above them, while Leary and Dervla had a bed divided off by a curtain. Moira and Fergal, she discovered later, had a place of their own, a tent erected on the back of a flat cart, and the other two men slept in what was called the bothy.

As they settled Sorcha said, 'You're English, aren't you?'

'Yes.'

197

'Where do you live?'

'I think I live here, now.'

'But where did you live?'

'A place called Liverpool.'

'What's it like? Is it a big city? I've never been in a city.'

Dervla's voice interrupted them. 'That's enough for tonight, Sorcha. Angel's tired. You can talk in the morning.'

She was woken as before by people moving around. The two boys had disappeared already and Sorcha was almost dressed, but when Angelina looked for her convent dress it had disappeared. Dervla came through the curtain with a bundle of clothes in her arms.

'That dress you were wearing shows you up as a convent girl to anyone passing, and besides the skirt was ripped. I've some cast-offs of Sorcha's here. Let's see if we can fit you out.'

Soon Angelina was dressed in a dark-blue skirt with two bands of embroidery round the hem, an apron, a blue blouse and a plaid shawl. Dervla's salve proved effective, as she had promised, and she was able to put on her own boots.

'There, you look more like one of us,' Dervla said.

When she had eaten her breakfast porridge Dervla came and sat beside her. 'Leary and I have been talking. It's likely that you are being looked for, don't you think?'

'I suppose so,' Angelina agreed. 'But I don't think anyone would look for me here.'

'Maybe not. But you never know. The polis like to come nosing around sometimes. I'm thinking one look at that fair skin and golden hair and they'd know you didn't belong to us.'

'What can I do, then?' Angelina asked.

'I can make a potion with walnut shells that will turn your skin brown. Maybe after a few weeks in the open air it will be darker anyway, but meanwhile I think we need to do something to help nature along. What do you say?'

'If you think that's the best thing to do,' Angelina said. 'I don't mind.'

Dervla stirred her potion over the fire for an hour and Angelina waited with growing impatience. It had not occurred to her until then that someone might look for her here, but now she was aware of the danger she was afraid that at any moment a policeman might appear and drag her back to the convent, or wherever her father awaited her. At last Dervla called her over and began to anoint her face with a rag dipped in the potion, smoothing it carefully over her ears and neck and up to her hairline. Then she treated her hands and arms the same way.

'Now,' she said sitting back, 'you're as brown as a berry, but there's not much I can do about that lovely hair, except cut it short and hide it under a cap. Will you let me do that?'

'Oh yes!' Angelina said. 'Please do it!'

Dervla picked up some scissors and took a lock of hair in her hands. Moira, sitting nearby nursing the baby, said, 'It's a shame, so it is, to cut such beautiful hair.'

'It'll grow again,' Dervla pointed out, and made a decisive cut. Very soon Angelina's hair was as short as a boy's and Dervla produced a peaked cap and set it on her head. It was slightly too large and sagged over her ears, but that, Dervla said, was all to the good. She delved into a carpet bag where she kept her things and produced a sliver of mirror.

'Take a look.'

Angelina looked and saw a brown-faced urchin. 'It doesn't look like me at all,' she exclaimed gleefully.

'Well, you'll pass a quick inspection,' Dervla said, 'but I wouldn't go further than that.'

Leary came by at that moment and said with a laugh, 'Well, who's this young scamp, then? I wouldn't have known you.' He looked closer and added, 'You've done a great job, Dervla. But if she's going to pass as one of us, she's going to need a new name as well.' He thought for a moment, with his head on one side. 'I think you should be Maeve. It means a song thrush. How do you like that?'

'Maeve,' Angelina repeated. 'Yes, I like that very much.'

'Maeve it is, then. It'll take a while to get used to it, I dare say, but you must try to answer to it, just in case someone should come inquiring.'

In the ensuing days, Angelina enjoyed greater freedom she had ever experienced before, even during the two weeks of the Easter holiday when she was left at the convent. It was true that she was expected to make herself useful. Everyone had their jobs to do, including Quinn and Danny, and no exception was made for her. She finally succeeded in producing a basket that met the standard Dervla required, but then to her relief she was given some cloth and told to make it up into small bags to contain sprigs of lavender, which she then embroidered with coloured wools. The scent of the lavender brought back memories of home, where bags like this had been kept in the drawers containing her underclothes. It had never occurred to her to wonder who had made them. She was allowed to create her own designs for the embroidery and she enjoyed the work much more than wrestling with canes and reeds.

Sorcha's particular duty was the care of the nanny goat, which produced the family's milk. Angelina was quickly co-opted as her assistant. As with the lavender bags, she had never wondered where milk came from, though she'd had a vague idea that cows were involved in some way. Her first sight of Sorcha tugging at the nanny goat's teats filled her with disgust. Worse followed.

'So, now you see how it's done you can try it yourself.'

Angelina drew back. 'No, thank you. I'd rather just watch you.'

'Just watch, is it? Nothing gets done by just watching. You drink the milk, you can help get it. That way we can share the work.'

Wrinkling her nose in disgust, Angelina took Sorcha's place on the low stool and took hold of the teats. The goat shifted irritably.

'She doesn't like me doing it. You'd better go on.'

'Not I! She'll get used to it. Just get a firm grip. You're only tickling her like that.'

Like it or not, Angelina could see no way of escaping and Sorcha refused to relent until she succeeded in filling the can which was used to carry the milk. From then on, milking the goat was a regular morning chore and one that Sorcha often found an excuse to escape.

When the chores were done, however, she was free to do as she pleased. She roamed the fields and lanes with Sorcha in search of herbs and early berries. They found mushrooms too, which Angelina regarded with grave suspicion, believing that anything found growing wild was probably poisonous; but Sorcha laughed at her and took back an armful of yellow chanterelles, which were greeted with delight.

Sorcha knew the names of all the flowers and plants and what they were good for, and could recognise birds by their songs; but she was a little too ready to laugh at Angelina for her ignorance of such matters. On the whole, Angelina preferred to join Quinn and Danny, drawing water, collecting firewood and learning how to set snares for rabbits.

There were aspects of this new life that were less enjoyable. She did not like having to relieve herself over a smelly pit behind a scanty shield of bushes, and as the summer weather grew warmer the atmosphere in the crowded caravan overnight became stuffy and oppressive. Worst of all was the lack of any opportunity to wash properly. The others seemed to be quite content to splash their faces and hands with cold water but Angelina soon began to long for warm water and soap and the privacy to have a good wash. Once, Sorcha took her to a place in the nearby river where the water formed a deep pool. Leaving Quinn on guard, with Sorcha's threats of what would happen to him if he looked round ringing in his ears, they stripped to their chemises and lowered themselves into the cool water. It was bliss, but Angelina was never able to persuade Sorcha to repeat the adventure.

One afternoon Danny asked, 'Will I show you where we get the eggs?'

'If you like.'

The boys led her across several fields until they came to a high stone wall.

'That's the laird's castle, in there,' Quinn told her.

'A castle? Like in the fairy stories?'

'Don't know about that. I never seen one. But there's a farm, too, with pigs and chickens. That's what we're after.'

'Suppose the laird sees us?'

'No chance. He doesn't live here. He'll be back in England, like all the others.'

'What others?'

'The men who own the land. They're all English. They've got castles and farms, but they don't want to live in Ireland. They have tenants and managers to look after it for them, and they just take the profit.'

'That doesn't seem right.'

'It's not, but that's how things are. Anyway, it's not the laird we need to worry about, but if the farmer sees us we'll be for it. This way.'

He turned along the line of the wall and Angelina followed, torn between excitement and fear. They came to a point where some of the stones from the top of the wall had fallen and lay in a heap at the base.

'Danny, you keep watch,' Quinn ordered.

He scrambled up, using the fallen stones as a ladder to reach the top, and Angelina hitched up her skirt and climbed after him. At the top he looked round.

'Stay down, till I see if the coast's clear.'

He raised his head cautiously and peered around, then turned back to whisper. 'No one about. Come on, but keep quiet.'

On the far side of the wall a small tree provided a way down. Angelina had never climbed a tree before and the drop below her made her heart thud. Encumbered by her long skirt it took her some time to lower herself down, while Quinn waited impatiently. When she joined him he led the way through a shrubbery and into an orchard. Ahead she could see farm buildings and hear hens clucking.

'I know the places where they lay,' Quinn whispered. 'They've got nest boxes where they're supposed to lay their eggs but some of them just like to wander. This way. Keep low.'

Within minutes he had located a clutch of eggs under a currant bush and another in the corner of a low wall.

'Here, you hold out your apron and I'll put the eggs in it. Don't drop them! We'll have some of these blackcurrants, too.'

Before long Angelina's apron was full of eggs but to scramble back up the tree without dropping them was an impossible feat. She took her apron off and wrapped the eggs in it to pass them to Quinn, who was already at the top of the wall. Then she struggled upwards and arrived scratched and panting at his side.

Once they were back on the other side of the wall he looked at her. 'You're not bad for a girl. Sorcha won't do it. She won't even try. She says climbing's for boys.'

Another memory rose in Angelina's mind. She looked at her skirt. It was patched with mud and green mould from the tree trunk, and there was a tear at the hem. 'Will Dervla be angry with me?'

'What for?'

'For spoiling my clothes.'

He drew back his head as if the question made no sense to him. 'You can brush the dirt off.'

'My skirt's torn, too.'

'Well, you can mend it, can't you?'

'Oh, yes I suppose so.'

'Well then.'

As they walked back to the camp Angelina wrestled with a problem of morality.

'These eggs, they really belong to the laird, don't they? We stole them.'

Quinn shrugged. 'So what?'

'Stealing's wrong. It's a sin.'

'See here. This land belongs to us, not the English. It's the laird who stole it from us, and now he sits in his fine house in England and feasts himself on the pork and beef that he fattens on our land, while the people who live here starve. There's no sin in taking what's ours by right.'

This seemed to make good enough sense, so she left it at that.

On another occasion, Quinn persuaded Killian to let them accompany him when he went to tickle trout. It seemed an odd thing to want to do, but Quinn was plainly excited by the prospect so she went along with him. The river ran through a little valley a short distance from the camp. When they came to the point where the ground dropped away into a thicket of trees and bushes, Killian said, 'Stay here.'

Quinn began to protest but Killian said, 'You're on guard duty. Keep your mouth shut and your eyes peeled, and if you see the keeper, whistle.'

Quinn's look of disappointment turned to one of self-importance. 'Trust me. I won't let you down.'

Killian disappeared among the trees and Quinn faced about and began to scan the landscape behind them.

'What are we looking for?' Angelina asked.

'Hush! You heard Killian. We're on watch for the keeper.'

'What keeper?'

'The laird's gamekeeper. We're still on his land. The trout belong to him – so he thinks.'

'The fish? Even the fish in the stream belong to him?'

'Aye. So do the rabbits in their warrens and the deer in the forest. Ordinary folks are not allowed to take any of them.'

'That doesn't seem right.'

'It's not, but that's the way the government in England has it.'

They stood for a while, watching the fields for any sign of movement, until Killian reappeared carrying a knapsack in which something writhed and wriggled.

'You got one, then?' Quinn said.

'Aye, a fine big fellow. But we could do with another. There's another pool further down. We'll try there.'

He led them downstream for a short distance, and when he stopped this time, Quinn begged, 'Let us come and watch. Maeve's never seen a trout tickled. And there's no one about.'

Killian hesitated, then nodded. 'Very well, but I don't want to hear a sound out of you, understood?'

'You won't,' Quinn promised.

They made their way down into the valley, to where the stream had formed a deep pool shadowed by a willow. Killian pointed to a spot on the bank. 'Still and silent!' he whispered.

Angelina sat beside Quinn and watched as Killian lowered himself to his knees by the pool. For a while he remained statue still, then he very slowly slid his arm into the water.

There was a moment of intense concentration, then a sudden movement and a gleaming silver fish landed with a thud on the bank beside him. It wriggled violently, thrashing its tail in an effort to regain the water but Killian reached into a pocket and produced a short, heavy club and struck it a single blow on the head. It lay still and he scooped it into his knapsack.

Quinn gasped as if he had been holding his breath in the effort to remain silent. 'Well done, Killian! He's a beauty.'

'He is that,' Killian agreed. 'Come on. Let's get them back while they're still fresh.'

As they walked back Angelina asked, 'How did you do that, Killian?'

'They call it tickling. When the trout's resting he's half asleep. You slip your hand very slowly underneath him and just let your fingertips stroke his belly. They seem to like that. Then one quick grab –' he jerked his arm in demonstration '– and he's out on the bank before he knows what's happening.'

'Is it difficult?'

'Well, it took me a while to learn. Many's the fine fish that's slipped through my fingers in days gone by – and some still do.'

The best day of all was when Leary lifted her onto Queenie's back and led her round the field. She had soon discovered that Quinn and Danny were almost as much at home on horseback as the older boys and even Sorcha could ride. She longed to be able to join them. Feeling the shaggy coat and the strong muscles under her legs, she had an inkling of how they must feel when their bodies and their mounts' moved as one. Up there she felt proud and powerful.

'Can I learn to ride properly, Leary?' she begged.

'Sure you can. Will we try a little trot now?'

'Yes, please.'

That was more difficult. She found herself bouncing up and down and would have slid off if Leary's strong hand had not been there to steady her.

'Relax!' he instructed. 'Let yourself sink down. Let your spine take up the movement.'

After that he gave her a lesson every morning and slowly her body adapted itself until she no longer needed him to hold on to her.

One morning there was an unusual bustle of activity in the camp. Fergal and Moira's tent was removed from the flat cart and it was brushed out. Dervla was collecting up all the baskets that were finished, and packing up Angelina's lavender bags. Moira and Sorcha appeared in clean dresses and had combed their hair.

'What's happening?' Angelina asked Dervla.

'We're going into town. There's things we need, and stuff to sell, and the lads are keen for a drop to drink and a bit of the craic.'

'The what?'

'A bit of chat and gossip. A bit of entertainment. You'll see.'

One of the horses was brought in and harnessed to the cart and the goods were loaded onto it. Dervla took the reins and Moira climbed up beside her. Leary lifted Angelina onto the back, beside Sorcha, then leaned up to her.

'Best you say as little as possible when we're in town. You may look like one of us but your English voice will give you away. And remember, your name's Maeve.'

All the men and boys were already mounted. Leary vaulted onto the back of his favourite black and white stallion and the cavalcade set off.

It took about half an hour to reach the town, which was little more than a large village. As they drove down the main street they were greeted by some with friendly shouts of welcome, but Angelina saw others draw away with frowns and shaken heads. The horses were tethered under the shade of a tree on a small green at the end of the street, and Danny and Killian were left to keep an eye on them, with the promise of being relieved later.

Dervla took Angelina's hand. 'You come with me. Here, you can carry these.'

She handed her a basket containing the lavender bags and strung a bundle of empty baskets on her free arm. Together, they set off down the street. At each house Dervla knocked and offered her goods. Sometimes they were well received; sometimes the door was shut in their faces. Dervla sold several of her baskets, but it was the lavender bags that went fastest.

The first woman they spoke to looked down at Angelina and asked, 'And what have you got there, my pretty?' Angelina mutely held up one of the bags and the woman took it and examined it. 'Now there's a pretty thing! Did you make this?' Angelina nodded. The woman looked at Dervla, and asked, 'Does she not have a tongue in her head?'

'She's shy,' Dervla said, and patted her on the head.

'Well, I'll take two of these, to bring a smile to that little face,' the woman said and pinched Angelina's cheek. As they walked on, Dervla murmured, 'Well, you're turning out to be an asset, for sure.'

At midday they picnicked beside the cart, but when the sun began to drop, and the shops in the village shut, they all headed for the inn, which stood where the two village streets crossed. Angelina hung back.

'Am I allowed in there?'

'Sure you are,' Dervla said. 'Who's going to stop you?'

There was only one room in the inn and it was already crowded. The air was full of tobacco smoke and loud with conversation, much of it in a language she did not understand, but which sounded different from the tongue the travellers spoke among themselves. There was a counter at one end, with shelves of bottles behind it, and rough tables and seats made from empty barrels took up most of the rest of the space. Leary and Fergal claimed a table and the women seated themselves round it. The younger men were already mingling with the crowd, trying to strike up conversations with any young women present. Pots full of what Angelina presumed was beer were brought and one was set in front of her.

'You'll not be used to strong liquor, I imagine,' Dervla said, 'but this is small beer. It'll not do you any harm.'

Angelina sipped. She didn't like the taste, but she was thirsty and there seemed to be no alternative on offer, so she drank it.

As the evening drew on and the conversation became more animated and louder still, Leary produced his fiddle and began to play. Very soon he was the centre of attention with people crowding round with requests, and some of the younger men and girls cleared a space in the middle of the room and began to dance. Then Leary changed the mood with a soulful ballad and suddenly called out, 'Maeve, come over here to me!'

Slightly fuddled by the beer Angelina was slow to recognise her new name until Dervla gave her a poke in the ribs. Shyly, she made her way across to where Leary sat.

'Now, you remember this song I taught you the other day?' he said, and played a few bars. Angelina nodded.

'Will you sing it for these folk, then? I've been telling them what a fine voice you have.'

Her first reaction was to refuse, but she loved Leary and did not want to displease him. She nodded again. He played the opening bars again and she started to sing, and was immediately aware of a hush spreading round the room. As always, once she heard her own voice she took courage and, as the last voices round the edge of the room died away, the sense of power over her audience brought a rush of pride. When the song came to an end it was greeted with applause and demands for more. She sang two more of the songs Leary had taught her. Then he said, 'Now hark ye. I know you're all God fearing folk, but you'll not hear anything to match this in any church in the land. Sing the "Agnus Dei", Maeve.'

She sang unaccompanied, each note dropping like clear water into the silence, and when it was over there was no applause, only a long, communal sigh.

Leary smiled and patted her shoulder and she went back to sit with Dervla and the others. It was only then that she saw that Killian and Quinn were going round the room holding out their caps and collecting money.

A little later, as shifting positions among the crowd brought Leary within earshot, she heard him saying, 'She's a changeling child, for sure. We found her wandering by the stone circle at Lough Gur, which is a magical place, as you all know. Did you ever hear a human child sing like that?'

The men round him nodded gravely and cast sidelong looks at Angelina. She hid her face in her apron, not sure whether to giggle or weep. She knew, with the part of her mind that clung to common sense, that Leary's story was a fiction; but there was another part that wondered if perhaps it might be true. After all, she had been told that she was a foundling. Maybe she really was a fairy child. One thing was certain: if everyone believed that she was, there was no chance that her father – if he was her father – would ever be able to trace her.

Fifteen

When James returned from the office on the day after his meeting with Lizzie Findlay, he was greeted in the hallway by Flossie, in a state of agitation.

'Mistress has had a visitor, and it left her in a right state.'

'A visitor? Who?'

'A lady, sir. A Mrs McBride.'

James felt a cold hand grab his stomach. 'McBride? Dammit! Is my mother in bed?'

'No, sir. She's in the drawing room. She's rallied now, but after the lady left she was taken quite faint.'

James turned to the door of the drawing room. 'Thank you, Flossie. I'll see what has happened. Leave it to me.'

Mrs Brackenridge was reclining on a chaise longue and appeared quite calm, but James saw the hectic flush on her cheekbones that always meant she was in pain. He crossed quickly to where she lay and knelt down beside her.

'How are you, Mama? Can I get you some of your drops?'

'Thank you, dear. There's no need. Flossie fetched them for me a few minutes ago. I shall be well directly.'

'Flossie says you have had a visitor, Mrs McBride.'

A faint ironic smile touched his mother's lips. 'Aren't I the favoured one? Marguerite McBride is very choosy about whom she visits, and I have been off her "at home" list ever since that time we met at the milliner's, when May recognised her little girl.'

'What did she want?'

'Ostensibly, to wish me a speedy recovery. She said she had heard from Laura Pearson that I was unwell and wondered of there was anything she could do to help.'

'But really …?'

'After a few minutes, she got to the point. She asked if I remembered Angelina. Of course, I said I did – but only vaguely. After all, it was some time ago. Then she said that it had come to her notice that you were making enquiries about her whereabouts; that you had even accosted the girl who used to be her nursemaid in the street and interrogated her. Of course, I made out that I knew nothing about it, that you never discussed your work with me.'

'That's good! Was that the end of it?'

'Oh no, far from it. She cast off any pretence that this was a social call at that point. She said that she understood that you had even been to see an old business rival of her husband's and that she and her husband resented anyone interfering in their affairs. She said I should warn you that there might be "unpleasant consequences" if you continued and I should remind you of what happened to the business rival in question when he crossed Mr McBride. What did happen to him, James?'

James drew a deep breath and sighed it out. 'His warehouse burnt down and as a consequence he went bankrupt.'

'Oh dear!'

He took hold of her hand. 'Don't let it worry you, Mama. It's only an idle threat, intended to intimidate me into keeping my nose out of McBride's affairs. Setting fire to a warehouse down on the docks might be blamed on an accident – as indeed it was – but burning down a house in a respectable street in the middle of the city is a totally different proposition.'

'All the same,' his mother said, 'I would be easier in my mind if you were not involved in this business. Do you need to take such an active part in Mr Kean's investigation?'

'Probably not, but I feel extremely sorry for him, and for Angelina if everything I've heard is true. But as it happens, I shall not be working with him for a while, at least. He has gone to Ireland, to see if he can pick up any clues as to her whereabouts, and I must get back to my regular duties in the office and to studying for my exams.'

He saw the relief on his mother's face. 'Yes, you should do that, my dear. I, too, have sympathy for Mr Kean and I hope his quest is successful, but you have to consider what is most important to you. I am afraid you have been neglecting your studies lately.'

'It's true, I have,' James agreed ruefully, 'but I'll put that right from now on. I promise.'

'That's good. That sets my mind at rest. Now, you must go and have your dinner. Cook will be keeping it hot for you. Don't worry about me.'

'You are sure?'

'Yes, yes. As long as I know you are keeping away from that horrible man.'

'I will, Mama,' he promised, but thought to himself as he sat down to eat: but all the same, I wonder why McBride is so keen to stop anyone from enquiring into his affairs.

He reported the conversation to Mr Weaver the following morning and the little man's nose twitched more violently than ever.

'I doubt very much if McBride would go to the lengths of sending his wife to threaten your mother if it was only a question of his daughter's disappearance. There's something more sinister behind this. I think we should have a word with my friend, the inspector.'

They met with Inspector Vane over steak pie and flagons of ale in the wood-panelled saloon bar of the Philharmonic Hotel. His eyes narrowed as he listened to James's account and at the end he nodded.

'We've been keeping an eye on McBride for some time now. We are pretty sure that he is using his tea-importing business as a cover for some illegal activity, but so far we haven't been able to come up with any definite proof. We suspect that he has a second warehouse somewhere, under another name, and that something other than tea is coming in in his tea chests, but we don't have enough evidence to warrant impounding his goods and conducting a thorough search. If we knew exactly when the next consignment was coming in it would help; but the fact that he is so keen to stop your enquiries suggests to me that it may be imminent. Thank you for bringing it to my attention.'

'I'm happy to do anything I can to put a stop to that man's activities,' James said, 'but at the same time I have to think of my mother's safety. I've told her that there is nothing to worry about, that what was implied is just an empty threat, but I can't pretend it doesn't worry me.'

'Quite right, too,' Vane replied. 'McBride is not a man to be crossed with impunity. I'm sure that the initial threat was just to warn you off and he has no intention of carrying it out, but to set your mind at rest, give me your address and I will tell my men to keep a special eye out in the vicinity of your house when they are out on the beat.'

James thanked him and handed him one of his cards.

As the inspector pocketed it, he added, 'Take my advice. Keep out of McBride's way and don't involve yourself any further.'

James took the words to heart and concentrated, as he had promised his mother, on his work and his studies for his final solicitor's examination. In spite of his good resolution, however, he could not dismiss Richard's quest for his daughter from his mind. He remembered McBride's connection with the Fenians and Lizzie's remark that he had got 'his own people' involved in the search. McBride obviously had more to hide than the origin of his adopted daughter, and James worried that his determination to stifle any investigation into his affairs might put Richard in danger.

A week passed without Richard's return, or any news of him. James was surprised, but concluded that he must have found some clues about Angelina's whereabouts, which he was following up. He hoped that it might be true, but logic told him that if she had not been found by now the likelihood was that she was either dead or in the hands of some unscrupulous person who was concealing her for his own ends.

Before long, however, something occurred that took his mind off both his studies and Angelina's fate. He returned home one evening to find his mother dressed for entertaining guests and looking brighter than he had seen her for some time.

'James, you will never guess who came to call on me this afternoon.'

'Who, Mama?'

'Felicity Forsyth and her daughter Prudence.'

'Yes?' He was at a loss to understand why this should be a cause for excitement.

'You must remember Prue Forsyth! You went to dancing classes with her when you were both children.'

'Oh yes, vaguely.' He recalled a plump, rather ungainly girl with unruly dark plaits and a tendency to spots.

'She has been away in Switzerland, being "finished", and has just got back. You would never believe the transformation in that girl! She has turned into a real beauty.'

James's heart sank. This was a familiar scenario. For the last two years his mother had been at pains to introduce him to a series of young women, whom she regarded as suitable potential wives for a rising young solicitor. Even before he met May, he had rebelled at the idea of having possible mates presented to him, and he had never felt any real attraction to any of them. They were, by and large, girls he had grown up with from families he had known since childhood and he had never experienced the excitement of meeting someone new and different – or not until he chanced to encounter a milliner's apprentice called May Lavender. What it was that enchanted him he had never quite been able to analyse. Perhaps it was her innocence of all the flirtatious mannerisms that more sophisticated young women used, almost by instinct. Perhaps it was her open-eyed wonder at every new experience. He could show her things and teach her things that were simply a matter of boring familiarity to the other girls he knew. More than anything, it was her fierce courage, which overcame her natural timidity when faced with any injustice or threat to those she loved. The combination of all these had stirred his heart in a way no other woman had ever done and made him prepared to face the disapproval of society and follow her to the other side of the world. It was only his concern for his mother, in her weak state of health, that had so far prevented him.

Mrs Breckenridge had made it clear from the start that she did not regard May as a suitable consort. James had the impression that when she had learned about how, largely as a result of her interference, May had decided to emigrate, she had felt that the threat was over, and for a while he had been spared her efforts to marry him off. Now it seemed it was all starting up again.

'Really?' He responded to her enthusiastic description in a tone as dismissive as he could contrive.

His mother was not to be put off. 'Now that she is back, her parents have decided it is time she came out. So they are organising a ball for her debut. It is to be quite a grand affair, and, of course, you are invited.'

James sighed. 'Really, Mama, I would rather not. I –' he thought of the only excuse that might carry some weight with her '– I can't spare the time away from my studies.'

'Rubbish! You spent quite enough time on that wild goose chase after little Angelina McBride. You can spare one evening to meet friends and see some society. You are becoming quite a recluse. Besides, the Forsyths will be most insulted if you refuse the invitation.'

James looked at her and saw how important this was and how the prospect had given her new energy. 'Very well,

Mama. I suppose I can spare one evening. You will have been invited too, of course?'

'Oh yes, but I have explained that I am not strong enough for anything of that sort. You must represent us both, and come home and describe it all to me. I shall look forward to that.'

So when the official invitation arrived, for the following Saturday week, James had no option but to accept.

Richard Kean had no difficulty in identifying the Convent of the Faithful Followers of Jesus from what Lizzie Findlay had told him, and on the evening following his parting from James, he drew up in a hired gig outside the main doors of The Laurels. When a lay sister opened the door he doffed his hat and proffered his card.

'I apologise for calling so late in the day, but I should greatly appreciate it if I could speak to your Mother Superior, or whoever is the senior person in charge of this convent.'

'May I ask what your business is with Reverend Mother?'

'It is a personal matter, concerning my daughter.'

'Please come in. I will ask Reverend Mother if she is at leisure to speak with you.'

After a short wait, Richard was shown up to Mother Mary Benedicta's office. She greeted him with her usual grave courtesy.

'You wish to speak to me about your daughter, I understand. Do you wish to enrol her as one of our pupils?'

'No, ma'am. I am afraid I may have slightly misled the sister who let me in. I am here to enquire about Angelina McBride, whom I believe to be my daughter.'

Mary Benedicta frowned. 'What grounds do you have for believing that?'

Briefly, Richard explained the circumstances that had led him to abandon his baby daughter at the gates of the workhouse. 'It is a story which does me no credit, I admit. My only excuse is that I was driven by necessity. But now I wish to make up for my previous neglect and give my daughter the loving home I believe she has been denied up to now.'

The Reverend Mother's eyebrows shot up. 'What makes you think that?'

'I have made enquiries in Liverpool about the people who adopted her and I have good grounds for thinking that she has not been well treated. The fact that she chose to run away, rather than return home, suggests to me that her fear of her adopted father was stronger than her fear of what might befall her, alone and unprotected, on the road. Please can you tell me what progress has been made in the search for her?'

Mary Benedicta folded her hands on the desk in front of her. 'Mr Kean, can you give me any proof that Angelina is, in fact, your daughter?'

Richard sighed and shook his head. 'So far, I must admit, the evidence is circumstantial, at best. I am hoping that if I can just see her I shall know.'

The Reverend Mother rose to her feet. 'I am sorry, Mr Kean, but under the circumstances I cannot discuss Angelina with you. You have told me a very touching story, but without concrete proof I must continue to regard Mr McBride as Angelina's legitimate guardian. I bid you good evening.'

Richard rose also. 'Can you not at least tell me if there has been any news of her?'

A glint of suspicion narrowed the nun's eyes. 'You are not from the newspapers, are you?'

'No! No, please believe me, my story is true. I am only concerned with my … with Angelina's welfare.'

Mary Benedicta's expression was austere. 'And I have explained that without proof I cannot tell you anymore. Good evening, Mr Kean.'

Richard saw that there was no point in continuing the conversation and took his leave.

As the lay sister was escorting him to the door, she remarked, 'I'm sure your daughter will be very happy here if you decide to entrust her to us. All our girls are really well-behaved and do extremely well.'

'I hope so,' Richard said, 'but I understand you have had one instance where a girl apparently was not happy here. Did I not hear that she had run away?'

'Ah!' the sister sighed deeply. 'Poor little thing. It's a tragedy, so it is. Such a beautiful child, and such a voice! You should have heard her sing.'

'Sing?'

'The voice of an angel, no less. But there, sometimes I think the angels wanted her for the heavenly choir, so they took her to themselves.'

Richard looked at her sharply. 'You think she's dead?'

The sister crossed herself. 'We must pray not. But if the worst comes to the worst it's a comfort to think of her sitting at the feet of Our Saviour and Him delighting in the sound of that pure, innocent voice.'

Richard drove back into the town in a sombre mood. Angelina had now been missing for several weeks and he had to face the fact that if she had not been found the outlook was grim indeed. It was too late to pursue his enquiries any further that night, so he took a room in a local hotel and spent a night haunted by images of the terrible fate that might have befallen his daughter.

First thing next morning, he sought out a small shop that offered engraving and printing services. A remark by Mother Mary Benedicta had given him an idea, which would save him from having to go over the wretched details again and again of how he had lost touch with his daughter. By the expedient of offering twice the normal fee, he succeeded within the hour in possessing a batch of business cards. He then made his way to the police station and asked to see the officer in charge of the investigation into Angelina's disappearance.

'Good morning,' he began when he was shown into a small, dingy office, offering one of the new cards. 'My name is Kean. I work for the *Liverpool Echo*. My editor has sent me over to enquire into the disappearance of Angelina McBride. I wonder if you could tell me how the investigation is progressing?'

The inspector, a thin-faced man with a lugubrious expression, regarded him with evident suspicion. 'What's your paper's interest in this?'

'I don't know if you are aware that her father, or her adoptive father rather, is a highly respected businessman in the city. The disappearance of his daughter has aroused considerable curiosity. Do you have any idea where she might be?'

'Dead in a ditch somewhere, most likely,' was the chilling response.

'But you have not found a body?'

'No. And we're not likely to. There's miles of countryside with not a living soul around. She could be anywhere.'

'But you have searched?' Richard persisted.

'Oh, we've searched all right. We've searched every back alley in Limerick and every barn and outhouse within five miles. My officers have trudged along every road leading away from the convent and knocked at every inhabited house. There's been neither sight nor sound of her. You can tell your readers that there's not a stone that hasn't been turned or a blade of grass that hasn't been lifted. They've no reason to think otherwise.'

'I'm sure they haven't,' Richard said. He rose heavily to his feet. 'Thank you, Inspector. I'll wish you good morning.' He paused. 'One more thing. Can you confirm the actual date of her disappearance?'

The inspector rummaged through some papers on his desk. 'May thirty-first. Sunday.'

His next call was to the office of the local newspaper. The editor was flattered that such a respected paper as the *Echo* should be taking a sufficient interest to send one of their own men to report on the affair, but could offer no further news.

'My paper might be prepared to offer a reward for information,' Richard suggested. 'Do you think that might produce a result?'

'It might,' the editor agreed. 'It might indeed.'

Richard mentioned a sum that was within his means, just, and large enough, he hoped, to encourage someone to come forward, and arranged that anyone with information should contact him at his hotel.

He spent the rest of the day tramping the streets of Limerick, knocking on doors and stopping passers-by. He concentrated on the narrow lanes and alleys of the old medieval city, shocked to find a degree of poverty and filth that surpassed even the mean streets of Liverpool. No one had seen a small girl wandering on her own. No one recalled a child of her description begging or attempting to steal food. He returned to his hotel thoroughly dispirited.

It occurred to him that she might have tried to stow away on one of the many vessels plying in and out of the harbour. From the harbour master he obtained a list of ships that had docked at Limerick around the 31st of May. All had sailed, for ports all over the world, and he realised with a heavy heart that is she had managed to slip aboard his chances of finding her were nil. Nevertheless, he haunted the docks for several days, questioning sailors and fishermen, with no result.

Next day he transferred his attentions to the new suburb of Newtown Pery. What a contrast he found here, among the elegant Georgian mansions situated in the squares and crescents. Here a knock at the door was answered by a butler or a parlourmaid, but no one had seen an unaccompanied child. No such child had asked for charity, or a job in the household.

The following morning he purchased a large-scale map of the area and a pair of compasses. In his room he spread the map and drew a circle five miles in diameter. How far could a nine year old walk in a day? he asked himself. How long could a child survive without food?

He hired the gig again and over the following days he traversed the roads leading away from the town in every direction. Limerick was a busy port and roads led to it from everywhere in Ireland. It was impossible to know which way Angelina's wanderings might have taken her. At first he followed the turnpike roads, west towards Shannon, north towards Parteen, east towards Annacotty and south towards St Patrickswell. Then he tried all the country lanes. The land was fertile. In some areas, fields of wheat were turning gold ready for harvest and cows grazed in rich pasture, but elsewhere he found empty cottages, neglected gardens and vacant pens, which had once held livestock. From time to time he came to large estates surrounding solidly built manor houses, and at each he stopped and asked the same questions, but at each he received the same answer. No one remembered seeing a little girl with golden hair.

He lay awake at night, wondering how it was possible that there was no trace of her somewhere within the circle he had drawn. The only solution was that she had somehow found her way further afield and he needed to extend his search; but to have gone so far she must have had transport of some kind. Berating himself for a fool, he made his way to the railway station. No one had seen Angelina there, either, and he was assured that it would have been impossible for her to board a train without first purchasing a ticket. There was a chance, he thought, that she might have slipped past the porters and the guard and stowed away, but if that was the answer his quest was hopeless. She could be anywhere in Ireland by now. He made enquiries about other forms of transport. Since the arrival of the railway there had been no regular coach service out of the city but there were various carters who carried goods to and from nearby villages. He tracked down as many as he could find but drew a blank. As the days passed he became increasingly despondent, and the police inspector's off-hand 'dead in a ditch somewhere' haunted his waking thoughts and troubled his dreams. In spite of all this, he stuck to his determination that he would go on searching until either he found his daughter, or had definitive proof that she was dead.

Sixteen

Richard made the convent the centre of his wanderings, since this must have been Angelina's starting point, and one day, driving slowly back towards the town and his hotel, he glanced across the fields and saw the roof of a house among the trees. There was a stile in the wall and a path leading across the field. He stopped the pony and got out. Why had he never noticed that before? If someone wished to avoid the outskirts of the town it was the obvious route. He tied the pony to a nearby tree and set off across the field. The house was off the beaten track and as he came closer he realised that, although he thought he had asked at every house in the area, he had never called there before.

When he knocked at the door, the parlourmaid denied all knowledge of a wandering child, but she carried his reporter's card in to her mistress and he was admitted. In answer to his usual questions he got the usual denials, but in a desperate last throw he said, 'Is it possible that one of your people might, perhaps unknowingly, have carried her to another town or village? I presume you keep a carriage and maybe a small trap, for visits to market and so forth.'

'Naturally,' the lady of the house responded, 'but I fail to see how the girl you are looking for could have got into one without anyone seeing her. But if you wish I can send for my coachman and you can ask him yourself.' She rang the bell and told the maid to fetch Michael.

In the room with the mistress of the house were two young ladies, who were introduced as her daughters. While they waited for the coachman one of them said, 'When did the little girl leave the convent?'

Richard named the date.

'Mama, wasn't that the day after Julia's party?'

'Yes. What of it?'

'I just thought, Michael brought the carriage to collect us that morning. Is it possible the little girl might have hidden inside?'

'I should hardly think so. I'm sure Michael would have seen her.'

At that moment the coachman appeared, looking a trifle apprehensive. 'You sent for me, ma'am?'

'Michael, do you recall fetching my daughters from Lady Astbury's after her party?'

'Yes, ma'am.'

'Did you, by any chance, take a young girl with you?'

'A girl, ma'am?' The man looked in equal measures anxious and offended. 'What young girl would that be?'

'Please don't disturb yourself,' Richard interposed. 'I am only seeking information about a little girl who ran away from the convent in Limerick. Did you, by any chance, come across a fair-haired child on your journey that morning?'

'A child, you say?'

'She's about nine years old.'

'Well?' his mistress prompted sharply.

'No, ma'am. I never saw any child that morning.'

'Is the coach house locked up at night?' Richard asked.

'No, sir. It can't be. It's just an open shelter.'

'So could a child have crept in there and hidden inside the carriage?'

'It's possible, I suppose.'

'But, Michael,' the lady of the house said, 'surely before setting out to collect my daughters you would have swept the carriage out, to make sure it was in a proper condition for them.'

The coachman looked embarrassed. 'It was an early start, ma'am. And I'd cleaned it the day before, to take the young ladies to the party, so I didn't see any need to do it again.'

'So a child could have hidden there, and you would not necessarily have seen her?' Richard said eagerly.

''S'possible, I suppose,' the man answered.

'But when you arrived at Lady Astbury's. Surely you would have seen her then?'

'Might not have done, ma'am. See, the ladies were not quite ready to leave, so I was told to take the carriage round to the yard and while I waited I stepped into the kitchen for a cup of tea.'

'So it is possible!' the daughter exclaimed, delighted at seeing her theory supported.

'It does seem so,' Richard agreed. 'Would you be so kind as to tell me where Lady Astbury resides?'

'At Palgrave Hall just outside Dooneen Bridge. It's about six miles away in the direction of Bruff.'

Richard thanked the ladies profusely and made a point of remarking that obviously no blame attached itself to Michael. Then he took his leave and walked back to where he had left his gig. An hour later he drew up outside the crenelated frontage of Palgrave Hall and asked to speak to the master or mistress. He was shown into an over-furnished drawing room where a fire was burning in the hearth in spite of the summer warmth. A thin-faced woman in middle age was reclining on a chaise longue.

'Sally says you are from the newspaper. What do you want with me?'

Richard explained his quest and added, 'I have been told that there was a party here on the day before the girl was discovered missing. I believe it is possible that she may have hidden herself in a carriage, which was sent to collect some of your guests the following morning. She would have been very hungry by then, I imagine. I was wondering if she might have asked here for food or shelter.'

The woman raised herself up on the chaise as if he had suggested something improper. 'If she did, she would have got short shrift, I can tell you. Lord Astbury and I do not hold with beggars.'

Richard bit back a cutting response. 'She was not, strictly speaking, a beggar. Just a helpless child looking for charity.'

'A child who, according to you, had run away from a place where she would have been cared for. It was an act of foolish disobedience for which she must take the consequences. I'll bid you good day, Mr Kean. Phoebe will see you out.'

As they reached the front door, the parlourmaid turned to him and said in a low voice, 'I didn't want to speak in front of the mistress, but I think I did see the little girl.'

'You saw her?' Richard's pulse leapt in response to this first real clue.

'The young ladies who had stayed here for the party didn't feel up to eating much breakfast, so I took the leavings back to the kitchen. When I got there Cook was just about to turn her away. A pretty little thing with fair hair?'

'Yes! Yes, that would be her. How did she look?'

'I only saw her for a moment. A bit … shabby. Dusty like and her hair all unbrushed. I think her dress was torn. Cook thought she was a gypsy child, but I said afterwards I never saw a gypsy with hair that colour.'

'You said Cook was about to turn her away. Did she?'

'She was going to. Like the mistress said, her and his Lordship don't hold with beggars and he'd like as not set the dogs on her if he saw her. But when Cook saw how much was left from the ladies' breakfast it made her angry to see good food going to waste. So she took an egg and some bread and gave them to the child, and told her to get out of the way sharp.'

'Thank heaven!' Richard said. 'And thank you for telling me. I don't suppose you have any idea where she went after that?'

The maid shook her head. 'I went back inside. She must have gone back out onto the road, I suppose, but I can't say for sure.'

Richard reached into his pocket for a coin. 'Thank you very much for your help – and please thank Cook for me, for her act of charity.'

'I don't know about charity,' the girl said with a shrug. 'More like cocking a snook at the gentry, if you'll pardon the expression. Anyway, I hope you find the little girl. Good luck.'

Back on the road Richard paused for a moment. The evening was far advanced and even in mid-summer it would be dark before long. Reluctantly, he turned back towards Limerick.

Next morning found him once again outside Palgrave Hall. There was only one road. Westward, it led back the way he had come. He headed east.

Some four or five miles further on he saw what he took to be a gypsy encampment a little way off the road. These people, he reasoned, would know the land round about very well and would certainly have noticed a strange child wandering about. He tied the pony to a tree and walked towards the caravan at the centre of the camp. Two women and a girl were sitting by the ashes of a fire, the younger woman cradling a baby and the others occupied in weaving baskets. A dog hurtled out from under the caravan, barking, and was called off by the older woman. She set down her basket and looked at him, her gaze not hostile but calmly assessing.

'What can we do for you, sir?'

Richard took off his hat. 'I am hoping you can help me. I am looking for a child, a young girl of nine years with very fair hair. She might have passed this way a few weeks ago. I thought you might have seen her.'

The woman looked at the other two and said something in a language he did not understand, and the girl got up and disappeared round the caravan.

'A young girl, is it?' The woman turned her attention to Richard. 'Fair haired, you said?'

'Yes. Have you seen her?'

The woman looked at her companion. 'Didn't we see a child on the road, would be about that long ago?'

The younger woman nodded. 'We did, so.'

'You saw her? What happened?'

'I called out to her, but the dog frightened her and she ran off. I thought she must have folks nearby. Do you mean to tell me she was on her own?'

'Yes, I'm afraid so.'

'How did that come about then?'

'She ran away from the convent where she was being educated.'

'And you are searching for her. What is she to you?'

'I'm a newspaper reporter from Liverpool. The child's ... her family live there and there is a good deal of interest in what has happened to her.'

The woman studied his face for a long moment. 'Is that so?'

'Yes.' He looked back at the road. 'She ran off, you say? That way?' He pointed in the direction he had been heading.

'Aye, that way.'

'Is there a town or a village in that direction?'

'Aye, Meanus. It's a couple of miles further on.'

'Perhaps she found shelter there. I shall go and ask. Thank you for your help.'

He turned to go but the woman rose to her feet and detained him with a hand on his arm.

'I was watching you come along the road. I'm afraid your pony is going lame.'

'Is it? I hadn't noticed anything. I'm afraid I don't know much about horses.'

'Oh, I definitely thought she was walking short, like something was hurting her. Here's my man, now. Would you like him to take a look? There's nothing he doesn't know about horses.'

A tall, rather swarthy man had appeared from somewhere beyond the caravan. The woman spoke to him in their own language and he nodded.

'Lame, is she? Will I take a look at her?'

'If it isn't too much trouble,' Richard said. 'I'd be grateful for your advice.'

They walked over to the gig and the man felt carefully down each of the pony's legs, murmuring to her as he did so. Then he picked up each foot in turn and examined it. As he did so, two younger men on horseback appeared from the field behind the caravan and set off down the road at a smart canter. The gypsy produced a knife and flicked something out of the pony's hoof.

'There! That might have been the trouble. Just a little stone. Walk her up and down a bit and let's have a look.'

Richard did as he said and he watched critically, pursing his lips. Richard had to walk the pony past him several times before he pronounced himself satisfied.

'She'll do, but take it gently for the rest of the way. She may still be a bit sore and I'm not sure that that was the root of the problem. You don't want her letting you down in the middle of nowhere, now do you?'

'No, of course not. I'll go slowly until I get to Meanus. Perhaps I can put up there for the night and give her a chance to rest.'

'Oh aye, there's an inn in Meanus. You'll be welcome there.'

'Well, I'm really grateful to you.' Richard put his hand in his pocket hesitantly. 'I'm not sure ...'

The man made a gesture of denial. 'No need, no need. I'm happy to help a fellow traveller.'

Richard mounted the gig, thanked the gypsy again and set off at a walk. It was hard to maintain the slow pace, because now he seemed to have picked up a definite scent he was eager to pursue it, but he reminded himself that he needed the pony to be fit for the rest of the quest, wherever that might take him, and forced himself to rein in. Halfway there, the two young horsemen passed him, heading back in the other direction.

Meanus was a poor sort of place; a cluster of thatched-roofed cottages round a cross-road with an inn at the junction. Richard drove the length of the main street, looking for someone who might give him information. An old man, squatting on his doorstep, took his pipe out of his mouth, spat and turned away without answering. Two women, gossiping over a garden fence, separated and went indoors as he approached. There seemed to be no one else about and, as it was past midday, he returned to the inn, tied the pony up outside and went in. The single room was empty except for a woman behind the table that served as a bar and two old men hunched over a game of drafts in one corner. The woman looked at him and he read hostility in her expression.

'Good evening.' Richard made his tone as emollient as possible. 'I wonder if you can help me. I'm looking for a little girl who is missing. I'm told she was seen heading in this direction.'

The woman shrugged and turned her head away, then called over her shoulder in her own language. One of the old men got up and went out. Another man, the landlord, Richard guessed, came out of a back room.

'What can I do for you?'

Richard repeated his request.

'You're an Englishman, by your speech,' the landlord commented.

Richard agreed that he was.

'And this child your looking for, would she be English too?'

'Yes, but what difference does it make? She's a child in need of help, whatever country she belongs to.'

'Aye, aye. I'm just trying to get the full picture. So what is she to you, that you're searching for her?'

Richard produced his card and told his usual fiction.

'The newspapers, is it?' The landlord studied the card with interest. 'Well, well, who'd have thought the English papers would take such an interest.'

'The child is from Liverpool. She was sent here to be educated at a convent school. Her ... her family are under-standably worried about her.'

'Oh, aye, aye. They would be, of course.'

Richard was beginning to lose patience. It almost felt as if the man was deliberately spinning the conversation out. 'So have you seen her?'

'Seen her? No, no. There's been no sight nor sound of her here.'

Richard let out a sigh of exasperation, then pulled himself together and forced himself to speak quietly.

'Do you think anyone else in the village might have seen her? Would someone perhaps have taken her into their home?'

The landlord pursed his lips and shook his head. 'No. If they had I'd be sure to have heard. Not much happens hereabouts that doesn't get talked about in here of an evening.'

'Do most of the local people come in here in the evening?'

'Aye, most of them.'

'Perhaps I could ask around then.

'You could, but I think you'll not learn much.'

Richard pulled out his watch. There was no point in driving back to Limerick now he had come this far, and there was the pony to think of. 'Can you put me up for the night?'

'Aye, there's a bed you can have.'

'I'll take a pint of your best brew – and something to eat perhaps?'

The man spoke to the woman, his wife Richard assumed, in their own tongue, and she nodded and went off into the back room. Richard took his beer and added, 'My gig is outside. The pony needs feeding and watering.'

'I'll send the boy to see to him.'

There seemed to be nothing else to be done, so Richard took his beer and sat down in a corner of the room. He tried to engage the old man in conversation but got only a blank stare in response. The woman brought him bread and cheese and when he had eaten it he wandered outside again.

The village seemed to be deserted, so he walked along the crossing road for some distance. Men were working in the fields, but they were too far away for him to engage them in conversation and he sensed that if he tried they

238

would resent his interruption. Depressed after the brief optimism of earlier, he made his way back to the inn and ordered another pint of beer.

The sun sank lower and at last people began to arrive, singly and in small groups, the men still in their working clothes, the women in shabby dresses with aprons. They glanced at Richard as they came in, but no one spoke to him, so when half a dozen or so were gathered he went over to them and asked his usual question. He was met with shrugs and shaken heads, but there was something in the looks that passed between them that made him uneasy. Returning to his seat, he reflected that what he was seeing was probably a general distrust and hostility to an English stranger, and knowing what he did about the tragedy of the famine, which was still fresh in people's minds, and the part his fellow countrymen had played in it, that was not surprising.

He was given a dish of greasy stew, containing some unidentified meat, which he suspected might be goat. By the time he had eaten it, the room was filling up, and the sound of voices grew louder as the pots of ale were emptied. At one point one voice was raised drunkenly above the rest.

'Where's the fiddler then and the little song thrush? Are we not to have any music tonight?'

Someone near him growled a reply and the man looked across at Richard and subsided, looking uncomfortable.

Richard began to wish that he had set off back to Limerick and sought a night's lodging somewhere else along the way. He was about to retire to bed when he heard hoof beats and the jingle of harness outside the door and two men came in. It was obvious from their appearance that they came from a different strata of society than the labouring men who filled the room. They wore tweed jackets and their breeches and boots were better cut and of better fabric. Also, there was something in their manner that suggested a degree of authority and, though they were obviously known to the locals, they were greeted with respect tempered, Richard thought, with a certain reserve.

The older of the two spoke briefly to the landlord and then came over to where Richard was sitting.

'I'm told you are looking for a small girl? Is that right?' His pleasant manner was a relief after the way he had been treated up to that moment.

'Yes.' Richard responded eagerly. 'Do you have any knowledge of her?'

'I think we do,' the man replied. 'Paddy here picked up a girl on the road a couple of weeks back and took her into Bruff.'

Richard's pulse quickened. 'He did? That's wonderful news. What happened when he got her to Bruff?'

'She was taken to a place where she could be looked after. We can show you where if you come with us tomorrow.'

'I can't tell you how glad I am to hear that! Thank you so much.' He half rose from his seat. 'Couldn't we go straight away?'

His companion smiled. 'It's a touch late to be setting out now. It will be dark before long. You've taken a room here, I think?'

'Yes.'

'Get a good night's sleep and we'll be on our way first thing tomorrow.'

'Are you staying in the inn tonight?'

'No. We've friends nearby who will give us a bed for the night. I'll wish you goodnight and see you in the morning.'

'Thank you. Oh, I don't know your name. I'm Richard Kean.'

'The name's Liam Doherty. Just call me Liam.'

'Thank you, Liam. Goodnight.'

Richard went to bed in a tumult of emotions. His long search was almost over and tomorrow he would see the daughter he so much longed to find – the daughter he had abandoned all those years ago.

And that thought cooled the joy of anticipation.

How would she receive him? Would she even believe that he was her father? He had no way of proving it. And if she did believe him, would she not blame him for all that she had suffered? Rather than a happy reunion, should he not expect bitter recriminations and hostility? He told himself that he must have patience; that eventually by kindness and understanding he would break down the barriers and teach her to love him. It was all he could hope for. On that thought, he fell asleep and slept surprisingly soundly, in spite of the fact that he found evidence in the morning that he had shared his bed with some unwelcome occupants.

There was only dry bread and some hard cheese for breakfast, but he choked it down without tasting it and was just settling his bill with the landlord when his friend from the night before arrived to collect him. A four-wheeled dog cart was drawn up outside the inn, with the man referred to as Paddy holding the reins.

'Hop in, and we'll be there in no time,' Liam said.

Richard was about to comply when a sudden thought halted him. 'I have a hired gig in the stables. It would be better if I followed you in that.'

'Oh, don't worry about that,' Liam said easily. 'I've had a word with the landlord. Your pony is lame, I'm told. You can pick it up on your way back, with the little girl. That will give the animal a chance to recover.'

That seemed the best plan, so Richard climbed into the dog cart and they set off.

'So you're a newspaper man?' Liam said. 'All the way from Liverpool.'

'That's right.'

'I'm surprised your editor is interested enough to send you all this way.'

'He is a personal friend of the child's father – her adoptive father, that is.' Richard felt a need to embroider his rather bald narrative.

'Is that so? And I'm told the paper is offering a reward for anyone who can discover her whereabouts.'

Enlightenment dawned. So this was why these two had come to find him. Some rumour must have reached them that he was in Meanus and making enquiries. Well, their motives were not important as long as they took him to Angelina.

'That's correct,' he said. 'And I'm sure the paper will be happy to give you the sum mentioned, to share with your friend.' He indicated to the taciturn Paddy.

'Ah, well, I won't say it won't be welcome –' Liam smiled '– but that wasn't our first thought, you know.'

'Of course not,' Richard murmured.

Bruff was a substantial town built along a river, which Liam informed Richard in English was called the Morning Star. Somewhat to his surprise they rattled straight through the high street and came to a stop outside a small, solidly built house set by itself on the river bank. From the look of it, he guessed, it had once been a mill.

'Is this where she is?' he asked.

'Come on in,' Liam said, jumping down from the cart.

Richard followed him inside, his heart thumping against his ribs. He would see her at any minute. Would he recognise her? Would she know him?

Liam led him into a back room. It was almost unfurnished, except for a deal table and a couple of chairs. The windows were small and high up, so that the room was gloomy in spite of the bright sunlight outside, and there was dirty straw on the floor. There was no one there.

Richard looked round. 'Is this where you brought her? Where is she?'

The expression of friendly good humour had vanished from Liam's face, as completely as if he had discarded a mask. Paddy, uncommunicative as ever, closed the door and set his back against it. Liam took one of the chairs and set it in the centre of the room.

'Sit there.'

'Why?' With a shock like a blow to the stomach, Richard realised that he had been the victim of a cruel deception.

'Sit!' Liam repeated, moving closer.

Richard looked from him to Paddy and contemplated punching him in the face and trying to make a run for it.

One glance at the immoveable bulk in front of the door told him that it would be useless. His only recourse was to try to talk himself out the situation. He sat, as ordered.

'Look, I don't know what you want with me. It's clear you haven't got my ... the little girl I'm looking for. Why have you done this?'

'I'll ask the questions,' Liam said. 'Now, tell me the truth. What brings you here?'

'I've told you. My newspaper sent me.'

'That's a lie for a start. I've friends in Liverpool and they tell me that the editor of the *Liverpool Echo* has never heard of you, and certainly never sent a reporter over here. So, what are you after?'

Richard struggled to bring his mind to bear. The disappointment, after being on the threshold of meeting Angelina at long last, was like a stone in his chest, making it hard to think coherently. But one fact emerged from the maelstrom.

'You've communicated with someone in Liverpool? You must have been following me for several days at least.'

'Oh yes, we've been keeping an eye on you, watching you snooping around. What I want to know is, what are you really looking for?'

'I'm looking for the child. All right, I'm not a reporter. I'll admit that was a fiction. But the rest is true.'

'Oh yes? And why would you be so concerned about a missing girl?'

'Because she's my daughter!'

'Ah, now we're coming to it. We were warned that would be the story.'

'What do you mean? Who warned you?'

'Oh, I've told you, we've friends in Liverpool. We were told you were coming and what the story would be. We've been watching you ever since you got off the boat.'

'I don't understand. Watching me? Why? What do you think I'm looking for?'

'That's the whole question, isn't it? What are you looking for? Let's stop beating about the bush. You're a British spy, sent here by the government.'

'I'm what?' Richard almost laughed aloud at the ridiculousness of the accusation.

'Don't play the innocent with me! Who sent you? And what are you looking for?'

'Nobody sent me. I came to look for my daughter.'

'This imaginary child you keep talking about. How much of a fool do you think I am?'

'She's not imaginary! Ask the Mother Superior at the Convent of the Faithful Companions of Jesus if you don't believe me. She will tell you that a child called Angelina McBride ran away at the end of May and has never been found.'

'McBride, is it?'

The name seemed to hold some significance for Liam. Richard pressed on. 'The McBrides adopted her from the workhouse in Liverpool and they sent her to the convent because she was becoming an embarrassment to them. They didn't want anyone to find out about her origins.'

Liam looked at him with a frown. 'And you say you are her father? Can you prove it?'

Richard shook head reluctantly. 'I can tell you why I think she is my daughter, but at the moment I have no proof.'

'So tell me.'

Once more Richard related the humiliating details of how he had abandoned his daughter.

Liam listened in silence, then he produced a sardonic grin. 'It's a good cover story. Now let's have the real one. You're a British spy and you've been sent here to find out what we are planning. I want to know how much you've discovered.'

'What do you mean by "we"? Who are you?'

The question was answered by a stinging open-handed blow to his face, which almost knocked him off his chair. 'Don't give me that! You'll be trying to tell me next you've never heard of the Fenians.'

'Fenians!' Richard pulled himself upright. 'Is that it? Look, I know nothing about you or your plans. I've lived in South Africa for most of the last seven years. I told you that. I'd never heard of you until a week or two ago.'

A second blow sent him sprawling to the floor. 'You're lying!'

'I'm not!' Richard wiped his hand across his mouth and it came away bloody. He hauled himself into a sitting position. Slowly something was becoming clear.

'Listen to me, just for a moment. Did Connor McBride tell you I was coming? Did he tell you I was a spy?'

'What if he did?'

'He wants his revenge because I am trying to take my daughter back. He has told everyone a pack of lies about her being the child of his deceased brother. I've discovered he never had a brother. I've been looking into his affairs, I admit, but only because I want to prove that Angelina was adopted from the workhouse where I left her. It seems he has other secrets that he doesn't want known and he is afraid I might uncover them. That's why he has told you I've been sent here to spy. He wants me dead and he's hoping you'll do his dirty work for him.'

He saw from Liam's expression that he had sown the seeds of doubt in his mind and pressed his advantage. 'Look, send someone to the convent in Limerick. I told the true story to the Reverend Mother there. I'm sure she will confirm that McBride left his daughter there and she has run away. Ask anyone in Limerick, ask the police or the editor of the paper there. I may have told them a falsehood about the reason for my interest, for shame of my part in the true story, but they will tell you that all my questions have been about the whereabouts of my daughter. It is the only thing that concerns me. You must have seen, last night, how affected I was by the prospect of finding her at last. Do you think I could counterfeit that?'

Liam stood silent for a moment. Then he said something in his own language to Paddy and turned back to Richard.

'There's a convent of the FCJs here in Bruff. If the child went missing from the sister house in Limerick they will certainly have been told. If they confirm your story I might begin to believe you. Meanwhile, you'll stay here, under guard. Don't make any attempt to escape. Even if you got out of the house, we've plenty of friends round here who will be happy to bring you back.' He looked round at Paddy. 'Give him some water and shut him in. Stay on guard. I'll be back shortly.'

He went out and a couple of minutes later a woman brought a bucket and a jug of water and a cracked mug and set them down on the floor. She left and Paddy followed and Richard heard the door shut and bolted after him.

Seventeen

The Donovan family was on the move. Moira and Fergal's tent and the bothy where the boys slept were dismantled and packed on the back of the cart. The campfire was extinguished, the cooking pots and other impedimenta stored in the caravan or hung on hooks on the outside. The horses were rounded up. The three young ones she had watched on her first day with the family were now accustomed to carrying a saddle and would walk, trot and canter to order and jump any obstacle that was put in their way. Leary pronounced them ready for market, along with two others that he had been schooling for some time. Two horses were hitched up to the caravan and another to the cart and the boys mounted up, leading spare horses on long reins. Leary mounted his stallion, and, as always, took the lead.

'Where are we going?' Angelina asked Dervla, as they climbed up onto the seat at the front of the caravan.

'To Buttevant,' was the answer. 'The Cahirmee horse fair starts tomorrow. With any luck we should make some good sales.'

As the cavalcade moved off, Angelina twisted round in her seat to look back at the abandoned campsite, and felt a stab of nostalgia. It was only a matter of weeks since she had found her way there but it had brought about such a change in her life that she almost felt she might have been born there.

Soon, however, her attention was captured by the passing scenery. It was pleasant to rumble down the country lanes at the pace of the plodding horses and her elevated seat gave her a view over walls and hedges. The sun was hot but there was a gentle breeze and the trees along the road provided welcome shade. She settled into her seat with a contented sigh. How much better it was to live like this than any other life she had known!

'What's Buttevant like?' she asked.

'Oh, it's a great place. It's very old and there has been a fair there every year for more years than anyone can remember. The fair field of Cahirmee has been famous in song and story for generations. You wait till you see it.'

It was evening when Dervla pointed ahead with her whip and said, 'Look there, on the hill. That's the ruins of Buttevant Castle.'

Angelina craned her neck and saw through the trees a line of crumbling grey walls and a topless tower. 'It's not like a castle in the stories,' she said, disappointed.

'Oh, it was once, I expect,' Dervla said. 'But there have been many battles fought over it and it shows its scars.'

As they approached the town, Angelina was amazed to see that the road ahead of them was clogged with a slow-moving line of carts and caravans and horses. They joined the end of it and soon she saw Leary riding ahead, calling out greetings to friends. The cavalcade moved slowly through a street lined with old stone houses and she gazed up at the ruined castle on one side and an ancient church on the other.

Eventually they came out at the far end, and there ahead of them was a wide expanse of grass, encircled by a bend in the river and dominated by a large grassy mound. Already the space was dotted with caravans and tents and fires were being lit and horses tethered. Leary led them to a spot not far from the mound and the process of setting up a new camp was begun.

While the women erected the shelters and unpacked the necessary equipment for cooking, Danny and Quinn were sent to fetch firewood and the men took the horses down to the river to drink. Angelina worked alongside Sorcha to prepare the meal and surprisingly quickly everything was in order and they were sitting around the fire to eat. Fergal had come in a couple of days back carrying four birds with handsome plumage, which had been hanging up in the caravan ever since. When Angelina asked what they were and where they came from, he had tapped the side of his nose and told her it was best not to ask questions like that. Now, plucked and gutted by Dervla's expert hands, they roasted on a spit over the fire, giving off a delicious aroma.

As soon as the meal was over, Sorcha and Quinn and Danny begged leave to go and find friends they had not seen since the last fair.

'Maeve can come too,' Danny said.

'I don't know.' Dervla looked doubtful. 'Come here a minute, Maeve.'

Angelina was used to answering to her new name and went to her. Dervla tucked a lock of golden hair under the cap that she always wore now and murmured, 'Your hair's growing. I'll have to cut it again. But at least with the sun you're almost as brown as the rest of us, even though the walnut juice is fading. Well, you'll pass, I suppose. But say as little as possible. Let Sorcha do the talking for you.'

This injunction was hardly necessary. Over the last weeks Angelina had begun to learn the language that the travellers spoke amongst themselves, and she could understand a good deal if people spoke slowly but she was less confident about speaking it.

'Don't worry,' Sorcha said. 'I'll tell everyone she stammers and doesn't like to talk.'

Angelina understood the reason for Dervla's caution, but she was convinced that no one could possibly be looking for her among these people, so she went off happily with the others. They seemed to know everyone in the great gathering of travellers and there was a warm welcome for them at one campfire after another and soon she found herself part of a motley crowd of boys and girls wandering among the caravans and the tethered horses, chattering and exchanging gossip, unfettered by any adult supervision.

Sorcha introduced her, but what she said to explain her presence was lost on Angelina. The other children looked at her curiously, but were friendly enough, and she was happy just to be with the crowd and take in the sights and sounds of the encampment.

Next day, the business of the fair started in earnest. All round the field, horses were being walked and trotted, their legs and teeth examined, bargains being struck. Leary seemed to have plenty of potential buyers and Sorcha told her that he was known 'all over Ireland' for being an honest dealer and having the best-quality animals.

'This place is famous for the horses that are sold here,' she said. 'Leary told me that a very famous general, I think his name was Napoleon, rode a horse that was bought here. There's a painting of him on it somewhere.'

A bystander overheard her. 'That's right enough. Marengo, the horse's name was. And what's more, the Duke of Wellington had a horse that came from here, too.'

They were watching a small group around two of Leary's horses. One was a pretty piebald mare with a long white mane and tail, which would, he declared, make a perfect mount for any lady in the land. Some days earlier he had fitted her with a side-saddle and persuaded Angelina to ride her. She had been nervous at first, but the saddle horn gave her something to hang onto and the mare was, in truth, a very gentle and biddable creature and she soon grew more confident.

Leary called her over. 'Now, gentlemen, I can promise you that this little mare is an ideal mount for a lady, or even for a child, and to prove it I'll put my adopted daughter up on her.'

Before she had time to object Angelina was lifted into the saddle.

'Now, just walk her around and let the gentlemen see how good she is,' Leary instructed.

Bursting with pride at being given such responsibility, she did as she was told, and even risked a short trot. The potential buyer was obviously impressed and the deal was closed with a handshake.

As he lifted her down, Leary said, 'That was well done. We'll make a horsewoman of you yet.'

'You said I was your adopted daughter,' Angelina whispered.

He grinned at her. 'Well, I have to explain you somehow. Do you mind?'

'Oh no. I don't mind at all.'

When they tired of watching the horses, Danny took her off to sample the delights of the rest of the fair. There were jugglers and fire-eaters and games where you had to throw little hoops over pegs or knock down skittles. There was a boxing ring, where a small man with gold rings in his ears was persuading challengers to take on a huge man covered in tattoos. There seemed to be no shortage of young men ready to try their luck, which surprised Angelina, since they all got knocked down very quickly. There were women selling toffee apples and sweetmeats. Leary had given them each a few pennies to spend as they chose, and Angelina used hers to buy toffee apples for herself and Danny. By evening, she was sticky and exhausted and full to the brim with new sights and experiences.

The day was not over, however. Men and women were gathering around a central fire. Bottles and flagons were passed round, and then the music started. Soon Leary was called upon to play and after a couple of jigs he called Angelina to his side.

She was not surprised. After that first evening in the inn at Meanus, they had made several visits, and each time she had been asked to sing and the boys had gone round with the hat. She understood that her singing voice had provided a useful addition to the family income and she was glad to feel that she was able to do something to earn her keep. Leary had been as good as his word and had taught her a number of songs, some of them in his own language, which she had had to learn parrot fashion, but whose melodies lingered in her mind long after the lesson had finished.

Tonight was a little different. The audience was much larger and she felt a little shy, but as always once she started to sing her confidence grew. It was good to hear how the hubbub of voices quietened and people turned to see where the sound was coming from and drew closer to listen. That night Leary did not ask for tips when she had finished.

Next day, Sorcha was sent into the town to buy some essential items and Angelina went with her. In several of the shop windows and pasted to walls there were brightly coloured playbills.

'Oh look!' Angelina said, tugging Sorcha's arm.

'What does it say?'

It had come as a shock to Angelina to discover that neither Sorcha nor Danny nor Quinn could read. She was fairly sure Leary could, but had no reason to believe that Dervla or Moira had learned. Questions about when or where the younger members of the family might go to school were met with laughter.

'It says, "FINNEGAN'S MUSIC HALL" and there is a list of people doing things, with their pictures.'

'What sort of things?'

'Well, there's a comedian – that's a man who makes jokes, isn't it? And a man and a woman who sing duets, and a performing dog – I wonder what he does? – and some people who do acrobatic dancing, and an ill–ill–illusionist. I don't know what that is.'

'When is it happening?'

'Tonight and tomorrow. In the theatre here. Do you think we could watch?'

'I don't know. I'll ask Leary.'

Back at the camp there was a brief discussion and then Leary agreed that they could all go that evening. They had to queue up to get in and Angelina was afraid that there might not be room, but they all packed in somehow.

The room was hot and there was a cloud of tobacco smoke, which made it hard to see across to where a slightly grubby curtain hid the stage. For a few minutes Angelina regretted that she had ever noticed the playbill and wished that they were all back in the field sitting round the campfire.

But then the curtain was rather shakily drawn aside and a new and magical world was revealed. There was a painted backcloth that was meant to look like a forest glade, and coloured footlights that bathed the stage in a warm glow. A large man with magnificent whiskers came on and told several jokes which she did not understand, but which made most of the audience laugh very loudly.

Then the man and woman, whose pictures were on the bill, came on and sang a love duet. She liked the man's voice but was not so impressed with the lady's; but she had to admit that she looked very beautiful and wore a lovely dress.

The performing dog was sweet and clever and the illusionist, which Dervla said was another word for a conjuror, performed tricks that made the audience gasp.

But it was the dancers that she liked best. The girl could bend her body into amazing contortions and the man picked her up and threw her around as if she weighed nothing at all. They appeared twice, and the second time they danced more gracefully and wore the most beautiful costumes.

On the way back to the caravan she walked as if in a dream, still half in and half out of a different world.

Next afternoon, she was surprised to see Leary deep in conversation with the man with the whiskers. After a while he called her over.

'This is Maeve, Mr Finnegan. Maeve, will you sing for the gentleman?'

'Now?'

'Does it make a difference what the time of day is?'

'No. But you haven't got your fiddle.'

'You don't need me to accompany you. Sing that song you first sang when you came to us: "The Last Rose of Summer".'

It seemed strange to burst into song in the middle of the field, while men and women were going about their every-day business, but she wanted to please Leary, so she sang. The man with the whiskers clasped his hands and raised his eyes heavenward, 'The voice of an angel, no less!'

'Isn't it, though,' Leary agreed. He smiled at her. 'Thank you, lass. That will do for now. I just wanted Mr Finnegan to hear you, and he'll be too busy with his own show to join us tonight.'

Later that day she saw Leary in earnest discussion with Dervla. It looked like an argument, which was unusual, but whatever it was about she finally seemed to give way.

The following day was the last day of the fair. Already some of the caravans were being loaded and tents packed away. There were fewer horses about, too. Leary had sold all those he intended to and was well pleased. Angelina joined Danny and Quinn as they made the rounds to say goodbye to their friends.

Around midday, Mr Finnegan appeared again and sat with Leary in the shade of the bothy and after some discussion she saw them shake hands, as if he had agreed to buy one of Leary's horses – except that he had not been anywhere near a horse, as far as she could see.

Leary called her over and she assumed he wanted her to sing again. Instead, Finnegan took her by the hand and drew her close to where he was sitting.

'Tell me, how would you like to be a grand lady?'

'I don't know what you mean.' She tried to withdraw her hand but he held onto it.

'How would you like to have your own carriage, and as many beautiful dresses as you wanted, and a serving girl to wait on you?'

It struck Angelina that he was describing the sort of life people like her mother enjoyed in Liverpool. That was a life that for her meant obeying rules and going to lessons with disagreeable people and being punished for crimes she did not know she had committed.

'Not particularly, thank you,' she said.

Finnegan drew back as if he had received a shock. 'Not want beautiful dresses? Not want fine food and a fine house and people to wait on you?'

'No, thank you.'

'Maeve, you have to think of your future,' Leary said quietly. 'You can't stay with us for ever.'

'Why can't I?' It was her turn to be shocked.

'Because you are born for something better than this. You have a wonderful talent. You should use it.'

'I don't understand.'

Finnegan leaned towards her. 'You came to see the show last night, didn't you? How would you like to be up there on the stage, singing?'

'Oh, yes, I'd like that.'

'That's what I'm offering you. Join us, be part of the company, and I'll put you at the top of the bill. You will be a star! People will come from far and wide to hear you sing, and when you are a little older young men will line up outside the theatre just for the pleasure of taking you to dinner. I've known actresses and singers with your sort of talent to marry into the aristocracy and end up living in grand houses. What do you think of that?'

'Would I have to go to lessons?'

'Lessons? Why? Perhaps we might find someone to teach you new songs, but that's all.'

'Would I have to do as I was told?'

'As long as you were there to sing every evening you would be as free as a bird.'

'I think I'd rather stay with Leary.'

Leary stood up. 'You can't do that, Maeve. We can't keep you with us all through the winter. You aren't strong enough or tough enough for the life we lead, and you wouldn't be able to pull your weight.'

'That's not fair!' she cried. 'I earn money for you, singing, and I help out. I fetch water and sew lavender bags. I'll do whatever you want.'

He shook his head. 'I'm sorry. I've come to an agreement with Mr Finnegan. It's a done deal. We can't be responsible for you any longer. You'll be much better off with him. Go along now and say goodbye to the others.'

She reached out and grabbed his sleeve, but he detached her hand and turned away.

Finnegan laid a hand on her shoulder. 'Come along, lassie. There's nothing to be afraid of. Say goodbye and we'll be on our way.'

Angelina looked round at the caravan. Dervla and Moira were watching and it was clear they knew what was happening. She went towards them, almost blinded by tears. Behind her, she heard the clink of coins changing hands and understood. Leary had sold her, with as little compunction as he parted with the horses on which he had lavished so much care and attention.

Sorcha ran to her. 'Is it true? You're going to be on the stage? Oh, you are so lucky!'

'Am I?'

"Course you are! If I was offered the chance, wouldn't I just jump at it?'

'I want to stay here, with you.'

Dervla put her arm round her. 'Don't cry. Leary is right. This will be better for you than staying with us. You'll sleep in a proper bed, in a warm house and eat better food and wear fine clothes. So dry your eyes and be thankful you have a voice that will buy you all those things.'

'But I won't know anyone.'

'You didn't know us when you came to stay with us, did you? You'll soon make friends. Now, here's your convent dress and the few things you brought with you – not that you'll be needing them – and I put in a lavender bag as a keepsake.'

She handed Angelina a small bundle and turned her to face Finnegan. 'Off you go, now. Good luck.'

Finnegan took her hand. 'That's the way. Come along. We've taken lodgings in the town with a Mrs Dailey and she'll have dinner waiting for us, and Mrs Finnegan can't wait to make your acquaintance.'

He was walking her away as he spoke. It suddenly occurred to her that she had not said goodbye to Danny and Quinn, but when she looked back they were nowhere to be seen.

Eighteen

Mrs Dailey's house was one of the larger buildings in the main street. Finnegan, who had not let go of her hand all the way, ushered her in through the front door and called out, 'Here she is, Mother. Here's our little song thrush.'

A door opened and a plump woman with the brightest red hair that Angelina had ever seen came into the hallway. She extended her arms and cried, 'Come here, my darling! Welcome to our company. I've heard so much about you and I can't wait to hear you sing.'

Angelina found herself smothered in a warm embrace. She extricated herself with some difficulty and remembered her manners. 'How do you do, ma'am?'

'Will you listen to that? Quite the little lady, isn't she? Come along in, my pet, and meet the rest of the family.'

She drew Angelina into the room, where a table was set ready for dinner. Three people came forward to meet her and she recognised one of them as the female part of the acrobatic dance team.

'Now, introductions,' the woman said. 'I'm Mrs Finnegan, but you've probably guessed that. Everyone calls me Ma. This is our daughter, Fionnuala. She's a dancer – but I think you've seen the show, so you know that. This is Darcy, her partner. And that there is our son, Aidan. He's our stage manager. Now, sit down. Here, you sit by me. I expect you're hungry.'

Angelina sat, too stunned to reply, and the family settled themselves around the table and fell to. Dervla had been right about one thing. There was more food here than she had seen for a long time. There was a pigeon pie and a round of beef and sausages and mashed potato, and an apple pie with cream to finish. Mrs Finnegan kept putting things on her plate and urging her to eat, but she was too upset and bewildered to swallow more than a few mouthfuls.

'Let her be,' Finnegan said. 'She'll eat when she's hungry. Now, I expect you're wondering what happens next, Maeve. We'll be leaving Buttevant this afternoon. Now the fair is over, there won't be enough people to make it worth our while to stay. We have an engagement in Cork, starting next Wednesday. That gives us two days to work out where you are going to fit into the bill and have a rehearsal. You'll meet the rest of the company tomorrow morning. This afternoon we have to pack up, ready to catch the five-ten.'

Angelina wondered what a five-ten was and concluded it must be another name for a stagecoach.

As soon as they had all finished eating, cases and boxes were brought down from the bedrooms and they all set off for the theatre, where the rest of the company were assembling. There seemed to be no time for introductions as everyone set to pack up the properties and equipment needed by the different acts. Even the painted backcloth was taken down and rolled up and put on the back of a handcart with the other boxes. No one had time for Angelina except to say a brief hello and she did not know how to help with the work, so she stood around feeling lonely and useless; but after a while she noticed the little dog whose act she had so much enjoyed tied up to a chair leg and looking rather disconsolate.

She went over and tentatively reached out to pat him. He immediately sat up and offered her a paw to shake. She squatted down bedside him and patted his head and he licked her face and nudged her with his nose to ask her to go on stroking him. For an hour, while what seemed like chaos reigned around her, she took comfort in the dog's unconditional affection and tried not to think of Leary and Dervla and Danny and the rest.

When they were almost ready, the man who owned the dog came over to her.

'Hello there. I'm Ronan. You must be Maeve.'

It was on the tip of her tongue to say, 'No. I'm Angelina,' but she remembered that her father might still be looking for her and thought better of it.

Ronan stooped to pat the dog. 'He's taken to you all right.'

'What's his name?'

'He's called Tinker. Listen, I've got my hands full. Would you like to bring him along?'

'Oh, yes, please.'

When everything had been packed, and the heaviest and bulkiest items loaded onto the hand cart, the entire company set off in procession, with Aidan pushing the cart and the rest following with suitcases on their shoulders and their arms full of boxes and bags. Angelina followed, leading Tinker. There were very few caravans or horses left now, but the local people came out of their houses and shops to watch the entertainers go by.

Some waved and called 'good luck' and Angelina heard others pointing out the different acts: 'Oh, there's the conjuror! He was good'; 'Isn't that the girl who dances?'

When she heard someone say, 'Oh look, there's the little dog who does the tricks. I suppose he belongs to that girl,' she lifted her head and felt quite proud.

The five-ten turned out to be a train, not a coach, bringing back memories of the day her father had brought her to the convent. It seemed a long time ago, but when she thought about it she realised it was only just over half a year. The gear was loaded into the guard's van, they climbed aboard and they were on their way. It was only a short journey to Cork and, once there, the company dispersed to various lodging houses where accommodation had been booked in advance. It seemed to be taken for granted that Angelina would stay in the same boarding house as the Finnegans. They had obviously been guests there before and were greeted like old friends and soon they were all sitting down to a splendid tea. This time, Angelina found she had recovered her appetite.

After they had eaten, Mrs Finnegan took her by the hand and pulled off the cap that she wore as a matter of habit. 'Will you look at that hair!' she exclaimed. 'What possessed them to cut it off like that?'

Finnegan came over and took a lock of it between his fingers. 'Voice of an angel,' he murmured, 'and hair to suit. Well, that's a bonus.'

'When it grows,' his wife said.

'It will. Till then we'll have to improvise. But first thing tomorrow you must take our little star out and find her some pretty dresses to wear. We can't have her looking like a gypsy when the public see her for the first time.'

That night Angelina slept in a proper bed and in a little room of her own. She had been given a bath in warm water and Fionnuala had loaned her a proper nightgown. As she dropped off to sleep she decided that her new life might not be so bad after all.

She had just finished dressing next morning when Mrs Finnegan tapped at the door and came in.

'Well, my dear, did you sleep well?'

'Very well, thank you ma'am.'

'There's no need to call me ma'am. Call me Ma, like everyone does.'

'Very good ... Ma.'

Mrs Finnegan took her by the shoulders and looked intently into her face. 'Now, Maeve, I'm going to ask you something and I want you to promise to give me a truthful answer. Will you do that?'

Angelina was beginning to feel some misgivings. 'I'll try, ma'am ... Ma.'

'You're not a gypsy child, are you?'

Angelina dropped her eyes and felt herself beginning to tremble. If she told Mrs Finnegan the true story, would she be handed over to her father and sent home?

'No,' she whispered.

'There's no need to shake so, pet. I don't mean any harm. Just tell me this. Did the gypsies steal you?'

'Steal me? No. I was lost and they took me in. They were kind to me.'

'Lost, were you? Did someone abandon you, leave you out there on the moor?'

'No.'

'So how did you get yourself lost?'

'I ... I ran away.'

'Now why would you do that?'

'Because I was frightened. I didn't want to be sent back and beaten and shut up in my room.'

'And who would have beaten you?'

'My mother ... but I don't think she is really my mother.'

'Not your real mother?'

'No. I'm ... I'm a foundling.'

'Ah, the gypsy man told Finnegan some wild story about finding you wandering. He said you were a changeling – a fairy child.'

Angelina looked up hopefully. 'Yes. I think I am.'

Mrs Finnegan laughed. 'Do you so? Well, well. From the way you speak I think it must have been English fairies who left you.'

Angelina gazed up into her face. 'Don't send me back. Please, please, don't send me back!'

'Hush, child. No one is going to send you anywhere. We want you here with us. Finnegan paid good money for you, apart from anything else. But just let me be sure of one thing. You are here of your own free will. There's no home you are longing to get back to, no loving family waiting for you?'

'No. They don't love me. I want to stay here with you.'

'Then stay you shall, and if you want to think of yourself as a fairy child that's up to you. Now, come and have some breakfast and then we'll go and find you something better to wear.'

As soon as they had finished eating, Mrs Finnegan took her by the hand and led her to a small dressmaker's shop in a side street, where she was apparently a regular client. An hour later, Angelina was provided with two new dresses. One was of white muslin, ornamented with bows of pink ribbon and artificial pink rosebuds; the other, slightly more practical, was of pale-blue silk poplin, with white lace trimmings. A visit to the milliner's shop next door produced a straw bonnet with blue ribbons, to hide her shorn hair. Attired in the blue poplin, she was introduced to the rest of the company, who had assembled on the stage of the theatre.

Aside from those she had already met, there was Dermot, the conjuror, and the duettists Catriona and Michael and Barney and Finn, who provided the music on accordion and fiddle. Ronan was there with Tinker, and Angelina was delighted when the little dog ran up to her and, without prompting, offered her a paw to shake. Finnegan introduced her as Maeve and assured them all that they were in for a treat when they heard her sing.

'This the little girl you bought from the gypsy?' Dermot said, tilting back his head and looking at her with half-closed eyes. 'Toothsome little morsel, isn't she? Come over here, my dear, and give your uncle Dermot a kiss.'

Dermot had bushy red whiskers and a nose to match. Angelina drew back.

'No, thank you. I don't like to kiss strange gentlemen.'

This roused a laugh from the rest of the company but Dermot looked affronted. 'Hoity-toity! Pardon my presumption, your majesty!'

Finnegan was handing round pieces of paper. 'This is the running order for this week. None of you need any rehearsal so you're free for the rest of the day. I want to work with Maeve here. We'll have a run through tomorrow morning. Be here at ten.'

Everyone was looking done the list he had given out. Michael exclaimed, 'You've put the girl in as the last act! That's a bit of a risk, isn't it?'

'You'll understand why when you hear her,' Finnegan said. 'Now off you go, all of you. I want to concentrate on Maeve. Barney, you stay. I shall need you.'

The company began to disperse, but Catriona came over to where Angelina was standing.

'My dear, you've been given a big responsibility. But don't worry. I'll give you a few tips. I could give you some lessons, too. After all, I am a trained singer.'

There was something condescending in her tone that Angelina did not like, but she replied meekly, 'Thank you, ma'am.'

'You leave her alone,' Finnegan said. 'I don't want her learning any of your affectations.'

'Oh, pardon me!' Catriona replied. 'Just wanted to give a beginner a bit of help.' She winked at Angelina and said softly. 'Take no notice. Anything you want to know, come to me. There's more to performing than just standing on a stage and singing, you know.'

When the others had gone, Finnegan said, 'Now then, let's decide what you are going to sing. I've given you two spots in the programme. For the first you can sing "The Last Rose of Summer" and one other. What else do you know?'

'I know some folk tunes that Leary taught me.'

'Right. What's your favourite?'

'I don't know what it is called, but it goes ...' she sang a few bars.

'Know that one, Barney?' Finnegan asked.

'To be sure I do.' There was a piano on the stage and Barney went to it and played the tune. She was glad to hear that he was as good on the piano as he was on the accordion.

'You can sing that, then,' Finnegan said. 'And for the second item, I want something religious, something angelic. Do you know any hymns?'

'I know the "Agnus Dei" from the mass.'

'You do? That's perfect. Sing that for me now.' He went down some steps at the side of the stage and seated himself in the front row. 'Right you are, whenever you're ready.'

When she had finished he clapped his hands and Mrs Finnegan rushed out from the wings and clasped Angelina to her bosom. 'Oh, that's the loveliest thing I've ever heard. You precious, precious child!'

'Mother,' Finnegan called from the auditorium, 'do we still have those angel's wings we made for the Christmas show?'

'Sure we do. I wouldn't throw them out, after the trouble I had making them.'

'Perfect! A simple white dress, and angel's wings. It'll bring the house down!'

After that, he made her sing the other two songs with Barney's accompaniment and expressed himself well satisfied.

When it came to the run-through the next morning, Angelina was much more nervous. She could sense that some of the company did not believe that she was up to the challenge of performing in front of an audience, and one or two were downright hostile; but in the event she managed all the songs perfectly and no one was able to find fault. Ronan, who seemed to have decided to take her under his wing, murmured to her as they prepared to leave the theatre, 'Take no notice if some of them seem to grudge you the success you deserve. Their noses are out of joint because you've been given star billing.'

Outside, Mrs Finnegan drew her attention to a brightly coloured playbill stuck on a board at the front of the theatre. In large letters were the words 'THE FIRST TIME ON ANY STAGE ... MAEVE THE IRISH SONG THRUSH. COME AND LISTEN TO THE VOICE OF AN ANGEL.'

For the first time, Angelina realised the enormity of the challenge facing her, and by the time she reached the theatre the following evening she was in a state of high tension. The sight of a long line of people queuing up for tickets did nothing to calm her nerves. In the dressing room, the other women were putting on heavy make-up. Mrs Finnegan sat her down on a stool and said, 'Right now. You can learn to do this for yourself in time, but for now leave it to me.'

She sat still while her face was daubed with a thick, greasy coating and then had to hold her eyes open while lines were drawn along her eyelids. At length Mrs Finnegan stood back and surveyed her.

'Yes, you'll do. Have a look at yourself.'

She held up a cracked mirror and Angelina saw someone she did not recognise; someone with a pale face and red cheeks and huge eyes with blue lids. She remembered how Dervla had darkened her skin and hidden her hair and how that had transformed her. Now she was changed again, but as before she welcomed the disguise.

'It doesn't look like me,' she said.

'Oh, it does. But if we left you as you were, all the audience would see would be a pale blob of a face. This way, you will look beautiful from the other side of the footlights. Now let's get you dressed.'

For her first appearance, she wore the white muslin and the bonnet and Mrs Finnegan declared she was as pretty as a picture. The assurance went some way to calming Angelina's nerves, but by the time she was standing in the wings her knees were shaking so badly she thought she might not be able to walk onto the stage. Ronan was waiting beside her, to go on after she finished.

She looked up at him. 'I don't think I can do it! I'm too scared.'

'Course you can!' he said. 'Listen, we're all a bit scared before we go on, But once we get there we're fine. Look at Tinker now. Don't you think he feels a bit frightened, going on in front of all those people? But he'll do his tricks, like he always does. You can be as brave as a little dog, can't you?'

She swallowed and agreed that she supposed she could. On stage, Mr Finnegan was announcing her.

'Ladies and gentlemen, prepare yourselves for a real treat. For the first time on any stage, please welcome the one and only Maeve, the Irish song thrush.'

Ronan gave her a gentle push, and she walked out into the glare of the footlights. Her first surprise was that she could not see beyond them. The audience was completely invisible, but she could hear them applauding. Finnegan gave her a pat on the shoulder and walked off into a corner of the stage and Barney played the introduction to "The Last Rose of Summer". Angelina opened her mouth to sing, but only a husky croak came out. She looked at Finnegan and he gave her a smile and made an upward motion of encouragement with his hand. Barney played the introduction again and this time she sang the opening lines, but in a voice that quavered.

From somewhere in the auditorium a voice shouted 'Get her off!', and one or two others took up the cry. Finnegan came out of his corner and went to the front of the stage.

'Ladies and gentlemen, please! You can see that this is a very young girl; a child, in fact. It's understandable that she's nervous. Give her a fair hearing.'

There was a mumble of response and someone said, 'That's right! Give the girl a chance.'

Finnegan came back to stand beside her. 'Now then, forget them out there. Sing to me.'

She sang, and suddenly her voice came back as clear and pure as it always was. She felt, rather than heard, the audience quieten and begin to listen and at the end they clapped loudly. When Barney began the introduction to the second number she did not notice that Finnegan was no longer by her side, and when she finished there was not only applause but cheering.

In the dressing room Mrs Finnegan kissed her and Fionnuala gave her a hug, and even Catriona said, 'Not bad, for a beginner.'

By the time she was dressed for her second appearance, in a long white smock with wings made of real feathers strapped to her chest, she was beginning to enjoy herself.

Finnegan introduced her again. 'Now, ladies and gentlemen, prepare yourselves to be transported to the heavenly realm, as you listen to the voice of an angel.'

Angelina walked out onto the stage and stood alone in a single spotlight. She drew a breath and sang, and the audience was so quiet she almost thought they had gone home. At the end there was a silence so prolonged that she wondered if, indeed, they had crept away while she was singing. Then the applause and the cheering started and she had to go back on stage and do it all again. When she came off, finally, Finnegan put his arm round her. 'I knew I was right, from the first moment I heard you. The voice of an angel indeed!'

Nineteen

James put on his dress suit with a mixture of reluctance and eager anticipation. Part of his mind was oppressed by a sense of guilt. He should not be occupying his time with anything as frivolous as a ball when his mother was so ill, and he had so much work to catch up on; and underlying that was the thought that he had never taken May to such an event, and never could have done.

The other half of his mind could not subdue a thrill of excitement. There had been a time when he had been a regular guest at similar entertainments and a frequent attender at concerts and plays. The thought of resuming that life was appealing and there were bound to be a lot of old friends at the ball, whom he had not seen for some time. He had lived like a monk for months, and there was really no reason to continue. It was just a pity that the cause of the celebration and the centre of attention was such an unattractive figure as Prudence Forsyth.

The Forsyths had spared no expense to launch their daughter onto the social scene. They had hired the ballroom at the Adelphi Hotel, the most prestigious venue in the city. A short flight of steps led from the foyer to the entrance of the ballroom and Mr and Mrs Forsyth were waiting at the top of it, with Prudence beside them, to receive their guests. When James arrived a line of people were waiting for their turn to be presented, so he had time to look ahead and take in the appearance of his hosts. For a moment, he thought he had arrived at the wrong ball. The couple at the head of the stairs did seem familiar, though he had only vague recollections of what Prudence's parents looked like, but he did not recognise Prudence herself. Gone was the puppy fat and the acne. Instead, smooth shoulders and rounded arms rose out of a white gown, the low-cut neck of which allowed a hint of the swell of perfect breasts. The once unruly dark hair had been disciplined into a centre parting and gathered into a luxurious chignon at the nape of the neck, decorated with white roses and pink ribbons. Beneath it was a perfectly oval face, set with very large dark eyes and an alluringly curved mouth. His mother was right. The transformation was amazing.

James just had time to take all this in before he reached the head of the stairs. He shook hands with Mr and Mrs Forsyth almost absentmindedly, his whole attention on his coming meeting with Prudence. She greeted him with a warm smile.

'James! I'm so glad you could come. We haven't seen each other for ages.'

'That's true.' He had to clear his throat before he could go on. 'I'm surprised you even remember me.'

'Of course I remember you. You were quite the best dancer at our dancing classes. I'm relying on you to take me onto the floor for the first dance.'

'Really?' That was a surprise indeed! 'Well, I'm most flattered.'

By this time the queue of people behind him was building up and he had to move on.

'Don't forget!' she murmured, as he turned away.

The dancing could not begin until all the guests had been received, so James had some time to kill. He looked around the room. Many of those who had already arrived were of the older generation, relatives or business associates probably, but there were plenty of young people and he soon spotted a group he had known since his schooldays. Among them were Peter, Prudence's elder brother, her older sister Isabel with her husband Laurence, and Ned Whitworth, who had been one of his closest friends. He took a glass of champagne from a passing waiter and went to join them.

'James Brackenbridge, by all that's wonderful!' Ned exclaimed. 'We have been wondering where you had got to. Opinion was divided between your joining a Trappist monastery and taking a vow of silence and having committed some heinous crime and got yourself transported.'

'Neither, so far,' James said with a laugh, adding with a mysterious wink, 'but I may be heading for one or the other.'

'No, seriously,' Peter put in, 'we've missed you. What have you been doing?'

James changed his tone. 'My mother is very ill, and I have been needed at home. And I have my solicitor's exams to work for, you know.'

'Tell me,' said Ned, 'what happened to that pretty little seamstress or whatever she was that we saw you out with once or twice? Have you got her hidden away in some secret love nest?'

James swallowed an irritable response. This was exactly the sort of thing he had feared when he was going out with May. 'She went away,' he said briefly. 'But come on, what's the news with all of you?'

Having successfully diverted the conversation he was happy to listen to what the others had to tell him. Peter had gone into the family business, Laurence was studying medicine, Ned was thinking of joining the army. This was a surprise. Ned's father was a baronet, with an estate out Knowsley way, and Ned himself was in receipt of a generous allowance, as James knew. There were several young ladies in the group, all fluttering their dance cards, and good manners required that he committed himself for a dance with all of them, but he carefully kept the first waltz free.

At length the guests were all assembled and the orchestra struck up. James made his way to Prudence's side and offered his arm. To his embarrassment, he found that for a few minutes they were the only couple on the dance floor. Then Mr and Mrs Forsyth joined them and after that the floor soon filled up and he was able to relax and enjoy himself. Prudence had been correct. He had been the best dancer in his class. He loved music, and the opportunity to move to its rhythm had always pleased him.

Prudence looked up into his face. 'Well, you haven't forgotten how to waltz. People have been telling me that you have forsworn society and shut yourself up with your books.'

'I have to spend a lot of time with my mother,' he explained. 'She suffers a great deal and it is only right that I should be with her.'

'Of course,' she agreed. 'I was so sorry to see her so worn down. Is there no hope of a cure?'

'None, I am afraid.'

'Poor James! I think it is very noble of you to give up so much of your time to her.'

'It's the least I can do,' he said, but even as he said it an inner voice called him a hypocrite. Was he not waiting for his mother to die, so that he could be free to join May in Australia? He forced the thought down and smiled at Prudence. 'Tell me about yourself. You've been in Switzerland, I hear.'

For the rest of the dance she chattered about her two years at finishing school and he was content to listen. After that, he was committed for several dances elsewhere, but when the supper dance was announced he moved quickly to claim her and took her into the dining room on his arm. It was a convivial occasion and they were soon at the centre of an animated group. After a time the talk turned to the subject of music. Prudence complained that the one thing she had missed most while she was away was the concerts at the Philharmonic Hall and St George's Hall.

'You used to go regularly, James,' she said. 'Do you still?'

'Not recently,' he confessed. 'I've been too busy.'

The conversation brought back memories of May and the sudden impulse that had prompted him to invite her to accompany him to a concert at St George's Hall. That had been the real start of their love affair. She had never seen or heard a full orchestra, and her wonder and delight had brought a new piquancy to his own enjoyment. After that he had been able to introduce her to so many of the things he loved best; not just music, but poetry and art and the beauties of nature. Every new experience had been an adventure. How she would have marvelled at the scene around him now, if only he could have persuaded her that she had as much right to be there as anyone!

'James!'

'What? Sorry.'

'I don't think you've heard a word I've been saying.'

'I'm sorry. My mind was elsewhere for a moment.'

'Thinking of your poor mother, I expect. But listen, there's a concert at the Phil next week – Mozart and Schubert. Emily and Peter are going, and Bella and Laurie. Shall we join them?'

For a moment he hesitated. 'Well, why not? I'm sure I can get away for one evening.'

To his surprise, his mother was still awake when he got home and called him into her room. She was propped up on her pillows and he could tell from her eyes that she had taken a large dose of the laudanum, but she was determined to hear about the ball.

'Did you enjoy yourself, my dear?'

'Yes, in the event I did. I'm glad you persuaded me to go.'

'And what did you think of Prudence?'

'She's turned out remarkably well. Quite a transformation, as you said.'

'I expect she was beset by young men wanting to dance with her.'

'Oh yes, she didn't want for partners.'

'And did you dance with her?'

'As a matter of fact, we had the first waltz and the supper dance.'

'The first waltz *and* the supper dance? Well, well.' His mother smiled sleepily. 'I think I'll settle down now.'

'That's right. Can I get you anything?'

'No, no. Nothing at all. Goodnight, my dear boy.'

He bent and kissed her. 'Goodnight, Mama. I hope you sleep well.'

The concert brought back to James how much he enjoyed music and how much he had missed it. He felt that his spirit had grown arid and shrivelled without it and the concert was like rain on dry ground. In the interval, Prudence was eager to discuss what they had heard and he discovered she was an informed and sensitive critic. They were soon deep in discussion, to the exclusion of the others.

Ned had joined the party and as they left the hall he suggested that they should all go to the music hall a few days later. This was less to James's taste but when Prudence declared herself keen to go and begged him to join them he agreed. In the event, it gave him almost as much pleasure as the classical concert. There was a good variety of turns, including some ballet and a solo pianist playing Chopin waltzes. Even the comedians were funnier than he'd expected.

When he somewhat reluctantly admitted his enjoyment, Ned chaffed him. 'You've let yourself turn into a dry old stick, and no mistake! You never used to be. We need to take you out and get you back to your old self. I prescribe a round of unalloyed gaiety and shall constitute myself master of the revels.'

He was as good as his word. In the days that followed, James found himself at the centre of a group bent on enjoying themselves. There were soirées and parties and at the weekend a trip on the ferry to sample the pleasures of Birkenhead Park. That was fraught with memories of May and her unfeigned amazement that there could be so much grass and so many trees and flowers, all open to the public; but he put them to one side and concentrated on his present companions. The most constant of these was Prudence, who seemed to be always at his side. She had a lively sense of humour and an almost unlimited capacity for enjoying herself, and her buoyant spirits were like a tonic. This, added to her beauty, attracted plenty of male attention and James felt flattered that she seemed to prefer his company to any other.

It was not long before he realised that he had a rival. If he bought Prue flowers, Ned would invariably arrive the following day with a larger and more luxuriant bouquet. When James gave her a book of poetry, Ned produced a copy of the latest novel. He was always ready to hand her on and off the ferry, or into and out of a carriage. And since he was a gentleman of leisure, he was available to squire her to afternoon concerts and tea parties while James was at work. Being a scion of the landed gentry, he had the means to keep horses and a reputation as an excellent rider and he frequently offered to procure a suitable mount for Prue and take her riding. It was an offer that she always laughingly refused. James, comfortable in the impression that in spite of all this Prue preferred his company to Ned's, found it all rather amusing. He thought of it as good sport.

One morning he was summoned into Mr Weaver's office.

'Have you heard anything from Richard Kean?' his employer asked.

With a jolt, James realised that he had not given a thought to his friend's fate for some days.

'No, nothing. I assume he is still searching for Angelina.'

'After all this time? Surely there cannot be any hope of finding her alive after so long.'

'I think Richard has sworn not to give up until he knows one way or the other.'

'Hmm.' Weaver looked troubled. 'I should feel more sanguine about his chances if McBride was not involved. Have you had any contact there?'

'No, sir. I promised I would keep away from him, and I have.'

'I'm glad to hear it. Everything I learn about that man makes me like him less. Vane tells me he managed to infiltrate one of his men into McBride's warehouse as a clerk. A week later he was washed up on Formby beach, with a knife in his back.'

'No!'

'Oh, yes. One of the Cornermen has been arrested on suspicion of the deed, but we can be pretty sure McBride was behind it.'

The Cornermen were a notorious gang of youths who hung around on street corners, usually outside public houses, and demanded money with menaces from passers-by.

'That's terrible!' James said.

'Did you know he has sacked young Miss Findlay, and her father?' Weaver asked.

'For talking to me and Richard?'

'Presumably.'

'But why? All she did was tell us about Angelina. It had nothing to do with any of McBride's business affairs.'

'I imagine it was as a warning to others not to discuss anything connected to him with anyone.'

'Poor Lizzie! The family must be destitute without her income and her father's. I think I should go and see if there is anything I can do to help.'

'You will not!' Weaver said firmly. 'You will keep well away – and that's an order.'

'Very well, sir. If you feel so strongly about it.'

'I feel strongly about preserving you from ending up like that unfortunate clerk,' Weaver said gruffly. He put his head on one side and looked at James with a curious half-smile and an expression of satisfaction. James was suddenly reminded of a robin which had just managed to swallow a particularly succulent worm. 'Quite apart from considerations of common humanity,' Weaver said, 'I have my own reasons for wanting you in one piece. How do you fancy the idea of a partnership?'

James caught a sharp breath. 'A partnership? You mean, here? With you and Mr Woolley?'

'Where else? Woolley is getting on a bit now. It won't be long before he thinks of retiring. I am going to need to take in someone else and it might as well be you. You've shown yourself to be a bright chap and a hard worker. Once you've passed your final examination, as I have no doubt you will, I cannot think of anyone better qualified for the position. What do you say?'

James swallowed hard. Once this offer would have been the summit of his ambitions, but now he had other plans. All the same, he was unwilling to give a blank refusal. He could see that Weaver was confident that he would accept and would be deeply hurt if he turned the offer down. He had come to like and respect him over the years they had worked together, and he knew that he could have been paid no higher compliment. But how could he agree? While he floundered Weaver himself came to his rescue.

'I can understand that with your mother's state of health to consider it must be hard for you to think of the future. You don't need to give me an answer now. Think it over. Talk to her about it. I'm sure your mother would be glad to know your prospects were secure. Let me know in a day or two.'

'I will!' James said, almost giddy with relief. 'And thank you, sir. Please don't think I am not sensible of the compliment you have paid me. I am truly grateful.'

'Well, well. We'll leave it there for the time being. You'd better get on with that conveyancing job now.'

Looking at his face, James could see that he was disappointed. He had expected an immediate and rapturous acceptance. He went back to his desk with a sense of guilt at what felt like disloyalty.

He felt guilty about another matter as well. It was his fault, and Richard's, that Lizzie Findlay had lost her job and he felt he ought to try to help her in some way, in spite of Weaver's direct order to the contrary.

As soon as he left work, he made his way to the address she had given him at their last meeting. It was a small, respectable place, not far from the docks, but when he reached it he found the door locked and the windows boarded up. He was tempted to give up at that point, but his conscience would not let him, so he made his way to McBride's warehouse and waited for the workers to come out. He was looking for the friend who had been so protective when he and Richard had first spoken to Lizzie. It was a long shot, because it was quite possible that she had been sacked as well, but to his relief he saw her coming out of the warehouse with the rest. She called goodbye to some other women and set off into the city. James followed her until they were well away and then he crossed the road and confronted her. She stopped and then drew back a pace or two.

'You again! I'm not talking to you. Not after what happened to Lizzie.'

'That's exactly why I am here,' James said. 'I feel really bad about Lizzie losing her job and I want to help if I can.'

'Help? You're a bit late for that.'

'Can you at least tell me where she lives now, so I can make the offer? I went to her house but it's all boarded up.'

The woman gave a brief, bitter laugh. 'Oh, I can tell you where to find her, but it's not round here. You'll have to go up the hill if you want to see her.'

'Up the hill?' James queried.

'Up Brownlow Hill. She's in the workhouse.'

'In the workhouse! Can matters have got so desperate so quickly? I know she and her father were both sacked, but had they no savings to fall back on?'

'Not a penny. Her da had been ailing for months. How he kept working as long as he did I'll never know. They'd spent every last penny on doctor's bills. The shock of losing his job finished him off.'

'He's dead?'

'Dropped down dead the day after he was sacked.'

'Dear God! Is there no other family?'

'No. Lizzie's ma died years back and the brothers are both away at sea. The mean bastard they rented the house from turned Lizzie out the day after the funeral. Where else was she supposed to go?'

James put his hand in his pocket and took out a coin. 'I shall go up there directly and see if there is anything I can do to help. Thank you for telling me, miss …?'

'Biggin, Flo Biggin. And I don't want your charity. Keep it for them as needs it.'

James had often seen the grim bulk of the workhouse at the top of the hill but he had never been inside. As he banged on the great door his heart seemed to twist in his chest at the thought that this was where May had grown up. When the porter opened a small wicket, he presented his card and asked to see the governor. The porter scrutinised the card suspiciously, but evidently decided that it was safer not to argue and led him along a narrow roadway to a bleak courtyard and up a flight of stairs to the door of the governor's office.

The governor was a small man with thinning hair and surprisingly bushy eyebrows and sideburns. He looked at the card and then at James, his expression wary, almost defensive.

'What does Weaver and Wooley, Solicitors, want with me?'

James made his tone reassuring. 'It's a small matter concerning one of your inmates. Elizabeth Findlay?'

'Findlay?' The governor appeared to search his memory. 'Ah yes, came to us quite recently. Is she in trouble?'

'No, no. Not at all. We just think she may be able to help us with our enquiries into another matter.' He was tempted to mention Angelina, but decided not to complicate matters. The truth was that, now he was here, he did not know quite why he had come.

The governor peered at him out of the thicket of eyebrows and whiskers and then shook his head impatiently. 'Very well. Very well.' He touched a bell on his desk and a lanky youth appeared from an inner room. 'Take this gentleman to Mrs Fosdyke's office. Mrs Fosdyke,' he added by way of explanation, 'is the superintendent in charge of all the female occupants.'

Mrs Fosdyke, a lean figure composed entirely, it struck James, of sharp angles, was less easily satisfied as to the reason for his request than the governor. In the end he fell back on the well-worn cliché of client confidentiality and, her curiosity baffled, she passed him into the hands of a thin, pale-faced girl with instructions to take him to the infirmary.

'The infirmary?' James queried with alarm. 'Is Miss Findlay ill?'

'No. She volunteered to help out as soon as she arrived here.' Mrs Fosdyke sniffed. 'It is unusual. Those who come to us are not usually so public spirited. No doubt she is hoping for favours of some sort.'

James thought that from what he had seen of Lizzie Findlay it seemed quite in character.

He had assumed that the workhouse was a single, large building but discovered that it was in fact a complex of buildings, like a small village. His journey through the narrow streets in the wake of his little guide filled him with a cold despair. He saw men and women reduced to a shabby uniformity in their workhouse clothes, listlessly engaged in repetitive tasks, their faces blank and without hope. What future could there be for them, he wondered? And how had May survived a childhood spent here and become the warm-hearted, vibrant person he knew?

His first sight of the infirmary surprised him. He had expected to find conditions of squalor and suffering, but the rooms were orderly and clean and nurses in uniform moved between the beds. His guide left him at the door of the female ward and he stood for a moment looking about him at a loss, until a woman who had been bending over one of the beds straightened up and came towards him. Her appearance struck him like a sudden burst of sunshine from a cloudy sky. Her skin was the colour of polished copper, her nose straight, cheekbones high and eyes like liquid amber. To be confronted with such unexpected and exotic beauty left him for a moment speechless.

'Can I help you?' she asked, her voice warm and slightly accented. 'You look lost.'

3

James swallowed and pulled himself together. 'My name is James Breckenridge. I work for a firm of solicitors. I am looking for Elizabeth Findlay.'

'Lizzie? I'll fetch her. I hope you have some good news for her. She does not deserve to be in here.'

She moved away, leaving James painfully aware that he had no such good news. What had possessed him to come here, he asked himself? What help could his apologies be to a woman who had been brought to this, and through his fault?

When Lizzie came towards him from the other end of the room he was shocked to see how much she had changed in a few short weeks. Her cheeks were sunken and her face had lost the healthy glow he remembered. She stopped in front of him, her expression telling him nothing.

'Mr Breckenridge? What do you want with me, sir?'

'Lizzie ... Miss Findlay ...' he floundered. 'I don't know what to say. I had no idea until today that that short conversation between us had such terrible consequences for you. I came ... I came to apologise. But now I see that apologies are totally inadequate. Is there anything at all I can do?'

He expected her to reject his apologies, to turn on him with fury and contempt. Instead she said with the faintest hint of an irony, 'Thank you for offering. But there's nothing, unless you happen to know of a respectable family that need a nursemaid and aren't too choosy were she comes from.'

'I'll make enquiries,' James promised, knowing there was little hope. 'I wish ... I wish sincerely that I had never involved you in my inquiries but I never imagined …' he trailed into silence.

There was an awkward pause, then Lizzie said, 'Did he find her – Mr Kean, was it? – did he find Angelina?'

'Not so far,' James said. 'We … we are still working on it.'

'That's terrible! Whatever can have happened to her?'

'We don't know, but we hope someone has taken her in and is looking after her.'

'Oh, I do pray they have! Poor little girl. Dumped here and then adopted by people who treated her so badly. She deserves something better.' She turned to the copper-skinned woman who was hovering nearby. 'Dora, you've been here a few years, haven't you. Do you ever remember a little girl with golden hair who was left outside the gates one night?'

The woman came closer. 'Golden hair? Did you say her name was Angelina? There was a child they used to call Angel.'

'Angel!' James exclaimed. 'Yes, that would be her? Did you know her?'

'Not exactly, but I heard tell of her. There was a fire here, a few years back, in the girls' dormitory. It turned out one of the girls had taken a child from the nursery up to bed with her – lord knows why – but when the fire broke out she gave the child to a friend and then went back to help another girl who was trapped. She got her hands burned and so she was sent here to be treated. The governor had her and the other girl put in a room to themselves – well, the other one had been badly disfigured when a burning beam fell on her. But the first one, the one who went back to help, all she was worried about was the child she called Angel. Couldn't wait to get out of here and go back to the nursery to make sure she was all right.'

James gazed at her in amazement. 'The girl, do you happen to remember her name?'

'It was a long time ago. Mary, was it? Mabel? No, May! That was it.' She looked at James. 'Why do you ask?'

'Oh, it's just that … I think I have met her – after she left here, of course.' He did not know why he prevaricated, why he did not say outright that she was his fiancée. Some lingering sense of shame, a wish to dissociate the May he knew from this place, prevented him.

Lizzie was staring at him in surprise and to change the subject he looked around him and said, 'I admire you both for volunteering to work here. But conditions are not as bad as I expected.'

'You wouldn't have said that three years back,' Dora said. 'It was terrible then, but since Miss Grey came here there's been a transformation. She's a trained nurse, worked under Florence Nightingale down in London. Mr Rathbone persuaded her to come and work here and she's done wonders.'

'William Rathbone?' James said. 'I know his reputation well. He is one of our leading philanthropists.'

'A very great man,' Dora confirmed.

A voice from further down the ward called querulously 'Nurse!' and Dora turned away. 'I must get on. If Miss Grey catches me gossiping I'll be for it.' She smiled quickly at James. 'I hope you find the little girl.'

'I must get on, too,' Lizzie said. 'Thank you for coming to see me.'

'Oh, please don't thank me! I wish I could do more.'

'Oh well, if you do happen to hear of someone who wants a nursemaid ...'

'I won't forget,' he assured her. He offered his hand and she shook it.

Over dinner that night he raised the subject with his mother, with little hope of success. To his surprise she said, 'As it happens, I can think of someone who might be interested. Jane Jackson came to see me the other day. Her daughter is married to Mark Winter and they are in desperation at the moment. They have three little ones, all under the age of five, and their maid has had to go off to look after her father, who was injured in an accident on the docks. I think they would be glad of anyone who would help out. It would only be temporary, of course, but it might be a fresh start for the poor girl. If you are sure that you can guarantee that she is reliable.'

'Oh, yes, I'm sure she is.' James did not know how he could be so sure, but he did not stop to question the fact.

Next day he called on the Winters and explained the situation, glossing over the reason why Lizzie had lost her job and simply saying that the girl she had been looking after had been sent away to school, making her redundant. Mark Winter went to the workhouse to interview Lizzie and twenty-four hours later she was happily installed in charge of the three little ones.

Nothing more was said about the partnership with Weaver and Woolley over the next days and James wrestled with a variety of different concerns. First and foremost was the question of how best to respond to his employer's offer.

Apart from his unwillingness to hurt Weaver's feelings, he sensed that once he had turned it down the atmosphere in the office would change. He would no longer be the up-and-coming pupil, but would be seen as an ungrateful dog who could no longer be trusted. As well as this, now that Weaver had recalled the quest for Angelina to his mind, he was worried about what might have happened to Richard, particularly in view of what he had learned about McBride's recent activities. On top of everything, it was clear that his mother's health was failing and she required more care and attention than he was able to provide. It was getting too much for Flossie as well, so he decided that the time had come to employ nurses, one for the daytime and another for the nights.

He continued to accept invitations to concerts and parties, as a much-needed reprieve from his worries. It was always as part of a group of friends, but once or twice he was surprised to find himself left alone with Prudence. One evening he walked her home after a concert and she asked him to come in while she found a book she had promised to lend him. Her parents had gone to bed and when she had handed him the book there was a hiatus, during which they looked at each other in silence. She was looking exceptionally beautiful that night and he found himself wrestling with an impulse to kiss her. Something told him that he would not be repulsed, but he controlled himself. If he let that happen, there could be only one outcome.

Next evening he was sitting beside his mother's bed, reading to her, when she put her hand over the book.

'That's enough for tonight. I want to talk to you.'

'What about, Mama?'

'About Prudence.'

'What about her?'

'She has been to see me once or twice, you know, with her mother.'

'Yes, you told me.'

'Such a pretty girl! And so accomplished. She will be an ornament to any man's home.'

James was beginning to feel uneasy. 'I'm sure you're right, Mama.'

She reached out and gripped his hand, with a strength that surprised him. 'There will be plenty of young men eager to carry her off. Don't wait too long or you will lose her.'

The words struck James like a slap on the face. He had been so glad to abandon his cloistered way of life and enjoy the companionship of his friends that he had sleep-walked into what he now realised was a very compromising situation. His mother was assuming that he intended to marry Prue. Was everyone else thinking the same? Was Prudence expecting it?

He murmured some soothing platitudes to his mother and settled her down for the night, then sought his own bed; but he had little sleep.

Next morning the same dilemma revolved itself in his brain. Had he gone too far to draw back? What would the consequences be if he did? How could he manage to convey to Prudence that all he wanted from her was her friendship and her company? How much pain would that cause? He was still brooding over that next morning as he sorted through the mail that was waiting on the doormat when he arrived at the office. He was brought up short by a letter personally addressed to him. It was not stamped and must have been hand delivered but he recognised the handwriting.

'Richard!' he exclaimed aloud. 'Thank God!'

He opened the letter and found a hastily scrawled note inside.

James.

I am in dire need of your assistance. I have been kidnapped and am being held to ransom. The sum demanded is £100, which I can meet, just, from my own resources, but under the circumstances I am unable to draw on them. I know you will not be able to lay your hands on such a sum, but perhaps Mr Weaver will be able to oblige. I can promise to reimburse him when I am free.

If you can raise the money you must bring it as soon as possible to the Gresham Hotel in Sackville Street, Dublin. Tell the desk clerk that you have a delivery for Mr Macready and you will be contacted. Do not go to the police or the authorities if you wish to see me alive.

I apologise for putting you to this trouble, but I fear that if you cannot come to my assistance things will go hard with me.

Your friend,
Richard Kean

James rushed into his superior's office without pausing to knock and thrust the letter in front of him. Weaver read it through, grim-faced.

'By God, I was afraid of something like this. I smell McBride's hand behind this.'

'You're right, I'm sure,' James agreed, 'though I'm surprised it's a case of ransom. I would have expected something ... well something more radical.'

'Murder, you mean? So would I. But we must be grateful for small mercies.'

'Can you find the money?'

'Oh yes, no problem there. But I don't like the idea of sending you to deliver it.'

'Why? It has to be me. I'm ready to go.'

'I just wonder if this isn't some ploy of McBride's to secure you both at one go. Once you are in Ireland what's to stop his associates, whoever they are, disposing of both of you?'

James swallowed and cleared his throat. There was a good deal of sense in Weaver's remark. 'I have to take that chance,' he said. 'We dare not involve anyone else. If we did and Richard paid the price I should never forgive myself.'

Weaver frowned in indecision for a moment, then he nodded grimly. 'You are right, and I applaud your courage. Can you be ready to take the night boat?'

'Yes.'

'Go home and make what preparations you need. When you get back here I shall have the money for you.'

James did as he was bid. He told his mother that he had to go away for a couple of nights on business, without giving any further details, and made sure that the nurses knew exactly what to do in his absence. As he kissed his mother goodbye, it occurred to him that it might be for the last time.

By nightfall he was on board the ferry, with a bulky parcel wrapped in brown paper in a briefcase under his arm.

Twenty

James entered the lobby of the Gresham Hotel with a queasiness in his stomach that was not just the after-effects of a rough crossing. He went to the desk and told the clerk that he had a delivery for Mr Macready, and the man told him that he was expected and should go up to room 201. Outside the door he stood for a moment, trying to slow his racing heartbeat; then he knocked and was told to enter.

There was only one man in the room, to James's relief – a middle-aged, respectable-looking chap. He rose from an easy chair as James entered and extended his hand, as if this were just an ordinary business meeting.

'I've been expecting you. How was your crossing?'

'Rough. How did you know I was here?'

'Oh, we've had our eye on you ever since your friend's letter was delivered. Do you have the money?'

'I do, but what guarantee do I have that Mr Kean will be released if I hand it over? I can't be sure even that he is still alive.'

Macready moved to the window and beckoned James to join him. With a gesture he directed his attention to the opposite side of the street. For a moment James's view was obscured by passing carriages and an omnibus, then he saw a group of three men. The one in the middle was Richard.

'See him?' Macready lowered the blind briefly and then raised it again. 'Now, this is what you do. You give me the money and then you head straight back to the docks and get on the first boat back to Liverpool.'

'But Kean! He must be released.'

'He will be. He will be brought to the boat before it sails.'

'Why should I trust you? How do I know you will let him go?'

'You don't have any option. You hand over the money, or your friend will not survive the night. Your choice.'

James looked from him to the figures across the street and as he watched Richard was hustled away by his two captors.

'The money!'

Unwillingly James opened the briefcase and handed over the envelope. Macready counted it methodically and tucked it away inside his jacket.

'Nice doing business with you. Now, the first boat, remember. Don't try anything funny if you want to see your friend alive.' Macready turned away and was out of the room before James had a chance to speak again.

James sank into a chair, feeling the strength suddenly leave his legs. He put his head in his hands. What had he done? What else could he have done? What were the chances that Macready would keep his word? He considered going to the police but put the idea aside. If Macready was to be believed, it would be tantamount to signing Richard's death warrant. There was only one course of action open to him, and that was to get on the boat and hope Richard would be allowed to join him.

There was no further sailing, he discovered, before the night boat that left at nine o'clock, so he spent the rest of the day either wandering along the roads around the docks or sitting in a small bar opposite the pier. As the sun began to set, he picked up his suitcase and went to the ticket office, where he bought two tickets. The ferry was tied up alongside the quay and people were going on board. James hung around near the ticket office, straining his eyes along the streets, hoping to catch a glimpse of his friend. The scheduled time for the sailing came closer and closer and there was still no sign of him. Then the ferry gave a blast on its whistle, and the ticket collector said, 'Better get aboard if you're going, sir.'

'I'm waiting for someone!'

'Looks like she's stood you up, sir, if you don't mind my saying so.'

'I do mind! I'm waiting for a friend, not a lady.'

'Well, if you wait much longer the ship will sail without you.'

James looked around at the ferry, and then back along the road. Should he let the boat go and hope Richard would appear for the next one? Or had the whole thing been a cheat? Perhaps they had never intended to release him.

He was about to head for the gangplank when he saw a figure emerge from a side street and come towards him at an unsteady run.

'Richard!'

Richard lifted his head towards the sound of his voice. 'James! Thank God!'

They hurried towards each other and James caught him in an embrace. 'My dear chap, thank heaven you're safe! Quick! The ship's about to sail!'

He grabbed Richard's arm and hurried him along the quay. They reached the gangplank just as it was about to be drawn up and staggered up it. Richard was clinging to him as if he was about to collapse and James was aware that the crew thought they were both drunk, but he managed to get him into the saloon and lowered him into a chair in a quiet corner.

'Are you all right?' he asked.

'More or less,' Richard said, with a shaky laugh. For the first time James was able to look at him properly and he was shocked to see that one side of his face was badly bruised and one eye was almost closed. He had been aware as he supported him of how little flesh there was covering the bones of his shoulders and arms.

'What have they done to you?'

'Just knocked me about a bit. It's nothing serious.'

He was very pale. James said, 'You look as if you could do with a brandy.'

'Wonderful idea!'

He went to the bar and ordered two double brandies. 'Do you have anything to eat?'

'I could make you a cheese sandwich,' the barman offered.

Returning with the brandies to where Richard was sitting, he drew a chair closer and said, 'What happened? Do you feel up to talking?'

'Give me a minute,' Richard responded. He took a large gulp of the drink and looked round the saloon as if half expecting his captors to reappear. 'I haven't thanked you for getting me out. You must have known you were taking a risk.'

'What else could I do?'

'You didn't inform the police?'

'No. But now you're free we can inform Inspector Vane when we get back.'

'Yes, no harm in that once we're back in England,' Richard agreed. He took another swallow of brandy and a little colour came back into his face. 'You want to know what happened.'

'If you're ready to talk.'

Richard rubbed a hand across his eyes. 'To be absolutely honest with you, I don't really understand it myself. But I'll tell you the story and you can see if you can make anything of it.'

'Tell me first, did you find any trace of Angelina?'

'I thought I had, but I lost the trail again just when I thought I was getting close.' He told James how he had traced his daughter as far as Meanus. 'The gypsies said she was definitely heading in that direction, but when I got there everyone I spoke to denied all knowledge of her. I almost got the feeling that they had been told not to speak. Then two men turned up and told me they had picked her up on the road and taken her to a place where she was being cared for.' He gave a rueful shrug and his voice cracked slightly as he went on. 'You can imagine how I felt, thinking I'd found her at last. I went with the men and they took me to a building on the outskirts of a town called Bruff and that's when I discovered the whole thing had been a confidence trick. They shut me in a room and started asking me questions.'

'What sort of questions?'

'That's the strange part of it. They seemed to think that I was a British spy, using the search for Angelina as a cover for some kind of investigation. They said they had been warned that I was coming and had been watching me all the time.'

'I can guess who warned them. McBride. He has been up to all sorts of no good while you were away.'

'I think you're right. They were under the impression that I had found out about something they were doing and they wanted to know what it was.' He touched his face gingerly. 'I couldn't give them an answer, hence the bruises.'

'My God, that man has a lot to answer for,' James said. 'But why set this whole charade up? Was it just to extract the ransom money?'

'Perhaps it was intended to warn me off – though there were times I thought the intention was to kill me, after they had got the information they wanted.'

'That's rather what I thought, too. So how did you persuade them to change their minds?

'I think I owe that to the nuns of the Faithful Companions of Jesus.'

'How so?'

'I kept insisting that I was only interested in finding my daughter, and I told them they could check my story with the Reverend Mother of the convent where she was being educated. It so happens that there is a sister house of the same order in Bruff. As far as I can make out, they checked with the nuns there, who had been approached by the Reverend Mother in case they had any knowledge of Angelina's whereabouts. They were able to confirm my story and I think that sowed a seed of doubt in the minds of the men holding me.'

'So what happened then?'

'Nothing, for a long time, except they stopped knocking me about. I was just left shut up with only the two thugs who had been set to guard me for five, maybe six days.' He lowered his head and ran both hands through his hair. 'I could never condemn anyone to solitary confinement, no matter what they had done, after that experience. You cannot imagine what it is like to sit for hour after hour in an almost-empty room, with nothing to occupy your mind except the thought that you may not live to see the open sky again.'

James reached out and laid a hand on his arm. 'You poor chap! It must have nearly driven you insane. It would me.'

A steward arrived with the cheese sandwich and Richard looked up. 'God bless you! They've kept me on bread and water the whole time I was a prisoner. I'm famished.'

'What do you think they were waiting for?' James asked.

'Not sure,' Richard answered with his mouth full. 'Maybe they had to refer to a higher authority. Maybe they were looking for further proof of my story. All I know is, one day the fellow who had talked me into coming to Bruff with them reappeared and told me to write that letter. Then, yesterday, they tied me up and gagged me and threw me in the back of a cart of some kind and drove me to another house, somewhere near here. This morning they untied me and told me to come with them. They had guns. They said if I attempted to get away or to draw attention to myself, they would shoot me. They took me to a busy street and made me stand there. I didn't know why at the time, but I guess they were waiting for a signal of some kind. Eventually they took me back to the house and kept me until an hour ago, when they brought me to a side street near the dock.

I could see the ferry and I thought they must be planning for me to get on it, but they waited so long I began to think something had gone wrong – the money wasn't right or someone had informed the police. Finally they let me go and told me to head for the boat. I can't tell you what a relief it was to see you standing there, waiting for me.'

'It was a great relief to me, too,' James assured him. 'I was beginning to think the whole thing had been a trick. But you're here now, thank heaven. Now, you look absolutely done up. Would you like another brandy?'

Richard shook his head. 'Nothing more, thank you.'

'Then why don't you put your feet up and try to sleep? Here, use this chair, and I'll see if I can find a rug or something to cover you.'

At James's request a steward produced a blanket and he spread it carefully over Richard's knees and within a few minutes it was apparent that he had drifted off into a doze, which soon deepened into a proper sleep and lasted until the boat docked in Liverpool. There was a small eating house near the docks, which opened at the crack of dawn to supply dockers on their way to work or passengers catching early boats, and James took him there and watched him eat a hearty breakfast before calling a hackney carriage and seeing him back to his hotel. Having made sure that he had everything he needed, he left him to rest and headed home.

He was greeted by an anxious Flossie. 'I'm that glad to see you home, sir. The mistress has been worse these last couple of days. She didn't leave her bed yesterday.'

'Has the doctor been?'

'Yes, sir. He came yesterday evening and gave her a draft. It seemed to help. She slept then.'

'Thank you, Flossie. I'll go straight up and see her.'

He found the room in semi-darkness and the nurse knitting by the light of a single candle. She rose as he entered and signed to him to be quiet and, approaching the bed, he saw that his mother's eyes were closed.

'She's peaceful now,' the nurse whispered. 'Don't disturb her.'

'No, of course not,' he responded. 'Please tell her when she wakes up that I am back from my business trip and have gone to the office.'

'Very good, sir.'

After a change of clothes, a wash and a shave, James presented himself at the usual hour at the office of Weaver and Woolley. Mr Weaver greeted him eagerly.

'Well?'

'All well, sir. Richard is back in his hotel room, resting. But he's been through the mill.'

'Tell me about it.'

James related the events of the previous day and what Richard had told him and Weaver nodded grimly.

'It's as we thought. McBride is behind it. He must have told his friends over there that a British spy was being sent to poke into their doings and would be using the search for Angelina as a cover. Thank heaven Kean was able to convince them of the truth of his story! Inspector Vane should know about this, now that Kean is out of danger, but perhaps we had better wait until he is fit to tell the story himself.'

'He promised to call in tomorrow morning, to bring you the money you lent him.'

'Well, there's no hurry for that, but I'll make an appointment with Vane so we can bring him up to date. Now, have you slept?'

'Not a great deal.'

'That's two nights on the trot, I imagine. Go home, my boy, and get some rest.'

James protested that he was quite ready to carry on as normal, but Weaver insisted and in truth he was glad to give in. Now that the tension of the previous couple of days was released he was suddenly aware how tired he was.

Back at the house he found his mother awake, but her mind was obviously clouded by the drug she had been given, so after reassuring her that he was well and unharmed, he left her to rest and went thankfully to bed.

Next morning, Richard appeared promptly at the offices of Weaver and Woolley.

'I have come to return the money you advanced to pay the ransom, sir. Will a cheque be acceptable?'

'Of course.'

Richard wrote out the cheque and handed it over. 'I'm most grateful for your help, needless to say. If I had not had friends who could raise the sum demanded, I do not like to think what might have happened to me.'

'As for that,' Weaver responded, 'I'm more than happy to help.' He glanced at the cheque. 'This will leave you somewhat short of funds, I imagine.'

'Not insupportably so,' Richard said, 'but it will mean that I shall have to draw in my horns somewhat with regard to expenses. I shall need to find somewhere cheaper to live, for one thing. And I must concentrate my mind on the job I was sent over here to do, which has been sadly neglected of late.'

'Does that mean you are going to give up the search for Angelina?' James asked.

Richard ran a hand over his face, which still bore the evidence of the beatings he had endured. 'What else can I do? If I really was on her trail before I was taken, it will have gone completely cold by now. My only consolation is that there has been no report of a body being found, so there is hope that she may have found shelter with someone – someone who, I pray, will treat her with more kindness than she has known up till now. There is no more I can do. Even if I thought there was a possibility of tracing her movements, I dare not set foot again in Ireland. It was made abundantly clear to me that if I did I would not get away with the payment of a ransom a second time.'

'I could go, I suppose,' James said.

'You could not!' Weaver responded. 'We've seen how far McBride's influence reaches. I'm not having you put yourself within his clutches on what looks more and more like a wild goose chase. Besides, you are needed here.' He glanced at the clock. 'I made an appointment with Inspector Vane. He should be here at any minute.'

Vane arrived soon afterwards and listened with a grim face to Richard's story.

'I ought to tell you that you did wrong to pay the ransom,' he said at its conclusion. 'That money will have gone to swell the coffers of the Fenians and to buy arms, in all probability. But I can't pretend I'm not glad to see you back here safe and sound.'

'It seems more and more certain that McBride is still involved with the Fenians,' Weaver said.

'Oh, there's no doubt in my mind about that. It's proving it that's the difficulty.' The inspector shook his head in frustration. 'I wish we knew what was in some of those tea chests that he brings in from India.'

'Can you not get a warrant to search them?' Weaver asked.

'Not without evidence that we have reason to be suspicious of the contents. And we can't go through the hold of every ship that docks, looking for chests addressed to this fictitious importer he has created to cover his tracks. If we only had some idea of when he's expecting a new consignment; that would be a step in the right direction.'

Richard sat forward. 'Something has just come back to me. I don't know if it has any relevance ...'

'Go on,' the inspector encouraged him.

'It's just a snatch of conversation I overheard while I was held captive. They were in the next room, so I didn't catch all of it. I think they were discussing what I might or might not have found out – this was while they still thought I was a spy. One of them said I'd been seen around the docks in Limerick, asking questions, and another man, I don't know who he was because I never saw him, said 'he won't have found out anything important there. The next shipment's not due until the middle of September.'

'The middle of September,' Vane echoed. 'The tea clippers start to arrive in early September. Gives time for the goods to be unloaded and repackaged as something McBride might legitimately be exporting to Ireland, and then loaded again for shipment to Limerick ... We might get a warrant to search any shipment leaving Liverpool for Limerick around that time.' His habitually weary expression was lightened by a brief smile. 'Thank you, Mr Kean. You may have given us just the lead we wanted.'

The meeting broke up soon after this. Vane returned to his police station, Richard left to look for cheaper lodgings and James tried, with varying success, to concentrate on the business of the law. Returning home that evening he found the doctor once again in attendance on his mother.

'The nurse sent for me again,' he said. 'Your mother's condition has worsened and she was very restless. I've given her a stronger dose of laudanum but I am afraid that is all I can do. She may rally again when that takes effect but –' he laid a hand of James's arm '– I'm afraid you must prepare yourself. It may be a matter of days or a week, but no more than that.'

James swallowed hard and blinked away tears. 'Do not grieve yourself too much,' the doctor continued. 'Your mother has endured with great courage for many months. The end will come as a merciful release. Perhaps this is the time to think whether there are any relatives you should contact.'

James nodded and spoke with difficulty. 'Yes, yes, you are right. I must think about it ... but really, there is no one, no one I can call to mind at the moment. But thank you for bringing it to my attention.'

He spent the rest of the evening and late into the night sitting by his mother's bed, holding her hand and moistening her lips from time to time with a sponge soaked in water. He tried to remember if there was anyone he should contact, but drew a blank. His grandparents were long dead. He knew that his mother had a sister – who had married against their father's wishes and cut off all communication with the family – and a brother who had been a seaman like James's father, but who had been offered a position as manager of a sugar plantation in the West Indies. They had received news more than five years ago that he had succumbed to some tropical disease and died without leaving any legitimate offspring.

Since his father's death in a shipwreck three years earlier, he and his mother had been sufficient for each other. He was her only child, an unusual occurrence, which she had once explained by telling him that his birth had been difficult and she had been warned that another child might be fatal. They had always been close, and his father's death had drawn them closer. And yet now the thought that most haunted his mind was the recognition that for almost a year he had been waiting for her to die, so that he could go to Australia to be with May.

He tried to reconcile his conscience by reflecting that he had delayed his engagement because it would have distressed his mother, and this long separation had been the price both he and May paid for her peace of mind. He had known for months that his mother could not live beyond the end of the year, but now it was upon him it was harder to bear than he had ever imagined.

Next day his pallor and heavy eyes soon drew Mr Weaver's attention and he told him to go home, but James begged to be allowed to stay. 'I need something else to think about,' he said, 'and there is nothing I can do at home except sit and wait. It might be days. I should go mad.'

'Very well,' Weaver said. 'Just remember that if you wish to go you do not need to ask for permission.'

Two days passed, in which his mother drifted in and out of consciousness. James went home in his lunch hour to sit with her and spent his evenings with his law books at her bedside. On the third day, when he was at the office, he was surprised to receive a note from Peter Forsyth, Prudence's brother.

There are matters which I need to discuss with you. I shall be grateful if you can meet with me at my club at six o'clock this evening.

It struck James that he had not given a thought to Prudence since the arrival of the ransom note that had sent him off to Ireland, and the formality of her brother's note set alarm bells ringing in his mind.

When he presented himself, however, at the address Peter had given he was received with a friendly handshake, which came as a considerable relief.

When they were both settled with a glass of Madeira, Peter said, 'We haven't seen anything of you for days. Have you been ill?'

'No, no,' James responded. 'I've … I've just been very busy.'

'Too busy to remember your friends?'

'No, of course not. I had to go to Ireland for a few days, on business …' He trailed off, unwilling to embark on the matter of his mother's illness.

Peter toyed with the stem of his wine glass for a moment, then he folded his hands on the table and fixed his eyes on James's face. 'Look, this is awkward so I'll get straight to the point. I want to know, we all want to know, what your intentions are regarding my sister.'

'Intentions?' James repeated.

'Oh, come on.' There was an edge of irritation now to Peter's voice. 'You are not so naive that you don't know what I'm talking about. You have been squiring Prue about all summer, taking her to concerts and parties and so on …'

'But always with you and the others,' James put in quickly. 'Just as a group of friends.'

'You really think that? Do you really think that no one has noticed how close you and she were? Do you think she hasn't noticed anything?'

'I … I like her very much, of course.'

'Well then?'

'I … I should be very sorry to hurt her feelings …'

'Are you saying that you're not serious?'

'Serious …?' James was completely at sea. He had got himself into a very difficult situation and had no idea how to get out of it.

'For God's sake stop repeating my words back to me. Do you, or do you not, intend to propose to my sister?'

James gazed into his glass. 'No ... no, that is, I don't know.'

Peter pushed back his chair. 'My God! I should call you out and put a bullet through your head.'

'Oh, for heaven's sake!' James responded sharply. 'What century do you think we are living in?' Peter sat down again and James went on more quietly, 'Look, I have enjoyed going around with you all this summer and I like Prudence very much, but I wasn't thinking of marriage. It simply didn't cross my mind.'

'Well, you had better think about it now,' Peter said. 'Because if you break her heart you will have me to reckon with.'

'Is she ... does she ... is she expecting me to say something?'

'She hasn't said as much, and I have too much affection for her to press her to expose her feelings to me. I just know that all summer we – that is her friends and family – have been waiting for you to make up your mind. So now is the time for you to do that.'

James bent his head. Too many thoughts were swirling through his mind for him to make sense of them. An excuse came to him.

'Look, Peter, I am sorry if I've upset you or her and I can see you need to have an answer, but the fact is I'm in no state of mind to decide anything at the moment. My mother is dying. The doctor says it is a matter of days. So you see, I can't really think about the future in any constructive way right now.'

'Oh, great heavens! I had no idea.' Peter reached across the table and laid a hand on James's arm. 'I'm so sorry.

I knew she was unwell, but I didn't realise it was so serious. Please forgive me for badgering you at such a difficult time.'

'No, no, it's all right. There's no need to apologise,' James said, sensing a rush of relief. 'I can quite understand your position and I realise I may have been … a little too casual. Give me a week or two to get my head clear and then I'll let you have an answer. And please explain to Prue why I haven't been in touch lately.'

'I will, of course,' Peter agreed. 'And I hope … well, what can I say? Our thoughts will be with you in this difficult time.'

'Thank you.'

'No hard feelings?'

'Of course not.'

They parted with a handshake and James made his way home with his mind in turmoil. For almost a year his plans for the future had been focussed on one point, the prospect of joining May in Australia; a new life in a new country. Now another possibility presented itself. His friends were expecting him to marry Prudence. It seemed likely that she was expecting it herself. And why not? She was a very attractive young woman. He had several times had to resist the impulse to take her in his arms and kiss her. They had so much in common, too – a love of music and poetry and the beauties of nature and he could talk to her as he could not talk to anyone else he knew. If he stayed in Liverpool he could continue to enjoy the civilised pleasures of a great city, which he suspected would be lacking in Melbourne, or wherever else he ended up.

Then, there was the offer of a partnership in Weaver and Woolley. He had every prospect of a prosperous and respectable career. Prue's father was well connected in the business community and would be able to put work his way. It was exactly the future his mother had envisaged for him.

On the reverse of the coin there was the thought of marriage to May. He tried to call up the image of her face but found he could no longer picture her clearly. He recalled what it was that had made him fall in love with her in the first place, and realised that it was the mirror image of what he saw in Prudence. Where Prue was sophisticated, May was a stranger to the mores of middle class society; where Prue was self-confident, May was afraid of causing offence or behaving improperly. Where Prue was well educated and had all the accomplishments expected of a young lady of her background, May had struggled to teach herself the things she felt she should know if she was to be his wife.

On the other hand, while Prue took all her advantages for granted and expected all the pleasures enjoyed by someone of her class to be readily available, for May those pleasures were a source of wonder and intense delight. Whereas Prue met him on equal terms in their discussions of music and literature, and was probably indeed better informed about such matters than he was, he had had the joy of introducing them to May and watching her grow in her appreciation and understanding. But in Australia, he would be the tyro, having to make his way in an unfamiliar society – and May was now the daughter of a wealthy man with an established position. In short, marriage to Prudence meant a life of comfortable familiarity; marriage to May was an adventure into unknown territory.

All these thoughts haunted his mind over the following days, while he divided his time between his work during the day and evenings spent at his mother's bedside, trying in vain to concentrate on studying for his exams. Most of the time his mother lay in a drugged sleep, but one night, just as he was about to hand over his watch to the nurse, she opened her eyes and focussed on his face.

'Oh, it's you, James.'

'Yes, Mama. I've been here all the time.' He leaned over and stroked her hair. 'Can I get you anything?'

'A sip of water, please.'

He poured water from a jug on the table and raised her head on his arm to hold the glass to her lips. When he laid her back she said, 'I'm glad you are here. I want to talk to you.'

'What about?'

'The little milliner's apprentice.'

'May? What about her?'

'You told me that you have been writing to each other. Do you still write?'

'Yes.'

'You were in love with her, weren't you?'

'Yes, I was.'

'Was it because of me that you let her go off to Australia?'

'Partly, yes.'

His mother closed her eyes and sighed. He squeezed her hand. 'Don't talk if it tires you.'

'No, there is something I want to say. It has been on my conscience. I did wrong to discourage you. She was a sweet girl, very talented and very well behaved, consider-ing her terrible childhood. Did you know she grew up in the workhouse?'

'Yes, I did. But I thought you didn't.'

'Oh, yes. Nan, the old milliner she was apprenticed to, told me years ago. That was why I felt she wasn't a suitable wife for you. I realise I was wrong. I was look-ing at her through the eyes of other people, who didn't know her, instead of seeing her for herself. And now she has gone away and you have been left alone. Can you forgive me?'

James swallowed. He could not suppress the thought that if his mother had said all this a year ago, May would have been at his side now. But at the same time, the fact that she had been struggling with her conscience ever since was a revelation that touched him deeply. 'Of course I can. I know you only wanted what was best for me.' It crossed his mind that if he were to tell her now about the offer of the partnership and that he intended to marry Prudence Forsyth, she would die happy. But even as the thought came to him, his mother spoke again.

'Do you still love her?'

An hour ago he could not have given her an answer; now, quite suddenly, there was no doubt in his mind. 'Yes, Mama. I do.'

'Then go to her, my darling, or tell her to come home. I can go in peace if I know you are going to be happy, in spite of my foolishness. Will you promise me to do that?'

'I will, Mama. I swear it.'

'That's good.' She sank back into the pillows. 'I think I can sleep now.'

He bent and kissed her on the brow. 'Goodnight, dear mama. Sleep well.'

'And you, my darling boy. Goodnight.'

Next morning, as he was dressing to go to the office, the nurse tapped on his door. As soon as he opened it he knew what she was going to say.

'Your mama passed away peacefully just before dawn. I didn't see any point in waking you. She was ready to go and now she is where there is no more pain.'

He nodded and drew a deep breath. 'Thank you. Yes, I believe she was. Can I see her?'

'Yes, of course.'

He knelt beside the bed for some time and tried to pray, but religion had been a matter of form for him rather than faith for many years, and although he repeated the well-known words he found little comfort in them. What did bring comfort was his mother's last words. 'I can go in peace if I know you are going to be happy.'

The following days were occupied with notifying her friends and making arrangements for the funeral. It was gratifying to see how many people were there; women she had known since childhood, old shipmates of his father's and their wives, widows of others who had been lost at sea. Richard came and gripped his hand warmly. Laura Pearson came and offered what seemed to be sincere condolences. The Forsyths came and Prudence kissed his cheek and murmured that she was sorry for his loss. Ned was there, and the rest of the group he had spent time with during the summer, but he felt a reserve that was more than simple respect to the solemnity of the occasion.

When it was over he sat down and wrote a note.

Dear Prudence,

I am sure you will understand that I must observe a period of mourning for my mother. So I shall not able to attend the concerts which we so greatly enjoyed together during the summer, or accept invitations of any sort. I want to thank you for your company and for the great pleasure it gave me to spend time with you. I am sure that you will not lack for escorts for future occasions and I wish you every happiness.

Yours sincerely,
James

She replied with a note saying that she understood and was sorry that they would not be able to enjoy the winter festivities together. Three weeks later he learned that she had accepted Ned's invitation to go riding with him.

Twenty One

Dearest May,

I am writing to tell you that my mother passed away peacefully in her sleep two nights ago. Her pain had become very much worse in the last few days and she was relying on very large doses of laudanum, with the result that she slept most of the time. When the end came it was a merciful release.

I find it hard to describe my feelings at this moment. There is grief, of course. The house seems very empty without her, although Flossie and Cook are still here, of course, and do their best to make sure that my every need is catered for. There is also relief, that her long suffering is over. But underneath all that, there is a kind of guilty rejoicing, in that I am now free to come and join you.

My guilt is lessened by a remarkable incident that occurred just before my mother died. I was sitting by her bed and she suddenly regained consciousness and wanted to talk. She asked me if I was still in touch with you, and, when I said I was, she told me that she knew I was in love with you and it was weighing on her conscience that she had kept us apart. She also said that she had been mistaken in judging you through the eyes of society and not for yourself. Finally, she made me promise that after she was gone I would come and find you and marry you. So you see, when all is said and done, we have her blessing.

Now I must tell you something else, which will sadden you I am afraid. I told you in my last letter about Richard Kean and his search for his missing daughter, whom we believe to be the child you called Angel. Matters have progressed since then. We managed to discover that she had been sent away to school, to a convent in Ireland, but that she had run away. That happened nearly three months ago and in spite of police searches no one has seen or heard from her since. Poor Richard went to Ireland and hunted for weeks for clues about what might have happened to her but without success. Our only comfort is that no body has been found, so we have hopes that she may have been taken in by someone, though by whom and for what purpose we shall probably never know.

I am sorry to give you this news, because I know it will grieve you. Of course, there has not been time for me to receive your answer to my last letter, in which I asked if you could think of any way we could prove that Richard's lost Amy and the McBride's Angelina are one and the same; but even if you can suggest something it appears it will be too late. She is lost to us, and lost it seems to the McBrides, and we can only hope that wherever she is now she is being treated better than she was by them. I feel very sorry for Richard. He may have acted badly in abandoning her in the first place, though it is hard to see what else he could have done. It is clear to me that he regrets his actions deeply and is desperate to find her again. He is a good man, a really nice fellow, and we have become great friends. I wish you could meet him.

So, that is my news for now. There is one more hurdle to leap before I can book my passage to Australia – I mean my examination, of course – but I am fairly confident of passing and I hope to leave Liverpool before Christmas. I have been reading in the papers that work is progressing at last on this canal project in Egypt and there is talk of it being finished by next year. If only it was sooner! It would make it possible for me to be with you weeks earlier. But we have been apart for almost a year now and my love for you has not diminished by one iota. I pray that you still feel the same. If that is the case, then a few more months will make no difference.

With all my love,
James

Twenty Two

Angelina studied herself in the dressing room mirror. Her bonnet hid hair that was still too short, and the thick grease-paint, which she had now learned to apply herself, covered the unbecoming tan her complexion had acquired during her time with the Donovans, but she was not satisfied.

'I hate this dress! Poplin is such cheap material. I ought to have something much finer, now that I'm the star of the show.'

'You are not the star of the show!' Catriona said sharply. 'You are *a* star, not *the* star.'

'It's my name at the top of the bill,' Angelina insisted complacently. 'Mr Finnegan said I bring in more customers than the rest of you put together.'

'That's rubbish! He only says that to keep you sweet. He's afraid you might decide to leave, or ask for more money.'

'Is he?' Angelina's confidence wavered for a moment. She looked round the dressing room and saw that Catriona was not the only one she had annoyed. For the first time it occurred to her that they must think her very conceited. She swallowed her pride and forced herself to apologise.

'Sorry. I expect you're right. We are all stars, really.' But she could not resist adding, 'I still think I ought to have a better dress.'

Catriona's tone changed. She came across and put an arm round her shoulders. 'Of course you should. But if you really want to be a star, a proper star, you need to learn to present yourself better. I told you when you first joined that there's more to it than just standing there and singing. I could teach you a few tricks of the trade, if you like.'

'Mr Finnegan said he didn't want me to learn that sort of thing,' Angelina responded doubtfully.

'Oh, pooh! What does he know? He's only interested in making money out of other people's talent. Why not let me show you what I mean?'

'Very well,' Angelina agreed, but without enthusiasm. She did not have a very high opinion of Catriona's performance, but the older woman had so much more experience than she had. She told herself that there must be things she could learn.

'Come to the theatre tomorrow morning,' Catriona said. 'There won't be anyone else here. We'll have a little rehearsal all to ourselves.'

Angelina duly presented herself the next day and found Catriona waiting for her.

'Now, let's think about how you present "The Last Rose of Summer". Sing the first few lines for me.' Angelina did as she was told, and Catriona broke in with, 'No, not like that. On that first line, come down to the footlights and pretend to pick a rose. No, really imagine you have a proper rose in your hand. That's better! Now, when you sing about all the rose's companions being faded and gone, look around the stage as if you can see them and it makes you very sad because they are all dead.'

The instructions went on all through the song … 'Now clasp your hands and look up to heaven … now wipe away an imaginary tear … that's better. Now do it all again from the beginning.'

Angelina felt awkward and rather foolish as she went through the actions, but she told herself that Catriona must know better than she did, so she did her best to follow the instructions. That evening, as she was preparing to go on stage, Catriona whispered in her ear. 'Don't forget. Do it the way I taught you.'

Obediently, Angelina performed the song as they had rehearsed it, but instead of the rapt attention she was used to from the audience she was aware of a certain restlessness, and even heard a few titters. The applause was less enthusiastic than usual, too.

As soon as the final curtain came down Aidan caught her arm.

'My da wants to talk to you. He's in his dressing room. You'd better get along now.'

Finnegan stood up as she came in and advanced towards her.

'Now, miss, just what do you think you're playing at? That's not the way I told you to perform that song.'

'I … I,' she felt herself squirming, 'I thought it would be better like that.'

'Better! You made a fool of yourself up there. Who put those ideas into your head?'

She dropped her eyes. 'Catriona said …'

327

'Catriona! I might have known. Did I or did I not tell you I didn't want you to copy her affectations?'

'But she said if I really wanted to be star …'

'If you want to be a star, you will do as you are told in future! Take no notice of Catriona. Go back to performing it just the way you always did. Understand?'

'Yes, Mr Finnegan. I'm sorry.'

He reached out and patted her cheek. 'Well, we'll say no more about it. Run along now, but I want you on stage tomorrow morning. There's a new song I want you to learn.'

As she reached the door of the dressing room she shared with the other women, Angelina heard Catriona's voice. 'Honestly, did you ever see anything so pathetic?! The poor child has no idea of stage craft.'

She pushed open the door in time to hear Fionnuala respond tartly, 'We all know who told her to do that, Cat. You're just jealous of that lovely voice. Leave the poor child alone.'

Finnegan was waiting for her when she arrived at the theatre next morning, together with Barney, the pianist.

'Can you read music?' he asked.

'Not really. I learned a little bit when … when I lived at home.'

He studied her face. 'You have never told us where home is, or was. Just that you don't want to go back there. Don't you miss it, sometimes?'

'No.' She hesitated. 'Well, sometimes, bits of it. I liked it when my mama was pleased with me, but …'

'But?'

'Most of the time she wasn't. I didn't like it then.'

'But you must think sometimes it would be nice to have a real home, with people who were always kind to you.'

'Oh yes! I should like that, very much.'

He handed her a sheet of paper. 'I want you to think of that when you sing this song. Go and stand by Barney at the piano and he'll play it through for you.'

Barney played and she followed the words on the paper: 'Mid pleasures and palaces though we may roam, Be it ever so humble there's no place like home …'

'Sing it for me,' Finnegan said.

It was not a difficult tune and she sang it without a problem until she came to the refrain – 'Home, home, sweet, sweet home' – and then her voice wavered.

'That's all right,' Finnegan said. 'Just keep going.'

He made her sing it three times and then told her to take the sheet music away with her and make sure she knew the words. 'We'll put it into the programme tomorrow.' As she turned to leave he added, 'By the by, I've been thinking you could do with a new costume. Ma will take you to the dressmaker's this afternoon.'

As she walked into the wings, she heard him say to Barney, 'I told you. There won't be a dry eye in the house if she sings it like that.'

The new dress was made of lavender silk, and there was a new bonnet to go with it.

Just as she was about to go on stage the following evening, Finnegan murmured in her ear, 'Just think about that lovely home we talked about yesterday.' When she got to the refrain she felt tears stinging her eyes, and for an instant her voice quavered. The applause at the end was thunderous.

It was over a month, now, since she had joined the company and each week they had packed up and moved on to play in a different town. From Cork they had gone to Waterford, then Wexford, Kilkenny and Portlaoise and now they were in Newbridge. Angelina had grown used to sleeping in a strange bed and being guided through unfamiliar streets by Ma Finnegan. Ma was always kind to her and made sure that she was eating properly and getting enough sleep. Staying up till nearly midnight on performance evenings had taken its toll, but she had adjusted to it after a week or two. Nevertheless, there were times, just before going to sleep or on first waking up, when an overwhelming sense of strangeness swept over her. She thought of her parents, or the people she had always believed were her parents, and wondered if they were still looking for her. She remembered the nuns and the girls she had known at the convent. What would they have thought if they could see her now? How long would she live like this? Until she was as old as Catriona? As old as Ma? She was unable to imagine the future. At times like these she remembered her beloved rag doll and wished she had her to cuddle.

It soon became evident that Catriona had not reconciled herself to Angelina's starring role in the company. Angelina had to put up with recurrent small annoyances. One night, just as she was about to go on stage, her bonnet was unaccountably discovered under a cushion, crushed so badly out of shape that it was almost unwearable. On another evening, one of the gold slippers she wore with her angel costume was missing and she had go on stage in bare feet. Later, it turned up in Tinker's basket, earning the little dog a scolding from his master. Next night, when she went to put on her angel wings, she discovered one had lost most of its feathers.

She was never able to prove that Catriona was the culprit and the other woman was always the loudest to exclaim in surprise at the loss and was the most eager to find the missing articles – except that she always looked for them in the wrong place. Angelina thought of complaining to Ma or to Mr Finnegan, but she was afraid of retaliation if she aggravated Catriona further and so kept quiet.

Their next engagement was in Bray, on the coast just south of Dublin. On the second evening, as soon as she began to sing, someone in the gallery started to boo and the sound was taken up by two or three other voices. Angelina had never experienced such a thing before. The audiences could be rowdy at times, shouting at Finnegan if they thought his jokes were unfunny or he was taking too long to introduce the next act, but he took all that in his stride. Sometimes they whistled at Fionnuala in her skimpy acrobat costume, and quite often there was rustling of programmes and fidgeting while Catriona and her partner were singing, but Angelina herself was always heard in hushed silence. Tonight was very different. As the noise increased she stopped singing and then ran off the stage in tears. Finnegan stepped into the breach.

'Now, see what you've done, you boys up there in the gallery. How can you treat a little maid like that? Shame on you!' This sentiment was echoed by members of the audience sitting in the pit. 'Shame! Shame!' Finnegan went on. 'Will I ask her to come back on stage and finish her song?' 'Yes! Yes!' the cry went up. 'Then let's give her a big round of applause to show our appreciation.'

The audience clapped and called, 'Maeve! Maeve!', and Finnegan came into the wings and took her by the hand. 'Come along now. Can you hear them calling for you? Take no notice of those louts in the gallery. You won't hear from them again.'

So she dried her eyes and went back onto the stage and this time the applause when she finished was louder than ever. Back in the dressing room, Ma put an arm round her shoulders. 'Don't let it worry you, pet. We all know who's responsible for that bit of nastiness, and it won't happen again.'

After the curtain came down, Aidan told Catriona that Finnegan wanted to see her in his dressing room. Angelina had no way of knowing what passed between them but Cat came back looking sulky and refused to talk to anyone. After that, there was no more barracking and the mysterious disappearances stopped.

Sometimes when they left the theatre after a performance, there would be men waiting at the stage door with flowers. Most often they were for Fionnuala, occasionally for Catriona, and once or twice there was a posy for Angelina. Then, one evening, when they were in Portlaoise, Ma came into the dressing room with a large box of sweetmeats and a beautiful bouquet addressed to her and inscribed 'from an admirer'. It happened again in Newbridge and again when they reached Bray. Angelina spent happy hours imagining who this 'admirer' might be. He would be young, of course, and very handsome; perhaps an officer in the army or even a knight. She had read about knights, who rode white horses and saved beautiful maidens, and she dreamed of meeting one in real life.

Their next engagement was in Dublin, where they were to stay for two weeks. On the second night Ma came into the dressing room where Angelina was taking off her make-up and drew her to one side, lowering her voice so that Fionnuala and Catriona did not hear.

'There's a gentleman asking to meet you. He's in Finnegan's dressing room.'

'A gentleman?' Angelina queried and felt a tremor of fear run through her body. Was it possible that her father has finally traced her and was waiting to take her back? 'What sort of gentleman?'

'It's the one who's been sending you presents. Don't you want to meet him and say thank you?'

'Oh!' It was a gasp of pure relief. 'Oh yes, I'd like to meet him.'

She was about to put on the workaday blue poplin dress but Ma stopped her. 'Here, put on the lavender silk. Let me help you.'

'Should I wear the bonnet?'

'No, I'll just brush your hair, so. And … yes … a touch of colour, I think.' Ma reached into the make-up box for a stick of carmine and touched Angelina's lips. 'There. We want you to look your best, don't we? Now, come along. We mustn't keep the gentleman waiting.'

When they reached the door, Angelina hung back. 'Will Mr Finnegan be there too?'

'Lord yes! Don't worry yourself. He'll stay with you all the time. Now, in you go.'

She opened the door and gave Angelina a gentle push. A man rose from a shabby easy chair to greet her. He was not young, and not particularly handsome, though he had splendid moustaches and a beautifully embroidered waistcoat.

'Ah, here she is! And even lovelier off stage than on! Come here, my sweetheart, and let me have a proper look at you.'

He held out his hand and Angelina went unwillingly towards him.

'This is the gentleman who has been sending you all the sweets and flowers,' Finnegan said. 'What do you want to say to him?'

Angelina made a little curtsy. 'Thank you very much, sir.'

'Come now,' the man said. 'Isn't it worth more than that? How about a little kiss?' He leaned forward and indicated his cheek. Angelina looked at Finnegan, who nodded encouragingly, so she stood on tiptoe and touched her lips briefly to the proffered cheek. He smelt of whisky and cigars, and she was powerfully reminded of the man she had called Papa.

'That's better!' he said. 'Now come and tell me all about yourself.'

He sat down again, keeping hold of her hand so that she had to stand close beside him. He looked round the room. Finnegan was occupying the only other chair.

'Dear me! There's nowhere for you to sit. I tell you what, why don't you sit on my knee?'

Angelina held back but Finnegan said, 'Go on, sweetheart. The gentleman isn't going to hurt you.' So she eased herself reluctantly onto the stranger's lap and he put his arm round her waist.

'Well, aren't you a little bundle of joy!' he exclaimed. 'Do you like to be tickled?'

She remembered vividly how her papa used to take her on his knee and tickle her. It had made her happy then, but he hadn't stopped her mama from beating her and he was the one who had taken her to the convent and left her there. She slid off the man's lap.

'Not really, no.'

'Oh, come now.' He made a little face, like a child deprived of a toy.

'Give her time, sir,' Finnegan said. 'She's not been used to this sort of attention. Maeve, there's a footstool under the table there. Why don't you bring that over and sit by the gentleman?'

She did as he suggested and the man reached out and stroked her hair. 'So, tell me. Where are you from, my pretty?'

She looked to Finnegan for guidance and he said, waving his cigar expressively, 'Ah, there now, there is the mystery. No one knows. She's a changeling, a fairy child, to be sure.'

'A fairy child?' The man looked down at her and she expected him to laugh, but instead he looked as if he believed the story and was delighted by it. 'So, you don't know who your mother and father were?'

She could answer that quite honestly. 'No, sir.'

'You don't need to call me sir. Call me Mr George. No mother or father? Well, well. A little orphan child. How sad!'

'I'm not sad,' Angelina said robustly. 'I like living with Ma and Mr Finnegan and singing on the stage.'

'And you do it most beautifully, like an angel, as the playbill says. We must look after you, if there is no one else. Isn't that so, Mr Finnegan?'

335

'Oh, quite so,' Finnegan agreed. 'And it's late for a little one to be out of bed. If she's to perform tomorrow I think I must take her home now.'

'Of course, of course,' the man said. 'We don't want to exhaust her. So, I'll say goodnight, Maeve. Sweet dreams.'

He leaned down and, before she could evade him, kissed her on the lips. She jumped up off the stool and retreated towards the door. 'Goodnight, sir.'

'Say, goodnight Mr George.'

'Goodnight, Mr George.' She opened the door and escaped into the corridor. As she did so, she heard him give a little chuckle and say, 'What a perfect little angel, Finnegan. So sweetly innocent. I'll be back tomorrow.'

Ma was waiting for her in the empty dressing room. 'Well, what did the gentleman have to say to you?'

'He kissed me and wanted to me to sit on his lap. I didn't like it.'

'Did he?' Ma patted her shoulder. 'Perhaps he hasn't got a little girl of his own, to sit on his lap. Do you think that might be it?'

'I suppose so,' she said doubtfully.

'If he's lonely and wants a little cuddle, where's the harm in that? And he sends you wonderful presents, doesn't he?'

'Yes.'

'And it wouldn't surprise me if he didn't give you something even better than sweets and flowers, when he gets to know you. You'd like that, wouldn't you?'

'I suppose so,' she repeated.

'Come along, let's get you back to the lodgings. You look worn out,' Ma said. 'I've got a treat for you when we get back. A nice cup of hot chocolate to help you sleep.'

The following evening she was sent for again to meet Mr George. He asked her to sit on his lap again and when she did so he reached into his waistcoat pocket and produced a slender box.

'See what I have for you here?'

'What is it?'

'Open it and see.'

She opened the box and found a necklace of pearls. 'Oh! It's beautiful! Thank you.' For a moment she forgot that he smelled of whisky and his moustache tickled and when he tapped the side of his face she kissed his cheek without being asked.

'There. That's good. Let me put it on for you.'

He took the necklace and she felt his hands on the back of her neck. 'So, turn round and let me look at you. Perfect! I knew pearls would be the right thing.' He stroked her cheek. 'They are real, you know. Not these artificial ones you can get these days.'

'Of course they are,' Finnegan put in. 'We wouldn't expect anything less from a gentleman like you, sir.'

Angelina continued to sit on his lap. It would have been ungrateful to do anything else; but she grew increasingly uncomfortable. He had his arm round her and pulled her close against him and there was something hard pressing into her hip. He asked her if she knew any other songs and if she had ever performed with anyone except Finnegan's company. Then he wanted to know if she had ever been to London. She shook her head.

'Maybe I'll take you there, one day,' he said.

'I don't think I want to go there,' she said.

'What? Not go to one of the greatest cities in the world? You should see London! The theatres there are much bigger and the ladies and gentlemen who attend them are the cream of society. You would be amazed to see them in all their finery. And they would love you. You would have the whole city at your feet.'

As soon as she could, she faked a yawn and Finnegan took the hint. 'Our little angel is tired. I must take her home.'

Mr George insisted on another kiss before he let her go, but finally, to her relief, she was out of the room. Ma threw up her hands in amazement at the sight of the pearls.

'What did I tell you? That's worth a few little kisses, isn't it?'

It was Catriona's reaction, when she arrived at the theatre the next day wearing the pearls, that made her feel that perhaps they were indeed worth a few kisses.

That night Mr George was not there, to her relief, but the next day was Sunday and at lunch Finnegan called her to his side and told her that she had been invited to take tea with him at the Gresham Hotel.

'Do I have to go?' she asked.

'Don't you want to? You don't know what he might have for you this time.'

'I don't want him to keep giving me presents,' she said. 'I don't really like him. I don't like sitting on his lap.'

'Listen,' Finnegan said, 'you have no idea where this could lead. A gentleman like that could open all sorts of doors for you. I mean he could introduce you to some very important people. Don't you want to be a real star? Not just here, in this little company, but in London or America. With a voice like yours you could go anywhere, but you need the help of a rich man like Mr George. Just think, if you were to perform on the London stage, all sorts of young men would be queuing up to take you out to dinner – wealthy men, men with titles. You could marry into the aristocracy if you play your cards right. Now, run and put the lavender silk dress on. I think we may have to fit you out with a few new gowns at this rate.'

They took a hansom cab to the hotel, an unusual extravagance. Angelina hoped that they would be sitting in the restaurant, where she saw other ladies and gentleman taking tea, but instead they were directed to a private room. Finnegan tapped on the door and when they received the invitation to enter he put his hand on her shoulder.

'In you go. I'll be back to collect you in an hour.'

He gave her a push and before she could protest she was inside and the door was closed behind her. She was alone with Mr George.

'Ah, here you are, my sweet,' he said. 'I've been waiting for you. Come over here and sit down.'

There was a table laid for tea with a lavish selection of sandwiches and scones and cakes. Mr George pulled out a chair for her, as if she was a grown up lady, and she sat down.

'Now, help yourself to whatever you like,' he said, pouring tea into delicate china cups.

The days were long gone when she had been glad to eat anything that Leary or Danny and the others could find or poach, but the normal fare at the lodgings where the company stayed was adequate but basic. Sandwiches of white bread with the crusts cut off and cream cakes were impossible to resist. Angelina decided that tea with Mr George was not as bad as she had thought it would be.

He waited until she had eaten her fill – or rather more than that – and then moved away from the table to an easy chair.

'Did you enjoy your tea?'

'Yes, thank you, Mr George.'

'Good. Now come over here and see what I've got for you.'

She went to him and he reached out and pulled her onto his lap.

'Let's see, I've got it somewhere. Now where did I put it?' He pretended to hunt in his pockets and finally produced another box, smaller than the last one. 'There, have a look in there.'

She opened the box to disclose a brooch, set with sparkling stones.

'That blue one is a sapphire,' he told her, 'and the little shiny ones are diamonds. Now what do you think of that?'

She had heard her mother talk of the jewels her friends wore, usually comparing them disparagingly to those she owned, and she knew that sapphires and diamonds were very costly. 'It's lovely,' she said, 'but I think it's too expensive for me. I should be afraid to lose it.'

'What a clever little creature it is!' Mr George said. 'You are right, of course. This isn't something you could wear every day. But one day, when you are a great lady, you will need things like this.'

'I shan't be a great lady,' she said, with a giggle.

'Oh yes, you will, if I have anything to do with it. I tell you what, suppose I keep it safe for you, until you are a little older? Is that a good idea?'

'Yes,' she said with relief. 'I think it is.'

'But then you won't have had a present for today.'

'That doesn't matter.'

'Oh yes it does. See that box on the table over there? Why don't you look inside that and see what you find.'

She slid off his lap and went to the table. Inside the box was a bonnet of fine straw, decorated with blue flowers and silk ribbons.

'Oh, it's beautiful!'

'Try it on. That's right. It suits you perfectly. Come here and let me tie the ribbon for you.'

She went to him and he tied the ribbons under her chin, then cupped her face in his hand.

'That's worth a kiss, isn't it?' She reached up and gave him a peck on the cheek. 'No, I mean a proper kiss. Like this.'

He slipped his hand round the back of her neck and pressed his mouth hard against hers, so hard that she felt her lips parting and then his tongue, wet and slimy, in her mouth. She struggled but he held on to her and his other hand, hot and clammy, slid under her skirt and gripped her buttock.

'Now then,' he whispered, still holding her, 'you've had a lovely present and there are plenty more where that came from. All you have to do is be nice to your Uncle George. It's not much to ask, is it?'

'Let me go! Let me go!' she sobbed. 'I'm going to be sick!'

His grasp slackened for a moment and she twisted away and threw up into the box that had contained the bonnet.

'Now then!' he exclaimed. 'This won't do. This is no way to behave when someone gives you a treat. Come along. Wipe your mouth and have a drink of water. You'll be well enough in a moment.'

He gave her a clean handkerchief and she wiped her face and took a sip of the water he offered her. She knew she needed to get away, but she was afraid that if she tried to leave he would prevent her.

'Too many cream cakes,' he said severely. 'You will have to learn when enough is enough.' His tone became conciliatory, almost wheedling. 'Don't worry about it. Come and sit on my knee again and we'll have a nice little cuddle.'

She backed towards the door. 'I want to go home.'

'You can't go until Mr Finnegan comes to fetch you. You can't go back on your own. You'll get lost.'

'I'll wait for him downstairs.'

'The hotel people will not like that. They will want to know what you are doing. Now, be a good girl and come and sit down.'

'I'll sit here, then.' She took a chair on the far side of the table.

He shook his head reproachfully. 'I really thought better of you than this. Such an ungrateful girl! Don't you want the beautiful brooch? Look, here.' He took the brooch out of his pocket and held it out to her. 'I tell you what. Why don't you keep it, after all. You can show it to your friends and make them jealous. I'll wager no one else gets presents like this.'

'I don't want it.'

His tone changed. 'You are being a very foolish child, you know. There are many, many girls who would love to have a rich uncle who gives them presents like this. And I've told you, I can make you a star, a real star. Don't you want to go to London and perform in a big theatre? You will live in first-rate hotel, or perhaps have a beautiful house of your own, and have a carriage with white horses to pull it and rich young men falling at your feet and asking you to marry them. Wouldn't you like that?'

She bit her lips and looked at the floor. The prospect he painted was tempting, but was the price too high?

'Well?' he said. 'What do you say to your Uncle George? All he wants is a little cuddle.'

She got up. 'Very well. But I don't want you to kiss me again like that. I didn't like it.'

'Then I won't do it again, I promise. Come here.'

She let him pull her onto his lap again and he folded her close and jogged her up and down as if she was riding a horse, singing a song about a 'galloping major'. The movement made her feel sick again, but she endured it without complaint until, to her enormous relief, Finnegan appeared at the door to take her home.

'Take her home, Finnegan,' George said smoothly. 'She's been a little unwell. Too many cream cakes, I'm afraid. Show Mr Finnegan the brooch, darling.'

She showed him and could see he was surprised and impressed. His manner to Mr George became almost obsequious.

'Well, sweetheart, we'll meet again soon,' George said. 'Kiss me good bye for now.'

She pecked his cheek and hastily drew back and he laughed. 'Such a shy little thing! Run along now.'

Outside in the street Finnegan said, 'Well, aren't you a lucky girl?'

'I don't like him!' she said fiercely. 'He tried to kiss me. He put his tongue in my mouth. That's why I was sick, not because of the cakes.'

'Oh?' Finnegan looked taken aback. 'Did he? Did you tell him you didn't like it?'

'Yes.'

'What did he say?'

'He said he wouldn't do it again.'

'Well, there you are then.'

'I don't want to go back there.'

'Listen, Maeve, he's given you that brooch and the necklace. You mustn't be ungrateful. I'm sure he won't kiss you like that again.'

In the hackney cab she sat back in her corner in silence. She did not want to have to spend more time with Mr George, but it was hard to see how she could get out of it. She began to cry, silently.

When they reached the lodgings, Ma took one look at her face and exclaimed, 'Goodness me, whatever is the matter? Are you ill?'

'He gave her cream cakes for tea and she ate a few to many,' Finnegan said, with a chuckle.

'It's not that!' Angelina cried. 'I don't like that man. I don't want to see him again, ever!'

She ran upstairs and slammed the door of her bedroom. Inside, she tore off the pretty bonnet and, throwing herself on the bed, wept as she had not done for many months.

Later, when she was calmer, she heard Finnegan and Ma talking. Their room was next to hers and the walls were not thick, and it was clear that they were having an argument.

'I want to know just what you think you are doing with that poor child,' Ma said.

'Nothing. Nothing wrong, anyway,' Finnegan responded. 'She doesn't know how lucky she is.'

'Lucky?'

'Yes. This could be the making of her – and of us.'

'What do you mean?'

'Think about it. She's got the talent to go to the very top, but she won't get there without help, the sort of help a man like that can give her – a man with money and influence and important friends. If he decides to take her up, the sky's the limit. And, as her manager, I go with her. That means us, Ma! No more flogging round the countryside with this crew of second-rate talent, trying to scrape a living. No more cheap lodging houses. The best of everything – first-class hotels, fine dresses for you, champagne, whatever you fancy.'

'And for that you would sell that sweet child's innocence to an old roué like that? Shame on you, Michael Finnegan. That's all I can say. Shame on you! I want no part of it and I won't stand by and let it happen.'

A door banged and feet stamped downstairs and then there was silence.

Later that evening, Ma came into Angelina's room with some soup and a slice of bread.

'I don't suppose you want much to eat, love, but try to get this down you.'

Angelina sat up on the bed and took the bowl. 'Thank you, Ma.'

Ma was silent for a moment, then she said, 'You don't like Mr George, then?'

'He's horrible. He put his tongue in my mouth.'

'Did he, so?' Ma's tone was grim. 'Well, you don't have to see him again if you don't want to.'

'Don't I?' Angelina's mood brightened. 'Really?'

'Really. But if you are not going to see him, I think we should send back the jewellery he has given you, don't you?'

'Yes, I suppose we should.'

'Give it to me, then, and I'll see he gets it back. You don't need to have any more to do with it.'

Angelina felt in the little bag she had carried with her and found the brooch. Then she fetched the pearls from the dressing table and handed them over. She was happy to part with the brooch but she couldn't help regretting the pearls.

'What about the bonnet?' she asked.

Ma smiled. 'I think you could keep the bonnet. Call it a reward for services rendered.'

For the next few days Finnegan was morose and uncommunicative, but the performances went on as usual and to Angelina's great relief there was no sign of Mr George. Whether Ma had taken it upon herself to return his gifts and tell him that the relationship was at an end or whether Finnegan had done it, she never knew.

On the last evening of their engagement in Dublin, Finnegan called the whole company together before the curtain went up. His whole expression was transformed. His eyes sparkled and here was a broad grin on his lips.

'Ladies and gentlemen, I have some wonderful news. Last night there was a manager from an English theatre in the audience and he was so impressed with the show that he has offered us an engagement over there. I need hardly tell you that this could be the beginning of great things for all of us. On the eighth of October, we open in the Cambridge Music Hall, Liverpool.'

Twenty Three

Freshfields
Rutherglen
Australia
July 25th 1868

Dearest James,

I read your letter, which I received today, with great excitement. A letter from you is always a cause for celebration, but this one gave me an extra pleasure. How wonderful that Angel's father has returned to look for her after all these years! I never believed that the McBride's were her real parents, or that she was his brother's child. No one could have looked less like a member of that family.

It is sad that Mr Kean had not been able to see her when you wrote, but as you say in your letter she must have come home from school for the holidays and the McBride's can hardly keep her shut away, so I expect he has seen her now. But that may not have been enough to persuade the McBride's to let her go. I do understand the problem of proving that she is the same child that I looked after in the workhouse. If only I had had the skill – or the materials – to draw her then! I have done a little sketch of her as I remember her as a baby, and again as she was on that fateful day when Mrs McBride brought her into Freeman's and I recognised her. (I say fateful, because after all it was the first time I saw you, and it was the fuss Mrs M. made about it that brought us together. If you had not had the idea of getting your mother to persuade all her friends to write to Mr Freeman on my behalf, I should have been sacked for sure.) I will enclose the sketches, but do remember that they are done from memory so they may not be accurate.

There is one more thing that might help. When Angel was left at the workhouse she was clutching a rag doll. She called it Raggy and adored it, would not sleep without it; but when she was adopted it was left behind. I don't think I ever told you about the fire in the dormitory, did I? I had taken Angel to sleep in my bed. It was against the rules, of course, but she was causing so much trouble in the nursery, crying all night, that the woman in charge turned a blind eye. I don't know how the fire started, but I woke up to find the room full of smoke. I gave Angel to Patty – you remember my friend Patty? – and then I stopped to help one of the other girls. I got burnt – not badly but enough to mean that I was sent to the infirmary. I was desperate to get out and make sure Angel was all right. I'll never forget how I felt when I finally got to the nursery and was told she had been taken away, and no one would tell me where she had gone or who had taken her. They found the rag doll in my bed when they were clearing up after the fire and thought it was mine. I kept it as a memento, until I saw her again in Freeman's shop. I knew it was her. I would have recognised her anywhere. I gave it back to her, that day I followed her to the park with her nurse-maid. She was playing hide and seek with some other children and I found her crouching under a bush. I hoped she would recognise me, but of course she didn't. She just took the doll and ran back to her nursemaid. I have put it into the sketch, to see if Mr Kean recognises it. If you get a chance, ask if she still has it. If she does, it would be absolute proof that she is the child I cared for in the workhouse.

Now, what other news do I have? Very little of any importance. It is winter here, of course, but the weather is much kinder than it was in Liverpool. There is one thing. Gus has a girlfriend, an Irish girl whose family came over here to escape the potato famine. Gus met her in Liverpool when they were waiting for a ship and that was what brought him out here in the first place. Her father is a cobbler and boot maker and he has set up in business in Beechworth, not so very far from here. Gus rides over to see her whenever he can find the time. Oh yes, I said 'rides'. All the men ride here, and a lot of the ladies. It is really the only way to get about. Father owns four beauti-ful horses and Gus has taken to riding as if he was born to it. When I see him, mounted on a big black horse, smartly dressed and with shiny boots, I remember the way we used to be and the poor half-starved, ragged little fellow he was once, and I can hardly believe how much things have changed for us.

Come soon, my dearest! I know it can't be before the end of this year and it will be high summer again when you get here, but I long to show you our new life and all the wonderful things there are here. Waiting is so difficult. But summer will come and bring you with it. I know you will keep your promise. I have faith in that and it makes the waiting bearable.

Your ever loving,
May

Twenty Four

After the funeral, James resumed the semi-monastic habits he had adopted the previous winter. He missed the company of his friends, and especially the concerts, but respect for his mother required him to observe a period of mourning and he was glad of the excuse to distance himself from his entanglement with Prudence. There was an added advantage, in that it gave him more time to concentrate on studying for his examination. He met Richard from time to time, but he was often away pursuing his quest to find up-to-date machinery for the mine in South Africa, and when they did see each other they tended to avoid the subject of Angelina.

It was October when he received May's letter and he set out the same evening for Richard's new lodgings and found him at home. It was not difficult to persuade him to join him for a drink and they made their way to their favourite watering hole, the saloon bar of the Adelphi Hotel. Once they were settled, James took May's letter out of his pocket.

'This came today. I'm afraid it isn't going to be much help under the circumstances, but I thought you would like to see these sketches. They are of Angelina – Amy – as May remembers her.'

'Let me see!' Richard said eagerly and James handed him the two pictures.

Richard perused them in silence for a moment and then he turned his head away and blew his nose hard. 'Sorry. Just give me a minute.' James waited and after a pause he turned back. 'This one, the one of her as a baby – it's so exactly as I remember her. It just brought it all back to me.'

'I'm sorry,' James said. 'I didn't mean to upset you.'

'No, no. Don't apologise. I'm really glad to have these.' He pulled out his pocket book and produced the faded sketch he had shown James on their first meeting. 'Compare this with May's picture. See what I mean?'

'Yes, I do.' It was true. The likeness between the two images was uncanny.

'May I keep them? It's the only memento I shall have.'

'Of course,' James said. 'They do seem to prove that Angelina is your daughter.'

'To my satisfaction, yes,' Richard said. 'I don't suppose it would be regarded as proof in a court of law.'

'Maybe not,' James agreed. 'There is one other thing, though. Listen to this.'

He read out the passage regarding the rag doll and Richard turned his attention to the picture of Angelina as a baby again. 'Yes! Yes, I remember that doll. She loved it so much. That's why I left it with her. I thought –' his voice cracked '– I thought it might be some comfort to her.'

'It seems it was,' James said. 'May writes that she was inseparable from it.'

'And May gave it back to her? How did that happen?'

James related what May had told him of how she had followed Angelina and her nursemaid to the park and secretly handed back the doll. 'It nearly cost her her job,' he added, 'when Mrs McBride found out.'

'I should think it's very unlikely that Angelina would have been allowed to keep it, then,' Richard said.

'I suppose so. But anyway, it's academic now. Unless she is found, or reappears somehow, the question doesn't arise.'

Richard sighed deeply. 'You're right, of course. I can't stop wondering what can have happened to her. I've half a mind to go and ask for a meeting with McBride, to see if he's had any luck looking for her – or the police, for that matter.'

'I wouldn't advise it,' James said. 'I doubt very much whether you'd get a straight answer and we both know what happens to people who pry into McBride's affairs.'

They finished their drinks and set off for home. It was a fine Saturday evening and although it was getting late people were still strolling through the city on their way home from visiting friends or from the pub. As they passed a shop window, Richard grabbed James's arm.

'Look!'

A brightly coloured playbill advertised FINNEGAN'S IRISH MUSIC HALL and below the title was a list of the items on the bill, with sketches of the performers. Prominent at the top was the name MAEVE THE IRISH SONG THRUSH and in even larger letters VOICE OF AN ANGEL. Beneath that was a picture of a little girl dressed as an angel, a halo encircling a head of golden curls.

'You're not thinking ...' James began.

'Yes! It could be her. Look at this.' Richard pulled May's sketch out of his pocket and held it to the lamplight from the shop window. 'See? It could be, couldn't it?'

'There is a resemblance,' James said dubiously, 'but how could it be her?'

'Think about it! We've always said that when no body was found and there was no other sign of her, she must have been taken in by someone – someone who wanted to keep her identity secret. And there's something else. When I went to the convent, one of the nuns let slip that Angelina had a beautiful singing voice – 'voice of an angel' – those were her very words. Suppose this Finnegan fellow heard her sing and saw her potential as a feature on his bill. People love to see children on the stage. He might have taken her in and given her a new name.'

'It's possible, I suppose,' James agreed. 'But she would had to have been willing to go along with the deception.'

'If she saw that as a way of escaping McBride's clutches, why not? Come on.' Richard was already turning to go.

'Where to?'

'To the theatre, of course. I'm going to see for myself.'

James looked at the playbill again and then consulted his watch. 'It's the last night, and the show is probably nearly over by now.'

'We might still catch the last acts.' Richard was striding down the street. 'Come on!'

They reached the Cambridge Music Hall, on the corner of Warwick Street and Mill Street, slightly out of breath. The theatre was situated on the first floor, above a public house, but the door leading to it was shut and the passage inside was in darkness.

'The curtain must have come down pretty early,' James said. 'There's no sign of life.'

Richard rattled the door and shouted, but there was no response.

'There must be a stage door, for the performers,' James said, 'round the back somewhere.'

'Let's try down here.' Richard indicated a narrow alley-way running along the side of the building.

As they hoped, it led them to a small doorway with a grimy sign, 'Cambridge Music Hall, Stage Door. No admittance to the public.' A man in a greasy waistcoat was just about to lock up.

'Please!' Richard said urgently. 'Is there anyone left inside? I want to speak to the manager.'

'You and a couple of hundred others,' the man replied. 'I'll tell you what I told the rest of them. You won't get your money back.'

'Has the show finished already?' James asked. 'It's very early.'

'Are you surprised, after the row we had tonight?'

'Row? What row? What happened?'

'You weren't in, then?'

'No, we only saw the playbill a few minutes ago. We were very anxious to see one of the acts.'

'Which one would that be, then?'

'The little girl, the voice of an angel,' Richard said.

'Well, you'd have been disappointed then. That's what all the trouble was about.'

'Can you tell us where we might find the performers now?' A half sovereign appeared in Richard's palm.

The stage door keeper looked at it regretfully. 'Gone! All gone. On the boat back to Ireland if they've got any sense.'

'What happened?' James asked again. 'What was the row about?'

'She didn't appear, did she? That's what most people came to see. When they heard she wasn't performing tonight there was a near riot.'

'Why didn't she appear?'

'Just before curtain was due to go up this fellow marched in and dragged her away. Claimed to be her father.'

Richard swore under his breath. 'This man,' James said, 'what did he look like?'

'Smart, well-off. Irish from the sound of him.'

'My God,' Richard groaned. 'McBride's got her. Did she go willingly?'

'Not her! Kicking and screaming and saying he wasn't her father. But he'd brought a couple of thugs with him and no one felt like arguing.'

Richard tossed the half sovereign into the man's waiting hand and turned away. 'Come on!'

'Where are we going?'

'To McBride's house. I know where he lives. I'm not leaving Amy in his clutches a minute longer than I can help.'

'Wait!' James caught his arm. 'What good will it be turning up there and demanding to see her? He'll just show us the door.'

'But she's my daughter!' Richard exclaimed. 'That must count for something.'

'But how can we prove it?'

'I know it's her.'

'That's not good enough. We need more than that.'

'What about the rag doll? If she still has that, it would be proof.'

'Yes, but McBride may deny all knowledge of it. We can't ask to search the house for it.'

Richard ran his hands through his hair. 'I don't care! I'll fight my way in if I have to.'

'Don't be a fool!' James said. 'You heard the stage doorkeeper. McBride had two thugs with him and he's probably got more he can call on. He's a dangerous man, Richard.'

'Well, what do you suggest?'

'I think we should speak to Inspector Vane. He might be able to send someone with us. A couple of burly police officers might give McBride pause for thought.'

'Will Vane be at the police station at this hour?'

'I don't know. We could try.'

At the police station they were told that the Inspector was out on police business and not expected back for some time. All they could do was leave a message, asking him to join them at McBride's address as soon as possible. As they turned away James had an inspiration.

'Lizzie!'

'What?'

'Lizzie Findlay looked after Angelina – Amy – before she was sent away. If Amy had the doll then, Lizzie would almost certainly have seen it.'

'That's true. Have you still got her address?'

'Yes, but she isn't there now,' James said. 'Come on, it's this way.'

On the way to the Martins' house, he explained to Richard how he had tracked Lizzie down to the workhouse and how he had succeeded in finding her this temporary situation. But when he rang the bell at the house occupied by Mr and Mrs Winter, the door was opened by a strange girl in the uniform of a nursemaid, with a grizzling baby in her arms.

'I'm sorry to call on you so late,' James said. 'I urgently need to speak to Elizabeth Findlay. Is she here?'

'Oh, yes. I'll get her. What name shall I say?'

'Tell her James Breckenridge wants to speak to her.'

'You'd better step inside. Mr and Mrs Winter are out but Lizzie's upstairs.' She called Lizzie's name and turned back to James. 'It's lucky you called tonight. She's leaving tomorrow. No place for her here, now I'm back.'

Before James could ask anything further, Lizzie came running downstairs. 'Mr Breckenridge! And Mr Kean! What are you doing here?'

'It's about Angelina.' Richard had been quiet up to now. 'Lizzie, we need your help.'

'Has she been found, then?'

'Yes, she has, and McBride's got her again.'

'Oh, poor little mite! She'll suffer for the trouble she's given them.'

'That's exactly what we are afraid of. But if I can prove that I am her real father we may be able to get the police to hand her over to me.'

'How are you going to do that?'

'That's where we need your help,' James said. 'Did Angelina have a favourite toy when you were looking after her?'

Lizzie frowned for a moment. 'Yes, now I come to think of it. An old rag doll. Raggy, she called it. She had dozens of beautiful, expensive dolls, but it was always Raggy she wanted if she was a bit upset.'

Richard pulled out May's sketch. 'Is this it?'

'Yes!' Lizzie's eyes widened in wonder. 'Where did you get that?'

'Never mind that for the moment,' James cut it. 'Do you think it might still be in the house?'

'Could be, I suppose. She kept it hidden away at the bottom of a chest, in case her ma made her throw it out. It might be there still.'

Richard held out a hand to her. 'Lizzie, will you come with us to the McBrides' house and help us to find it? I'm frightened of what they might do to my daughter if she's left in their hands. I promise you won't lose by it, if it causes a problem with regard to your work.'

'No need to worry about that. I don't work here anymore.' She stood for a moment, looking from him to James, then she nodded. 'I'll get my hat.'

Minutes later they were threading their way through the city streets in search of a hansom cab. When they found one, Richard gave an address in Toxteth.

'That's a long way out of town at this time of night,' the driver grumbled.

'I'll make it worth your while,' Richard promised. 'We need to get there as quickly as possible.'

With the promised reward in mind, the driver applied his whip and a short time later they drew up outside a handsome, detached house in Devonshire Road.

'This is the place, isn't it?' Richard asked Lizzie.

'Oh yes,' she agreed. 'This is where they live.'

'They may be in bed,' James said.

'No, look. There's a light in that window,' Richard responded.

While Richard paid off the driver James had a quiet word with Lizzie. 'You told me that you were friendly with the parlourmaid here.'

'Jane. Yes.'

'Can you ask if she will help us? Perhaps you could slip away without the McBrides knowing you are with us.'

'Suits me,' she said. 'I don't want to meet them if I don't have to.'

Richard rang the doorbell and a rather flustered Jane answered it. 'Richard Kean to see Mr McBride,' he announced.

'I'm sorry, sir. Mr McBride doesn't receive visitors at this time of night.'

'He'll receive me,' Richard said brusquely and pushed past the girl into the hall.

He threw open the door of the room where they had seen the light and discovered the McBrides sitting close together at a small table, apparently engaged in an urgent consultation. McBride jumped to his feet as Richard entered.

'What is the meaning of this? How dare you force your way in here at this time of night?'

'I want my daughter,' Richard said bluntly.

James paused in the doorway and looked back to see Lizzie whispering to Jane, and then the two of them headed up the stairs. Good girls! he thought.

McBride and Richard were squaring up to each other across the table. 'You want what?' McBride said.

'My daughter. You abducted her from the theatre earlier this evening.'

'Abducted? I don't know who you are, but you are labouring under a very strange misapprehension. I removed my own daughter from a place where she was being held against her will and brought her home.'

'You know very well who I am,' Richard said. 'My name is Kean, Richard Kean. You tried to have me killed as a spy in Ireland when I went to look for Amy – Angelina, as you call her.'

'I don't know what you are talking about,' McBride said. 'We have never met, to my knowledge, and that accusation is libellous.' He looked beyond Richard to James. 'I know you, though. You're the solicitor's clerk who has been poking his nose into my affairs. You had better advise your friend here to mind his language if he doesn't want to end up in court.'

'Never mind that,' Richard said. 'Angelina is my daughter. We know that she is not the child of your dead brother, as you claim. You never had a brother. You found Angelina in the workhouse and adopted her, and ever since you have been afraid that someone will find out that she is a doorstep baby. That's why you sent her away.'

'This is a farrago of lies,' McBride said, forcing a laugh. 'You must be mad. Get out of my house.'

'Not until you give me my daughter.'

'If you are under the illusion that we found Angelina in the workhouse, how do you imagine that she got there?'

'Because I left her there. It was an act of desperation which I have always regretted and I am determined to put right.'

'My dear sir –' McBride's voice had taken on a sarcastic tone '– if you abandoned your daughter, you have no further rights over her. Even if Angelina was taken from the workhouse, which she was not, you have no right to burst in here demanding to have her back.'

Richard's voice lost its aggressive self-confidence. 'What you say has some truth in it. If I thought that you had given her the sort of life I would wish for her, a life where she was cherished and cared for, I would leave her with you, however hard that might be for me. But it is not so. I know that she has not been happy here. I know that she was beaten, severely.' He turned his eyes to Mrs McBride who had sat still, silently staring with wide eyes from one man to the other. 'How could you do that to a helpless child?'

Marguerite McBride drew herself up. 'Spare the rod and spoil the child. Have you never heard that before? She was a disobedient, wilful girl and she had to be taught a lesson.'

'There are better ways of teaching,' Richard said. 'What you did was far beyond any acceptable punishment. You made her life such a misery that she preferred to run away and trust herself to the mercy of strangers rather than come back to this house.'

'This has gone far enough!' McBride said. 'You have no reason to believe that our daughter is the child you abandoned. You had better leave before I call some of my men to throw you out.'

'She was taken from the workhouse, and she is my daughter.'

'Prove it!'

Up in the nursery, Angelina sat shivering on her bed, straining her ears for the sound of approaching footsteps. The lavender silk dress in which she had been taken from the theatre had been torn off her by Marguerite as soon as she reached the room and she was left in her chemise and stockings.

'Hussy!' her adoptive mother had screamed at her. 'Look at you! With your face painted like a whore! Get that cleaned off, while I decide what to do with you. You're going to suffer for the trouble you've put us to.'

There was no lamp or candle, so the room was in darkness, but then, to her despair, she saw light appear under the door and heard movement. She scrambled off the bed and huddled in a corner of the room, whimpering with fear. The door opened and the lamp was held high, and then a familiar voice said, 'Angelina? Come here, sweetheart. It's me, Lizzie.'

'Prove it!' McBride reiterated.

At that moment the door opened and Lizzie entered, holding a tear-stained Angelina by the hand. Richard spun round and for a moment James thought his legs were going to give way underneath him.

'Amy!' His voice shook. 'It is you! I'd know you anywhere.' He dropped on his knees in front of her. 'Darling, I'm your real papa. Do you remember me?'

Angelina shrank back against Lizzie's skirt and gazed at him. The stage make-up, which she had not tried to remove, had run and her eyes were rimmed with black, making them larger and more appealing than ever.

Lizzie bent down to her. 'Don't be frightened. This man isn't going to hurt you.'

'That's enough!' McBride interrupted. 'What are you doing here, miss? I gave you the sack months ago. How dare you come creeping in here?'

James spoke for the first time. 'Angelina, what have you got there?'

The child looked at him and then down at what she had clutched in her free hand. 'It's Raggy,' she whispered.

'Richard,' James said, 'show Mr McBride the pictures.'

Richard straightened up and pulled out his pocket book. From it he extracted two sheets of paper, unfolded them and held them where McBride could see them. 'This is a picture of our daughter drawn by my wife just before she died. You can see that in it, Amy – Angelina – is holding a rag doll identical to the one she is holding now. This one is a sketch drawn by May Lavender who looked after her in the workhouse. She also shows her holding the doll. Do you need any more proof?'

'May Lavender?' Mrs McBride said sharply. 'That's the chit of a girl, the milliner's apprentice, who tried to say she recognised Angelina. She gave her that toy. It doesn't prove a thing.'

'May?' Angelina spoke above a whisper for the first time. 'Where is she? I want to see May.'

James turned to her. 'May isn't here now, Angelina. She had to go away, but she still remembers you. Do you remember her?'

'I ... I think so. She was kind to me.'

'Can you remember where that was? Was it while you lived here?'

Angelina shook her head, her face puckered with the effort to remember. 'No. I think it was somewhere else.'

He looked round at the McBrides. 'Isn't that enough for you? Why go on pretending? We all know the truth.'

'Forgeries and lies,' McBride blustered. 'Get out!'

'Is that what you want?' Richard said. 'Do you really want to read in tomorrow's papers that the child you call your daughter was left on the doorstep of the workhouse. That you have treated her so brutally that she ran away? That you never had a brother, and that your name is not Connor McBride but Finn O'Connor, who was sent away from his village in disgrace and is known to have links with the Fenian movement?'

'The papers will never print that. They know I should take an action for libel and I should win. You've shot your bolt, Mr Kean. If I were you I'd get out of here while you still can. I'm a dangerous man to cross, as you already know. You won't get a second chance.'

Richard and James exchanged glances and Richard swooped down and gathered Angelina into his arms. 'I'm going, but I'm taking my daughter with me.'

'Just try it!' McBride's tone was scornful. 'Look behind you.'

They swung round to find the doorway blocked by two hefty men carrying short clubs.

'I rang for them while you were ranting on,' McBride said. 'I'm perfectly entitled to use force to eject unwanted visitors who threaten me and my family and try to kidnap my child.'

The silence that followed was broken by a sudden loud hammering on the front door and a moment later a white-faced Jane rushed into the room.

'Sir, it's the police!'

The two thugs swung round, hastily concealing the clubs behind their backs. Into the room strode Inspector Vane, followed by three uniformed policemen.

'Inspector! Thank God!' James exclaimed.

Vane stopped short and stared round the room. 'What the devil are you two doing here?'

'We sent you a message, asking you to meet us here.'

'You did? Well, never mind that. I'm here on different business.' He moved to McBride. 'Finn O'Connor, alias Connor McBride, I am arresting you on suspicion of smuggling arms, with the intention of supplying them to Her Majesty's enemies, namely the Fenians.'

'This is ridiculous!' In spite of the bluster it was obvious that McBride was scared. 'Where's your proof?'

'In the hold of the *Rose of Tralee*, which was about to set sail for Limerick, under police guard,' Vane said. 'Cuff him.'

Two policemen stepped forward and handcuffed McBride. James noticed that the two thugs had quietly slipped out of the door.

'Inspector,' Richard said, 'I have proved to my own satisfaction that this little girl is my missing daughter. Is it acceptable to you for me to take her with me?'

'It strikes me as the best solution, in the circumstances,' Vane said.

'We'll be on our way, then,' Richard said. 'Come along, Amy darling, I'll take care of you.'

She struggled in his arms. 'No! I don't know you! Let me go!'

James stepped in. 'Perhaps if Lizzie came with us …?'

'Will you?' Richard asked. 'She trusts you.'

'Of course I will.' Lizzie took Angelina from Richard's arms. 'Come upstairs, pet, and we'll find you some clothes to put on. You can't go anywhere dressed like that.'

She carried the little girl out of the room, leaving Richard looking distraught. James laid a hand on his arm. 'It's not surprising that she doesn't know who to trust any more. She'll come round when she gets to know you.'

'Right!' Vane said. 'We'll be on our way. Take him out and put him in the Black Maria.'

'Stop!' Mrs McBride was on her feet. 'You cannot just leave me here alone. What is supposed to happen to me?'

'That is for you to work out for yourself, madam,' Vane responded. 'Meanwhile, don't go anywhere. We may have questions to ask you later.'

He followed McBride and his men out of the room.

Marguerite sank down on a chair and put her head in her hands. 'What am I going to do? I shall be penniless.'

Richard looked at her, stony-faced. 'I cannot give you any answer to that. Do you wish to see Angelina before I take her away?'

'Angelina?' She raised a bloodless face. 'Oh, take her! Take her! I'll be glad to be rid of the wretched child.'

Richard looked at James and in silence they left the room. In the hallway, Richard stopped suddenly. 'I don't know where I can take her. My lodgings are quite unsuitable. I only have the one room.'

James hesitated only a moment. 'Come to my house. There's plenty of room for both of you – and for Lizzie, too.'

'Can we? I can't think of a better solution. It's ideal. Are you sure?'

'Of course. Stay as long as you like. I'll be glad of the company.'

Lizzie came downstairs, leading Angelina, who was wearing a simple blue dress. 'It's a bit too short,' she said. 'But it's all I can find to fit her. She's grown that much in the last few months.'

'Never mind,' Richard said. 'We'll get her something more suitable as soon as the shops open. Lizzie, we are going to stay with Mr Breckenridge for the time being. I was wondering – would you be prepared to stay, too, as Amy's nursemaid?'

'Me?' Lizzie's thin face took on a radiant smile. 'Oh yes. I should like that very much.' She looked down at the little girl. 'Would you like that, Angel … oh, I suppose I'd better get used to calling you Amy now.'

Angelina looked up at Richard. 'Is my name really Amy?'

'Yes – well, that's how you were christened. But you can go on being Angelina, if you would prefer it.'

She thought for a moment. 'May used to call me Angel. I remember that now. But Amy is nice, too.'

'It means "loved one",' Richard told her. 'And we did love you, very much. One day I'll try to explain to you why I had to leave you, but not tonight.'

'But you are my real papa?'

'Yes, darling, I am.'

'Do I have a real mama, too?'

'No, I'm sorry. Your mama died, a long time ago.'

'Oh.' She was quiet for a moment. 'Never mind. It's nice having a real papa. Shall we go now?'

'Yes, let's go.' Richard held out his hand and Angelina let go of Lizzie's and took it and they walked out of the house together.

The following afternoon, James and Richard sat together in the drawing room of James's house. Through the window they could see Lizzie playing ball with the child James still thought of as Angelina. They had eaten an excellent Sunday luncheon and James had opened a bottle of the claret his father had left stored in the cellar, and there was a mood of relaxation after the emotional turmoil of the previous evening.

'I still can't get over the extraordinary story of how she came to be appearing in that music hall show,' Richard said. 'I mean, look at her now. I'm no expert but I should say she's behaving just like any normal child. You would never think she had been through those incredible experiences.'

'I can't help wishing we had spotted that playbill a day or two earlier,' James mused. 'I should like to have seen her perform.'

'It seems as though she was good at it,' Richard said. 'If there was a riot when she didn't appear, people must have been given to expect something remarkable.'

'Maybe you can get her to sing for us one day, when she's a bit more settled,' James suggested.

'Yes, I should like that.'

Richard produced a cigar case and offered it, and there was a pause while they both lit up.

Then James said, 'Have you though about future plans? Will you take Amy back to South Africa?'

'I don't know,' Richard said slowly. 'Having had a break from that job, I'm not sure I want to go back. I shall have fulfilled my contract, so I'm free to go elsewhere if I want to.'

'Fresh fields and pastures new?' James quoted and was instantly reminded of May.

'Something like that.'

'Do you know, Freshfields is the name May's father gave to the property he bought in Australia?'

'No, really? That's a strange coincidence.'

'How so?'

Richard did not answer immediately. Then he said, 'Are your plans still the same?'

'Oh yes. As soon as I've done my exams I shall be on the first boat.'

'I was wondering … do you think May would like to see her little Angel again?'

'I'm sure she'd love to.' James put down his cigar. 'You're not thinking …?'

'Well, why not? I know there are plenty of openings for a mining engineer in Australia, and I fancy a complete change. What do you think?'

'I think it's a wonderful idea! And May will be absolutely delighted.'

'That's settled, then.' He put down his own cigar and held out his hand. 'All we need now is for you to pass that exam.'

Later that evening, there was an incident, which disrupted the earlier tranquillity. Tea was over and Lizzie said that it was time for Angelina to go to bed.

'I'm sure you're right, Lizzie,' Richard said. 'You are much more experienced in these matters than I am.' He held out his hand to Angelina. 'Come and kiss me goodnight.'

She stepped back. Memories of horrible Mr George flooded her mind. 'I don't want to. I don't kiss men. And I don't want to go to bed!'

Richard looked puzzled and hurt, but Lizzie said gently, 'Don't worry, sir. She'll come round to you after a bit. Come along, pet, bedtime.'

'No!' Angelina raised her voice. 'I'm not going to bed! I'm a grown up girl. I don't go to bed like a baby.'

'Now then!' Lizzie's voice took on a harder note. 'We'll have none of that, if you please. It's bedtime. Don't argue.'

She tried to take hold of Angelina's hand but the little girl sat down abruptly on the floor and refused to move.

'I won't! I won't! You can't make me!'

Richard stepped in.

'Perhaps, as today is a rather special occasion, we might stretch a point? Another half hour? Would that be all right?'

Lizzie pursed her lips disapprovingly but she stepped back. 'Will that be all right for you, Amy?' Richard said. 'In half an hour, you'll go up to bed without any further argument?'

She hesitated, looking from him to Lizzie. Then she nodded, gracious in victory. 'Yes, thank you, Papa.'

Later, when Lizzie came downstairs after putting a reluctant Angelina to bed, Richard sighed ruefully.

'I hope this is going to work out. I'm afraid my experience of fatherhood is very limited. Are we going to have more scenes like that?'

Lizzie smiled reassuringly. 'I don't think you need to worry, sir. It's not surprising that she's unsettled. She's spent her life, as far as I can tell, being spoilt and indulged one minute and then punished the next. She's always liked to get her own way, and I suppose while she's been with these theatrical people she's more or less been allowed to have it. So we can expect the occasional tantrum. But under it all she's a sweet-natured child. She'll come round after a bit.

Curled up in yet another strange bed, though a more comfortable one than any she had slept in for months, Angelina tried to make sense of the crowded events of the last two days.

She had not wanted to come to Liverpool when Finnegan had announced it, and she had tried to persuade him to change his mind and turn down the offer to perform there; but he had laughed at her and assured her that this was the best thing that could have happened.

She had explained that she was afraid of being recognised, but he had brushed her fears aside, telling her that there was no chance of that when she was made up and in costume.

During the day, all the time they were in the city, she had stayed inside, resolutely rejecting any suggestion that she might like to see the sights, and as the week went by she had begun to believe that Finnegan was right. Then, on the last night, as she was preparing to go on stage, she had heard shouting and before she had a chance to hide, her father – she corrected herself mentally ... the man she had thought of as her father – was there, grabbing her in his arms and carrying her off. She had screamed and struggled and begged Finnegan and Ronan, who were nearby, to rescue her, but her abiding memory was of their stunned expressions as McBride carried her out of the stage door.

What had followed had been the most terrifying hours of her life. There had been the journey in the hansom cab with her wrist held in an iron grip and a voice that warned her in a harsh whisper, 'One sound out of you and you'll regret it!' Then the arrival at the house, her mother dragging her upstairs, stripping her and calling her a whore, and the wait for the promised punishment. Then, suddenly, everything had changed again. Lizzie had appeared and taken her downstairs to meet this stranger who said he was her real father.

That had been just last night and now she was here in this comfortable house, being cosseted by Lizzie. This morning she had had a long talk with her new papa and his friend, who said he was going to marry May. They had wanted to hear all about her adventures and no one had been cross about her running away or appearing on the stage. Her new papa was kind, and had promised to buy her some new dresses and anything else she wanted. Lizzie had tutted at that and said he should not spoil her, but he had said he had nine years of not being able to spoil her and now he was going to make up for lost time.

She was sorry now that she had refused to kiss him good-night. He had looked so sad that she made up her mind next time he asked she would do it.

He had told her that were all going on a long boat trip to Australia and she was going to see May again. She tried to remember what May looked like, but all she could recall was being held in gentle arms and a soft voice singing 'Lavender's Blue'. Then she remembered the lady who had given her back her doll. Was that May? It was all too confusing and she was getting sleepy. Papa had said they would have a wonderful life in Australia, and when she had asked if she could still have piano lessons, he had promised that she would. She had asked then if she could have a puppy dog, and he had laughed and promised she could have a whole kennelful if she wanted, and a pony to ride as well.

Growing drowsier, remembered faces drifted through her mind: Leary and Dervla and Quinn and Danny – did they ever think of her? Did they miss her? Ma Finnegan and Finnegan himself. She had never had a chance to say goodbye, but Papa said they would be back in Ireland by now.

She thought she would miss the excitement of appearing on stage and hearing people clap when she sang, and she remembered what Finnegan had promised, that one day she would be a famous star with young men queuing up to take her out. That would have been fun, but perhaps it would never have happened. She was wise enough to know that the leap from Finnegan's Irish Music Hall to the London stage was too great for most people.

On the other hand, she need not give up the idea completely. Perhaps in Australia there would be concerts where she could sing. Her new papa might help. After all, he had promised her whatever she wanted ...

She turned over and snuggled down. Everything was going to be wonderful from now on. On that thought she fell asleep.

Twenty Five

Liverpool
December 12th 1868

Dearest May,

I am writing this in haste as I have much to do and think about, but I want to let you have the good news. I have passed my examination and am now a fully qualified solicitor!

I have booked my passage on the Royal Standard, leaving Liverpool on December 23rd, so I should be with you not long after you receive this letter. As I told you in my last letter, Richard and Angel – I must learn to call her Amy – are travelling with me, so after all this time you will see her again. She is very well. It is remarkable how quickly she has adapted to a completely new life and a new set of relationships, but I suppose she had to get used to that during the time when she was 'on the run', to coin a phrase.

Now she understands that nobody is going to beat her, and she is going to stay with us permanently, she shows herself to be a remarkably self-possessed little person.

Richard dotes on her and I must admit that she takes advantage of the fact, but it is so good to see her happy after all she has been through. Lizzie is a great standby and a good influence. While she can get away with anything with Richard, Lizzie takes a much firmer stand and insists on good behaviour. It works very well for all of them.

A week or two ago Richard asked her if she would like to sing for us and without having to be asked twice she stood up and sang 'The Last Rose of Summer' and the 'Agnus Dei', which is apparently the one that got her into trouble in the convent. I understand now why the playbill advertised her as 'voice of an angel'. She has an amazingly pure tone and a real musical sense. I haven't said anything to Richard yet, but I really think that once we are settled we should try to find a good singing teacher for her. I think she may have a great future on the concert platform.

I can't wait to see you again, and to bring Angel to meet you. I have put the house on the market and found a buyer almost at once, so now it is a matter of packing up what I can bring with me and disposing of everything else. I shall miss Flossie and Cook, but I have found a new position for Flossie with a very good family and arranged a small pension from the money my father left me for Cook. I think they will do perfectly well without me.

On a more difficult topic, I had to tell Mr Weaver that I am not accepting his offer of a partnership. He was shocked and disappointed, but when I explained about my promise to you he seemed to understand. At least, he has written me a glowing reference, in case I want to join a firm in Melbourne or somewhere. I don't know whether it will be better to set up on my own account or look for a position with an established firm, but I can start to sort that out when I get to Australia. Richard will need to find a job, too, but he doesn't think that will be a problem. Meanwhile, we are grateful for your father's generous invitation to stay at Freshfields until we get settled.

So, you can start making arrangements for the wedding! I leave all the details to you and I know you will make a perfect job of it. For my contribution, I am bringing my best man and a pretty little bridesmaid for you.

Please give my regards to Gus and your father.

Your loving and impatient husband-to-be,
James